HEIRS *of* TIRRAGYL

Books by Joan Campbell

The Poison Tree Path Chronicles

Chains of Gwyndorr (Book 1)
Heirs of Tirragyl (Book 2)
Guardian of Ajalon (Book 3)

Illustrated Collections of Short Stories, Reflections and Prayers

Encounters: Life Changing Moments with Jesus
Journeys: On Ancient Paths of Faith
Soul Search: Questions Jesus Asked

www.joancampbell.co.za

HEIRS *of* TIRRAGYL

THE POISON TREE PATH CHRONICLES

BOOK 2

JOAN CAMPBELL

Heirs of Tirragyl by Joan Campbell

ISBN: 978-1-991222-93-0 (Print)
         978-1-991222-94-7 (eBook)

Heirs of Tirragyl
The Poison Tree Path Chronicles series, Book 2
Copyright © 2017 by Joan Campbell

Cover design by Charles Bernard
Interior design/typesetting by Beth Shagene
Edited by Ramona Richardson

To Nicole and Ashlyn

Now that you are
"old enough to start reading
fairy tales again."
(C.S. Lewis)

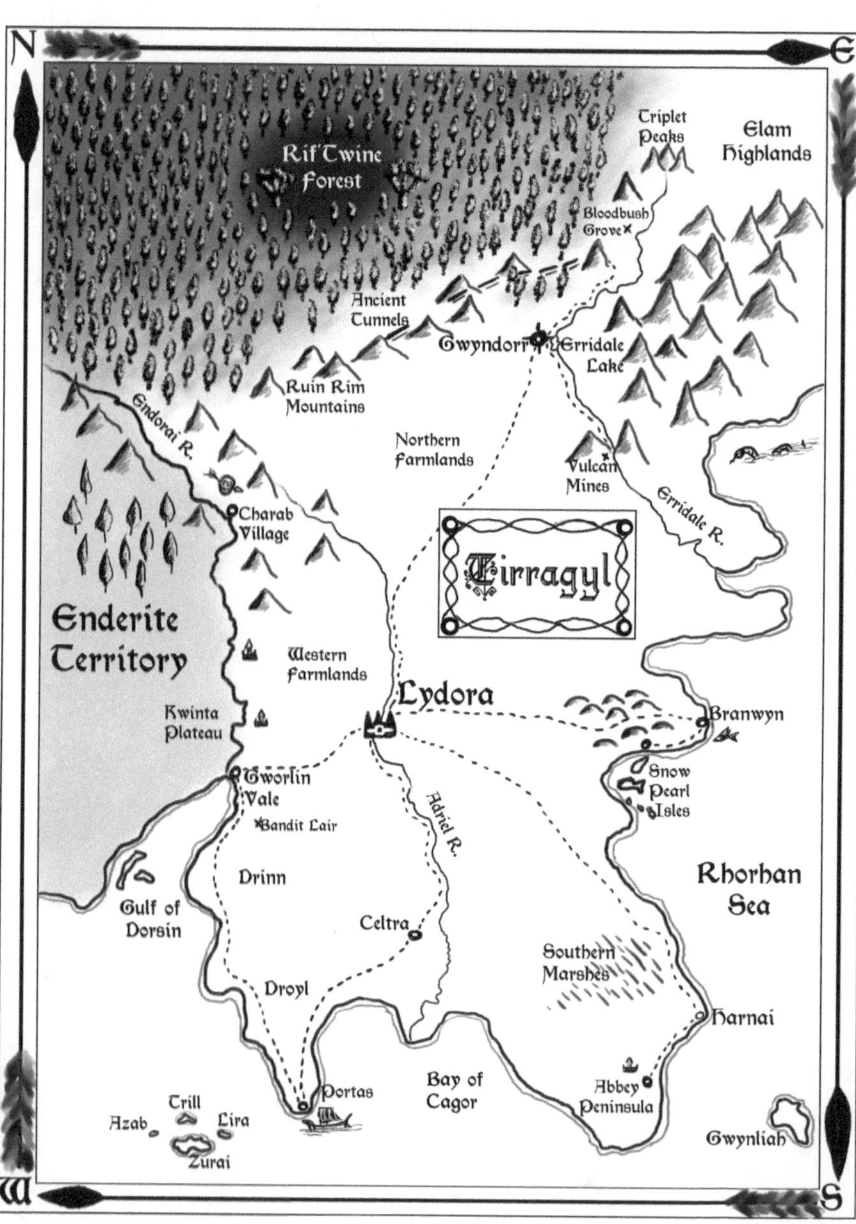

N
E
W
S
Rif'Twine Forest
Triplet Peaks
Elam Highlands
Bloodbush Grove
Ancient Tunnels
Gwyndorr
Erridale Lake
Ruin Rim Mountains
Northern Farmlands
Vulcan Mines
Erridale R.
Gindorai R.
Charab Village
Tirragyl
Enderite Territory
Western Farmlands
Kwinta Plateau
Lydora
Branwyn
Snow Pearl Isles
Gworlin Vale
Bandit Lair
Drinn
Adriel R.
Celtra
Rhorhan Sea
Gulf of Dorsin
Droyl
Southern Marshes
Harnai
Bay of Cagor
Abbey Peninsula
Portas
Trill
Azab
Lira
Zurai
Gwynliah

ACKNOWLEDGMENTS

Many of the same people I thanked in *Chains of Gwyndorr* played a significant role in bringing *Heirs of Tirragyl* to life. It is with the same heartfelt gratitude that I acknowledge them again. Thank you . . .

Steve Laube, for believing in me and supporting me through the process of publishing my second book with Enclave.

Ramona Richards, for working with me on the edit of this book at a particularly sad time in your life and for still giving so whole-heartedly of your time and wisdom.

Charles Bernard, for another imaginative cover. In your masterful hands my world looks even better than I imagine it.

Susan Mathis, for being the one to say, "Why don't you turn it into a trilogy?" and for spending an afternoon talking to me about what it entails to be a professional writer. That conversation and your incredible work ethic changed the way I approach my writing.

My family for their continued support. Roy, it means so much to me that you are reading my books when they're not really your "cup of tea." Telling me that you're proud of me makes my heart melt. Nicole, thank you for loving this book as much as the first one. Ashlyn, thank you for saying that I'm an inspiration to you. That means a lot coming from someone with your creativity and imagination.

My many friends, who continue to show interest and give

encouragement. A particular thanks to the "Hooks and Books" ladies for your enthusiasm at the approaching release dates of my books. I'm both excited and nervous to finally share them with you. Go easy on your critique of this new author!

And finally to the One who walks every step of this journey with me. *"You hem me in behind and before, and you lay your hand upon me."* (Psalm 139:5, NIV).

Thank you, Lord.

PROLOGUE

*S*ky *omen.* The words pulsed through the palace courtyard, and the morning bustle died away as men and women stared upward. The spy's gaze followed, finding an almost perfectly round halo of colored light shimmering in the sky. He had never seen anything like it before.

An uneasy hush settled over the crowd. *What could this mean, this day of all days?*

"It is a sign of good fortune," an elderly Brethren monk called out. "Taus bestows his blessing on the joint rule of King Alexor and Queen Nyla."

There were murmurs of agreement as people slowly returned to their work. *Yes, it is a portent of good,* their nods and smiles conveyed, even as they glanced nervously at the sky.

The spy stared a moment longer at that halo of light. He was not a particularly superstitious man, but it struck him as strange that the last sky omen had appeared on the day the royal twins were born. That day, eighteen years ago, a double rainbow with a single base had arced across the sky above Tirragyl. It had heralded chaos and conflict, for the birth of the royal half-souls had almost torn the House of Taus apart. Now here was another sky sign on the day of their crowning.

With his attention on the strange sight, the spy did not notice the kitchen boy until he brushed up against him.

"A letter for you, Raven," his messenger whispered, deftly slipping something into the pocket of the spy's robe before turning and melting back into the crowd.

As his fingers felt the weight and smoothness of the envelope, the spy smiled, the omen all but forgotten. It had been quiet these last few months and an assignment from a wealthy Highborn was just what he needed. Curious, he slipped the envelope out of his pocket and looked down at the seal. But at the sight of the serpentine 'L' pressed into the red wax, the spy's smile faded.

The Warrior's High Commander stared at the strange ring of colored light in the sky and felt a familiar sense of unease.

The same feeling had come over him in his War Chamber a few days earlier. He had been talking to his commanders when a sudden wave of disquiet lapped through his thoughts, there one moment, gone the next. The brooding emotion had also gripped him several times at night as he startled awake, hearing a bell ring its clarion call through his dreams. Even yesterday, as he read an ancient manuscript and his gaze fell upon a passage of destruction and war, a tingle of apprehension had coursed through him. And now this omen of doom.

Mikel dropped his gaze from the sky to the steel glint of the river far below and let his eyes follow the Feyn's course through the valleys and hills. Could an enemy be following that winding river even now, right to the Guardian Grotto's entrance? Surely the Guardian rock would have warned him, imparting a sense of clarity and knowing, as it had before.

But this sense of foreboding was as useless to him as a warped arrow. It did not tell him if someone approached. Nor if they were friend or foe.

The young Charab steadied his breath, drew back the bowstring, and released the arrow, watching it thud into the center of the target.

Smoothly, he drew another arrow from his quiver and turned his body fractionally for a better aim at the next target.

Then he stopped and lowered his bow.

Behind him, his village was silent as a grave. Strangest of all, no sounds carried from the boys' training turf. No clunk of wooden swords. No elders' berating voices.

The Charab swung the bow across his shoulder and bounded across the boulders to a point above the sandy turf. As he looked across to the training field, he saw that the constant dance of thrust and parry had ceased and that the elders and boys stood motionless, staring upward.

He followed their gaze and took in a sharp breath of wonder at the rainbow circle, beautiful and other-worldly, in the sky. The elders claimed such sky omens warned of approaching battles or deaths of kings or even power shifts in other realms. The young Charab had never paid much heed to their foretellings. The pain of the people he was destined to lead would not lessen with such events. Approaching battles did not frighten them. On the death of one king, an equally brutal one was sure to rise to power. And he suspected that the Charab people had long been forgotten in other realms.

Even if they were still remembered, he doubted that a shift there could undo what held the Charab captive here.

The ancient curse that bound his people to Taus could never be broken.

CHAPTER 1

The crown grew heavy. Nyla cast a quick look at her brother standing next to her on the palace balcony. Their crowns were identical—a latticed gold circlet encrusted with rare snow and fire gems. As always, Alexor sensed her gaze and winked at her before turning his attention back to the procession.

Nyla did the same, although her attention soon wandered from the jugglers and dancers below her to the streets thronged with people. *Her subjects.* The thought filled her with a surge of trepidation. Would she make a good queen? The needs were so great—poverty, injustice, the encroaching Rif'twine. What if they failed?

The music stopped and the procession ended. Lord Briskyl stepped forward, between her and Alexor, and lifted their arms in the air. His voice boomed across the crowd.

"People of Tirragyl, I present to you King Alexor and Queen Nyla of the house of Taus, joint heirs to their father Altaus's throne. May they be graced with wisdom and goodness, as their father was before them, and may their reign be prosperous and peaceful."

The crowd's approval was a deafening roar in Nyla's ears, stopping only when Alexor raised his left hand to silence them. Nyla had agreed that Alexor should do the required Sovereign Speech; she didn't think her voice would carry over the crowd. He did it with his usual ease and charm and, when he finished, the crowd's roar seemed even louder than before.

When all the cheering and waving ended, Nyla slipped between the guards and royal counselors, across the marble courtyard of the palace, and into her serene wing. Her light and spacious rooms encircled courtyards where water trickled and plants flourished. They had always been her sanctuary. Several of her attendants fluttered to her side and removed the crown, the heavy coronation cloak, the gold bracelets and earrings, and the Octora spider-silk slippers.

She chased the ladies away and sank gratefully onto the soft feather bed, her head pounding from the heat and noise of the long coronation service.

"My queen?" Lohlyn's voice woke her from her light slumber. "I am sorry. Did I wake you?"

"Not to worry, Loh. And none of this 'my queen' prattle. I'm still Nyla to you." She grabbed her lady-in-waiting's hand and squeezed it. "Did you see any of it, or were you stuck in the palace all the time?"

"I only saw you on the balcony." Lohlyn smiled. "You know all the rules about who is allowed in formal chambers, don't you?"

Nyla sat up and rubbed her aching neck. "Something I'll have to change soon."

"Water?" Lohlyn held out a silver goblet. "I thought you'd need it after standing in the sun all that time."

Nyla took it gratefully. Somehow, Lohlyn knew every one of her needs, just as Alexor knew every one of her thoughts.

"I wish you'd been there, Loh. You should have seen Duke Frankyl's expression when that crown was placed on my head. You'd think Tirragyl had just been thrown into the abyss for having a woman on the throne."

Lohlyn smiled, but there was a hint of worry in her dark eyes. The Duke was not the only one who thought Nyla should not be joint-ruler with her brother. In fact, probably most of the noblemen felt that way. It had been a point of contention from the time the twins were born.

"Shall I help you dress for the Lords of the Realm Banquet, Nyla?"

"Festering breath! I'd all but forgotten about that pompous affair. How long do I have?"

"The first lords have entered the banquet hall, but there is plenty of mead to entertain them. And it is, after all, the sovereign's right to arrive when she sees fit."

"Just help me into the gown quickly." Nyla tugged at the loops that fastened the silk dress, and Lohlyn quickly came to her side, her deft fingers loosening the fasteners.

"I still want to go see Mada, but that will have to wait," Nyla said as she stepped into the deep purple gown that had been made for the banquet. The dark fabric contrasted sharply with Nyla's pale skin and almost white hair, and the wide skirt drowned her small figure. The only reason she was wearing it was because Alexor's cloak was made from the same cloth, and he thought they should match.

She pulled a face as she saw herself in the looking glass. "It's vile, isn't it?"

"Nonsense. It's a beautiful dress."

"Maybe, but it looks dreadful on me. Now on *you* it would look exquisite." She studied her friend's warm skin tone, chestnut hair, and hazel eyes. What a pity, she thought, that Lohlyn's beauty was not appreciated in Tirragyl, where only the fair and pale were considered attractive.

"I'm far too large for it," Lohlyn laughed. "Anyway, I'd be too terrified to drink a goblet of anything, knowing I could spill a drop on fabric so valuable."

"Now there's an idea." Nyla's serious eyes sparkled with momentary mischief. "Maybe if I spill a goblet of mead on it, I can come and change into something I actually like."

Lohlyn rearranged Nyla's long hair into a series of plaits, winding them together into one long strand, before accompanying her to the banquet hall. As the two doormen saw their queen approach, they dropped to their knees with their foreheads to the ground.

"Oh my, Loh," Nyla said under her breath. "I'm not sure I'll enjoy having people so close to my feet all day."

"We'll have to wash them every time you set foot out the door."

"And I'll have to make sure I put my best foot forward."

The two friends laughed. Lohlyn pointed to the men on the floor and mouthed something that looked like "up."

"Oh!" Nyla composed herself and said in her most regal voice, "Thank you, guards. You may rise and open the door."

"Try not to die of boredom," Lohlyn whispered as the grand doors swung open.

With the noise of the banquet far behind her, Lohlyn wound her way through the dark passages that lay at the heart of the palace. The Palace Administrator and his staff had their sleeping quarters here, but most of the other rooms leading off the passages were filled with old documents, parchments, and objects from forgotten reigns. It seemed almost appropriate that the previous king had tucked his mother into one of these rooms.

Mada, as Nyla called her grandmother, was indeed old and forgotten, and King Altaus had hoped that hiding her away in a deep part of the palace would silence her outspoken criticism of his all-too-brief reign. It hadn't worked. Mada had used everything in her power to undermine her son's reign, which had reminded her far too much of her husband's. Altaus had had the same cruel streak as his father and, had a hunting accident not claimed his life, his reign might have become as infamous as King Tausorlin's.

She knocked on the wooden door and heard whispering inside. Hesta, Mada's nurse and companion, opened the door cautiously and peered out, her relief evident as she saw Lohlyn.

"Lohlyn, it's you. Come in."

Lohlyn stepped into the dimly lit room. The stale air accosted her with its sharp, sour smell of illness and old age. Mada lay under a pile of fleeces and tsebee skins, only her face visible. In the week since Lohlyn had last seen her, Mada seemed to have shrunk even more, her cheeks sinking in, her mouth pinched in pain. Yet her light blue eyes were filled with the usual sharp intelligence and her voice had lost none of its authority when she said, "Leave us alone, Hesta."

The nurse cast a grateful glance to Lohlyn and closed the door behind her.

"How is my granddaughter, Lohlyn? And why aren't you by her side?" Her words may have been slower, but they were as direct as always.

"She is at the Lords of the Realm Banquet, my lady, and King Alexor saw fit to leave me off the guest list."

"Pretentious affair. You are not missing much." A cough wracked Mada's body, but once it subsided and her breathing steadied, she continued, softer than before. "It worries me that Nyla is alone."

"Klyden is there as part of the Royal Guard."

The old woman nodded, apparently satisfied. "Have there been any more threats to her life?"

"Not since last year."

"This is a dangerous time." Mada's voice dropped. "These transitions always are. You need to be on your guard at all times."

"Of course, my lady."

Mada smiled. "Looking at your beautiful face, it is easy to forget just what you are. And you were, of course, trained by the best."

"The very best." Lohlyn swallowed away the lump in her throat.

"Remind me. How long have you been here?"

"Seven years, my lady. Nyla was eleven when I arrived."

"I remember." Mada's brow furrowed. "My husband was still king at the time. You were little more than a child yourself."

"I was eighteen."

"Seven years," Mada said wistfully. "You've done well to keep the secret."

"Thank you. Still, now that she is queen, wouldn't it be a good time to tell her the truth?"

"The truth?" The old woman's voice quivered. "What truth would that be, Lohlyn? The truth that, when she was born, every one of my husband's counselors recommended she be put to death? The truth that her own mother and father wanted to drown her so that her half-soul would be free to return where everyone thought it belonged—her brother? The truth that many still think her death would benefit Tirragyl, for finally Alexor would be a whole person? Is that the truth you wish her to know, Lohlyn?"

"No, my lady." Lohlyn dropped her head. "I mean the truth about me."

"That would require explaining everything else." Mada paused for a long time, catching her breath after her emotional outburst. "I forbid you to tell her."

"But if she ever—"

"I forbid it." Mada's voice was as hard as steel. "There are secrets that should never be told, for they can steal a soul as quickly as the waters of the Adriel River."

"Yes, my lady."

"Do I have your word, Lohlyn?"

"Yes, my lady." Lohlyn pushed down the surge of sorrow. "By the Creed, I will not tell her about me. Or her past."

Nyla sat at the head of the banquet table and let her eyes wander down its length, pausing to take in each face along the way. Before her sat the twenty-four lords of Tirragyl, each of whom came to swear fealty to her and Alexor. Their expressions were grim, their tones hushed as they drank from their goblets and picked at the rich fare on the table. They were all much older than she was, and she sensed their wariness at what they were required to do. Bowing their knees to rulers so young—and one of them a woman—did not appeal to these powerful men.

She frowned, leaning over to Alexor. "They don't seem very glad to be here, do they?"

Her brother snorted. "Must be uncomfortable as chewing on gristle for these old carcasses to give us fledglings their loyalty."

"Perhaps with time we'll win their trust," she said.

"What does it matter?" His dazzling smile loosened a little of her anxiety. "We hold all the power. They don't have to like us. They only have to be loyal to us. And if they're not . . ." He made a cutting motion across his throat. When she didn't smile, he grabbed her hand. "Nyla, loosen up. I mock."

"Being someone's liege-sovereign is no light matter. At times we will hold their very lives in our hands."

"That crown is already too heavy on your head." He flicked her crown forward and laughed as she swiped away his hand. "I think you need some mead to help you see the lighter side of this."

"I don't want—"

But Alexor had already told the steward to fill her goblet, and when his own was brimming, he clinked it against hers. "To a long and prosperous reign, Nyla." His blue eyes sparkled with boyish excitement and she couldn't help but smile as she took a sip of the sweet rich mead. Other than his youth, Alexor looked like a king. He was tall and strong with a thick golden mane of hair. Surely their subjects, and even these lords, would grow to admire him as much as she did. Nyla might not look like a queen should, but if Alexor could win hearts, their joint rule would succeed and bring change to Tirragyl.

"Your Majesties." Lord Briskyl stood behind them. "Shall we start the proceedings?"

"Yes." Alexor rose to his feet and held out his arm for Nyla. Together they swept into the adjacent throne room, followed by their subject lords. The throne from which her grandfather had ruled so long, and her father but a few brief years, had been replicated. The old throne, dark with age, and the new, in a much lighter wood, now stood side by side on a platform. The king and queen climbed the three steps and turned to face their lords before lowering themselves onto Tirragyl's double thrones, Alexor on the original, Nyla on the copy.

At a signal from Alexor, Lord Briskyl's loud voice boomed across the room, calling the first lord.

"Lord Lucian of Gwyndorr, of the Northern Cantref. Step forward to pledge yourself to your sovereigns."

A tall, powerfully built man rose to his feet. He wore a dark blue robe of spun silk that made their own look almost drab, and it flowed around him like liquid as he strode forward. Even though she sat on a raised throne, Nyla felt strangely insignificant as the lord's eyes swept over her. He bowed low and, as he straightened, his golden brown eyes came to rest on Alexor.

"I, Lucian, pledge myself and all my possessions to the service of the crown," he said in a deep, resonant voice. "I will willingly die at the command of King Alexor and Queen Nyla. If I fail them in any way, my treachery will be punishable by death."

"Rise, Lord Lucian. We accept your allegiance," Alexor said. As the lord turned away and the next lord was called forward, her brother winked at her and whispered, "See how very easy this task of ruling is, Nyla?"

CHAPTER 2

Shara had lost count of the weeks since she had fled from Gwyndorr. The long days of walking and climbing ever upward into the highlands had melted together into one continuous blur. Her skin had grown darker from the weeks in the sunlight. Even her tousled dark curls now held hints of the golden sun. Blisters dotted her feet, and her legs ached.

Yet, as difficult as it had been, she felt strangely content. She was with Nicho, and the hours of walking had provided them with time to talk. The division that had existed between them in Gwyndorr—she, a Highborn, he a low—had evaporated like the mist that cloaked the highlands in the early morning. Here they were equals and friends, and over time something deeper had begun to grow between them.

A shudder passed through her body, thinking how different her life would have been if her uncle Randin's will had prevailed and she had become Maldor's wife.

"What is it, Shara?" Nicho asked, concerned.

"Just thinking where I would be right now if you hadn't come for me."

"Gwyndorr, you mean?"

"With Maldor."

Nicho's expression darkened. He had experienced Maldor's

cruelty firsthand. It was one of the reasons Eliad and Andreo had been able to convince him to rescue Shara on her wedding day.

"Strange, isn't it?" Shara continued. "To grow up in Randin's house for almost fourteen years, and not miss it at all."

"Not much for you to miss, is there?"

"Only Marai. I wish we could tell her we were safe."

Nicho nodded but didn't reply, almost as if he didn't trust his voice to speak about his mother.

Shara reached out and grabbed his hand. "Eliad said we could send a message to her once we reached the Grotto."

"Yes, she will know soon enough that we are well."

They lapsed into silence, and Shara thought about Marai, the cook, who had filled her life with motherly love. For her to lose Shara and Nicho on one day was a cruel blow indeed. Not knowing what had happened to them must be driving her nigh-on crazy. Shara felt guilty at the thought.

They walked in a ravine and Shara turned her attention to the cliffs that towered above them on both sides. Most of the walls consisted of stark rock, but against all odds, small plants had taken root in the cracks, clinging defiantly to the mountain face. *Tenacious.* She smiled as the word crept into her mind. Yes, the plants were just as tenacious as she had been living in Randin's house, nourished only by the soil of Marai's love.

"We'll break for the night here," Eliad's voice penetrated Shara's thoughts. "Tabeal seems to think it a good place."

Shara glanced at the Gold Breast perched on a ledge above them. How strange she would have considered it a few weeks earlier, to be following a bird into the unknown. Yet, since the rainy day on which the bird had come to find her—and Shara knew without a doubt that she had—Tabeal had proved herself completely trustworthy. After all, Tabeal had led them to the buried book which Eliad claimed would unravel the mystery of her past. At night, as they huddled around the fire, Shara often paged through it and traced the unknown letters of the Old Tongue script. Every time she begged Eliad to read it, he shook his head. *Not yet, my love. The time will come, but it is not yet here.* So she pushed down her gnawing impatience, and focused instead on the journey.

Yes, Tabeal had proved herself trustworthy indeed. Hadn't she come to them all in their hour of greatest need? Brother Andreo, when his brethren had thrown him out of their fellowship; Nicho, when the town guards were closing in on him; and Shara, on the day of her wedding to Maldor. Shara knew Tabeal was no ordinary bird, but even on this topic, Eliad was his usual tight-lipped self. *Where does she come from, Eliad? How does she know things? How does she do the things she does?* He answered all Shara's questions with a gentle smile and his usual reply. *Patience, my love. You will understand as you learn to trust.*

Andreo and Eliad dropped their bags onto the ground of a small enclosure carved into the cliff wall. It wouldn't give much shelter in a storm, but the sky was clear and the night would be dry. Soon the four of them would fall into their familiar routine. Eliad would arrange all their soft clothing and blankets into a bed, as Andreo gathered stones for a fire circle. Nicho and Shara would scour the area for kindling and firewood. Then, as darkness fell, they would huddle around the fire. Andreo would prepare the hot, somewhat spicy tea from the leaves of the yoran bush, which he claimed helped induce sleep. Shara didn't like it much, but at least it softened their small ration of pan bread.

"We need water, lad." Eliad passed Nicho the two skins.

"I'll come with you," Shara said. It had been two days since she had bathed in the river and the thought delighted her.

Nicho and Shara picked their way down a steep slope to where the river tumbled into a small pool of water.

"It's perfect!" They both took off their outer robes and lowered themselves into the icy water. Shara laughed as Nicho splashed her, marveling at the sound of her voice echoing back to her.

"Listen, Nicho!" she said. "Hello!" *Hello . . . hello . . . hello,* her voice reverberated around them.

"Let me try." Nicho's boyish face dimpled with mischief and

delight. "Shara is beautiful." *Is beautiful . . . beautiful.* The words spun around, mixing with their laughter.

Suddenly a shout filled the air around them, and the laughter died on their lips. They looked up to the place where Eliad and Andreo had been sitting.

"Eliad?" Nicho called out, but the only voice that replied was his own.

"Brother Andreo?" Shara added uncertainly.

Nicho pulled himself out of the pool and grabbed their clothes. "Quickly, Shara." He dragged her from the water and over the smooth rocks, toward the thick foliage on the side of the river.

"What's going on, Nicho?"

"Hide here while I go check on Eliad and Andreo." He pushed her into the cover of the bushes.

"I'm coming with you."

"No, Shara. Lord Lucian is after you, remember?"

Shara pulled her outer robe over her dripping undergown and watched as Nicho edged his way back up the bank, cursing the fact that she was stuck here. By the time he disappeared, she had made up her mind. Sitting here served no purpose at all.

Shara fingered the knife tucked into the pocket of her gown. It had been with the buried book and her constant companion since the escape. She pushed her way clear of the bushes and started in the direction Nicho had taken. Yet, she had taken less than ten steps, when a familiar sound stopped her in her tracks. The sound of swords being drawn. Slowly, she turned.

Four dark-haired men stood in a semicircle behind her, each one with a sharp blade pointing her way. A large, muscular man with a scar across his face stepped forward. There was a flint of anger in his green eyes. Shara took an involuntary step away.

"Another Highborn!" He spat on the ground and lifted his sword, grazing her throat with its tip. "How did you find this place?"

"Where are my friends?" Shara asked.

"You're not in Gwyndorr anymore, *my lady,*" the man snarled. "Here I ask the questions and you answer them."

Shara swallowed, trying not to look at the blade pressed against her neck.

"A bird led us here. The Gold Breast."

"You would have me believe that?" he sneered. "Obviously you don't value your life very much."

"It's true, whether you believe it or not," Shara said evenly. "Now tell me what you've done with my friends."

"I've done with them what I'm soon going to do with you."

Fear clenched Shara's chest. Had he killed them in cold blood? A monk and an old man? What kind of person did such a thing?

"You killed them?"

At the flicker of amusement on the man's face, a hot rage flooded through Shara. Everything grew strangely quiet as she focused on his face. Never before had she felt such hatred. Not for Randin when he told her of her betrothal, or even Maldor when he looked at her with his lustful eyes.

Her fingers closed on the knife under her cloak and she slowly pulled it from its sheath. She knew that she could not beat her captor—he had the look of a fighting man—but she didn't care. She would die, like the others, but she would hurt him in the process.

The man lowered his sword and turned slightly to say something to one of his companions. It was the small gap Shara needed. She threw herself at him like an injured lioness, her knife slashing wildly through the air. She saw surprise in his eyes, and then pain, before he reacted. He dropped his sword and his right arm came down on the wrist of her knife hand in a vice-like grip, as his left hand threw a jarring punch to her jaw. The world felt off-kilter for a moment until her opponent's face came back into sharp focus.

"Drop it!" he hissed.

Her hand was immobile in his grip. She had little choice but to let the knife fall to the ground. He kicked it away toward his companion, not once taking his eyes off her face. His left hand now held his own knife. She could feel it pressed against her ribs. She was inordinately satisfied to see blood flowing from a gash on his arm.

"You *really* don't value your life much, do you?" he said through clenched teeth.

"You're a beast," she spat out at him. "Killing people in cold blood."

"Who said I killed them?" The mocking look was back on his face. "I said I did to them what I would do to you." He signaled to his companion, who passed him a length of rope. "Which is truss you up like a gaggle of wild fowl." The rope bit into her wrists as he wound it tightly around her hands.

"They're alive?" she asked weakly.

He nodded. "We always interrogate our prisoners before we kill them."

There was a scrambling sound from above and Shara glanced up to see Nicho standing on the ledge. Before she could shout a warning, he spoke.

"Let her go, Pearce."

Two of the men leapt toward Nicho with the speed of highly trained warriors, but her captor's commanding voice barked out an order. "Leave him. He's one of us!"

"If that's true, why in the abyss did he lead the Highborns to the Grotto?"

"He has some explaining to do, doesn't he?"

Nicho and her captor's eyes locked and Shara sensed an undercurrent of emotion passing through that gaze. Her captor was the first to look away. He turned to her, prying the knots loose as roughly as he had tied them.

Nicho pushed past the two swordsmen to where she stood. He fingered a graze on her cheek. "Are you hurt, Shara?"

"I'm fine. Who is this man, Nicho?"

Nicho looked steadily at her captor, something unreadable in his expression. "Someone I knew back in Gwyndorr."

Her captor's eyes narrowed as he looked at them. "Festering carcass, Nicho! You and this Highborn are lovers?"

"No, Pearce," Nicho said. "We are friends."

"A Parashi and a Highborn friends?" Pearce spat out the last word. "How far you have come from your roots. Crif, give me a blindfold." He took the piece of rough material from his companion and held it out to Nicho. "Blindfold your *friend*."

"Why?"

"Because she's the enemy. Not all of us have forgotten that."

"I won't."

"I give the instructions here and if you do not follow them, I will have you both tied up and blindfolded and shoved all the way to the Grotto," Pearce said softly. "Or you can gently lead her there. You choose."

"Just do it, Nicho," Shara whispered.

Nicho had little choice but to comply. After he had tied the binding around her eyes, he led her by the arm, keeping up a running account of all the pitfalls on their path. Shara could hear Pearce's impatient calls from far ahead, but Nicho kept the same steady pace.

"Who are they, Nicho?" she whispered.

"The Parashi Warriors," he answered brusquely.

"What do they do?"

"They're the Parashi resistance."

"Does that mean we've finally reached the Guardian Grotto?"

"Yes."

After what felt like an eternity, she heard Pearce's voice. "Take it off."

Nicho gently pulled the blindfold away from her eyes and she looked around in wonder. They stood before a towering cliff, decked with moss and creepers. A wide curtain of water cascaded from a point far above their heads.

"The entrance to the Guardian Grotto." Nicho's voice held a note of wonder. "Just like the legends describe it."

Pearce nodded. "That's right, Nicho. What we always dreamed of, right?"

Nicho's expression lost some of its awe as his gaze turned back to Pearce.

"We were slow in coming here, given Eliad's age. But for hardened soldiers like you, it can't be more than a two or three week journey, right?"

"Four if you are trying to avoid the patrols."

"Still, it's not so hard to send word back, is it? Some word to tell us that Derry was safe."

Pearce dropped his gaze. "I'll take the girl." He grabbed Shara's arm. "Step only where we step, Nicho, or you'll trigger an arrow trap."

He took care picking his way across the large stones littered at the foot of the cliff. Nicho was always just a step behind them. Shara looked intently for the entrance of a cave, but she could not see it. Their path took them to the pool into which the waterfall tumbled. Shara could feel its spray on her face. Here Pearce stopped.

"There are four flat rocks in the pool." He pointed. "You will need to jump from one to the other, and then through the waterfall to the ledge where the cave entrance lies."

"The entrance is behind the waterfall?" Shara marveled at how well hidden it was.

"Nicho, you go first. Then the girl. I will come in behind you."

"Just to make sure we don't escape?" Nicho said.

"Escape through that maze?" Pearce laughed. "You've always thought very highly of your abilities, haven't you?"

Shara's body trembled as she leapt from stone to stone. They were farther apart than they had appeared from the shore. Her final leap through the waterfall proved to be the most frightening of all because there was no way of seeing where she would land. But, as the water rained down on her, she already felt Nicho's hands reaching for her.

He laughed with a child's delight. "Amazing, isn't it?"

"I suppose. Although I am drenched!"

Nicho's laughter stopped as soon as Pearce appeared.

"Come." Pearce led them back along the ledge, to a dark crack in the cliff. "Welcome to the Guardian Grotto," he said, as they stepped into the darkness.

CHAPTER 3

The door to Nyla's chamber flew open and she flinched. Lohlyn, who a moment before had been calmly brushing her hair, suddenly stood between Nyla and the newcomer. For just the briefest of moments, Nyla imagined that a glint of steel had replaced the brush in Lohlyn's hand. Yet Lohlyn's hand was empty as she dropped into a deep curtsy.

"Festering breath, Alexor. Would you have us faint with fright?" Nyla said. "Whatever happened to knocking?"

"Kings don't knock." He indicated Lohlyn could rise.

"They do when they enter the chamber of a queen."

"Even if the queen is his sister?"

"Especially then." Nyla rose from the bench, her irritation eased by his disarming smile. "So what's so important that you have to burst in here unannounced? I'm just getting ready for the meeting with the cantref commissioners. Couldn't it wait until then?"

"I cancelled the meeting."

"Why? There were important decisions to be made."

"Nothing that can't wait until tomorrow." Alexor breezed past Lohlyn to the table containing all of Nyla's jewelry and perfumes. He idly picked up a vial of perfume and wafted it under his nose.

"Would you like me to leave, Your Majesty?" Lohlyn asked quietly.

"Yes," Alexor said just as Nyla said, "No. Stay Lohlyn."

Alexor spun around and laughed. "I almost forgot that there are two Majesties present." His eyes narrowed on Lohlyn, who hadn't moved from Nyla's side. "Well, there's no doubt where your lady's loyalty lies, is there?"

"Why are you here, Alexor?"

"I need you."

"Need me? For what?"

"A hunt. There have been sightings of a wildwood pig in the hills north of the city. I want to take care of it before it becomes a menace."

"The wildwoods are shy, aren't they? Shouldn't harm anybody." Had her brother really cast aside an important meeting to go on a *hunt*?

"This one's already causing some problems. It's injured. You don't want to mess with an injured pig."

That was the truth. Wildwoods were the largest breed of forest pigs and the most elusive. They would rather run away than put up a fight, but Nyla had heard stories of hunters being impaled on the triple tusks of cornered wildwood pigs.

"Why don't you let the Rangers take care of it?"

"Oh, come on, Nyla! It's good sport, that's why. And in the two weeks since our coronation, I've done nothing but listen to the whining of the lords and commissioners. I need a break." His expression was pleading. "So are you coming or not?"

"I think not. Maybe I can meet with the commissioners myself?"

"No. Come with." He grabbed her by the hand. "You know you are my fortune finder, don't you? I don't hunt half as well without you."

"Nonsense." She pulled her hand from his grasp.

"Anyway, I know how good you are with a bow and arrow," he continued. "We need all the expertise we can get."

"Who's going?"

"Just a few palace nobles and one or two lords who haven't returned to their lands yet."

"Fine," Nyla sighed, "but Lohlyn goes with us this time."

"Why?" Alexor cast a disparaging glance at Lohlyn. "Your hair won't need brushing on a hunt."

"Because I don't want to be the only woman in a group of foolish young men, that's why."

Alexor sighed. "Fine. Just make sure she keeps up."

Straddling Skybreeze's back felt wonderful, feeling the power pulsing through his galloping limbs as the wind swept her hair behind her. Alexor had been right—they needed this.

"*Yaaarraaaa!*" Nyla shouted. The wind snatched her voice away, but Alexor, just ahead of her, turned and laughed, echoing the Tirragyl war cry. They led the hunt into the northern hills. On Skybreeze and Skyflame, nobody could catch them. The two steeds were the offspring of the finest stallion in all Tirragyl.

Alexor pulled in his reins sharply as they crested the hill. "Didn't I tell you this would be wonderful?"

Nyla stopped by his side. "As always, you know best, Your Majesty," she laughed, turning to watch the rest of the group pounding up the hill. She was glad to see that there were at least two riders behind Lohlyn.

Waiting for the others to arrive gave Nyla a chance to admire the view. Behind them stood the royal citadel of Lydora, soaring high above the plain. Its position and strong wall ensured it would remain an impenetrable fortress for as long as the heirs of Taus sat on Tirragyl's throne.

The city had almost tripled in size over the last twenty years, as the encroaching Rif'twine forest forced people south. It now sprawled out of the confines of the wall, and seeing it from this angle, Nyla's joy dimmed. The many thousands living beyond the walls were vulnerable. There was always the possibility that the Enderites would attack again from the west, and there was no protection for the "Outsiders."

Nor were there many opportunities for them to make a livelihood. A lucky few might trickle into the city in the morning to sell wares, or do some small tasks for a loaf or two of bread, but the city guards only let a few hundred pass before shutting the gates. Many Outsiders now slept at one of the five city gates, hoping to be one of the lucky few granted access. Every week there were stories of deaths caused by stampedes at the gate.

"Whoa!" shouted the first rider to reach them. Their cousin, Troyl, had a broad grin on his face. "You set a fast pace, Alexor."

"But of course," her brother countered. "Wildwoods wait for no man."

"Or woman," Nyla added.

Troyl appeared only now to notice her. "Well ridden, Queen Nyla," he said.

Nyla had decided some time ago that certain men were uncomfortable in the presence of women, for, as familiar as Troyl was with Alexor, he was as formal with her.

Lohlyn and three other riders reined in right behind Troyl.

Duke Frankyl's son slapped Alexor on the back. "My word, Your Majesty. Shouldn't you be pacing yourself somewhat?"

"Blame my sister. I couldn't exactly be beaten by a girl, could I?"

The Duke's son nodded, but he did not look at Nyla. How like his father, she thought. Duke Frankyl didn't think she should be on the throne, and his son didn't think she should be on a hunt.

As the last two riders appeared, Alexor urged Skyflame into an easy canter, and all of them fell in behind him. Their attention was now on the ground and small shrubs, looking for a trail or signs of foraging. It took another half hour of riding before they saw droppings that were relatively fresh, and found the spoor leading into a small vale between the hills.

Silently they picked their way down between the scrub. Nyla loved this part of the hunt. Every one of her senses heightened in the quiet. Her eyes saw every sway and scurry in the bushes, her ears heard the rustling underfoot, her nose picked up the distinctive whiff of a wild animal. The wildwood was close now. Her skin prickled with anticipation.

Alexor pointed at a small grove of trees. Wildwoods favored this kind of hiding place.

"Nyla, Troyl, Uzzer, and I will stay here," he whispered. "The rest of you go around and make some noise on the other side of the trees. That will beat him out and send him in our direction."

A few men looked disappointed but they followed Alexor's orders and skirted the grove. Only Lohlyn blatantly disobeyed his command, drawing her horse in next to Nyla's.

"Can I stay, Nyla?" she whispered.

Nyla nodded, casting a quick glance at her brother whose full attention appeared to be on the trees.

After awhile, Alexor whispered, "Spread out a little." His forehead furrowed when he spotted Lohlyn. He seemed about to speak, but the sound of voices from the far side of the grove distracted him. "Spread out," Alexor hissed again, and Nyla and Lohlyn edged away from the others.

Nyla lifted her bow and eased an arrow from her quiver as the voices increased in volume. She hardly dared to blink as her gaze roved over the trees, but nothing stirred there.

Suddenly there was an explosion of sound and movement—not from the grove, as they had all expected, but from the rocks that lay just to the right of Nyla. The pig was on them so quickly that Nyla was unable to release her arrow. Skybreeze reared in fright. Had she not been holding the bow and arrow, Nyla would have kept her seat, but instead she found herself flying through the air. Years of horsemanship saved her from what could have been a brutal fall, for in the split second that it took to crash back to the earth, Nyla bundled herself into a tight ball and rolled onto the hard ground. She would have frightful bruises the next day, but at least there was no searing pain to indicate broken bones.

No sooner had the comforting thought formed than she became aware of a pawing sound. She looked up to see the wildwood pig a mere fifteen paces from where she lay, lowering his head. He was about to charge, his tusks aimed right at her. She was dimly aware of shouting. It may have been Alexor or even a voice in her head telling her to move, but her limbs seemed paralyzed. All she could do was watch in grim fascination as the pig raced toward her.

An arrow plowed across the pig's back, momentarily slowing him down and swinging him off course. Yet his red eyes filled with an even greater rage when they found Nyla again. He let out a high-pitched shriek as he continued his murderous charge.

At the last moment, Nyla closed her eyes, waiting for the fatal blow. But it never came. Instead, there was a loud thumping sound as the pig fell to the ground and slid to a halt a few paces from where she sat. Nyla opened her eyes. A knife was embedded deep into the pig's side.

Lohlyn was the first to reach her. She dropped to her knees and pulled Nyla's shaking body into a tight embrace.

"It's fine, Nyla. He's dead. He can't hurt you," she whispered.

Alexor was there too, bending over her. "Nyla! By Taus, why didn't you move? Didn't you hear me calling?"

"Leave her alone, Your Majesty." Lohlyn said. "She's in shock."

Alexor moved away, joining Troyl at the body of the pig.

"Festering bait-breath!" Troyl whistled. "That's the cleanest kill I've ever seen. Look at that."

He reached for the knife and pulled at it. It didn't budge. "Straight into the heart and with incredible strength," he said. "It all happened so fast, I couldn't tell. Whose hand loosed it?"

Alexor turned and looked toward Lohlyn, whose full attention was on Nyla. "The handmaiden," he said softly.

"Well, I'll be." Troyl followed his gaze. "What a lucky shot. I mean, she hit the heart of charging pig. It's incredible."

"Yes." Alexor's eyes did not leave Lohlyn's face. "Incredible, is it not?"

CHAPTER 4

The Grotto was a surprise to Shara. She had expected little more than a basic, rough cave, but instead discovered a well-lit underworld settlement. Paths and carved-out steps led to huge caverns. The largest of these were common areas, such as the dining area with its ordered arrangement of tables and benches, and the barracks with its sleeping pallets. They also passed through a kitchen where several women glanced up at them in surprise. The sound of hammering could be heard through the cave wall to their right and, at Nicho's enquiring glance, Pearce said, "Armory."

Pearce led them through a maze of passages until they reached a small cavern closed off by a grid of iron bars. The slouching guard pulled himself to attention as he saw Pearce.

"Commander." He put his left fist over his heart in the Warrior salute.

"At ease," Pearce said. "Open the door, Taygor. We have two more prisoners."

Through the bars, Shara now saw two other figures. "Eliad? Brother Andreo?" She rushed forward, but Pearce grasped her arm in his iron grip.

"Not so fast, *my lady.* Here I tell you when and where you go." He smirked. "And I promise you'll spend plenty of time in the dungeon. No need to rush the experience."

"Let her go, Pearce!" Nicho hissed.

"As you wish." By now, the guard had unlocked the door, and Pearce thrust Shara through it. "You too, Nicho."

Nicho did as he was told and Pearce swung the door closed behind him.

"Pearce." Nicho turned back. "Please tell Derry I am here. I have news of Hildah and Jed."

There was a long silence before Pearce spoke. "The only one you will be speaking to is me, until we have this whole mess sorted out. What in the abyss were you thinking, bringing Highborns to the Grotto?"

"Please, Pearce. Your brother will want news of his wife and child."

"Someone will come for you so the interrogations can begin." He marched away without another word.

Shara knelt beside Eliad, fingering a dark bruise on the old man's forehead.

"It's nothing, my child," he said, a slight quiver in his voice.

"Are you fine, Brother?" Nicho asked.

"I am unhurt," Andreo said. "Am I right in assuming we have been captured by the Parashi Warriors?"

"Yes," Nicho said, "and this isn't exactly the warm welcome I had imagined." He slumped down next to Shara.

They sat in silence for a long time. A solitary wax candle lit the cavern, and Shara watched it shrink in size. There was no natural light to judge the passing of time, but her aching back and dry mouth attested to the fact that they had been here for several hours already. She was cold, too, her clothes still damp from the leap through the waterfall.

Finally, a key rattled in the lock.

"Dry clothes," the guard said, throwing a bundle of brown material at them. "Put them on then I'll take you to the High Commander."

Shara went alone to the back of the dungeon and took off her wet clothes, pulling the dry robe over her head. Quickly she knelt down and took the Cerulean Dusk Dreamer out of the wet robe's pocket. She held it reverently in her hands, feeling the familiar and comforting warmth tingle through her fingers.

How fortunate that the Warriors had not searched her. The beautiful blue rock was strictly forbidden in Tirragyl, its powers considered too great. Only the Guardian and Mind Rocks were more powerful. Yet, since she had found the rock in her uncle's study, Shara had grown rather attached to it. Sometimes Andreo's warning against the use of magic still rang through her mind, but Shara needed the rock to uncover the secrets her uncle had kept from her. Every time she fell asleep clutching the Cerulean Dusk Dreamer, it drew her into a dream that revealed something of the past or future. Although Shara didn't like the magic's side-effects—dizziness, weakness, and nausea—it was worth it if helped her unravel the mystery of who she was.

"The guards are back, Shara," Nicho's voice called. "Let's go meet this High Commander."

"I'm coming," she said, slipping the Cerulean Dusk Dreamer into the pocket of the shapeless brown robe.

Nicho looked around in amazement as two guards lead them through a maze of passages. Only now did it become evident how large the Guardian Grotto was. They passed through different barracks and dining areas and, incredibly, Nicho heard the sound of horses neighing. But he studied only the faces around him.

There were many, each looking at them in thoughtful, and occasionally hostile, appraisal. However, not one of them was the face Nicho sought—Derry, whom he had been unable to keep from following his brother Pearce to the Grotto.

The guards led them to a large, well-lit room. Maps were pinned to the wall and in the center stood a long wooden table. Pearce stood behind this, a tall man to his left. The only sign of this man's advanced age was his granite-grey hair, for he stood as strong and upright as a young oak. His face was dark and lined, that of a man often in the sun, and his green eyes flickered over the prisoners with sharp astuteness.

Their personal belongings were strewn across the table—food, water bags, and weapons—but it was on the book that the man's hand rested.

"Good day, travelers." His voice was deep and confident. "I am the Parashi High Commander, Mikel. Take a seat." He pointed at the wooden stools behind them, and the four of them each sat down as the two guards took up position at the door.

"Pearce tells me you were at the Echo Pool. No one has ever found us without a guide. Tell me, how did you get to be here?"

"We had a guide," Eliad said. "A Gold Breast bird called Tabeal."

"Gold Breast?" Mikel's eyes narrowed. "The ancient writings speak of such a bird. But if it exists, it has not been seen in many hundreds of years."

Eliad smiled. "The bird is real enough and it led us here after our escape from Gwyndorr."

"Escape? What were you escaping from?"

"Shara was escaping a marriage arranged by the Town Guard Captain, Randin."

"Do captains arrange marriages in Gwyndorr?" Mikel turned his appraising gaze to Shara.

"Randin is my uncle," Shara said. "I lived in his house for fourteen years, after my parents perished in the plague. Or so he told me."

"But you have reason to doubt his words?"

"I have always had the sense that there is far more to my past," Shara said. "And I'm determined to discover what it is."

"How exactly will you do that?"

Shara dropped her gaze, but not before the color rose to her cheeks. "I'm not sure, sir."

"So who did this Randin betroth Shara to?" Mikel turned his attention back to Eliad.

"Lord Lucian's son, Maldor," the old man answered.

"Lucian, Lord of Gwyndorr?" Nicho heard the coolness in Mikel voice. "But wouldn't that have been a good match for you, Shara?"

"No! I hate Maldor," Shara said, with all the fieriness Nicho remembered so well from childhood. "He's cruel. You should have seen how he beat Nicho almost to death."

Nicho squirmed under the High Commander's sharp and appraising gaze. "How is it that you have come to be at the Grotto, Nicho?"

"I was Captain Randin's groom, sir. The captain found out that I was teaching the Parashi boys their letters. He sent out some guards to arrest me."

"Indeed? How did you escape a whole group of guards?"

"Tabeal warned me. She took the three of us"—he pointed to Andreo and Eliad— "to rescue Shara from Lord Lucian's house."

"And then she led you here," Mikel said, "past all the defenses of the Guardian rock. An unheard of feat." His gaze dropped to the book lying on the table. "What of the book?" he asked. "If I'm not mistaken, it is written in the Old Tongue, very similar in structure to ancient Parashi, the language almost lost to our people in the Great Purge."

"Almost?" Andreo spoke for the first time. The High Commander looked up sharply. "I'm sorry, sir. We learned in the monastery that Parashi was completely eradicated after it became a crime to speak it."

"Not completely. In fact, I have several Old Parashi documents in my possession. I have also begun to teach it to our children. Andreo, was it?" His eyes studied the monk's face.

"Yes, sir."

"You are of the Brotherhood of Taus?"

"I was, sir."

"Is Andreo the name given to you at induction into the Brotherhood?"

Andreo nodded. "We are not permitted to speak our childhood name. We renounce it to become a new person."

"Yet one never forgets one's true name, for it is a part of who we are."

"Yes, sir." Andreo had dropped his gaze to the ground and his voice was soft as he said. "I was Riagall."

"A Parashi name," Mikel said. "How is it that the Brotherhood accepted a Parashi into their midst? Their codes are rather strict on such matters, are they not?"

"My mother was a Parashi servant, and my father a wealthy noblemen of some integrity. I inherited his Highborn features, and his money bought my position in the monastery. Only one other monk knew of my past and he, Brother Gladson, became my friend and ally. But toward the end of my days in the Brotherhood, another, Brother Angustus, started to suspect that I was not all I claimed to be. He initiated my disgracing." Andreo's voice was raw with pain. "The Gold Breast and Eliad found me on the cliff above the monastery just as I had decided to end my life." He looked down to the ground. "I know it is a shameful thing, but the next day I would have had to face Brother Angustus's mind powers. He would have stolen every part of me, and filled my mind with nothing but bland devotion to the Brotherhood. Death seemed the better option." The confession had tumbled out of him, surprising all present. There was a long silence before the High Commander spoke.

"I would have chosen death as well," he said softly.

"This is all very interesting," Pearce drawled, "but rather irrelevant. What we need to decide, sir, is what to do with this Highborn and her cohorts."

"*This Highborn*, Pearce?" The High Commander looked intently at Pearce. "You speak as if she is the enemy."

"Isn't she?"

"I have said it before. We are not fighting individuals. We are fighting a system."

"With respect, it's a system upheld by her people."

"I doubt this young woman has had much to do with oppressing our people." The High Commander's smile warmed his stern features, and Shara returned it.

"They all oppress in their own way."

"Somebody who befriends a Parashi groom does not carry the Highborn hatred in her blood, Pearce. We must learn to look beyond the names we call each other."

"It's irrelevant. She's one of them." Pearce's gaze found Nicho. "And by association, so is *he*."

"In fighting hatred, let us not learn to hate, Commander." Mikel turned back to the travelers. "We need to talk about your plans. Whether you are to stay or go."

"Go?" Pearce asked. "Sir, you plan to let them go? They know where the Grotto is!"

"We have established that they are not the enemy." The steeliness in the High Commander's tone seemed to dissuade Pearce from further argument.

"Perhaps we could stay, sir?" Nicho asked softly. "Bring those we left behind and join in the struggle."

"I would like that, Nicho. I am sure you have much to offer the Warriors. But Lord Lucian is a dangerous man." The High Commander turned to a map behind him, which showed the contours of the Highlands. He pointed to a spot on the map's edge.

"Gwyndorr. In the early years of his lordship, Lucian tried to find the Guardian Grotto. Like all before him, he never made it past Two Plague Pass, the access point to the Outer Peaks. You know that we are protected by the magic of the Guardian rock?"

"How does the Guardian rock do that?" Shara asked.

"Confusion. Disorientation. In the Old Times there were accounts of foghounds and other plagues overtaking our enemies. Also, those with mind powers—such as the Brethren of Taus—cannot seek us out with those powers. They cannot breach the Rock's defenses with their minds. It has kept us safe for more than four hundred years." Mikel smiled. "It also forewarns me of visitors."

"So you knew we were near, even before we reached the Echo Pool?" Nicho asked.

"I knew a few days ago, Nicho." Mikel's eyebrows furrowed together, "Although there was some unusual distortion that did not allow me to know if you were friends or foe."

"Maybe because they are both," Pearce muttered under his breath.

"If Lord Lucian is determined to wed his son to Shara and

suspects you are hiding here, he may well turn his attention to finding us again," Mikel said somberly.

"It is a risk indeed," Eliad said. "We are here only for a short respite, High Commander. Another, longer journey lies before us. With your permission, sir, could we stay awhile to renew our strength and replenish our stocks?"

"Of course. You will be our guests." The High Commander's smile contrasted sharply with Pearce's scowl.

CHAPTER 5

Klyden waited for his sister in the little-used storeroom behind the barracks, their usual meeting place. They always chose their time carefully—the early evening before Sacred Day, when all the off-duty guards visited the taverns of Lydora. Even if he and Lohlyn were seen together, Klyden knew his fellow guards would merely slap him on the back and congratulate him on conquering the queen's lady-in-waiting. They teased him often enough for the effect he had on women, an effect he wasn't even aware of. *Unwitting Loverboy,* they'd taken to calling him.

His sister slipped through the door he had left slightly ajar. Only when he heard the grating of the door as she pushed it closed again did Klyden light the candle. She made her way around the trove of rusted, broken weapons and shields and then sank down next to him on the dusty floor.

"Good to see you, little brother." Her smile wavered at his solemn expression. "Why so serious, Kly?"

"News of your wildwood kill is all over the barracks."

"I can imagine," she said wistfully. "A remarkable kill. Even for me."

"Even so, it was a mistake to show them your abilities."

"What could I do? The animal was about to maul the queen to death."

"There were other capable hunters around, weren't there?"

"I waited as long as I could. Come now, we have so little time." She threw her arm around his shoulder. "Let's not chew on this."

"You're a lady-in-waiting. You're not meant to know the blade of a knife from its handle." This could be the very thing that exposed her.

Lohlyn's intense gaze went right into him, as it always had. She saw beyond the anger in his words, to the fear.

"Kly, I'm being as careful as I can." She squeezed his shoulder. "I know what is at stake. We've always known the cost of keeping the queen safe."

Klyden recalled his father's solemn gaze and words. *Protectors give up everything—hopes and loves and dreams. They sacrifice everything, even life itself, for those they commit to protect.*

"We chose this," Lohlyn added gently.

Yes, he had chosen. At sixteen he had spoken the oath of a man, promising Mada he would do everything in his powers to keep her granddaughter safe.

"I know." He gripped her hand, still resting on his shoulder. "I've always known it could cost me my life, Loh. But the one thing I didn't consider is that it could cost you yours. Only that, I fear."

"Well, then it's a good thing I'm better at it than you," Lohlyn grinned.

"Pah! Better?" He smiled back at her. "Have you forgotten the time I smashed your wooden sword clean out of your hands and it landed in that pile of dung?"

"Perhaps you've forgotten how I made you fall *into* a pile of dung after one particularly long duel."

"There was foul play involved, I'm sure of it." He laughed at the memory. "You and Elxa were in on that together."

"The only foul play was on the seat of your pants."

They stayed a few more moments, sitting amongst the broken weapons of Tirragyl's army, remembering a lifetime long gone. Then they both slipped into the dark night to fulfill their oaths and offer their all in service to Queen Nyla.

· · ·

Lohlyn felt a pang of anxiety as she entered the queen's chambers. She couldn't have been gone for more than half an hour, but Nyla was nowhere in sight.

And sitting in Nyla's chair, her back to the door, was a dark-haired stranger.

Lohlyn forced herself into a state of calm, even as her fingers curled around the hilt of her knife. "Who are you, and where is the queen?"

The stranger spun around with a peal of laughter. "I fooled you, Lohlyn."

"Nyla!" Lohlyn's relief was great when she saw the familiar pale features of the queen, framed by the unusual dark hair. "What are you doing?"

"Trying out my disguise," Nyla said, lifting off the dark wig. "And if I fooled you, I can definitely fool others."

"Disguise? Why do you need a disguise?"

"Because I'm going to the Merchant Gate tomorrow morning."

"You can't go to the gate, it's not safe for—"

"I'm going," Nyla said with all the authority inherent to her position, "and you're going with me. That's an order."

Wrapped in a commoner's cloak, Nyla crept through Lydora's streets in the early morning light, Lohlyn by her side.

Her lady-in-waiting had almost persuaded her against this venture. Nyla had waivered when Lohlyn pointed out that their own close acquaintance was at stake should they be caught. Yet in the end, Nyla had decided that, as supreme ruler over Tirragyl, she would be able to protect her friend. Lohlyn had seemed surprised by her determination, but Nyla was beginning to realize that her subjects' lives were in her hands. If she couldn't keep them safe, who could? There was too much at stake for her to fade into the background, as she had always done before her coronation.

"What time do the gates open, Lohlyn?"

"Sunrise. There is a guard posted on the eastern wall who blows a trumpet."

"Should be soon then. Will we make it?"

"It's not much farther."

They moved through the still-slumbering streets in silence. Rows of stone buildings lined their way. Pictures hung over the arched doors in this row, depicting the trades practiced by the merchants within. This street and the two squares it connected were the commercial heart of Lydora. It was here that the people now crushing at the gate would come, hoping to sell their wares or make a few bronze coins for a service.

The sound of a trumpet pierced the silence.

"Come." Nyla grabbed her friend's hand. "We must hurry."

The two women ran over the cobbled stones toward the square, a low creaking sound indicating that the guards had begun to open the gates. As they reached the square, the doors swung fully open and the guards raised the portcullis. Nyla could now see the throng of people and hear the roar of their voices as they clamored for entrance.

"By Taus," Nyla whispered, "it's worse than I had imagined."

Like a course of water released from its blockage, the mass of people streamed through the gates, heading straight for Nyla and Lohlyn.

"Come." Lohlyn grabbed her hand and dragged her to the side of the square and up a flight of stone steps leading to the top of the wall. From this high vantage point, they could see the crowd outside the gate. The people shouted and pushed their way forward before the gates closed. All were dressed in the somber greens, greys, and browns of the lower class. A splash of orange drew Nyla's gaze to a young woman with a bright scarf wrapped around her head. She was pale and thin and had a baby strapped to her back. Nyla watched her anxiously in the crush of the crowd, hoping she would make it through the gates unharmed.

But she was still some way from the gates when Nyla heard the voices of the guards bellowing, "Step back from the gate or face death!" A large group of guards, linked together and brandishing shields, pushed into the middle of the stream of people, crashing their heavy batons down on everyone around them.

Nyla watched as the young woman tried to fight her way to the side, away from the guards, but the force of the crowd kept moving her forward. Fear was etched on the woman's face as she drew nearer and nearer the guards, who still swung their batons wildly. Nyla screamed as she saw the baton crush down on the woman's head, and watched as she stumbled to the ground, under the feet of the people. She continued searching the crowd for the woman's face. Maybe her scarf had come undone as she clambered back to her feet? However, there was no sign of her, although occasionally Nyla thought she spotted a flash of orange on the ground between the milling feet.

"Go home, Parashi scum!" the guards shouted as several of their companions dragged the gates closed.

Nyla shakily turned to Lohlyn. "By Taus, Loh. Did you see that woman with the orange scarf falling? We must go and see—"

"I saw her. She won't be the only one who fell today."

"She had a baby on her back. Did you see it?"

Lohlyn shook her head, a flicker of sorrow in her eyes. "There are at least ten or fifteen fallers a day, I hear."

"It's outrageous!"

"It's the risk they face for trying to make it through the gates," Lohlyn said matter-of-factly. "Let's go back before you are missed."

"No." There was a note of steel in Nyla's voice. "I want to go check that the woman and her baby are fine."

"They're probably not fine, Nyla." Lohlyn said gently. "Fallers seldom rise again."

Lohlyn stood uncertainly outside Nyla's chambers. The queen had never locked her out before. Yet on their return from the gate, she had barred the door and insisted nobody enter. She had refused the midday meal and ignored every offer of companionship.

"Nyla." Lohlyn spoke through the keyhole. "Can I come in now, please? I've brought some hot-herb."

After a long pause, she heard something shift inside and the tap of light footsteps. Then a heavy scraping sound as whatever Nyla had pushed in front of the door was moved out of the way. After another long wait, a voice said, "Come in."

Lohlyn pushed the door open. Nyla was sitting, barefoot, on the floor, a circle of paper around her and an inkpot at her knee. She was biting the end of the quill in concentration. Her eyes were puffy and red.

"What are you doing, Nyla?"

"Making plans."

Lohlyn sank to her knees and picked up the paper nearest to her. Covered in Nyla's neat scrawl, it contained a list of gates, names, and numbers.

"For what?"

"Helping the Outsiders."

"Right." Lohlyn picked up another and studied it. It was a map of Lydora. "And this one?"

"A rough drawing of where the new walls will be."

"Really?"

The queen looked up sharply. "You seem skeptical, Lohlyn."

"No. Well, not exactly. But the king and council will have to approve this."

"I know."

"And not everybody is as concerned about the Outsiders as you are."

"That's just because they haven't seen the desperation on their faces," Nyla said. "They all need to go and stand on top of the wall and see it with their own eyes."

Lohlyn thought there was little chance of that happening.

"Did you do as I asked?" Nyla asked softly, not looking up.

"Yes," Lohlyn said. On their way back to the palace, the queen had asked her to send somebody to the gate to check if the orange-scarfed woman and her baby were among the dead. After Nyla had barred her chambers, Lohlyn had decided to go herself. "She and her child were among the fallen." She could still see the bloodstained scarf and their bruised bodies in her mind.

"You were right, then. The fallen do not rise." Bitterness laced Nyla's voice. "What becomes of their bodies?"

"They leave them by the wall for a day or so. Sometimes a brother or father will come and take them away and bury them."

"And if they don't?"

"The guards . . . dispose of them."

"How?"

"The rubbish pile to the south of the city walls."

A bright anger burnt in Nyla's eyes as she looked at her friend. "In their minds, that's all they are. Rubbish."

CHAPTER 6

They had been at the Guardian Grotto for two days with no sign of Derry. Nicho had expected to find his friend swiftly, but he now realized it would not be that easy. Pearce was particularly uncooperative and the Grotto had an extensive network of caves. If Derry was stationed on the other side of it, he might not have heard of the new arrivals—or if he had, did not realize that Nicho was among them.

The High Commander had assigned them comfortable quarters. They consisted of two adjoining chambers containing six sleeping pallets. Torch sconces hung on the wall, providing a warm, flickering light during the day. The low table between the sleeping pallets contained additional oil lamps, water jars, and goblets. In a chest against the wall, they found some heavy tsebee skin blankets and a game of dice. After their many nights of sleeping under the stars, the group reveled in these small luxuries.

The exhaustion and stress of their long journey had caused them to sleep much of the first day, rising only for a late afternoon meal with Mikel and several of his commanders. Pearce had been absent.

On this, the second day, Mikel had told them to feel free to explore the Grotto. Shara headed for the kitchen, while Andreo and Eliad followed Mikel down a narrow passage to see his collection of old manuscripts. Nicho declined the invitation to join them, deciding instead to look for Derry.

He asked everyone he came across where Commander Pearce's brother was stationed, but the afternoon of questioning and searching proved fruitless. Nicho only received blank stares and shaking heads in response.

He was close to giving up when he heard the sound of muffled voices ahead of him. He followed the dimly lit passage to a large cavern, where several men sat polishing their swords. They looked up at him in surprise as he emerged from the passage.

"Good day," he said. "I am Nicho."

One of the men grunted something that might have been a greeting. The other three merely turned back to their swords.

"Could you help me?" Nicho persisted, turning his attention to the grunter. "I'm looking for a man called Derry. He is Commander Pearce's brother."

The grunter lifted his shoulders in a sign of indifference, but one of the other men looked up. "The Commander's brother, you say?"

"Yes. Derry. Surely you would have seen him?"

The man shook his head. "Never heard of him. Didn't even know the Commander had a brother."

"He came with the last batch of men." Nicho's exasperation was growing. Was everyone in the Grotto just hampering his search on Pearce's orders?

"The last batch of men the Commander brought?"

"Yes."

"The Grotto is big. More than a thousand men here now. I don't know them all." The man turned his attention back to his work.

"Surely you would have taken note of the Commander's brother?"

"You'd think so."

Another dead end.

"Wait," Nicho said. "There were others with him too. Curtis. And . . . I can't remember now . . . Madoc, I think."

"I know a Madoc," the grunter drawled. "Sleeps in my barracks. He's in the armory."

"Where's that?" Nicho had lost all sense of direction in the shadowy underground world.

The grunter pointed a thumb toward a passage at the rear of the cavern, and Nicho flung a word of thanks over his shoulder before he dashed down it.

A few more men had to point him in the right direction, but eventually he could make out the sounds of hammers beating against steel and he followed it to a large, hot cavern where eight men worked. One tended a fire which held two red-hot rods of metal. Others hammered rods into sharp blades. Their faces were streaked ash-black, and it was hard for Nicho to recognize Madoc through the sparks and heat radiating through the cave. His voice, too, was lost over the hiss of the fire and clanging blows. Finally, one of the men glanced up. He looked displeased to see a stranger in the forge.

"What is it?" he bellowed.

Nicho moved closer to him and shouted as loudly as he could, "Madoc!"

The man frowned and glanced around, his eyes coming to rest on the fire-tender. "He's busy!"

"The Commander needs him," Nicho lied.

The man huffed in irritation, but shouted something to the man next to him, who in turn gained Madoc's attention and pointed toward the stranger at the armory entrance.

Nicho, unable to bear the heat, slipped outside and waited for Madoc to join him. It didn't take long before the sweat-streaked youth appeared.

"I'm on duty," he shouted, still accustomed to speaking over the noise. "What the—" A look of confusion passed over his face. "I've seen you before. Gwyndorr slum, right?"

"Yes. At Pearce's house the evening before you left."

"I remember. The Commander said you were too cowardly to come with us."

"Pearce doesn't understand true courage," Nicho said under his breath.

"When did you arrive?" Madoc hadn't heard his last statement.

"Two days ago."

"Are you in the armory? Hope not, for your sake. It's a real abyss-hole."

"I'm not sure. But I wanted to find Derry. Do you know where he is?"

For a moment Madoc's features froze, and Nicho heard his sharp intake of breath. "Derry?"

"Yes, Derry!" Nicho felt a surge of anger. "Pearce's brother!"

"I know who Derry is," Madoc said softly, glancing up and down the passage before turning his gaze back to Nicho.

"So where is he?"

Madoc let out a long sigh and then said, "Derry didn't make it."

"Didn't make what?" Nicho shook his head in confusion.

"Derry . . . is dead."

"Derry is dead?" The words seemed wrong to Nicho, the notion impossible. "No, he can't be dead. You're all here."

"When we left Gwyndorr, there were patrols on the eastern road, but we skirted around them. We usually stayed about five hundred meters from the road. The Commander warned us not to get too close. Derry went out one morning alone before the rest of us even woke up. I think he wanted to find some wood to carve or something. He was always doing something crazy like that. But that day he went too close to the road. They caught him. We woke up to his screams."

Madoc shook his head as if to rid himself of the memory. "They tortured him because they wanted the rest of us to come running, too. But the Commander remained really calm. Told us to go ahead and get as far away as we could. He went back alone."

Something heavy pressed down on Nicho's chest, making it hard to breathe. *Derry was dead.* Hildah and Jed—Derry wasn't going back for them. Ever. He would never carve another horse or bowl or table. Derry. Sweet, innocent, trusting Derry.

Madoc's voice broke through his thoughts again. "The Commander caught up with us two days later. We were glad to see him. Thought they might have got him, too. He told us then what they had done to Derry. Barbaric, these Highborns." His voice choked with rage. "They had left his body. The Commander buried him under the ancient oaks in the Bloodbush Grove." He paused, taking in Nicho's shocked expression. "He was your friend, wasn't he?" After an uncomfortable pause, he said, "It's an honorable burial place for a Warrior. He would have liked it."

Nicho heard himself ask, "Why does nobody here know what happened?"

Madoc looked down, fidgeting with his fingers. "Commander Pearce told us that it served no purpose to speak of it."

"He told you not to?"

"Yes." The look of fear that suddenly crossed Madoc's face made him look like a young boy. "I've just disobeyed his command, haven't I?"

"I'm sure he won't mind that you told me," Nicho said. "I was Derry's friend, after all." His reasonable tone sounded as if it came from a great distance. How could he sound so very calm when he had just discovered that his best friend—more a brother than a friend—was dead?

"I'm going to find Pearce," he heard himself say. "You'd better carry on working."

"You won't tell him I told you?"

Nicho was already a few paces away. He heard the anxiety in Madoc's voice, but he did nothing to ease it. Everything in him was focused on two thoughts.

Derry was dead. And Pearce had to pay.

CHAPTER 7

Nyla stood before the Royal Council and looked into the faces of the twelve men. Two or three returned her gaze, but most averted their eyes. Duke Frankyl even whispered to the man next to him, a clearly defiant action as far as Nyla was concerned.

She drew courage from Alexor's presence on her left. He had promised that she could count on his support in this matter, and few on the council would dare to go against the will of both the king and queen.

She cleared her throat. "In summary, gentlemen, I propose that we extend the walls of Lydora to include the area where the Outsiders now live." She pointed to the map, which she had already explained to them in detail. "The workmen will be drawn from among the Outsiders, providing employment and enabling them to feed their families. The walls will mean that they are safe should Lydora ever come under attack.

"In the meantime, we will also let the Outsiders into the city on a rotation basis, using access to all five of Lydora's gates. And widows and orphans will be given a portion of grain every week. Are there any questions?"

"Your Majesty." Duke Frankyl rose. He was a short man with a sharp, beak-like nose. "Your ideas are most becoming of a great queen concerned for her subjects." His voice dripped with deference. "However, I would encourage the council to consider the great cost to the Crown of such an extensive project. Have you been able to determine just how much this would be?"

"I have indeed, Duke Frankyl. The stonemasons who were in my father's employ are calculating the costs. By the end of this week, I will be able to give you the exact amounts. Any other questions?"

"You can hardly expect us to approve a project this size before we have all the facts," the Duke continued. "We are men of age and experience and have seen many such projects fail when the gold runs out. It may require raising taxes, in which case the noblemen are likely to revolt. Or the Parashi will expect more than we can deliver and turn on us. You may be giving them the spark they need to start a raging fire."

"Hear, hear." Most of the men around the table nodded their agreement.

"If we do nothing and just allow them to die outside our city walls, will that not be a more likely cause for them to revolt?" Nyla stood her ground.

Lord Briskyl, ever the diplomat, rose to his feet. Nyla liked the tall, grey-bearded man for, unlike some of the others on the council, he treated her with respect. "I suggest we hear the king's position on this matter," he said.

Nyla took her seat, relieved to allow Alexor to address the meeting. She had told him about the woman and child crushed to death. He had pored over her maps and nodded thoughtfully. He had understood, had seen the need to help the people. If there was one person who could swing the council in their favor, it was Alexor.

"Gentlemen, I think the queen has raised some interesting insights into the problems Lydora is facing, with the many Parashi camped outside our city," Alexor said. "We can't deny that the situation requires action. She has proposed several plans to deal with the Outsider difficulty, but I think as a council we may be able to agree on several less costly options."

"Aye, there must be other solutions to this problem," one of the men said.

"As I see it," Alexor continued, "Lydora does not have the

resources to provide for so many Parashi. I think we should consider ways of encouraging them to leave."

"Leave?" Nyla was back on her feet. "They have nothing and nowhere to go, Alexor. That is why they are desperate enough to risk being crushed at the gate. Where else would they go but the capital city, where there is trade and money?"

"We can't just give them grain, Nyla. We would incur the wrath of the lords if they hear we are spending their tax money on handouts to the Parashi."

"Indeed, Your Majesty. You are endowed with great foresight," Duke Frankyl said smoothly. "But how do you propose we rid the city of this scourge?"

"Rid the city? Scourge?" Nyla's body shook with rage. "You speak as if they are a plague of rats, Duke. These are people. Our subjects, deserving of our protection and care." She tempered her rising voice. "We have an obligation to these people. We need to do what is right for them. For if we wrong them any more than we already have, I fear we become their enemies as much as the marauders from the west."

Nobody replied, but as she looked at them, she suddenly saw what Lohlyn had warned her of—her words fell like seeds on stony ground. They did not care about the Outsiders. Their only concern was their own welfare. How could she have been so blind all this time?

She turned to her brother. "Alexor? Surely you see what needs to be done?"

He dropped his gaze and cleared his throat. "I think we will adjourn this meeting for now. Let us all take time to think about these issues. We will reconvene tomorrow to hear other proposals."

Alexor and the men hurriedly filed from the room, but Nyla sat for a long time at the head of the long table. Everything in the room mocked her. The marble floor, inlaid with precious stones. The ivory chairs. The sparkling chandeliers. The gold goblets and spider-silk curtains. The crown on her head sang out that she had wealth and power in abundance, yet she understood, as never before, that it was a façade. She was powerless, an inconvenient accident of birth.

As much as Mada had tried to protect her, she knew. She had heard the palace whispers that spoke of the troublesome princess carrying within her a portion of the rightful king's soul. Never before had Nyla considered just what those words meant, but finally she understood. She was a half-soul, maybe even less, and because of that, she was powerless. Woman and children would continue to fall and be crushed and she, Nyla, would never have the strength to raise them to their feet.

The king was seldom free of lingering counselors and courtiers, but Lord Lucian finally found him alone in the palace gardens. Alexor leaned against the stone pillar of a previous ruler's arbor, his clenched fist repeatedly striking the crumbling structure.

"The heights of power are lonely places, are they not, Your Majesty?"

The king spun around.

"Forgive me, sire," Lucian bowed. "I startled you."

"You did," the king said petulantly. "I thought all my lords left many days ago. What still finds you in my palace, Lord Lucian?"

"Urgent, unfinished business, Your Majesty. I was hoping for an audience with you in the next few days to discuss the matters."

"There are channels," Alexor muttered. "Accosting the king in his garden does not win you much favor."

"My intention was not to accost you, be assured," Lucian said smoothly. "I just sensed an inner turmoil in you that I thought I might be able to alleviate."

"How do you propose to do that?"

"As king, you never know who to trust. Those closest to you could be plotting your destruction. It is a lonely and frightening place to be, and you need at least one person near you to watch your back."

"You think I do not have such a person? I've had such a person since birth." Alexor looked past Lucian to where his guards stood a stone's throw away. One snap of his fingers and Lucian's time alone with the king would be over.

"You may *believe* you have someone," Lucian said carefully, "but if you consider the situation closely, the people supposedly closest to us are often the ones who benefit the most from our demise." Lucian stepped on dangerous ground. What he implied came close to treason.

Yet he had read the king's mood well. Alexor's eyes widened slightly and he nodded as if Lucian's words had merit. Still, years of loyalty were not undone in a single conversation and he said, rather stiffly, "You do not need to fear for me. The queen and I have very capable people around us."

"Of course, sire. Now I will leave you to your thoughts." Lucian made as if to go, then turned back. "One more thing, King Alexor. I heard about the wildwood hunt. Your sister had a most narrow escape, did she not?"

"Indeed. It was a frightening experience for us all."

"How fortunate that the handmaiden handles a knife so well. Where was she trained? I have a good mind to send my son there for some lessons."

"It was an exceptional kill," Alexor said grudgingly. He did not seem to like his sister's lady-in-waiting—Lucian tucked the useful insight away. "But I myself attribute it to Taus's intervention. You would expect Taus to protect those of us divinely chosen for the throne, would you not?"

"Indeed, sire." Lucian nodded. "But such skill usually comes with years of practice. The woman is of noble birth?"

"I believe. She would have to be to serve my sister."

"Surprising. In my experience, noble ladies spend more time selecting wardrobes than practicing knife tosses." Lucian forced himself into another low bow. "I have intruded too long, Your Majesty. Thank you for your time."

Alexor gave a dismissive wave. "That audience you asked for, Lord Lucian? We will grant it tomorrow at noon in the throne room."

"Most kind of you. But could I propose I meet only with you, sire?"

"As opposed to the council?"

"As opposed to the queen." Lucian glanced down at his fingers, aware that he was again touching on forbidden territory.

"Why? We are joint rulers and make joint decisions."

"Of course, and I would not suggest it, except that it concerns the Parashi situation, and I hear the queen is"— he cleared his throat —"slightly *soft* when it comes to the Lowborns."

"Where do you hear that?"

"It is common knowledge that seeing the fallers at the gate moved her deeply."

"You think that is a bad thing?"

"I admire compassion as much as any man does. However, the greatest rulers make decisions with their heads and not their hearts. I believe you are that wise ruler, King Alexor."

Lucian could sense the king's turmoil. Loyalty to his sister warred with the pride of being declared greater and wiser than she. Lucian had known men such as the king before and he knew the outcome of Alexor's inner battle long before the king spoke.

"Fine. I will meet with you alone, Lord Lucian."

CHAPTER 8

Nicho had little recollection of how he found his way to the War Chamber. Maybe he asked someone, or maybe his burning grief drove him there in some inexplicable way.

Pearce sat alone behind the long table. The High Commander was nowhere in sight. It wouldn't have mattered to Nicho if he had been there, except that Mikel might have tried to stop Nicho from doing what he had come to do.

Pearce looked up as Nicho stumbled in. "I was wondering how long it would take you to find out," he said in a flat voice.

"You killed him, Pearce. You killed him! I begged you. Do you remember? *Begged* you not to take him." The cold rage that had taken possession of Nicho's body propelled him forward.

"I remember." Pearce's usual fearless bluster was gone. He hunched over as if all of Tirragyl's weight rested on his shoulders.

"Do you remember what I said I would do to you, Pearce? Do you remember that too?"

"Hunt me down like a wild pig. Well, here I am. No need to hunt me. Finish me off right here. Right now."

"That's exactly what I intend to do. Draw your sword!" Nicho glanced down at the sword in his own hand, not even sure where it had come from. It mattered little. Soon it would have accomplished its purpose.

"No."

"Draw it, Pearce!" Nicho cried. "You deserve to die for what you did to your brother. He was as innocent as a boy. How could you have done that to him? How could you?"

Pearce sat unmoving, head down, seemingly indifferent to the sword pointed at his neck.

"I said draw your sword!" Nicho's voice broke on the last word.

"I won't," Pearce said calmly. "If you want to kill me, do it. I won't defend myself."

How easy it would be to give vent to all that cold rage and drive the sword through him. He deserved it. To take innocent, simple Derry into the line of danger the way Pearce had done was tantamount to killing him with his own hands. Yes, Pearce deserved to die.

But Nicho couldn't do it. He had been prepared for the old Pearce—the hard, bristling, angry Pearce. How easy it would have been to fight him! But this pathetic, broken man?

After a long pause, Pearce looked up. "Well?" The hard edge was back in his voice. "Are you going to keep your promise? Or are you too weak to avenge my brother's death?"

"You know I'm not, Pearce."

"Then what are you waiting for?"

Nicho suddenly understood. Pearce *wanted* Nicho to kill him. The pain of losing his brother was so great that he had no desire to live anymore. Strangely, seeing his grief mirrored in Pearce's eyes softened something in Nicho's heart.

"It won't bring him back." Nicho sank down on the stool opposite him. The sword dropped from his hand. He cradled his head in his arms. "He's gone."

"Yes. Gone . . . forever."

They sat in silence for a very long time before Nicho asked, "Why did you tell the men not to speak of him?"

"I'm the strong second-in-command. The one who puts the Warriors above everything else. I didn't want them to see me as weak." Pearce shrugged. "Maybe I thought it would help me forget."

"Forget Derry?"

"Not Derry. The pain. The images seared in my mind. By the abyss, Nicho, you should have seen . . ." His voice choked with tears. "If you had seen what they did to him, you wouldn't be gadding around with Highborns, of that I'm sure."

"Leave Shara out of it, Pearce. She bears no responsibility in this. You, yes. Me, yes. I should have tried harder to talk him out of it. But Shara? Absolutely not."

Another sorrowful silence stretched between them before Nicho asked, "What now, Pearce?"

"Now?" Pearce looked up. "What is left to do now but carry on fighting?"

"What about Hildah and Jed? And Nana?"

Pearce looked away. "This is no place for women and children."

"That's not what you told Derry!" The rage simmered through Nicho's blood again. "You said you would send for them."

"Maybe, but not soon. There is much to be done before we have room for any more families."

"Were you even planning to send word to them about Derry's death?"

"They would have heard soon enough. There's always someone coming and going between the Grotto and Gwyndorr."

"By the abyss! You have a cold and cowardly heart." Nicho rose to his feet. "I should have run my sword through it. Everybody would have been better off."

"It's not too late," Pearce mocked.

"How could Derry have looked up to you?" Nicho suddenly wanted to stab Pearce, not with the sword, but with his words. "You would have his own wife and child starve to death in Gwyndorr. What would Derry say to that?"

"As I recall, Derry left them in *your* care." Pearce's voice was cold, calculating. "If they starve, it's because you are gallivanting around with your Highborn whore."

Nicho slapped him. For a Parashi, a slap was an act of humiliation, but the surprise in Pearce's eyes instantly changed to triumph.

"You'll have to choose now, won't you, Nicho? Do you follow a wench who has lured you through her Highborn charms, or do you follow the promise you made to your best friend?"

Nicho turned without speaking and stumbled out the door. Pearce's parting words tolled like a death-bell through his mind all the way back to the chamber.

Shara had made her way to the Grotto's kitchen that day and offered her help. The women's companionable chatter reminded her of Marai's kitchen, and by the time she helped serve the food in the dining hall that evening, she felt truly happy.

She finally dished herself a ladle of the stew and sank down on the bench next to Nicho, Andreo, and Eliad.

"How's the food? Any good?"

"Very good," Eliad said. "Is this your creation?"

"Well, I did chop the carrots and leeks."

"Tastiest carrots I've ever had." Andreo winked at her.

"What about you, Nicho?" She elbowed him in the ribs. "Best leeks you've ever tasted?"

He looked up at her, seeming to notice her for the first time. His mouth was pinched in a tight line, as if he was in pain, and dark smudges shadowed his eyes. "What did you say?" he asked.

"Do you like the stew?"

He looked down at his plate uncomprehendingly. "It's fine."

"Are you unwell?" She reached out to touch his forehead, but he swept her hand away. "Nicho. What is it?"

"Nothing. Can everyone stop asking me that?" He rose and stepped over the bench, stalking from the table without another word.

The joy of the day was quenched in that moment. Shara turned questioning eyes to Eliad, but he merely shrugged and stared after Nicho with puzzled eyes.

That night Nicho was nowhere to be found, and as Shara crept under her blanket, she was conscious of the empty sleeping pallet in the adjacent cavern. The first night they had arranged their beds on either side of the wall separating the caverns. They had tried to place them near each other, had tapped messages through the wall and giggled at the thought that only a hands width of wall separated them. But tonight there were no secret messages and no laughter, only silence.

Sleep eluded Shara. Her thoughts turned to the Cerulean Dusk Dreamer, hidden deep in her travel sack under her cloak. She hadn't used it since she came to the Grotto, but the more she thought about it, the greater her urge to hold it. She recalled its beautiful dusk-sky color and its comforting warmth, imagined the pleasant swaying sensation as its power took hold of her and wrapped her in its vivid dream world. She gave no thought to the sickness and headaches that inevitably followed.

Shara pushed the blanket aside and sat in the dark, listening to Eliad's rhythmic breathing through the cavern opening. She stretched out her hand and felt for the sack at the base of her bed. As she lifted it, she tugged open the neck and burrowed her hand deep within, feeling for the stone. All she felt, though, was the soft cloak.

A moment of panic engulfed her. Had somebody discovered the stone and taken it? But no—her fingers finally felt its cold, hard surface. She drew it out, holding it tightly as the surge of anxiety seeped from her body.

Shara lay down again, gripping the stone to her chest. It seemed to take longer than usual for it to pulse with warmth, but finally her palms began to tingle, the sensation inching up her arm and into her neck. As the familiar heat crept through her body, the rock's powers called to her own weariness, and she yielded to its strong pull.

The effect was immediate and stronger than ever before as a dream wove its way into her mind. She stood on a hill, towered over by stark, black rocks. Dark clouds swirled close above her head. Light flashed and thunder growled from deep within their layered folds.

Andreo had taught her that lighting always struck in high places, and she had an urge to climb down the mountain and seek shelter, but she saw no footpath leading from its heights. So she pushed herself into the cleft of two of the towering rocks and gazed down at the mighty city sprawled below her.

Shara had never seen a city like it. At least three, maybe four times larger than Gwyndorr, the walls could not contain all its inhabitants, for she could clearly see the mass of people camped beyond its boundary walls.

A crash of thunder made her jump. She felt it trembling beneath her feet. The dark mass of clouds now seemed close enough to touch. At their center was a deep hole—the eye of the storm.

She had to get away. She jumped from the cleft and began to run, but a black rock stood like a sentinel, blocking her way. She turned and ran another way, only to find a new rock hindering her. Surely there was a gap somewhere! But as she frantically grasped around to find it, it seemed as if the rocks moved in closer. She was completely hemmed in by their menacing height.

Shara fell to her knees. The wind died down and an eerie still-ness swallowed the sound of the thunder. To Shara it was even more frightening than the violent peals had been.

There is no escape. The thought was not her own. It came from somewhere outside herself, and was followed by another: *I see you.*

Shara was surprised to find, beyond the terror, a numbed sense of calm. Despite her shaking body, she slowly lifted her head and looked deep into the gaping hole in the clouds. At first, it looked like a huge mouth that could swallow her in a single gulp. But after awhile, the clouds brightened, catching some gilded sunlight or perhaps the brilliance of the lightning flashing deep within. Now only one small dark circle remained and around it, an oval of gold. She realized then that she was looking at an eye—a golden eye that watched her. She was mesmerized under its stare, until a pulse of pure white light shot down, searing her with its heat. The crash of the strike reverberated around her, a mixture of words and laughter: *I am coming to find you, Shara.*

· · ·

Mikel startled awake. He listened intently. Had he heard a scream? No—all was quiet in the Grotto. Yet not all was well. Deep within him, even as he slept, he had felt the flash of malicious power directed at the cave. Where had it come from? Even more importantly, how had it broken through the strong Guardian powers that protected the Grotto?

Somewhere there was a crack in their defenses.

He rose from his sleeping pallet, lit a lamp, and ran a finger over the spines of the books on his shelf until he found the one he sought. This was the oldest document in the Grotto, dating back almost four hundred years to the time just after the Great War and just before the Purge began. It was written in the Ancient Tongue, and the mere act of breathing in its scent of dust and ink filled Mikel with a peculiar mix of sorrow and joy. Sorrow at all that was lost. Joy at the small treasures that remained.

He had read the manuscript's words many times. It was an account of the simple life of freedom before the Highborn invasion and of the Great King who ruled in those days of peace. It told of the war in the mountains, of how the Parashi defense had finally been crushed, and the oppression that followed. *That continues to this day*, Mikel thought, turning the pages, looking for one particular passage.

Mikel did not seek the well-known history, but rather a single passage near the end, one he had read often but never understood.

Here it was. His fingers traced the lines as his mouth formed the ancient words. He read it again, slowly, emphasizing each word. Before, he had always attributed his lack of understanding to an error in translation. Now he knew that he had not understood the words for one simple reason—they had not yet come to pass. The words were a prophecy.

> *The Guardian, once strong, grows weak*
> *As evil pierces through the Dusk*
> *Midnight darkness follows*
> *And mountains shake at the wrath of the foe*
> *Before Dawn releases her light.*

Mikel slowly closed the book. *The Guardian grows weak. Evil pierces through the Dusk.* He sensed, in the deepest part of himself, that fulfillment of the prophecy had begun.

Nicho spent the night trawling through the caves. The endless, twisting passages of the Grotto confused him. They turned back on themselves, constantly leading to places he had already been. He wanted to get as far away as he could from his companions, Pearce, and the thoughts twisting in his mind. Thoughts that always returned to the same dark place. Instead, his journey into the bowels of the Grotto only mirrored the turmoil in his mind.

Finally he sank down on the hard ground of a small, empty cavern and curled his legs tight against his body. There were only two options open to him. Both filled him with dark dismay.

The first was to stay here—free—with Shara. To forget his promise to Derry. Forget about Jed, Hildah, and Nana waiting for their father and husband to return, not knowing that he was dead.

The second was to leave the Grotto, to turn his back on freedom, on Shara and their love, and return to Gwyndorr to take care of Derry's family. Fear filled him at this thought, for he had left Gwyndorr a fugitive with soldiers looking for him. Even if he managed to slip back in through the town gate, how would he find work to support Hildah and Jed?

What was more, the thought of leaving Shara pierced him and left him feeling vacant and bereft. How could he have grown to care so much for her? Beautiful, strong Shara, who had slowly shown him the deepest places of her heart? At the sight of her, his heart pounded and warmth spread through his body. Her laughter lifted him, her smile soothed him and chased away his doubts that they could be together. When he was with her, he felt whole, like the man he was meant to be. He could not bear losing Shara.

Yet, when he thought of staying, his mind returned to the last time he had seen Jed. Already the joyful light that had always shone in the young boy's eyes had dulled. Hildah's dark cares had become his own—Hildah, little more than a child herself. They had been desperate when he'd left a few weeks earlier. How would they be now?

Nicho stayed in that dark cave for a long time, his thoughts swirling into an abyss of despair. When he finally stretched out, his body aching from the cold and lack of movement, Nicho had made his decision. He knew what he had to do.

CHAPTER 9

Lucian followed the king's servant to a little-used room at the back of the palace. Obviously the king did not want his sister to know of their meeting. It showed just the smallest of cracks in their seemingly inseparable relationship. With enough time and patience, Lucian felt sure he could widen it.

His thoughts returned to the night before when he had been drawn to pick up his Mind Rock. The smooth black rock, swirling with flecks of light, had been unusually hot to his touch. Initially he had allowed its powers to take his mind into the thoughts of those in the palace. But soon Lucian had become aware of another, far more distant, mind.

Shara.

He had thrilled at the realization that the girl had once more picked up the Cerulean Dusk Dreamer. Since all the power rocks were connected, Lucian could access her mind despite the distance between them. And since the girl had reached the base of the Parashi resistance, Lucian could look into the very heart of the Guardian Grotto.

His excitement had made him careless, however, and he had shown himself to the girl. In future he would have to be more subtle. Her terror had been so great that she might not use the Dreamer again. If he was to locate the Grotto, he needed more time with her.

"Wait here, Lord Lucian." The servant stood aside and swept his hand toward the room. "The king will join you shortly."

Lucian stepped into the room and walked over to the tall, narrow window that looked over the Royal Guard barracks.

As he looked at the grey buildings, he thought again of the night before. During the connection with Shara, he had sensed the Grotto's vastness. He had also felt the presence of another person—an older man with steel grey hair and wise eyes. In their split-second encounter, Lucian sensed the man had authority and strength. It was unfortunate the man had realized the brief breach in the Grotto's defense. Lucian may have lost the element of surprise.

"Lord Lucian." The king's voice broke through his thoughts.

"Your Majesty." Lucian bowed with all the reverence he could muster.

"Why did you want a meeting?" The king positioned himself on a broad wooden chair and indicated for Lucian to take the one beside it.

"A direct ruler, I see. I appreciate that." The young king flushed with pleasure at the compliment. "I come with a proposal that could greatly benefit us both." Lucian paused to let the thought sink in. "Have you heard of the Guardian Grotto, Your Majesty?"

"Of course."

"The Grotto has been a hotbed of dissension for almost four centuries. Ever since the invaders conquered Tirragyl."

"I know that," the king said petulantly.

"Of course you do, Your Majesty. You also know that, in all that time, many have searched for its location and failed."

"Because it's protected by a Guardian Rock."

Lucian nodded. "The Grotto is the seat of the Parashi resistance. Prohibited documents are kept there. Rebels are trained and organized into an army. Plans are made for the overthrow of your throne."

King Alexor snorted. "You make them sound like an actual threat."

"Because they are, Your Majesty."

"Have you seen my army? A few rebel soldiers would be nothing more than an annoying bee to a grubear."

"The odds may appear to be in your favor, but I would not underestimate them, King Alexor. They have powerful weapons at their disposal."

"Really?" The king stretched out languidly and stifled a yawn. "Such as?"

"The discontentment of the Parashi. The Lowborns have little to lose and if the Parashi Warriors spur them to take up arms, you will be faced with a problem."

"An army of poor, hungry peasants, with the odd pitchfork for a weapon." Alexor laughed disdainfully. "I think we'd be able to handle them."

"They won't be attacking during the day. They will be setting alight buildings, destroying roads, poisoning water. Insurgent tactics designed to cause mayhem. And with such a vast population of Parashi, it could be difficult to eradicate."

For the first time, the king shifted in his seat, his smug expression slipping a little.

Lucian continued. "The other weapon they have is the Guardian Rock."

"Useless! Other than hiding their location it's absolutely useless to them." The king rose to his feet. "It's nothing more than a chunk of stone. I should know. I have its twin locked in my vault."

"I know a little about the power rocks, Your Majesty, and you are essentially right." Lucian had to tread carefully now. "The Guardian Rock needs its companion for its full powers to be released. Yet the two rocks do have some powers individually, too. It is, as you pointed out, the only reason we haven't located the Grotto."

"Besides shielding the Grotto, what more could they do with it?"

"I'd rather we were not in a position to discover that, Your Majesty. Which is why I come to you with a proposal."

The king sat down again and stared warily at Lucian. "Out with it then."

"I have discovered the location of the Grotto."

"How in the abyss . . . ?" The king's expression was incredulous.

Again, Lucian was on dangerous ground. The higher-level power rocks were outlawed, and if it was known that he had a Mind Rock, he would be forced to relinquish it.

"My son, Maldor, was betrothed to a young woman who fled to the Grotto a few weeks back. I had her followed," Lucian lied.

"Why did she flee?"

"It matters little, Your Majesty." Lucian's even voice did not betray his irritation. "But it showed us the location of the Grotto."

"So where is it then?"

Lucian had expected this question, and drew out a map of the highlands, on which he had marked the so-called location of the Grotto. The fact that he guessed did not overly concern him. By the time he led a campaign against the Warriors—and captured Shara again—he would know exactly where it was.

The king studied the map intently. "Who would have known?" His eyes lit up with boyish excitement. "I will convene my war council immediately so we can plan our attack. I will be known as the king who found the Guardian Grotto and annihilated the Resistance."

"May I suggest we proceed with some caution?" Lucian interjected quickly. "My men have been scouting the area and know it well. They are trying to determine the number of rebels and the weapons at their disposal, as well as any weaknesses in their defense."

"Good, good. You will be on the war council then."

"I think, Your Majesty, we should meet privately a few more times before we call together the council. That way I will be able to give you valuable information that your counselors will not have access to. The old, experienced generals will not be able to dominate you. You will have all the power."

The king nodded vigorously.

"Also, there might be some opposition. We must ensure our plans are well worked out before sharing it with a council."

"Opposition? Who would oppose removing a four-hundred-year-old thorn from our flesh?"

"Women are peace lovers and do not always have the stomach for war," Lucian said smoothly.

"Women? You mean my sister?" The last word carried a load of contrasting emotions.

"I was thinking of her, yes." Lucian bowed his head and let the dissentious thought take root.

"My sister and I almost always see eye-to-eye," the king declared. "I do not expect her to oppose this."

"Of course. But let us not concern her with the small strategic details. Let us meet, you and I, in the next month and have an attack plan in place to present to the queen and war council."

The king stroked the stubble on his chin and nodded. "Fine. We will meet as often as required to plan this. Is there anything else you need?"

Lucian bowed and considered just how well the meeting had gone. Everything had fallen into place just as he had planned. Everything, except one thing. He had thought to bring it up at a later stage. Yet, with the king this enthusiastic, maybe he would be open to the suggestion now.

"There is one more thing, Your Majesty. Could you perhaps bring the Guardian Rock to our next meeting? I think it will play an important part in our plans."

The king's brow furrowed slightly. No doubt he had been told the Rock was dangerous and needed to be kept out of sight, secured by chain and lock. It was therefore an indication of the trust Lucian was gaining when he said, "I will see what I can arrange, Lord Lucian."

Nyla's warm hand curled around Mada's bony fingers. They felt cold and twig-thin, almost as if they could snap with the slightest pressure. Hesta had sent word that Mada was weaker.

"Mada?" Nyla whispered. Fear fluttered through her when there was no response. She tried again, a little louder. "Mada."

Her grandmother's eyes opened and for a moment, confusion etched her face. Then her eyes came into sharp focus on Nyla's face.

"You are here," she whispered.

"Yes, Mada."

"Your brother?"

"I will send for him immediately." Nyla turned to Lohlyn and Hesta, standing in the shadows of the room, but before she could call them over, Mada tightened her grip on Nyla's hand. The strength in it surprised Nyla.

"No!" Mada's voice cracked. "No."

"Of course. There will be plenty of time to speak to Alexor. This can just be our time."

Her grandmother's eyes flickered to where Lohlyn and Hesta stood, watching anxiously. "Leave us," she muttered.

The two of them slipped from the room. Mada pointed a trembling finger to the goblet of water, and Nyla lifted her up slightly to give her a sip. It shocked her just how light Mada felt—like a young child. The water revived her slightly, and again she squeezed Nyla's hand in a vice-grip and turned earnest eyes on her.

"Nyla, there are things you need to know . . . should have told you before." She sank back on the pillows and breathed a few shallow breaths before she continued. "The Tirragylins believe twins are cursed. Half souls." The few words had tired her.

"I know, Mada. They think I have part of Alexor's soul in me." Why was Mada wasting her precious breath telling her this now?

"Who told you? Lohlyn?"

"No." What did Lohlyn have to do with all of this?

"Who?"

"I don't know, Mada. I'm eighteen. I've heard people speaking. It didn't seem all that important."

"It is . . . very . . . important." Her grandmother's voice rose a notch, causing a fit of coughs to rack through her body.

Nyla gave her another sip of water. The coughing had weakened Mada and she sat solemnly looking at Nyla. Her long, silent gaze was uncomfortable and, to fill it, Nyla told Mada about some of the lighter aspects of life at court.

She did not mention her disagreement with Alexor or the council on the Parashi issue, nor the woman with the orange scarf crushed at the gate. Instead, she spoke of the antics of ladies trying to court her favor and the strange meals the new chef had been preparing in an attempt to impress her and Alexor. However, in the middle of a sentence, Mada interrupted her.

"Nyla, listen. You . . . *you* are the rightful ruler. You care." She caught her breath again. "Never believe you are less or half."

"Alexor and I are joint rulers, and will be for life, Mada. It's written into the laws of the country."

"Many . . . want you dead." There was another long pause. "They . . . want Alexor to rule."

"No. You are wrong." Yet even as she said the words, she saw Duke Frankyl's pinched face in her mind.

"Be careful." The words were a whisper, and Nyla leaned in closer to hear them. "Be careful of Alexor."

"Are you saying Alexor would harm me?" Anger pulsed through Nyla. How could Mada imply something like that? Didn't she know how close they were? How they loved each other?

Mada's sunken body trembled slightly, and a surge of compassion replaced Nyla's anger. Her grandmother was old and her thoughts no longer clear. She had lived through difficult times and witnessed atrocities, many committed by her husband and son. Could anyone blame her for her paranoia? She could no longer tell good from bad, safety from danger.

"Hush now. Everything is fine." She stroked her grandmother's face. "Get some rest."

"Promise, Nyla . . . promise to be careful."

"Yes, Mada. We'll be careful."

A smile ghosted over Mada's lips before she closed her eyes again.

CHAPTER 10

On the morning after Shara's terrifying dream, Andreo convinced her to go to the Grotto's classroom with him, where Mikel had put him in charge of tutoring the Grotto children. Andreo thought Shara might enjoy meeting them and, if she agreed, would let her tutor the younger children, while he focused on the older ones.

Shara returned from the classroom elated, her nightmare all but forgotten as she regaled Andreo with an account of her first day. The children had drawn pictures, made letters with stones, and sung funny alphabet songs. They had created plays and fought imaginary battles to learn about history.

"You're a natural teacher, Shara." Andreo beamed at her as they made their way down the passage leading to their chambers.

"Tomorrow I think I will make them mark out a big map of Tirragyl with stones and I'll teach them about the different towns and . . ."

Shara's words trailed off at the sight of Eliad and Nicho sitting on the floor near the chest in deep conversation. As he saw her, Nicho jumped to his feet. The haunted expression in his eyes was one she had never seen before. Where yesterday he had seemed angry, today he seemed . . . sorrowful.

"Shara." He came over and reached out to take her hand, but then reconsidered, dropping his arm to his side. "You're back."

"So are you."

"Yes." They stood looking at each other as if a deep vale lay between them, one that neither words nor touch could breach.

"Where were you?" he finally asked.

"I helped Brother Andreo teach. You?"

"I went deep into the Grotto." He paused, before adding, "To think."

"About what?"

He looked away and shook his head. "It's difficult to explain. Come sit."

Shara looked at Eliad, who smiled fleetingly and patted the floor. Reluctantly she sank down next to him. Andreo did the same.

"Is that what you and Eliad are talking about?" she asked.

"A little." He cleared his throat. "I heard some news yesterday." His voice grew thick. "My best friend Derry, Pearce's brother, was killed on his way to the Grotto."

"Oh, Nicho." She reached out her hand to him, but let it drop as he continued.

"Derry has—I mean, *had*—a wife and son. Before he left, I promised to take care of them should . . . should anything happen to him." His gaze on her was steady, resolute. "I'm going back to Gwyndorr."

"No!" The single word punched all the air out of her, and a hollow ache crept through her midriff. "Please don't go."

Eliad spoke quietly into the long silence: "Are you planning to return to us, lad?"

"I don't know. It's a long way there and back. And the child is young." His voice trailed off. "But I want to. I really, really want to."

Shara dropped her face into her hands. The ground under her seemed to shudder and tilt.

"The town guards might still be on the lookout for you," Andreo said. "Randin, too."

"I know the risks. But I cannot go back on my word."

Shara glanced up at Nicho then. Their eyes met briefly, before they both looked away.

"Take this." Eliad drew a long, narrow object wrapped in oilskin from his sack and put it, almost reverently, into Nicho's hand.

"What is it?"

"The best weapon for such a perilous journey. Unwrap it and I will explain."

Nicho unrolled the skin to reveal a thin reed pipe.

"I'm no musician, Eliad," he said. "And that's the weakest weapon I've ever seen."

"It's no ordinary pipe." Eliad lifted the pipe from the cloth and ran a finger over its smooth surface. "It calls the Gold Breast."

"Tabeal comes if you play the pipe?" Andreo asked.

"Every time." Eliad smiled.

"But if I'm in Gwyndorr and Tabeal is here somewhere in the mountains, how will she hear it?" Nicho asked skeptically.

"She will hear. And she will come. No matter where you are." He placed the pipe back in Nicho's hand. "Take good care of it, lad. I think of it as the Hope-Caller."

They sat awhile longer, Eliad speaking the most—words of encouragement and strength, even of hope that they would all be reunited one day. Shara wanted to believe them, and she saw in Nicho's eyes the same longing, and the same doubts.

At some point in the evening, the two older men retired to bed, leaving Nicho and Shara in uncomfortable silence.

"You should probably get some sleep too," Shara said.

"Yes." But he did not move. She felt his gaze burning on her face but looked away.

"I'm sorry I have to do this, Shara."

"Me, too."

"It doesn't mean I don't . . ." He shook his head. "I care for you, but I—"

"It's fine." His words meant nothing. Only his actions mattered now. And his actions were to choose another over her. "Are you packed?"

"Yes."

"When are you leaving?"

"Sunrise."

"Be careful." She rose, and he scrambled to his feet. For a moment, she thought he would draw her into an embrace, so she quickly turned away. "Good-bye, Nicho."

"Good-bye, Shara."

Long after the lamps were doused, Shara lay awake, thinking of what had come to pass since the day the Gold Breast found her. She recalled all the times she had spent in the stable with Nicho—naming the newborn foal Kharin, speaking of their dreams, laughing. She remembered the day she had first left Gwyndorr, hidden under a horse blanket. How free and joyful they had been.

That day she had first sensed Nicho's feelings might be as deep as her own. Then came the shock of her intended wedding to Maldor and the realization that she would never see Nicho again. But he had come back for her, had risked everything to break into Lord Lucian's estate and save her. Why wasn't she worth anything to him anymore?

Sometime in the early hours of the morning, sleep overcame Shara's turmoil and grief, and she would never know that Nicho, too, had laid awake deep into the stretches of the night, until he finally rose. She never saw him pause beside her sleeping form to bend down and stroke her hair—so softly she didn't even stir—before creeping from the bedchamber.

All she knew was that, when she awoke in the morning, Nicho was gone.

CHAPTER 11

Two weeks had passed since Lucian started meeting with the king. Two weeks since he had first laid eyes on the Guardian Rock, had touched it and felt its wild, untamable power lash through his fingers again.

Lucian had forgotten how ordinary it looked. Whereas the Mind Rock was as mysterious and dark as a midnight sky and the Dusk Dreamer was an exquisite blue, the most powerful rock of all, the Guardian Rock, was an ugly grey color. One part of it was rough and misshapen, while the other—the part which had been hewn from its other half—was flat and smooth, with dark striations swirling through it. It had been heavy as he cradled it in both his hands.

Briefly, its power had seared into his mind and he'd directed it outward, searching tentatively for its companion rock. But pain had exploded through his head as he did so. He had stumbled backward, almost dropping the rock as the king reached out to steady him.

Even now the memory filled him with rage. He had looked like a fool. Just as it had before, the power in the King's rock mocked him. But not for long.

He had hoped the king would entrust the Guardian Rock to him. Had felt sure that, with enough time and practice, he could tame a small portion of its energy and twist it for his purposes. However, the king had dutifully carried the rock back to its hiding place and had not brought it out again.

They met every second or third day and, at least on that score, Lucian was pleased with his progress. Slowly, he was starting to breach the king's defenses. Alexor was sharing his thoughts and feelings with him. This morning he had even asked Lucian's advice concerning a matter of state.

Lucian turned his attention to the chest that had just been delivered to his chambers. No ordinary chest, it had a small mechanism in its base that, when released, revealed a hidden compartment containing a sealed letter. He studied the mark on the letter's wax seal—a bird's claw. Lucian had used the services of the one called The Raven once before. The spy's cloak and dagger tactics were legendary. He was a master at creating a sense of danger and mystique.

Lucian tore open the letter.

Lord Lucian,

As you requested, I have investigated those closest to the queen and, in particular, her lady-in-waiting. After an extensive search in the western cantrefs, I can confidently say that there is no trace of a noble lady by the name Lohlyn of Lorren. The woman is clearly an imposter. I have placed myself in grave peril, but I believe that I am close to discovering her true identity. If you wish to continue using my services, place another eight sovereigns in this chest and have it delivered to The Nest.

Anger flared inside Lucian. He had already paid the Raven an exorbitant fee. Should he allow the man to extort even more from him? Did the spy realize just who he was playing with?

Still, the Raven's note confirmed his own instincts that the queen's lady-in-waiting was more than she appeared. When the king told him how she had slain the wildwood pig, he had been even surer that she was more than a pretty companion to the queen. Just what that "more" was, he had not understood. Every discreet enquiry he made unearthed the same information. The girl's name was Lohlyn of Lorren. She was twenty-five and the daughter of a minor landowner in the small, far western cantref of Droyl. She had come to the palace seven years ago as a companion to Princess Nyla. She had no living relatives, for her father had died the year she came to Lydora. Lucian didn't believe a word of it.

He continued reading.

I will need two other things in order to proceed. If it is true that you have the king's ear, the first should not be too difficult. I will require a letter bearing the king's seal, stating that my investigation is under his authority. However, the second may prove to be the death knell to this investigation. I need a single word from the king—a word he may have been told never to utter. I need to know the Charab arming word. Should I continue this search without it, I am a dead man. If the money and letter reach me before Tuesday, you will hear from me soon. If not, I will consider the investigation closed.

Lucian crumpled the letter into a tight ball and threw it into the fire, watching the flames devour it. His thoughts stumbled to another time and another place.

The Charab. The name was almost lost in the dusty recesses of his past. Could the Raven have discovered a link between them and the girl? Unlikely. The Charab—king's assassins—were always men. Yet if he could even hint that such a link existed, it could be the spark he needed to set the palace, and kingdom, alight.

Lucian sat by the fire until the flames dwindled to embers, sifting through the old memories until he uncovered the one he needed. The Charab arming word was a word so potent, it was whispered only on the deathbed of the king, and only to his successor.

Lohlyn cast another anxious glance at the queen. Nyla may have agreed to come for a walk in the palace gardens, but the sunlight had not lifted her mood.

"Look here, Nyla." She pointed to the purple butterfly settled on the frisia bush. Lohlyn's finely honed senses picked up a waft of the sweet perfume that had attracted the insect. "Can you smell the flowers?"

Nyla came over and bent toward the blooms. She straightened with a smile. "That's lovely. Let's sit here for awhile, Loh."

A sense of lightness, as fragile as the butterfly, finally seemed to settle on Nyla as they sat in silence, looking over the rolling gardens of the palace. Lohlyn knew better than to splinter it with words.

Nyla's last few weeks as queen had been difficult and unsettling. The girl and her child crushed at the gate. Then the rejection of her proposals by the council. Mada's death had shaken her, too, but Alexor's decision to bury their grandmother outside of the royal plot had spiraled Nyla into despondency.

He said she didn't deserve it. Said she did nothing but hamper the kings. Nyla had wept as she reported her brother's words. *I told him she should be honored for hampering such evil reigns. We just don't seem to agree on anything anymore.*

"Did you ever run a Two-Tied race?" The queen's voice brought Lohlyn back to the present.

"A what?"

"Two-Tied race. Where your leg is tied to that of your partner's?" Nyla smiled. "We used to do it down there between the trees, with some of our cousins." Her voice was wistful. "So did you?"

"I don't think so."

"You would have remembered. It's difficult until you get the hang of it. You have to work together. Alexor and I knew just how to do it. We'd throw our arms around each other's neck and call 'in, out, in, out,' and it would be as if we were one body. Nobody could beat us."

"They weren't just letting you win because you were the royal heirs?" Lohlyn grinned.

"We were always in tune with each other. I thought it would be like that always." Sadness pierced the fragile happiness the memory had evoked. "I thought we would go through life tied together, two people working as one."

"Life's not a game. It's more complicated than moving your feet at the right time," Lohlyn said. "Maybe you just need a new system."

They sat awhile longer watching the sun edge toward the horizon.

"You know, Loh? I think you might be onto something?" Hope echoed through Nyla's words.

"I am?"

"We need a new system. And to get one, Alexor and I need to sit and talk all this out." The queen clambered to her feet.

"Talking is always a good place to start," Lohlyn said cautiously.

"I'm going to find him. Come!"

"Maybe you should do this tomorrow, Nyla."

"We've wasted enough time already."

Lohlyn followed Nyla back to the palace, her eyes ranging over the tree trunks and shifting shadows for one single, out-of-place movement. As good as it was to see Nyla's mood lift, Lohlyn remained wary. She had spent far too many hours with Mada to let down her guard where Nyla was concerned. For Mada's dark musings always concluded in the same way—Nyla's life was in danger.

Nobody could tell them where the king was, and it was sheer chance that they walked past a quiet passage as he and one of the lords stepped out of it.

"Alex! We've been looking for you." Nyla flung an arm around her brother's waist. "Where were you?"

As the king indicated Lohlyn could rise from her curtsy, she sensed the lord's gaze on her. He looked at her with such intensity that her skin crawled with a sense of danger. *Your body talks to you. Listen to it*, her father had always said. If she listened to her body now, she would turn and run. Instead, she edged closer to Nyla.

"Nyla, do you remember Lord Lucian of Gwyndorr?" Alexor said.

The man's eyes left Lohlyn's face as he bowed at Nyla. "Your Majesty. A pleasure to be in your company again." His voice was soft and musical, like a brook of water. It soothed away some of Lohlyn's disquiet.

"The pleasure is mine, Lord Lucian."

"And this must be Lohlyn of Lorren," the lord said, turning those strange golden eyes on her again. "Slayer of wildwood pigs. How well you did to keep our cherished queen safe."

The queen beamed at Lohlyn, pleased at the acknowledgement

of her lady's bravery, but Lohlyn felt a fist of dread clench inside her, for she heard the undertone of suspicion in his words.

Nyla turned back to the king. "Remember how nobody could beat us at the Two-Tied race?" At his bemused shrug, she said, "We need to start running this ruling race like that. And we can. We just need a new system." She linked her arm into his, and for just a moment Lohlyn imagined the giggles of the young twins running arm-in-arm down a green hill. "You will excuse us, Lord Lucian? My brother and I have much to discuss."

The lord bowed as the king and queen left, but as Lohlyn made to follow, he reached for her hand. She began to pull away, but his grip was strong as he lifted her hand to his mouth.

"It's been a delight, Lohlyn of Lorren."

Strange how, despite his cold lips, that kiss burned its memory onto her skin for the rest of the night.

CHAPTER 12

Almost three weeks had passed since Nicho left. Shara moved unthinkingly through the routine of her days. Other than the few hours she spent each day in the Grotto classroom, she found little joy in life. Under the watchful eye of Eliad and Andreo, she dutifully ate something at each meal, yet it tasted bland and felt difficult to swallow. The talking and laughter at the dining tables swirled around her, but to Shara it seemed as if she stood far from it, only hearing faint echoes of words. With Nicho lost to her, her life felt colorless and bleak.

Only at night did the color return. She had sworn, after that last fearful dream, never to touch the Dusk Dreamer again. Yet its warm comfort had drawn her back, and never before had her dreams been so beautiful, so vivid and filled with hope. She and Nicho walking in a field of yellow flowers. Nicho riding on a beautiful stallion and pulling her onto his saddle. The sound of children—*their* children— laughing as Nicho chased them down the twisting paths of a beautiful garden. Every night, the Dusk Dreamer reflected all her hopes and dreams back to her, as if they would truly come to pass. It was all that kept her going.

Tonight, she gripped the rock to her chest again and let the dream carry her to the man she loved.

Nicho stood a few paces away, his back to her. He was throwing a stone into a large body of water as small waves lapped at his feet. The sky was awash with the golden light of sunset. He turned, saw her, and his eyes lit with pleasure. She ran to him, her bare feet sinking into the fluid sand. She had never stood at the edge of a sea before, but she had eyes only for Nicho.

"You came," he said.

"Of course, my love."

They held each other. Shara breathed in the familiar smell of his skin—warm and alive, and slightly salty from the sea spray. She did not need to speak. If all she did was stand here for the rest of her life, she would be content.

Then he pulled back from her embrace, and for one strange moment, it seemed as if he was looking through her, almost into her. But then his eyes were back on her face, his smile melting away all the day's sorrow.

"Where are we?" she said, finally looking at the beauty around her.

"The edge of the Rhorhan Sea. Lovely, isn't it?"

"What are you doing here when you were going back to Gwyndorr?"

Surprise flashed on his face. "Why would I go back there?"

"For Derry's son and wife, remember?"

"Yes, of course." He waved his hand as if it was of little concern. "We have so little time, though. Tell me what you've been doing. How are things at the Grotto?"

"Lonely without you, Nicho."

"I will come back for you. I said I would, didn't I?"

No, you never did, Shara thought.

Nicho continued, "But what of the others?"

"Brother Andreo is tutoring. I'm helping him. And Eliad? He seems to spend much time with the High Commander, poring over old books and maps."

"The old man with steel grey hair?"

"Yes." Shara narrowed her eyes. "Mikel."

Something shifted under her feet as she said the name. A sharp crack broke through the sound of the lapping waves, and a discordant keening grew in volume. The edge of her vision began to blur.

"What is happening?" Shara shouted over the jarring sound.

Nicho looked around furtively before turning to her and grabbing her hands.

"Listen to me. Hide the Dusk Dreamer. This High Commander knows about it. If you don't hide it, you'll never see me again."

"But why—?"

"Do you trust me, Shara?"

"You know I do, Nicho."

"Then don't admit you've got it. Hide it. Go! Now!"

Nicho and the dream vanished. Shara was back in the dark Grotto. Her heart pounded with fear and a wave of nausea assailed her. But she didn't have time to let the side-effects of the rock's power wear off. She had to hide it.

She fought the dizziness as she fumbled in the dark for her cloak and shoes. It felt like an eternity passed until she found them. She gingerly felt her way around the chamber to the entrance. But she hadn't even taken four steps down the passage when she heard the sound of running feet and saw the glimmers of light bouncing off the passage walls. At any moment someone would burst around the corner, and she would be caught with the Dusk Dreamer in her hand.

Think, Shara. Think.

Under Nicho's sleeping pallet, they had found a small indent in the cave wall. She remembered it well because she had told Nicho she would hide some love notes for him to read in the night. Shara stumbled to the empty bed and felt around for the hole, pushing the rock down into it. She straightened up just as two men with flaming torches appeared.

"Get up!" Pearce's voice shattered the silence. "The High Commander demands to see you right now."

Mikel looked up as Pearce herded the three into the war chamber. Eliad, in the lead, was calm and composed. Andreo seemed a bit more agitated, but he also met the High Commander's gaze steadily.

Shara, however, kept her eyes to the ground as Pearce pushed her forward.

"What is this about, Mikel?" Eliad broke the silence. "Since when do the Parashi Warriors treat their guests like criminals?"

"That would be when they start *acting* like criminals." Mikel spoke softly, deliberately, fighting to keep the rage from igniting his words.

"We were fast asleep one moment and yanked from our beds the next," Eliad said incredulously.

"Not much criminal activity in sleeping, is there?" Andreo added.

"You would be surprised." Mikel's eyes narrowed on Shara, who was gazing at a point on the wall behind his head.

"Please inform us of the crime we have committed," Andreo said.

"For four hundred years the Grotto has been safe," Mikel said. "And in less than a month following your arrival, our security has been breached. Not once." He slammed his fist down on the table. "But twice, that I know of."

"Breached?" Eliad and Andreo shared a glance. "What do you mean, *breached*?"

Mikel strode toward Shara and stood in front of her, forcing her to meet his eyes. "Do you want to explain what you've been doing, Shara, or shall I?"

Her jaw clenched, but she stared mutely ahead of her. In all his years fighting against the Highborn invaders, he had never felt such singular resentment for one of them. It shocked him.

"Fine, have it your way. I will tell them, and you can fill in the blanks." He turned, directing his words to Eliad and Andreo. "Shara has been using a power rock. I suspect a Cerulean Dusk Dreamer."

Eliad's eyes widened in understanding. Andreo cast a puzzled glance at his former pupil.

"A power rock?" Andreo spoke. "Where on earth would she get a rock so rare?"

"I do not know. But she brought it here, of that I am sure."

"I didn't," Shara finally spoke. "I've never even laid eyes on one."

"Don't lie to me, Shara." Mikel spun back to face her. "You have already done irreparable damage. But if you tell us all you saw and heard, we might be able to control it."

"What damage could she possibly have done?" Pearce asked from the back of the chamber. "Don't dream rocks do nothing more than give you a good night's sleep, and perhaps a few pleasant imaginings?"

Mikel shook his head. "The rock is charged with Old Magic, infused with power from the earliest eons when the world was created. Only the Mind and Guardian rocks hold greater power. Power is dangerous. And every time Shara used the Dreamer, she became a channel, not only for the rock's power, but for every other power-bearer out there. Foolish girl!"

"You're lying." Shara's voice quivered. "It's not like that at all!"

"No? Then tell us how it is, Shara."

"I . . . I don't have a rock."

"Then why did I hear a scream and feel the malicious power in the Grotto just before Nicho left?" He paced around her. "I didn't fully understand it then. But tonight I sensed you speaking my name to a power-bearer. Who was he, Shara? And what else did you show him?"

"I don't know what you mean."

"A scream?" Eliad reached for Shara's hand, and spoke gently. "There was one night when you woke up screaming. Do you remember, Shara?"

"No. I mean, yes, I remember. I just had a—"

"Bad dream?" Mikel said sharply.

"Yes, a bad dream." Her eyes blazed. "Have you never had one of those?"

Eliad raised his eyes and hand to the High Commander. Mikel understood, and he paced back to his seat behind the desk, allowing Eliad to talk gently to the girl.

Not that she deserved gentleness after what she had done. Everything was in jeopardy because of her actions. His people. His plans to help the Parashi. The Guardian Rock. The old writings. Everything he cherished in life could have just been undone by one senseless girl.

"I don't know what he's talking about, Eliad." Shara wiped a tear from her face.

"You asked me about the power rocks when we were still in Gwyndorr," Andreo said. "Had you found one then?"

The girl kept denying it. Mikel signaled Pearce over and whispered, "Go search their chambers for an unusual rock. Turn over everything if you have to. Bring it to me immediately."

The three continued their hushed conversation. Mikel said no more.

Finally Eliad turned to Mikel. "We seem to be at an impasse, Mikel. You say she has it and Shara says she doesn't."

"And you believe her?"

Eliad hesitated. "I do."

"And you, Andreo? Do you believe her?"

"Shara's never lied to me before," Andreo answered.

"Then, as you say, we have reached a standoff."

"I think not, High Commander." Pearce stood in the doorway. He marched toward the table, dropped something into the High Commander's outstretched hand and cast a vindictive smile at Shara.

Mikel slowly lifted the rock into the air, and the candlelight pierced its many facets. It was alluringly beautiful—deep blue, the color of the night sky just before all the light seeps away.

As Mikel held up her Dusk Dreamer, anger clawed deep inside Shara, creeping upward until she felt it might burst through her skin. Instead, it constricted in her throat, a hard lump that she could only release with a scream.

"*Nooo!*"

She flung herself at the High Commander, all her attention on the rock in his hand. She hit him, bit him, dug her nails into his face. Only her Dusk Dreamer mattered. She had to get it back. If she didn't, she would never see Nicho again. Her fingers were on it now. She could feel the tingle of warmth it gave off. She tried to twist it from Mikel's grip, but he was stronger than she was, and he pulled his hand away.

"Step back, Shara." The authority in his voice stopped her. She became aware of Pearce standing to Mikel's left, sword drawn. Eliad and Andreo had moved closer and were reaching for her.

"You have no right to it," she snarled. "It's mine."

"It doesn't belong to you." At any other time she might have recognized the note of kindness in Mikel's voice. "Rather, you belong to it."

"Give it to me. Please." She fell at his feet. "I'll never see Nicho again if you don't give it to me."

"It's destroying you. And the destruction will not stop with you. It's not your friend. It's a foul enemy."

"No, I'll die without it."

She felt arms lifting her, pulling her from the floor, but she refused to cooperate, keeping her legs and arms limp. Pearce tried to pick her up, but she screamed until he dropped her again.

"Leave her here. We'll talk to her in the morning," Mikel said.

"I will stay." Andreo dropped down next to her.

Feet shuffled away. Torches dimmed. Only one flickering candle remained when she finally looked up.

"Where did he take it, Brother?" she asked weakly.

"Shara." He stroked her hair as if she were a young child. "Everything will be fine now."

"You don't understand. Nicho came to me in my dreams. Talked to me. How will he reach me now?"

"Hush. We will talk about it in the morning."

"The High Commander can't just steal my Dreamer like that." She grabbed Andreo's arm. "You can make him give it back. You and Eliad. Demand he give it back to me."

"No. Look what it's already done to you."

"I won't even use it again. I promise. I'll just keep it safe. You heard what he said. It's powerful. If it falls into the wrong hands, it can wreak havoc. I've been managing it fine."

"No, you haven't. It's turned you into . . . this."

"But I know now to be careful with it, Brother."

No amount of talking convinced Andreo that the Dusk Dreamer was hers, and that she was responsible enough to keep it safe. She finally allowed herself to be led back to the sleeping chamber. She did not sleep that night, thinking only of one thing—how to get her Cerulean Dusk Dreamer back.

CHAPTER 13

The Raven edged forward on the ledge and peered into the gorge below. His movement dislodged a small stone, which hurtled into the abyss. He drew back quickly, fighting the vertigo. By all cursed things, was there really no other way to reach this dreadful village?

His guide—an Enderite—spoke halting Tirragylin. He was short and stocky, more agile than the mountain lynx, and as strong as a wildwood pig. Galling as it was to seek help from an Enderite, the Raven had had no option. The village he sought lay in the western rim mountains, and although it lay within the borders of Tirragyl, the route from his own country was almost impassable. The safer approach was to cross the Endorai River in the Gworlin Vale, and take the Enderite road onto the Kwinta Plateau. From here, a narrow bridge crossed back over the Endorai River gorge to the small village of Charab, said to be perched in the folds of the mountain.

"Bridge near." His guide pointed to their left.

The Raven thought he saw something snake across a narrow part of the gorge. From this distance it looked as thin as a thread.

"Bad men in Charab," the guide said as they headed toward the bridge. "Men arrow kill"—he pointed to the center of his forehead—"every time. Cross bridge is very"—he groped for a word—"very dead."

The Raven merely nodded. He didn't doubt his guide's words,

but he was not a man to waste his own. True to their agreement, the Enderite led him to the bridge and hastily departed with his coins.

The Raven considered the wood and rope construction, and calculated how many steps it would take to reach the other side. At least a hundred, he thought. A hundred steps on a flimsy, swinging bridge, with the arrows of the deadliest men in Tirragyl pointed at his heart and a plummeting fall beneath his feet. He had been surprised—and, perhaps, a little disappointed—that Lord Lucian had managed to pry the Charab arming word from the king.

The Raven was a cautious man. One did not survive long in his line of work by being foolhardy. Yet he did not lack courage, for a coward would have chosen a safer livelihood many years ago. Caution and courage now warred inside him as he stood by the bridge.

Courage won. He stepped onto the first narrow plank and felt the bridge sway with his weight.

He must not show fear. The Charab would see it and despise him for it. He stilled his breathing and started moving slowly but steadily to the other side. To keep himself from looking down into the gorge, his eyes scanned the area around the end of the bridge, looking for movement. Surely they were watching him, but even his trained eye could not find the scouts in the thick bushes.

When he was five paces away, they materialized—four men dressed in mottled green and brown cloaks. Two of them had armed bows pointing in his direction, and a third held a curved sword. The fourth man did not carry a weapon, although the Raven didn't doubt that he could draw one in the blink of an eye. The Raven stopped and raised his hands to show that he carried no weapon. The unarmed man beckoned him forward.

As soon as his foot touched solid ground, three men surrounded him. Two patted down his body, searching for concealed weapons, while the other took the bag off his shoulder and emptied its contents on the ground. The Raven's short knife was one of the items that spilled from it, and the man nimbly threw it to the fourth man, who caught it by its hilt.

"A good knife," he said, studying the blade with interest before turning his intense green eyes onto the Raven.

He was young, the Raven realized, in his early twenties maybe, yet he appeared to command the older men.

"What is your name and business here?" the young Charab asked.

"I am known as the Raven. I carry a message from the new king." He watched the young man's face for a reaction but saw none.

"What is your real name?"

"I prefer the Raven."

"Your preferences carry little weight here, *Raven*." There might have been a hint of amusement on the young man's lips, but even this was well concealed. "We will take you to our village." He pointed to the Raven's bag, and one of the men knelt down and stuffed the contents back into it.

"Can I carry it myself?"

"My man will bring it."

He followed the young leader along a winding path, over rocky outcrops, then through deeper vales into a thick forest. Deep within the woodland they finally came upon a slight clearing with wooden houses built along either side of a fast-paced river.

The uniformity of the houses struck the Raven first. Each was the same size and faced down-river. If there was a hierarchy in the Charab society, it was not visible in the construction of their houses.

Their entire journey had been made in silence, but now the young man spoke. "You will start your stay in the cell, until you have met with the Charabian. He will decide your fate."

"When will I meet with him?"

"When he chooses."

"My business is rather urgent."

"You will abide by our time, Raven." There was no reprimand in the words. They were flat and emotionless. The Raven had expected hostility, not this cool, almost indifferent, reception.

"It's a matter of life and death, sir."

"It usually is." The young man led him to one of the wooden houses and opened the door. For a prison cell, it was one of the more comfortable the Raven had seen, with a fresh grass-bed, blankets, a bowl of water, a lamp, and oil. Still, the Raven preferred not to be surrounded by walls and locks.

"If he cannot see me soon, I demand to be taken back to the bridge." He spoke with as much authority as he could muster. "I need to report to the king immediately. One does not make one's royal liege wait."

"You will not return to the bridge, Raven." The complete control in the words sent a small shudder down the Raven's back. "Unless the Charabian acquits you."

"Acquits me? Am I on trial?"

"Of course. You were from the moment you stepped onto the bridge." Finally, there was a smile on the young man's face, although it held no warmth. "Most men are sentenced long before they reach our side, though."

"Why wasn't I?"

The man tilted his head slightly. "You look like a man with secrets," he said, "and secrets are valuable in our trade."

Lucian turned the smooth black rock over in his hands. His mind reached out for Shara, but all it found was a deep, grey void. There was little doubt that the one called Mikel had found the Dusk Dreamer.

In the last dream Lucian had spun for Shara, he had sensed the moment the High Commander woke. He had felt the shock of the older man and the commander's dawning realization of what had happened. He was a perceptive one, this Mikel. Dangerous even, for Lucian sensed in him some of the ancient wisdom that the Purge should have eradicated hundreds of years ago.

Even more reason to attack the Guardian Grotto and destroy its influence on the Parashi. Yet Lucian had not quite pinpointed its location. He had been careful with Shara these last weeks, had spent more time convincing her that he was Nicho, than trying to breach through into the Grotto. He needed a few more moments of contact with her, though. Then he would know where it was.

He turned his mind inward to the palace. He had skimmed over the mind of the king several times, but always cautiously, not wanting to hamper his influence in any way. An unpleasant mind to visit, it was a jumbled tangle of arrogant ambition and feeble guilt, of love sullied with resentment.

Tonight he sought another mind—the one who called herself Lohlyn of Lorren. He had seldom seen a more beautiful woman, although the Tirragylins would not value her dark loveliness. She was an enigma, and Lucian enjoyed a challenge. He felt his pulse quicken at the thought of exposing her. Maybe, once he had stripped her of her lies, she would come begging him for her life and be indebted to him for granting it. The idea was delightful.

He sensed her, asleep in the room adjacent to the queen. He probed her thoughts cautiously and found that, unlike any other mind he had ever stolen into, hers was not a muddle of images and thoughts. In fact, only one image appeared—that of a dead-still lake in the early morning light, mist coiling over it. Mountains towered beyond the lake, strong and impenetrable.

He stayed very still for a long time, watching the lake, seeing if a new image would emerge. He noticed the undercurrents in the water, sweeping the occasional ripple across the lake and belying the sense of serenity in the image. However, besides this, nothing changed.

Growing impatient, Lucian pushed his thoughts inward, feeling for a chink in the armor of the woman's mind. Yet the more he pushed, the hazier the scene grew, until even the mountains were covered, and all he could make out was mist curling around him.

His hand burned. The shock of pain brought him back to reality. He dropped the fiery rock. Instantly, the lake and mist disappeared. What in the abyss was *that*? The woman's mind was completely inaccessible to him, even in sleep.

He thought of the Raven. The spy's last request had been for the arming word of the Charab. What had he uncovered to make him think that the one who called herself Lohlyn had links to the mysterious group? Although he had given the Raven the word he sought, Lucian had not believed that a young woman could be connected to the dangerous tribe.

But after what he had experienced tonight, he was starting to change his mind.

CHAPTER 14

Mikel considered Shara, and for the first time since confiscating the Dusk Dreamer, felt a surge of compassion for the girl. This was the second day he had her brought to him for questioning, and once again she stood in stony silence. The only words that had passed her lips the day before were, "I'll only talk if you show me the rock."

Her face was sallow and her eyes puffy. After two sleepless nights, Mikel expected her resolve to waver. Yet the firm set of her jaw warned him that he would not win this battle easily. He admired strength in others, no matter how misdirected it might be.

"Shara," he said gently, "shall we go on a bit of an exploration today? It's been awhile since you've been in sunlight, and a few hours out of the cave will be good for you."

Suspicion and curiosity warred on her face. "I still won't talk about it."

"That's fine. I won't ask you any questions."

"So what's in it for you then?"

"The Grotto is made up of two extensive, unlinked cave systems. I try to visit the Deep Caves every week or so, just to make sure everything is fine. And I enjoy the sun."

"But you have a reason to take me, don't you? Some plan?"

"Two reasons, other than getting you into sunlight." Truth was always the best tactic, especially with one as perceptive as Shara.

"Firstly, I want you to see the Grotto and its people the way I do. They are my family, Shara. I'd die to protect them, and I want you to understand that."

She glanced away. A twinge of guilt colored her expression, then vanished. "And the second?"

"To spend time with you and remind myself why my first impression of you was positive."

"It isn't anymore?" There was hurt in her eyes.

"My anger obscured it for awhile." He reached out and squeezed her arm. "I'm sorry, Shara." It was the truth. The ferocity of his anger had frightened him.

"Well, my first impression of you was wrong, too." She shook off his hand. He recalled what Eliad had told him of her past. No parents. Little love. This one's heart was a fragile bird in a cage of steel.

"Why's that, Shara?"

"You didn't strike me as a man who would take another's property."

"I only took something away that was destroying you. The way a father would take a poisonous snake from a child."

"It wasn't destroying me. I slept. I was happy. I could talk to Nicho." Her eyes blazed with renewed rage. "But look at me now!"

"It was a lie, Shara. Nicho couldn't speak to you, not unless he also had a power rock. There was somebody else behind those dreams."

"No!" She spun away from him. "You said you wouldn't ask me any more questions."

"True. Let's not talk about the Dreamer. Do you want to come with me to the Deep Caves?"

She stood, arms folded tightly. Coaxing her to open up to him would be more difficult than prying a stream-mollusk from its shell.

"I would enjoy your company, Shara."

"Fine," she finally relented, "I'll come."

Their party of eight—fortunately Pearce was not included—set out in the morning. Eliad, Andreo, and four armed men had accompanied Shara and Mikel as they wound their way through a complicated series of tunnels to the exit they called The Burrow.

When they stepped into the sunlight, joy surged through Shara, reminding her of the day she and Nicho had escaped Randin's homestead in search of the Gold Breast. The memory made her wonder, had she run away from Gwyndorr only to be trapped in another prison?

No, the Grotto hadn't felt like a prison while Nicho was with her. Then it had felt like home. Even in the weeks since he had left, she could still escape its walls in her dreams. Only now that both Nicho and her Dusk Dreamer were gone did the Grotto's dark and musty interior feel oppressive.

The exit wasn't as well hidden as the one behind the waterfall, but it was small and shielded by large boulders. It opened onto a plateau where two sentries were posted. They spoke a soft greeting to Mikel and their fellow Warriors before turning back to scan the rocky crags that jutted around them. The view from this high point was breathtaking and Mikel allowed her a few moments to take it in. Far below them wound the river which, Mikel told her, they must have followed to reach the Grotto entrance. Hills and mountains stretched out as far as she could see until they disappeared into the hazy distance.

Shara fell in behind Mikel as they started out toward the Deep Caves. Two of his men had gone ahead as scouts. The other two positioned themselves behind her, with Andreo and Eliad at the rear. Mikel proved to be a fascinating guide. He pointed out animal tracks in the dust between the rocks, and he and Andreo discovered a shared interest in plants and alchemy. Shara didn't say much on the walk, but she savored the warm sun on her face, the breeze that tugged at the loose strands of hair, and the deep breaths of crisp mountain air.

The last part of the trek was the most difficult, requiring a climb down a rather steep incline, but even this Shara enjoyed. And now they stood in a moisture-laden dale that abounded with plant life.

"Do you see it?" Mikel smiled.

"See what?" Eliad looked around.

"The entrance to the Deep Caves."

Shara let her gaze trail across the rock face, looking for a darkening or a crack, but it appeared solid. Mikel gave them a few more moments, then chuckled and led them toward a towering, gnarled tree.

"The Deep Caves don't lie in the cliffs, as you would expect. They lie under our feet."

Shara peered at the ground, looking for a hole.

"That's what makes them such a good and unusual hiding place," Mikel continued. "The entrance is equally surprising." He held aside a robust shrub that grew against the old tree and Shara saw the large oval hole in the thick, weaving trunk. "It's so well hidden, we don't even post a sentry here. Come."

He pushed into the tree and Shara followed him, looking around with wonder. They stood in a large hollowed-out enclosure, its roof and walls ribbed with thick twines.

"Mikel, how does the tree survive if it has a large gaping hole for a heart?" Shara spoke in a whisper. A sense of sacredness pervaded the ancient tree.

The exit darkened with Andreo's head. "Is there still room for us in there?"

"One more," Mikel said.

Andreo stepped through the hole and peered around. "Incredible," he breathed. "I've never seen anything like it. What kind of tree is it, Mikel?"

"In the Old Tongue it's called a *Chay'ets*. A Life-tree. There are not many left." Mikel smiled. "Except, of course, in the Rif'twine, where they have another name."

"Indeed?"

"The poison tree."

"Poison?" Shara withdrew her trailing hand from a thick twine.

"They are not poisonous here," Mikel added hastily. "Come, let us descend into the caves."

He led them toward an opening strangled by the twines.

"These are roots," he said. "We have to keep cutting some of them away, but the tree has many others. Careful now. You have to go the rest of the way down the rope ladder." Shara saw the ladder firmly secured to several thick roots. "Will you go first, Shara?"

Shara grabbed hold of the ladder and gingerly placed her foot on a rung. Slowly, she felt her way down through the narrow space, twines all around her. It seemed to grow darker the farther she went down, but finally the twines grew away from the ladder until, in a pale orange glow, she saw that they now crept over the roof of a cavern. Without the embrace of the roots, she suddenly felt vulnerable clinging to the small ladder in mid-air.

She forced herself to keep moving, humming a tune Marai had taught her, and trying not to look down to see how far above the ground she was. It felt like an eternity before her foot finally reached solid ground. Only then did she allow herself to study her surroundings.

She stood in a relatively small cavern, and looking up, she could just see the point where the ladder broke free of the twines on the roof of the cave. Those roots crept over the roof and down the walls, and gave the cavern a warm, woody sense, different to the cold stone in the other Guardian Grotto. The light came, not from flickering torches, but from several glowing Vulcan power rocks. As she went over to study one, a woman's voice, muted in the timbered cave, startled her.

"You are with the High Commander?"

Shara spun around and found herself facing a woman only a few years older than herself, dressed in a Warrior robe and headband, a sword sheathed at her side.

"You're a Warrior?"

"Yes," the woman smiled, glancing up at the ladder. Shara followed her gaze to where Andreo was steadily moving down. "I assume you came with Mikel. Otherwise, I will have to run my sword through you."

"No! I mean yes. We came with the High Commander," Shara said quickly, before she saw the laughter in the woman's eyes.

"You must be Shara." The woman reached out a hand in greeting. "I am Kella, commander of this cave."

"Oh. I didn't know there were women warriors, much less commanders."

"It is the Parashi way," Kella shrugged. "We have stories of very brave and capable women fighting against the invaders. Hundreds of years of oppression took away women's strength and courage, but slowly we are finding our place again."

Andreo stepped off the ladder and stared around in amazement, his gaze coming to rest on Kella.

"Welcome," she said with a smile. "I am Kella. Come, let me take you through to the common room while we wait for the others."

They followed her through a passage into a much larger cavern free of roots, where torches flickered in sconces on the stone walls. Kella led them to several benches and tables at the back of the cave. Some warriors glanced up and nodded a greeting before turning back to their game of dice and stones.

"It's called Garrison and Gallows," Kella said. "An ancient strategy game requiring great concentration, which explains why my warriors hardly pay you any heed."

"Is that the game they called Gargal?" Andreo moved in closer to have a look. "I've heard of it, but never seen it played."

"It was outlawed in the Great Purge."

"What could be so dangerous about a game?" Shara asked.

"Or some plant potions?" Andreo muttered.

"My father told me about your skills in plant alchemy, Andreo," said Kella. "Something we can definitely use around here."

"Your father?" Shara asked. "You're the High Commander's daughter?"

"The one and only." Kella smiled.

When Mikel arrived with Eliad and the other men, he and Kella walked arm in arm to the dining hall, where a meal of fresh bread and watered-down mead awaited them. After that, Kella led them on an inspection of the caves.

To Shara, they didn't look all that different from the other caves, except that many of the warriors here were women. Maybe because of this, there was something softer and more homely about these caves. Vulcans, glowing a warm orange, lit up many of the passages. The occasional wall had been painted with circular patterns of bright yellows, reds, and greens.

"We have some skilled artists among us," Kella laughed, as she saw Shara studying the walls.

Some of the rooms also contained woven carpets, and they passed a room with several weaving looms, where two women unbundled thread.

The passage narrowed and curved. Mikel stopped at the top of some uneven steps that led downward. Shara, standing behind him, counted seven steps before the flight was obscured by the bend in the passage.

"At the heart of this cave lies our most treasured possession," Mikel said solemnly as his eyes found Shara's. "The Guardian Rock."

Shara had hardly thought about the Dusk Dreamer today, but mention of the cave's power rock brought hers to mind again. Did Mikel have it with him? Maybe his fingers wrapped around its comforting warmth even now. Her eyes strayed down to his hands. When she looked up, his gaze was still on her and she flushed.

"Come. I will show it to you."

Shara lost count of the number of steps. The constant curve in the passage left her feeling disoriented. What's more, only the first few steps were lit by Vulcans. After that, they had to rely on the light from their torch, and the flickering shadows as they circled deeper and deeper into the earth made her feel queasy. Finally they spilled out into a large, dark room.

Kella moved past her, and Shara heard a flare striking. The torch on a sconce in the wall flickered to life. She lit a few more until a circle of light surrounded them. In the middle of the room, on a small stone table, lay a grey rock.

"The Guardian Rock," Mikel said.

"That's it? It's so ugly compared to—" Shara cut off the sentence, aware of their eyes on her. "It's so plain, isn't it?"

"Plain, yes." Mikel moved closer to the rock but did not touch it. "True power does not need to masquerade as beauty."

"What does it do?" Shara tried to hide her skepticism.

"This is only half of the rock, Shara. But even so, its power has shielded us for close to four hundred years."

Didn't that just prove her rock was more powerful, Shara thought? Hadn't it broken through the Guardian's power?

"Why didn't it stop Shara from bringing in the Dusk Dreamer, then?" Andreo asked.

"Her intentions were not evil," Mikel smiled at Shara. "Her heart is good, and the Guardian sensed that."

"What would happen if the other part of the Guardian was joined to this one?" Eliad asked.

"There are some prophecies, Eliad, that seem to refer to such an event. But they are difficult to understand. All I know is that evil wrought them apart and evil will try to bring them together. For its own selfish means, of course." Mikel shook his head. "But evil only destroys, it never restores."

"It could be the end of everything," Kella said.

"And maybe a new beginning." Mikel smiled at his daughter.

CHAPTER 15

The Raven sat in his cell, listening to the silence. Two days had passed since his arrival in the Charab village, and other than three daily visits from an older girl who had the same startling green eyes as the young leader, the Raven had seen—and heard—no one.

It was as if he were in a ghost village. No sounds of women going about their domestic chores. No sounds of children laughing. No villagers calling to each other.

"Where is everyone?" The Raven asked the girl on the first day she brought him a bowl of hot stew.

She looked at him intently but gave no reply.

On the second morning, he had asked her name, but again she stared at him without any reaction. Whether she was deaf and mute or just obeying orders, the Raven did not know. After that he asked no more questions.

He was a fool to have come here, he thought now, staring at the light that streamed through the gaps between the wooden walls. Curse the day he spoke to the renegade leader whose territory stretched from Gworlin Vale to Drinn!

The Raven had crossed paths with the one they called the Bent Bandit many years before, and securing his own freedom had cost him dearly. However, the man with the misshapen back had his own form of honor. On the day he freed the Raven, he had solemnly declared that should the Raven ever need to come through his territory again, he would fall under his protection.

So, on his way back from the western cantref of Droyl, the Raven left the main road and headed toward Drinn in search of the Bent Bandit. There had been no evidence of a noblewoman called Lohlyn in Droyl, and on a hunch, the Raven decided to pay a visit to his previous captor.

He had been welcomed as an old friend and spent two happy days reacquainting himself with the strong friga berry beer that the Bandits brewed. At the end of the stay, he had told the Bent Bandit about the girl called Lohlyn, and her incredible feat with the knife that brought down a wildwood pig.

"Sounds like something only a Charab could do," the Bandit had said.

"The Charab? King's assassins, you mean?"

"Aye. Unrivalled skill with bows and knives. With anything sharp, mind you."

"I've heard the Charab are only men, though."

The Bent Bandit had nodded, staring thoughtfully into his beaker of friga beer. "Aye, but there are rumors. They say the old Charabian rebelled against the last king."

"Rebelled? But aren't they . . . what do you call it?"

"Aye, blood-bound to the king. Obey or die. But he got away. Rumor is he had a daughter who was as good as any of the Charab, some say even better."

"Are you saying this girl could be her?"

"Not saying nothin'. Just telling you a story, Raven-boy. Now drink up, lad."

From that moment, The Raven had been unable to keep his mind off the mystery of the girl. He should have told Lord Lucian that the search had been futile, that there was no evidence of a woman called Lohlyn in Droyl. Instead the Raven had started to think. Where could he discover if the girl was the old Charabian's daughter?

There was only one place—Charab—and only one way he would gain access to it—with the king's arming word.

He was here now, in the Charab village, with the arming word tucked into his mind. Yet it availed him nothing if he could not gain access to the Charabian. Yes, he was indeed a fool to have come.

He heard the key in the door and looked up. He expected to see the girl, but the young commander stood in the entrance. The Raven rose to his feet.

"The Charabian will see you now," the young man said matter-of-factly, as if only a few minutes had passed, instead of two whole days.

"It's about time."

A glint of amusement flashed in the young man's eyes. "Remember what I said before. You are on trial. Arrogance does nothing to advance your case."

"I've never been treated like this before."

"You've never invaded Charab before."

"Invaded? I came with a message from the king." The Raven knew he should rein in his temper, but it felt good to vent a little after two days of complete solitude. Better to do it with this young man than with the Charabian himself. "Where is everyone in this cursed village, anyway?" he added as the man led him from the hut.

"We are skilled in the art of silence and self-control, Raven." He cast a somewhat disparaging glance at the Raven. "Have you heard of it?"

"Even the children?" The Raven glanced through an open door and saw two children eating at a table. They had been here all the time? Incredible! He had been so sure the village was all but empty.

The man led him toward the river and across a feeble rope bridge. The Raven felt his hands turn clammy as he carefully edged across the bridge. The young commander watched him with an indifferent expression on his face. Once across, the man led him on another path that wound parallel to the river before turning into the forest. Ten minutes of walking finally brought them to a clearing. A huge wooden deck stood at the height of the trees, and the Raven became aware of faces staring down at him. Most of them were attached to a bow and arrow.

"So this is where you all hide out."

Two knotted ropes dropped from above, and the young commander climbed effortlessly to the top. The Raven struggled, but finally reached the platform. The Charab guards watched him clamber onto the deck with the same expressionless eyes as the young man. Curse this place and these people!

"This way." The young man led him toward a round, enclosed wooden structure that stood in the center of the giant platform. "This is our Tribunal Rondel."

The Raven had to duck down to enter the building. The first thing that caught his eye was a girl sitting on a carpet in the center of the room. It was the same girl who had fed him all his meals. She sat cross-legged, and in front of her, lying on a small brown pillow, was an opaque rock. Behind her stood a bearded man, short and muscular, with black and peppered-grey hair. Thick hair covered his arms and the small triangle of chest that peaked from below his green and brown robe. Even his eyebrows were thick, meeting in the middle.

He smiled as the Raven entered and dipped his head in the first sign of respect that the Raven had received. Behind him stood two gangly boys, nearly men.

"You enter the tribunal, Raven, requesting an audience with me, the Charabian," the bearded man said.

"Yes, indeed." The Raven bowed slightly. "I have come with a message from the king."

"In due time. First I will introduce my kin." He pointed to the young commander who stood next to the Raven. "You have met my son Elxa, the next Charabian." The Raven glanced at the young man with a measure of newfound respect. That explained why the older men deferred to him.

The Charabian continued, "This is my daughter Frey. She has been serving you." The girl looked up at him with a smile. "And my two other sons, Sira and Brun."

"It is an honor to meet your family. And what shall I call you?"

"Charabian. Now, sit." The Charabian pointed to a cushion next to the girl. "My daughter is skilled in the use of the Verity Gem. You have heard of it?"

"A little." The Raven glanced nervously at the rock as he sat down. "Isn't it outlawed?"

The Charabian smiled. "I am the law here, Raven." He sat down on a slightly raised platform and his three sons sank to the ground. "Let me tell you what will happen. I will ask the questions, and you will answer them. If my daughter detects one lie, I will give you a chance to correct it. If she detects another, Elxa will execute you. Do you understand?"

The Raven swallowed and glanced at the rock before looking at the girl. "I understand. The rock goes grey if I tell a lie and clear if I tell the truth?"

"Let my daughter worry about the details. You concern yourself with telling the truth," the Charabian said. "Think carefully before you answer."

The Raven nodded.

"You can start by telling me who you really are. Your name, place of birth. Who you work for."

"No one . . . um . . . I mean, few know my name, sir." The Raven glanced at the rock to see if it changed. "Much as yourself, I prefer it that way."

The Charabian said nothing, but continued to look at the Raven with an expectant expression. As the silence stretched out, the Raven again glanced at the girl and rock. He had little choice but to answer. "My name is Gart. I was born to farmers on the central plains. I was expected to take over the farm, but I hated it. So I changed myself. Became a master-spy, and a particularly good one at that."

He glanced at the girl and caught the slight nod she gave her father.

"Good, Gart. You are doing well," the Charabian said. "And how did you hear of our village?"

"I . . . I'm not sure exactly when I heard of it. It's part of Tirragyl legend, isn't it?"

"Yes, but few venture to find it."

"I had little choice. I have a question that only you can answer."

"A question from the king?" The Charabian asked, and the Raven noticed the first sense of unease in the man.

"Yes, sir. From the king."

The girl suddenly stretched out her hands toward the rock. Her hands trembled, and the rock—which till then had been growing clearer—suddenly began to darken.

"He lies, Father," she said in a crystal-clear voice.

"That was your first, and only, chance, Gart," the Charabian said calmly. "Now, who sent you?"

The Raven glanced at Elxa, seated a mere pace away from him, and wondered just what a Charabian execution entailed. He could not afford to make any more mistakes.

"Lord Lucian sent me."

"Lucian, Lord of Gwyndorr?"

"Yes." He had seen the momentary look of displeasure on the Charabian's face.

"Why?"

"I have been trying to discover for him the identity of the queen's lady-in-waiting."

"Really? And for this he sent you to the most dangerous place in Tirragyl?"

"So it appears."

"What makes him think he could find the answers here?"

"The girl is rather special. She is unusually gifted with a knife. It is a skill seldom seen among nobility. So I thought she might have links to the Charab."

The Charabian seemed to relax somewhat. "Our women do not acquire weapon skills. They also never leave our community. You must be mistaken, Gart."

"It's what I thought, sir. But then I heard of the old Charabian's daughter."

Something changed in the room as he said those last three words. The Charabian's body tensed and a furtive look passed between him and Elxa. The girl, who had been watching the rock, looked up at him, shock evident on her face. Even the two younger boys reacted. Almost in unison their heads swiveled toward their father.

The Charabian took some time to compose himself before he said, "We do not speak of my predecessor to strangers."

"It's what I suspected. But is it true that you are blood-bound to honor the king's wishes, and if he wishes you to talk to me, you will be required to do so?" The Raven sensed the subtle shift of power in the room.

"You are not the king and neither is Lord Lucian." The Charabian's words sounded clipped, angry.

"I come with the king's authority, Charabian."

"We have already established that is a lie. Which means you have just told your second." He signaled to Elxa.

"Did the rock indicate I lied?" The Raven swung around to the girl.

She shook her head. "He speaks the truth, Father."

The Charabian let out a long sigh. "The king did not send you, but you come with his authority? It seems improbable, Gart."

"Not if Lord Lucian is close to the king. Close enough to be granted the king's favor in this matter."

"What are you saying, Gart?"

"I am saying *ra'aph-aqeb*."

As he spoke the arming word, the Charabian dropped to his knees, face to the ground. The two boys, and Elxa, too, were suddenly pressed down to the floor, as if by an invisible force. Only the girl was left sitting on the carpet staring at him, a look of terror on her face. Finally, she grabbed the Verity gem, rose to her feet, and ran from the Rondel.

"Right." The Raven said, somewhat shakily. "Now *I* will ask the questions. And you will all start calling me Raven."

CHAPTER 16

Elxa had only heard the arming word spoken twice before. The first was on the prime-day of his twelfth summer, when the Charabian handed him his coming-of-age blade. His uncle had spoken it in a hushed voice, infusing the word with a somber sense of responsibility. Elxa had thrilled to hear it for the first time. His people's history and identity were contained in that single word, and that day Elxa became a true Charab, a king's assassin, the most highly trained warrior in the known world. That day the word had filled him with a sense of honor and pride.

Yet the second time he heard it, he had seen it for what it truly was, and for what it made of him. That day it had filled him with revulsion. He had been fourteen, the age his brother, Brun, was now. His uncle and cousins had recently fled and Elxa's father had just started to wear the Charabian cloak.

A king's man had arrived, and his father had called Elxa to meet with them in the Rondel, together with two older Charab. Elxa could still recall the man's arrogant bearing as he spoke the arming word and watched the unseen force push them all to the floor.

"Well, well. That is rather something," the man had drawled. "The oh-so-mighty Charab groveling at my feet."

"What is the king's command, sir?" Elxa's father had asked through gritted teeth.

"Ah yes, rather an amusing one, I think." The man had paced

around the room, studying the swords on the wall. "The king wants to dispose of a very dangerous rebel in Tirragyl. You are to eliminate him."

"As the king commands, sir," his father said. "Who is this man?"

The messenger rubbed his hands together gleefully. "Very dangerous in fact, but I'm sure you will know how to handle him. He's known as the Old Charabian."

His father's voice had sounded as hollow as an echo in a tomb. "The king commands me to kill my own brother?"

"Yes. And his son, too, of course."

At those last words, Elxa had fought against the supernatural weight pressing him to the floor, and raised his eyes to look at the man—a mistake he would regret.

As the man caught his eye, he smiled and said, "Rumor is that your son Elxa, who will be Charabian after you, has yet to make his first kill. It has come to the king's attention that the old Charabian has a daughter he is particularly fond of. She will be Elxa's assignment. What better way to prove his loyalty to King Tausorlin?" His smile had turned to a sneer. "And rather a good reminder of the cost of rebelling against the crown, no?"

"As the king commands, it will be done," his father had said, and pain had thudded through Elxa's heart, like nails driving through a coffin.

Today, Elxa did not raise his eyes to look at the man called the Raven. Only when his father asked if they could rise did the heavy power of the arming word lift, and Elxa straighten his back to look warily at the tall, wispy spy. He should have shot him off the bridge when he had the chance.

"Come and sit," the Raven said, sitting down in the same place he had earlier. It showed a measure of humility that he didn't take the Charabian's seat for himself. He sounded almost apologetic as he said, "I only require answers, nothing more."

"Answers cost dearly, Raven."

"Secrets cost more. Trust me, it's my living." The Raven's smile was fleeting. "Tell me about your brother."

"What do you want to know?"

"Why did he rebel against the king?"

The Charabian swallowed and looked away from the spy. "An order came to kill an entire village occupying land that the king coveted."

"And he refused?"

"He refused."

"But aren't you blood-bound to obey the king's instructions? All the way back since Taus's time?"

"Yes. Our disobedience requires our death."

"Did your brother die?"

"Not then." Elxa watched his father shift in his seat. "He fled."

"And his daughter went with him?"

"Yes."

"Where did they go?"

"An island in the Rhorhan Sea, south of Droyl."

The Raven didn't speak for a long time. He rose to his feet and circled around the room, fingers stroking his chin. Elxa's brothers looked down as he passed them, but Elxa noticed his father's eyes following the spy closely.

"What does this arming word do, exactly? It's more than a mere code word, isn't it?" he finally asked.

"It's a curse Taus spoke over my forefather, binding all the men in our line to Taus's heirs forever."

"I watched you all fall to the ground," the Raven said quietly. "I saw the power for myself. How in the abyss did your brother break free of it?"

"I . . . I never got to ask him."

The Raven sat down again. "What of your niece? How old is she?"

The Charabian furrowed his brow in thought, but the answer rolled from Elxa's tongue with ease. "Twenty-five. Three years older than I am."

"Indeed?" The Raven turned his attention to Elxa. "You were close to her?"

Elxa nodded, not trusting his voice.

"What was she like?"

Elxa smiled as he thought of his cousin. "Joyful. Always playing pranks. She didn't seem to belong in this place. This village is built on . . . death." Elxa glanced briefly at his father. "But she—she was full of life."

"Yet she was also good at handling killing weapons?"

"Exceptional," the Charabian answered. "Better than almost everyone, except perhaps her father."

"Why did she receive the training as a girl?"

"My brother taught her. He wanted her to be able to defend herself, almost as if he knew what was to come."

"Where is she now? Still on the island?"

"No, she is not."

"Did you go looking for her?"

His father gave Elxa a long, sorrowful gaze, before he spoke. "She is Elxa's . . . assignment, but praise the blades, he has not found her."

"By Taus!" The Raven's shock was genuine. "The king commanded you kill your cousin?"

"Kings give little thought to small matters like family ties." Elxa's steady voice hid his bitterness.

"What does she look like?" the Raven asked Elxa.

"Black, shiny hair and eyes that are sometimes green and sometimes brown."

"They're hazel," Elxa's father said.

"Her skin is darker than our own," Elxa said.

"Her mother was not one of us," the Charabian added. "She was from across the Rhorhan sea and had skin the color of polished Chay'ets."

"What is this girl's name?"

"Shorlrihoan, from her mother's native tongue," his father answered.

Sira looked up at Elxa just then, and Elxa knew his brother's thought for the same went through his own mind. Since his cousin's fourth year, she had been known by another name, one that his own infant tongue had devised to replace the impossible foreign one.

Lohlyn.

The Raven stayed another two days, this time as a guest in one of the Charabian's two homes. The Charabian had two wives and it was into his second wife's home that Elxa brought him. She was the mother of the two younger boys, Sira and Brun, as well as a younger daughter of about five.

A small, docile woman named Gria, the Raven initially thought her an uneven match for the commanding Charabian, but over the course of time, he came to realize that she was a formidable force, especially where her children were concerned.

The village had not been as quiet as the first few days of his stay, and when he asked Gria about it, she told him that her husband always sent out an instruction for silence when there was a stranger in their midst. How had she kept her daughter quiet for that long, he asked. They were taught to control their minds and bodies from a young age, she replied.

Elxa came for him early one morning to show him the boys' weapon training. The boys ranged from the ages of four to twelve, and they were drilled intensely—and rather harshly, the Raven thought—by several older Charab. The men demanded absolute concentration. If just one of the boys failed to reach the high standards demanded, the entire group was kept for additional drills.

"They are rather severe on those boys," the Raven said as they walked back to the village.

"If we fail to make them the best, they will die. Our business is death, Raven, and we have to be very, very good at it."

"How many wives did the old Charabian have?" He sensed the young man tensing. It happened every time he raised the subject of his uncle and cousins.

"Three."

"And Shorlrihoan was the daughter of the first?"

"Yes, his oldest child. My uncle brought her mother with him from one of his first assignments. He was probably about Sira's age at the time." Elxa laughed. "My grandfather was apparently livid. Our community is a closed one and he forbade his son from marrying this dark, foreign girl. But it was too late. She was already with child." Elxa looked across at the Raven with a wry smile. "Many call us barbarians, but we are not. We have a noble code of honor, and my uncle married the woman. They loved each other deeply."

"What happened to her?"

"She died in her second childbirth, and the child with her. Shorlrihoan was a mere baby herself. After that my uncle took two more wives."

"Shorlrihoan was his favorite child? That's why he taught her everything he knew?"

"You are a good spy, Raven. Your insight is keen. Shorlrihoan was everything to him—his treasure. The bond between them was . . . "Elxa shook his head, at a loss to describe such love. "It's the reason she left with him."

"She didn't have to leave?"

"No, women are not blood-bound. She could have stayed under our protection."

"Then why did the king send you to kill her?"

"Only one reason I can think of besides revenge," Elxa said. "He was afraid we would follow my uncle in rebelling against him. It was his reminder to us of what rebellion costs."

Early on the fifth day, Elxa led him back to the bridge and the Raven stood staring across the gorge with a measure of regret. He was not so sure he wanted to return to his life of secrets and intrigue. In Charab he had found a close-knit community. Men and women who lived simply and uprightly. Sorrow hung over their lives—the long shadow cast by the king's powerful hold—yet they still enjoyed simple pleasures of family and friendship. The Raven felt a sense of kinship with them, even of acceptance.

He grasped Elxa's hand and looked intently into the young man's eyes. "What now, Elxa? King Tausorlin and even King Altaus are dead. Do their orders die with them?"

Elxa shook his head. "I wish it were that simple."

"So if you hear word of Shorlrihoan's whereabouts, you will . . . ?"

"I will comply with the king's orders. It is my duty." He spoke the words coldly, the emotion hidden by a lifetime of control.

"By all Taus's mercies, I hope no news reaches you then, my friend."

"Taus is anything but merciful, Raven."

On the first day the Raven crossed the bridge to Charab, only one thought had occupied his mind: would an arrow suddenly appear and pierce his skull, felling him into the gorge? Today, another thought gripped his mind as he crept across the rope bridge: what should he do with the information he had gathered here in the last few days? He had no desire to hurt these people—or, if she was indeed the old Charabian's daughter, the woman who called herself Lohlyn of Lorren. Could he just go back to Lord Lucian and tell him that the woman had nothing to do with the Charab? That every trail had gone cold?

A long trip lay ahead of him, and by the end of it, the Raven would need to make one of the most difficult decisions of his life.

CHAPTER 17

I think you have a fever, Nyla. Why don't you rest, and I'll bring you my remedy."

Nyla brushed Lohlyn's hand away from her forehead. "I'm fine Loh. Just . . . worn out. From ruling. And arguing. And persuading. How I wish . . ."

"Yes?"

Nyla sighed. "Sometimes I wish I had just been Alexor's younger sister instead of his twin."

"Your birth was no accident," Lohlyn said. "The Ancient One ordained it thus."

It wasn't the first time Lohlyn referred to the old god that the Parashi favored over Taus. Nyla always wondered where such a strange belief had crept into Lohlyn's thinking, but, as always, she let it slip past without a challenge. What did it matter what her friend believed? Sometimes she wondered herself how her human ancestor Taus could now be revered as a god.

"All I know is that ruling a kingdom is far more difficult than I could ever have imagined. Especially when my voice is so different from the rest of the council."

"You had another disagreement today?"

"Every time we meet I seem to be at odds with them. With Alexor. If I say we should spend money on houses for the Parashi, he says the first thing we should build is a monument to our grandfather. He suggests increasing our merchant fleet to increase imports while I say employ our citizens to produce more goods. Palace affairs, defense, trade, royal appointments, banquets, the Rif'twine—we don't see eye to eye on anything anymore."

"Perhaps it requires more time. The crown is still new on both your heads and ruling is not easy."

Nyla shook her head. "It's more than that. He says I'm always driveling on about the needs of the common man, and don't give any thought to the importance of our royal position. It's like we're in a Two-Tied race and he is pulling to the left and me to the right."

"You will win them over eventually. Keep following your good heart. Now, I insist you rest."

"You insist?" Nyla laughed. "How outrageous—a lady-in-waiting giving instructions to her royal mistress."

"Only because her mistress is so obstinate."

"Fine," Nyla said. "I think that remedy is just what I need. Remind me what it's made of?"

"Just a concoction of herbs. The recipe was passed down in my family over the generations." As always, when Lohlyn spoke of her family, sorrow crept into her eyes. Nyla had asked her once about her parents, but Lohlyn was tight-lipped and proffered only the bare facts.

"Go make this secret remedy, then. I'll rest."

Nyla lay down on her bed and pulled the thick grubear fur over her. At first her mind raced back to the council meeting, but soon the warmth and softness of the fur eased her to sleep. When she awoke, her lips were dry and her body hot. She must have kicked the fur off in her sleep. It took her a moment to realize that it was not morning, but late afternoon. The sky outside her window was darkening.

Lohlyn sat in the shadows by her door. She rose and came to her.

"You've been restless. I didn't want to wake you." She felt the queen's forehead. "You're still so hot. Should I send for the physician?"

"That fool? I think your remedy works better than all his concoctions." She looked around. "Where is it, by the way?"

"Here." Lohlyn reached for a stone cup and held it to Nyla's lips.

"Unh!" It burned her throat as she swallowed. "I forgot how vile it tastes."

"Keep sipping it through the night, and you should feel better in the morning. If not, I will call the physician."

Nyla looked at her lady-in-waiting and smiled. Things between Alexor and herself had been strained lately, but at least she knew Lohlyn would always be by her side.

Lucian hurried down the passage leading to Alexor's private chambers, to which only the king's closest advisors were ever summoned. This was Lucian's first time.

Had he been in doubt as to its location, the king's bellowing voice would have directed him. Servants scuttled away from the direction of the shouting.

One man cast him a pitying glance. "The king just ordered everyone from his chambers, my lord. Are you sure you should be—?"

Lucian swept past him without a word.

Two Royal Guards stood stoically outside the double doors, from which a young crying servant girl, carrying several large jagged mirror pieces, now emerged.

"The king called for me," Lucian said. One of the men looked at him questioningly, but he enter the room before the guard could object.

Alexor, dressed in his rich purple coronation gown, stood looking out of the window. Lucian noticed an oval frame to which a few shards of mirror still clung. When he saw the king's bandaged right hand, Lucian allowed himself a flicker of amusement. Anger served Lucian's purposes well.

"Your Majesty. I came as soon as you sent for me." Lucian bowed as Alexor spun around.

"Lucian!" The king's voice sounded slightly high and breathless. "Finally someone with sense. I am surrounded by fools."

"How can I serve you, my liege?"

The king shook his head. "I need to be with someone I can trust. Drink, Lucian?" He walked over to a cabinet containing a jug and several goblets.

"Allow me, my king," Lucian reached for the jug. "I see you have an injury."

"It's nothing. A small accident with a mirror." Alexor grimaced. "Do you see this robe, Lucian?" He held the rich fabric out and swirled it around. "This was the very robe Taus wore. It has rested on the shoulders of every great Tirragylin king since him." He laughed bitterly. "Did my sister wear it? No. She wore a replica. *I* wore the real one."

"Of course you did, Your Majesty. You are Tirragyl's king. She is merely the queen."

"Then why am I not treated with the respect granted my predecessors? I'll tell you why. It's because I am a *half-soul*." He spat the word out. "Every one thinks that I am less. Less than them! Curse Nyla for turning me into this."

"You are destined to be a great king, Your Majesty," Lucian said smoothly, handing the king a goblet.

Alexor took a long sip of the wine. "But if she has a piece of my own soul, why does she oppose me? Wouldn't our souls agree on decisions? Like today. She started talking of irrigating the Southern Plain. *Irrigating!* Have you ever heard anything so foolish?" He didn't wait for Lucian to respond. "What's worse is that Lord Briskyl called her plans ingenious. The old codger has always had a soft spot her, but what if he's not the only one? What if she is slowly turning the entire council against me? What then, Lord Lucian?"

"It will not come to that, Your Majesty. Briskyl is misguided, but the others are firmly on your side."

The king's growing suspicion toward his sister pleased Lucian. He had been subtly planting the distrustful seeds into the king's mind from the time he arrived at the palace. However, it would not serve his purposes to have the king turn on the entire council. He would have to ensure those relationships stayed intact for some time longer.

"They could be plotting against me right now." The king bit his lower lip.

"Duke Frankyl is firmly a king's man, as are the others. They never liked the idea of a woman on the throne. They are loyal to you only, Your Majesty."

"Do you think so, Lucian?"

"Undoubtedly, sire. But if you are concerned, could I suggest something that might lead to a better outcome for you?"

"You are the advisor I trust the most. What should I do?"

"Why not start recording some of the queen's opposing behavior, Your Majesty? A time might come when you could present this to your council. I could also start looking if there is any treachery to be found in those loyal to her. Together we could construct a case to depose the queen as Tirragyl's ruler."

"Depose?" The word startled the king. "Is that even possible? It's never been done before."

"True, but then the kingdom has never had two rulers. It will be better for the kingdom to have only one."

"But what of . . . what of our . . . joint spirit?" Alexor lowered his voice as he spoke the shameful words.

"Let us not concern ourselves with that at the moment," Lucian appeased. "For now, we will just keep a note of any disloyalty to you, Taus's *rightful* heir."

"A good plan, Lucian. I am grateful to have a man such as you by my side."

"Your hand is bleeding again, sire. Should I call for a physician?"

The king glanced down at the blood seeping through the bandage, and cursed. "He was here already, the useless dolt. Just send in one of the guards. Soldiers are better at wounds, I find."

Lucian bowed and retraced his steps back to his quarters. This had been a most profitable afternoon. The king trusted him and now called on him for counsel over all his other advisors. Alexor was starting to turn on his sister, which could only strengthen Lucian's position. All that Lucian still required was to pinpoint the location of the Grotto.

Back in his room, he drew the black Mind Rock from its hiding place and held it until he felt the first warm surge of power. He pushed the power outward, searching, searching.

It was Shara's mind, filled with the dusky haze of the dreamer rock, which he sought, But still he could not find her. It had been many days since he had entered the Grotto through her mind and sensed the commander Mikel's shock of truth. He had warned the girl to hide the rock, but he suspected it had been found, for he could no longer reach her in the guise of the one she loved.

He pulled his mind back to the palace and lowered the rock carefully onto the table. He had come so very close to discovering where the Grotto was. One more time in the girl's mind and he would know, he was sure of it.

Yet Lucian knew something of the power rocks that Mikel did not. If Mikel had indeed found the rock and confiscated it from Shara, all was not yet lost. As long as the rock was in the vicinity of the girl, it would call to her with its alluring powers. One did not simply walk away from a power rock that had you in its grasp. And if it did not draw the girl, possibly it could draw another.

Maybe even Mikel himself. Lucian laughed at the thought.

No, all was not yet lost. As long as the Dusk Dreamer was in the Grotto, Lucian had a chance of breaking through its defenses. The Grotto was still within his reach.

CHAPTER 18

Twenty-nine sunsets and sunrises had passed since he'd left the Grotto. Already, it felt to Nicho that it had all been a figment of his imagination—Shara, the Warriors, the caves hidden behind a veil of water.

Dressed in the unfamiliar clothes of a farm hand, Nicho sat in the back of a cart loaded with hay as it rolled steadily toward the gates of Gwyndorr. The thought of entering the city he had fled as a fugitive should have frightened him, but Nicho was too weary to care. A strange numbness had crept over him on his long trek back. More than physical tiredness, it was seeing the mound of soil at the Bloodbush grove where his best friend's body lay. And letting go of his dreams of a life with Shara. And realizing that the bright spark of hope he had felt as they left Gwyndorr had been nothing more than an ember already turning cold.

You will go back. How often had he told himself this as he lay under the shifting stars? *You will see her again. You and Jed. Hildah, Nana, and Marai. You will all go back to the Grotto and start a new and beautiful life there.*

Now, as the cart drew closer to the towering walls, Nicho saw just how impossible it would be. He had to slip into Gwyndorr and then out again with a whole family of un-papered Parashi. Then he had to take a senile old woman and young child across mountains. Nana would definitely not make it, and Jed would struggle. But Nicho had to try. Trying and failing was better than the guilt that would consume him if he didn't try at all.

"You ready, Nicho?" a voice spoke from the front.

"Ready as I'll ever be."

He glanced up at the farmer and felt a stirring of appreciation. The man was taking a risk, bringing a wanted fugitive into the city. Nicho had sought him out only because there was nobody else to turn to.

This was the same farmer who supplied Randin's hay. Nicho had told him everything on the night he stumbled into his small house. The farmer and his two sons had listened with rapt attention. The only comment the man had made was, "I knew she was trouble. Didn't I tell ya, lad?" After that, he set about feeding Nicho, finding him clothes, and devising a plan to get him into Gwyndorr.

"I'll never be able to repay you, Ruhan. Thank you," Nicho said as they neared the town guard.

"Don't get caught. That'll be payment enough."

"What's your business in Gwyndorr?" The guard said crisply, looking up at the famer.

"Hay delivery, sir."

"For who?"

"Owner of the tavern over on Brothel Road." The farmer pointed. "A man called Yamiel."

"Yamiel. Yes, I know him well." The guard looked at Nicho. "Who's this then?"

"My son, Zurgi. Helps with the unloading. I'm getting too old for that." The farmer rubbed his lower back for effect.

"All right, you can go through. Just make sure you're out of here by dusk."

"Yes, sir."

"That was easy," Nicho said as they drove down the dirt road that led to the part of town where the taverns and brothels lay. "You want some help unloading this hay, Ruhan?"

"No, off with you. You have a great deal to do here." The farmer stopped the cart and looked around. "This seems a good place to say our farewells."

Nicho clambered from the back of the cart to the front and threw an arm around the farmer. "Thank you, Ruhan. Not many people would lay their lives on the line for anyone else in these times."

"Nonsense." The man said gruffly. "Just hitched you a ride, is all." He squeezed Nicho's arm. "Be careful, lad."

Nicho watched the cart pull away, then glanced around. This street was always busy with travelers arriving and leaving, traders bartering, and harlots smiling at passersby. No one seemed to be paying much attention to him.

He headed for the Parashi slum, even though the person he wanted to see the most in Gwyndorr was his mother, Marai. It took effort not to run up the street to Master Randin's house as he passed the intersection. When they had fled, he had had no time to say his good-byes. One moment he had been in the stable, brushing down the horses, and the next he was fleeing for his life. In the long watches of the night, he had imagined his mother's heartbreak at never knowing his and Shara's fate. A son should never put his mother through such pain. He would send word to her as soon as he was at Hildah's house.

As he reached the outskirts of the Parashi slum, the squalor in which his people lived struck him anew. The stench and decay over-whelmed him as never before. Had he simply forgotten how bad it was, or had things deteriorated since he left? He kept his eyes to the ground as he passed a group of men, all smoking the foul driva-grass. The slum had eyes of its own. The fewer people knew of his return, the better.

When he reached Hildah's door, Nicho hesitated. Fear clawed at his throat. How would he break it to Hildah and Jed that Derry was dead? He took a deep breath and pushed open the door.

It was uncharacteristically dark inside. Hildah loved the light and always opened the curtains, but now they were drawn. The quiet was also unsettling. Nicho had expected a child's shout of joy to welcome him. The anticipation of that call had infused him with strength on his long journey here.

Someone moved in the deep shadows at the back of the house.

"Nana?" Nicho said uncertainly.

"What do you want here?" A man's voice, not particularly friendly. He moved closer, and in the light spilling in from the door, Nicho could see a heavy, middle-aged man.

"I . . . I'm sorry. I'm looking for Hildah."

"Hildah?"

"Yes, Hildah—a young woman—and her son, Jed."

"Oh, yes. *Her.*" There was something in the way he said "her" that Nicho didn't like. "She's taken her services elsewhere." He laughed. "Somewhere with a higher standard of clientele, probably. Might not think much of the likes of you."

"What? What are you talking about? Hildah. She used to live here. With her son and an old woman."

"Yes, I had the pleasure"—the man licked his lips—"of making her acquaintance. She's not here anymore. Try the brothels near the town gate."

"Brothels?" Nicho felt the blood rush to his face at the man's implication. "Are you trying to say that . . . that Hildah . . . ?"

"Isn't that what you came for?"

"No, by Taus! She's a married woman. She'd never do that!"

"I remember that dimwit of a husband she had. He upped and offed. Left her to fend for herself, he did."

"No!" Rage propelled Nicho forward. He grabbed the man's shirt with one hand and punched him with the other.

"Get off me, you mutt!" The man shoved Nicho back and started to advance, his hands balled into fists. Nicho darted out of the door and ran. Behind him he could hear the man bellowing insults. Thankfully, he didn't give chase.

Nicho ran until his chest ached. He couldn't make sense of what he had just heard. Maybe he had been in the wrong house, and the man thought he was talking about somebody else. No, the man had known Derry. *I remember that dimwit husband she had.* And he had known that Derry had left with Pearce. *Upped and offed. Left her to fend for herself.*

No! It couldn't be. Nicho dropped to his knees in an alley, hardly noticing that he sank into something slimy and wet. How could Hildah . . . ? And where were Nana and Jed?

Nicho sat in the alley for a long time, oblivious to the rats scurrying around him. As the darkness encroached, he pushed himself up and headed back to the main road. The curfew bell rang as he reached it. He watched people scatter, heading for their homes. Nicho had nowhere to go.

Except . . .

Why hadn't he thought of it earlier? He ran along the twisting slum roads until he reached the one he knew so well. Nicho knocked softly, not like the loud rap of the town guards. He didn't want to frighten Rosa and Simhew. He heard a scraping noise from inside.

"Who's there?" Rosa's voice whispered.

"Nicho."

There was a sharp exclamation and the sliding of bolts. The door opened and his friend stood looking at him as if she were staring at a spirit.

"By the abyss! Nicho. We thought you were dead." She flung her arms around him, then pulled away to let him in, quickly bolting the door behind him. "Where have you been?"

"It's a long story." One that he suddenly didn't feel like telling. He caught sight of her plate of gruel sitting on the bench, and his stomach rumbled.

She smiled. "Want some?"

"Please." It suddenly struck him that something was wrong. There was only one plate. *Simhew!*

"Where is Simhew, Rosa? Not . . . ?"

She shook her head. "No, he's fine. They came looking for you here." Her mouth twitched. "It was horrible. The more I said I didn't know where you were, the more they hit me."

"No!" He stepped to her and pulled her into his arms. "I'm sorry."

"And then . . ." Her body shuddered with a sob. "Then they threatened to take Sim to a Rifter Gang. But thank the Ancient One, he wasn't here and they didn't have time to wait. I sent him away for awhile after that, scared they would come back. But they didn't."

"Is he back home now?"

"He should be here soon. He's apprenticed to the old cobbler. Remember him?"

"Mm. He's half blind isn't he? I'm glad he *saw* Sim's potential."

They shared a smile.

She passed him her own plate of food and dished up another for herself. Then they sat together on the bench where they had shared so many cups of origo and ate in silence.

"Why are you back?" she asked finally.

"For Hildah and Jed. I'd promised Derry I'd look after them if anything happened to him." He looked away from her gaze. "Derry is dead, Rosa."

A small breath escaped from her lips.

"I was at Derry's house this afternoon, and this fat man told me . . . he told me that Hildah was . . . was working at a brothel or something." He looked at Rosa. "It's not true is it, Rosa?"

She looked down as she said, "It's what I hear, Nicho."

"But what of Nana? And Jed?"

"Nana died a few days after you disappeared." She squeezed his hand. "She was special to you, wasn't she?"

"Yes, like my own grandmother." Yet relief mingled with his sadness. Nana had been spared the sorrow of Derry's death.

"I don't know what Hildah did with Jed. Maybe Yasmin knows?"

Of course—Derry's twin sister! The only problem was that, like his mother, she worked for Master Randin, and Nicho couldn't exactly march into the homestead of the very man looking for him and demand to speak to her.

Rosa read his mind. "Why don't you stay here tonight, and we'll send word to your mother and Yasmin in the morning."

As he curled up on the floor that night, Nicho thought how, from the moment Derry had left, the threads of their lives, once so intricately connected, had started to unravel. Nicho feared to discover what would remain.

CHAPTER 19

Y ou are lying!"

The words had little impact on the Raven, still reeling from the shock of finding himself in the palace in the middle of the night. How had Lord Lucian tracked him down? He had always been so very careful.

"Why would I lie, Lord Lucian? You gave me a task and I completed it." Annoyance made him add, "It is you who has reneged on our agreement by contacting me directly."

"You expect me to believe this?" Lucian's tone was mocking as he read aloud, "'There is no contact between the woman called Lohlyn and the assassins . . . women are not trained in weapon use . . . spoke to the Charabian and he does not know the woman' . . . blah, blah, blah." Lucian crushed the letter in his fist. "Why are you lying, Raven?" His gaze was dark and unsettling. There was something about those eyes that made it difficult to look away, and even more difficult to tell a lie.

"I did not discover a direct link between Lohlyn and the Charab."

"What did you discover?"

"I have told you already. I went across the bridge. They kept me locked up a few days, and then I had an audience with the Charabian and his son. I spoke the arming word and asked them if they knew a woman called Lohlyn and they said—"

"Wait!" Lucian, who had walked toward the tall window, spun

around and glared at him. "That's probably not her real name and you know it."

The Raven dragged his gaze away. The man was insightful.

Lord Lucian continued, "Let's go back one step. Tell me why you thought there was a connection with the Charab in the first place."

"A last resort. There were no other clues, and I was with a man in Droyl and mentioned the girl and the pig. He said it sounded like something a Charab would be able to do, so I thought—"

"No, no, no." Lord Lucian shook his head and for the first time that night, the corners of his lips turned upward into the smallest of smiles. "Everyone knows the dangers of crossing that bridge. It was more than a whim. You knew something more, didn't you?"

"I knew nothing for sure."

"What exactly did this man say to make you willing to do something that dangerous?"

The Raven didn't reply, even though those strange golden brown eyes beckoned him to. This was the heart of the truth—if he folded now, he endangered Lohlyn's life and maybe even Elxa's. Above all, he wanted to protect his new Charab friends and the daughter of the old Charabian.

"Well?"

"I have answered all your questions, Lord Lucian. Now maybe you can tell me how you tracked me down."

"Maybe you are losing your touch, Raven. Maybe you are not quite the spy-master you think you are, if I can track you down."

The Raven flinched inside. He took pride in being the best spy in Tirragyl. He still found it difficult to believe that Lord Lucian had breached all his careful security measures, sending palace guards to fetch him in the middle of the night. "Am I free to go now, Lord Lucian? My sleep was rather interrupted."

"You will be free to go as soon as you tell me what this Droyl man said to you—the words that made you risk crossing the bridge."

"And if I don't?"

Lucian laughed. "Do you realize how powerful I am? I am the king's thumb-man. With a whisper in his ear, I could have you"—the lord twirled his fingers thoughtfully—"thrown into a dungeon. Or tried for treason. Or maybe I'd just start by exposing you as the elusive Raven. The mystery of who you are is rather valuable in your trade, I'm sure. But you can always go back to being a . . . farrier? Farmer? Whatever you were before you became the great, revered spy-master."

The Raven's temples pounded with rage. Lord Lucian had read him like a scroll. He understood the one thing that the Raven would place even above loyalty or love—his identity.

"Are you threatening me?"

"Yes, Raven." The lord's smile was victorious, that of a warrior on the verge of delivering the deathblow to a helpless foe.

In that moment, the Raven felt an urge to tell him to do whatever he wanted. That he, the Raven, would never be controlled by another man's threats. But he was a man of common sense. It's what made him such an effective spy. If he let his pride dictate this one decision, he would pay for it the rest of his life. He was defeated.

"Fine, I will tell you what the Bandit said, but it proves nothing." The Raven took a deep breath. "He told me about the previous Charabian who rebelled against King Tausorlin."

"Rebelled? Impossible. They are blood-bound to Taus and his line."

"Somehow the old Charabian broke the bond and refused to destroy some village on the king's instructions."

"What's that got to do with Lohlyn?"

"The old Charabian had a daughter whom he had trained himself. She was exceptional at weapons."

"You think it is her?"

"I can't be sure, but it's possible." The spy felt a twist of grief inside him—grief for the woman called Lohlyn, who, although he had never laid eyes on her, the Raven had grown to respect. And grief for himself as he realized that he was not the man he had always thought himself to be. A man of honor would never betray an innocent woman into the hands of one as treacherous as this man.

"Why didn't you tell me this earlier?"

"I deal in certainties, sir, not speculations."

"Or because you've come to care for these Charab in some way?" The Raven shook his head.

"Don't worry, Raven," Lucian said. "I have interesting plans for her. And now . . ." He tore up the letter the Raven had written and pointed to the scroll and inkwell on the desk. "If you would be so kind as to rewrite the letter, including this new evidence, of course. Then," he smiled broadly, "you can be on your way, and the secret of who you are will be safe."

Yet even as he picked up the quill to do the lord's bidding, the Raven sensed that he would never again be safe now that Lord Lucian knew his identity.

Lucian enjoyed the sense of power that came from being the sole bearer of a secret. Once he exposed the queen's lady-in-waiting, that feeling would fade. So, like a pearl hidden in a shell, he carried it around with him for several more days. He went out of his way to catch glimpses of the dark beauty. At night he lay on his sleeping pallet and imagined her terror as he publicly uncovered her deception. His fantasy ended with her begging for her life at his feet.

When his anticipation grew to the breaking point, he began to set into place the steps of his plan. True, he wanted to humiliate Lohlyn, but he could not lose sight of his more significant goal—that of deposing the queen. Again he marveled at the stroke of providence that had led the Raven to discover Lohlyn's ties to the Charab. He could not have wished for more damaging evidence.

It came at a good time, too, for Lucian had noticed that the ever-vacillating king was taking strides toward reconciling with his sister. Some afternoons he even saw the two of them walking and laughing in the palace gardens. When he'd asked the king about this, Alexor had been defensive.

"We are joint rulers, Lucian. It's to our advantage to work together, and there's no reason we can't. We've been best friends since the womb, for Taus's sake."

"Have you been recording some of the rebellious things that are said in the council?"

A look of confusion had passed over the king's face. "Maybe I was wrong about that, Lucian. Maybe nobody is trying to rebel against me. They're just trying to do what they believe is best."

"Possibly, but I would still be wary, my liege. Many are power hungry, and the closer they are to the power, the hungrier they are. You recall what happened to your great-grandfather, don't you?"

The king had nodded. Everybody knew the story, still told in taverns across Tirragyl, of how King Critaus's own guards, who had fallen under the spell of the charismatic young prince, Juwer, had butchered the king in his bed. The usurper prince was crowned by the council and held power for almost two years before being defeated by the supporters of the rightful heir, Critaus's young son.

"You and I need to be on our guard that there isn't a Juwer in your court, my liege. We can never be too careful."

"I appreciate your wise counsel," the king had said. "It is good to have a trustworthy man by my side."

Yes, this evidence was perfect and came at just the right time. Now all Lucian needed to do was ensure that the time and manner in which he exposed Lohlyn would cause the most damage to the queen.

CHAPTER 20

Shara watched as Eliad and Andreo toasted one another over the dinner table. It was a happy day in the Grotto, a day of celebration. For once the mead ran freely and the table groaned under the unusual weight of platters of food. There was singing and laughing as they recalled some age-old victory of the Parashi over the Invaders. It all seemed rather pointless to Shara—everyone knew the ultimate outcome of that particular war. Even so, it should have been a day to enjoy, a change from the dreary and disciplined monotony of life in the Grotto.

But she could not enjoy it. Not without Nicho. And not without her Dusk Dreamer. At the thought of her rock, Shara's eyes flickered to Mikel seated at the head of their table. Since he had confiscated the Dusk Dreamer, she had been watching him. Where he went. What he did and when he did it. Who he ate with and what he said to them. At times she had the sense that he was watching her, too. When she felt his eyes on her, she would turn to the person nearest her and pretend to be in deep conversation. She would even throw back her head and laugh at something they said, funny or not. Shara wanted Mikel to believe that she had forgotten the Dusk Dreamer. If he believed that, he might let down his guard.

"More mead, Shara?" Andreo held out the jug.

"Why not?" She smiled broadly. Her companions also needed to believe she had carried on with her life. Hadn't they supported Mikel in his decision to take the rock away?

"You didn't eat much of your food," Eliad said.

"There's just been too much of it today. Hasn't it been wonderful?"

Mikel heard her words and looked up. He smiled, a genuine and warm smile. "You've enjoyed your day, Shara?"

"Of course, Mikel. Who wouldn't?" *A girl who has lost everything she holds dear, that's who wouldn't.* But what did they know of loss?

"I'm glad. You haven't seemed that well these last few weeks."

She hadn't been well. Sleep eluded her. The Dusk Dreamer called to her in the dark. If only she could hold it for a brief moment and let in envelop her in soothing rest. Mikel had explained that other power bearers could reach her through the rock, but she wouldn't let that happen anymore. All she needed was to hold the rock and let it draw her into sleep.

The sleepless nights were taking their toll on her days. In her class, the children's laughter pierced into her head. She often snapped at them to keep quiet. They seemed wary around her now, but she didn't care. In fact, she hardly thought of them. Shara forced her way through the lessons only because she did not want Andreo or Mikel to hear that she wasn't teaching the children anymore. There were no longer games, songs, or plays. And if she felt an occasional pang of guilt at the children's downcast faces, she told herself that it was not her fault. Mikel's theft had changed her. The moment she found the rock, everything would be fine. She would once more be the teacher they all loved. She would laugh and play and live again.

Mikel reached for something in his robe. For a moment, Shara imagined him pulling out the Dusk Dreamer and her heart quickened with hope. Perhaps he had decided to trust her with the rock again.

Alas, it was not a rock that lay in his hand. It was a wilted plant.

"I found this on the way to the Deep Caves, Andreo."

Andreo reached out, his eyes growing wider. "It's a hloring bush!"

"I will take you there the next time we go. There was a whole cluster of them growing in the shade of the Chay'ets."

"A remarkable plant with diverse uses."

Andreo expounded on about the virtues of the bush, but Shara turned her attention away. She studied the folds of Mikel's robe, wondering—as she had many times in the last weeks—if this was the hiding place of her Dusk Dreamer. If so, it would be particularly difficult to reach. He might also be hiding it in his chambers. Shara had followed him there a few nights before, but had turned back when she realized a guard was stationed outside the room. Why would he post a guard at the door if not to protect something as precious as the rock?

Shara looked around at the full dining hall with sudden insight. Almost everyone was here. Could it be that the guards were no longer at their post? If so, now was the perfect opportunity.

She reached for the mead goblet and took one last, long sip of the sweet drink. For courage. For providence. Then she cleared her throat and began to rise.

"I'm going to my chambers early tonight. The children have tired me out."

Eliad looked up. "I will come too, Shara. I'm feeling rather tired myself."

"No, no." She hoped the words didn't sound too hasty. "Stay awhile, Eliad. It's not every day you can enjoy a feast in the Grotto."

Mikel watched Shara leave the dining hall alone. At the entrance, she turned briefly and cast a look back at the table, flushing slightly as she met his gaze. Instantly, a smile came to her lips.

He had seen that smile a lot lately. *I'm fine*, it said, and it might have had most people convinced, but not Mikel. Mikel had spent too long studying the subtle shifts in people's expressions to be taken in by that thin smile. No, Shara was not fine. The Dusk Dreamer, and the powerful force that had entered with it, still had her in its clutches.

"Follow the girl," Mikel whispered to Pearce, seated on his right.

"But don't let her see you. Just report back to me tonight where she goes."

His commander nodded, seemingly pleased with the assignment. Pearce had never liked the Highborn girl and seemed to delight in every mistake she made.

Mikel turned back to the festivities, although his lighthearted joy was gone. He suspected that Shara was heading to his chambers to look for the power rock. Just as well that he had come up with the perfect hiding place a few days after he had confiscated it—somewhere she would not be able to reach. How he wished the most beautiful of rocks had never found its way into the Guardian Grotto.

Shara had been right. On this high feast-day, no guard was stationed outside Mikel's quarters. The door made a loud grating sound as she pushed it open. A small oil lamp flickered on a chest at the far side of the chamber. The room was smaller than she had imagined, and the furnishings were as humble as those in her own room. The High Commander was obviously not one to take advantage of his position. *Except when it comes to my Dusk Dreamer,* she thought with a rush of anger.

There weren't many hiding places here. She opened the chest and rummaged inside. It contained parchments, a heavy cloak, two daggers, and a small oil painting of a dark-haired woman who could only be Kella's mother. There was no power rock, though. Shara felt under the sleeping pallet. She had hidden the Dusk Dreamer under her own sleeping pallet after discovering it in Randin's study. Yet here, too, Shara found nothing.

Her attention turned to the bookshelf. Briefly, interest surged through her as she looked at the old books stacked on the shelf. Then the desire for her rock washed over her again. She carefully lifted the books off the shelf so she could look behind them. No rock.

As she returned them back to the shelf, her eye caught on something familiar. Under the top book lay another one. She pulled it free, a surge of conflicting emotions coursing through her. It was the leather-bound book she and Nicho had found in the Birch Grove. She had almost forgotten that Andreo had carried it with him to the Grotto.

She dropped onto her haunches, cradling the book in her lap. Vivid, light-filled memories filled her as she opened it. The Gold Breast leading them to the book's hiding place. The joy and freedom of the day on which they had found it. The sense of promise that tingled through her fingers, even now, as they followed the curve of the ancient script.

Because Tabeal had led them to the book, she had thought it contained something of value. Something that would tell her of her past and explain why Lucian was determined to join her to his son. But the book had proved useless. Yes, Andreo had managed to translate a few passages and he and Eliad claimed that Tabeal could give them all understanding of the words. Yet the Gold Breast was gone and here the book now lay, undeciphered, gathering dust.

Shara slammed it closed again. Nothing but dried ink on paper. The words held no power. No power at all compared to that which pulsed deep in her rock.

She suddenly knew that the rock was not here. If it was, she would have sensed it, for that's how close they had become—Shara and the Dusk Dreamer.

Mikel had hidden the Dusk Dreamer well. Yet Shara would not rest until she found it.

CHAPTER 21

Rosa had sent word to Yasmin and Marai that Nicho was staying with her, but it was three full days before Nicho's mother appeared. It was late afternoon, and Marai was on her way back from tending a woman who had shown signs of early labor.

Rosa opened the door at the soft knock. Marai didn't even greet her. Her eyes found Nicho's face and tears streamed down her cheeks as she crossed the room and pulled him into a tight embrace.

"I'm sorry, Ma," Nicho said over and over again as his own eyes clouded with tears. "I'm sorry I just left like that."

"Nonsense. You didn't have any choice." She pulled back and looked at him. "I'm upset that you came back."

"In that, too, I didn't have any choice. Derry is dead. I came for Hildah and Jed."

"Dead?" Her face was a mask of shock.

"Yes, on the way to the Grotto. A patrol got him."

"Oh, Nicho." She drew him back into her arms. *If only the world were as safe as a mother's embrace,* he thought. For just a moment, nothing could harm him.

They sat on Simhew's sleeping pallet, drinking origo and eating the bread his mother had brought. He told her everything, from the time he realized the town guards were looking for him until the time he drove back into Gwyndorr on Ruhan's wagon.

She didn't say much, but when she heard that Shara was safely at the Grotto, she covered her mouth and said softly, "Thank the powers that be!"

When his words stopped, tears were in her eyes. "I was right, wasn't I, about Shara? You always told me she was a mighty Highborn, but she's nothing of the sort."

"You were right, Ma." He smiled.

"You care for her, Nicho?"

"I love her."

"Well, I be . . ."

"Some more origo, Marai?" Rosa interrupted.

"No, my girl. I can't stay too long. Curfew bell will be ringing soon."

"What about you?" Nicho asked. "Did Master Randin question you, too?" The thought had haunted Nicho from the time he left.

"'Twas not too bad. He realized soon that I was more surprised to find you gone than he was. And Master Randin had bigger problems than a missing groom, I can tell you that."

"What do you mean?"

"Lord Lucian was furious that Shara was gone. You ask Rosa—he had eight of the town guards executed. Their rotting bodies lined the streets to the gates for days."

"By the abyss!"

"He might've had Master Randin killed, too, 'cept Lady Olva's father is such a prominent elder. As it is, he took away his position as Town Guard Captain." She nodded at Nicho's exclamation of surprise. "Master Randin's just a common guard now, and I can tell you, I've never seen such a bruised ego. Comes home shouting and lording it over us like never before."

"Does he know I was one of the men who rescued Shara?"

"I don't think so. It even surprised me when you told me." She winked. "In a good way, mind you."

"Did Yasmin say anything about Hildah and Jed?"

"Never a word, Nic. Though she was crying one morning when Nana died. 'Twas much for her to bear, especially with Pearce and Derry gone."

"I hear Hildah might be working in one of the brothels." The words felt like shards of glass in Nicho's mouth. Knowing it was bad enough. Speaking it out, even worse.

"Poor girl." Marai shook her head sadly.

"Poor girl?" Nicho looked up sharply. "Her husband's away a few weeks, and she starts whoring around? And you pity her?"

"No woman chooses that. 'Tis desperation. Survival. Nothing more."

"But she could have . . . surely there are other ways to earn a living."

"She's young. Never worked a day in her life. Gwyndorr is bursting at the seams with Parashi looking for work. She had no choice. Don't judge her."

"But what did she do with Jed?"

"Maybe Yaz knows. She told me to tell you to meet her at the Wool and Wench tonight." His mother pursed her lips. "Be careful, lad. Word in the kitchen is that the only reason the town guards haven't shut it down is that the owner pays them a bribe each month. But with new Captain Issor, things might be changing. It sounds like he's a stickler for the law and probably doesn't look too favorably on taverns serving Parashi after the curfew bell. If they come and shut it down, and you're there . . ."

"I'll take care of myself, don't you worry."

"What will you do once you find Hildah and Jed, Nicho?"

"I'm taking it one day at a time. But I want to try get you all back to the Grotto. That freedom . . ." He closed his eyes, remembering. "It's like nut pies tasted on the day of the Spring Fair. Sweet. Blissful."

The Wool and Wench was a tavern not far from where Ruhan had dropped Nicho a few days earlier. Unlike the other taverns in the area, it did not lie on the main road, for it did not draw its clientele from the merchants and travelers to the city. Instead, its entrance was in a narrow, dark alleyway that lay behind the popular taverns. This was also where all the refuse from the hostelries ended up, and the stench was overwhelming.

"By the abyss, I thought the slum was bad," Nicho said under his breath as he tried to find the entrance. In this, too, the Wool and Wench was different. It did not publicize its presence with flaming torches and seductively dressed women. In fact, Nicho passed the closed door and had to retrace his steps to find it, knocking tentatively when he did.

"Who's there?" a deep voice growled.

"Um, Nicho."

"What you want?"

"I . . . I'm meeting someone here."

"Who?"

"Yasmin."

"Why didn't you say so?" The door swung open and a tall man peered down at him. He had a surprisingly friendly face. "Any friend of Yasmin's is always welcome here."

It was warm and airless inside. Torches flickered from wall sconces, and oil lamps sputtered on wooden tables where men huddled over beakers of frothy beer. For such a large gathering of men, the talk and laughter seemed rather restrained. Still, it was a welcoming place. The proprietor led him to a small table near the back, then returned with a large beaker of beer.

"First one's on the house," he smiled.

"Thanks. Is Yasmin here?"

"Should be here soon. She works the night shift."

"She works here?"

"Yes." The man's brows furrowed. "You a friend of Yaz and you don't know that?"

"I've been out of town."

"Really? A Parashi? How'd you get that right?"

"Long story."

"Right. Would have to be." The man left and Nicho watched him bustle around with more beakers. Nicho sipped the beer slowly. It had a peculiar taste—sweeter than most beers—but, if his spinning head was anything to go by, even more potent.

He hadn't noticed Yasmin come in, so he startled when she suddenly slid onto the bench next to him and pressed her body against his own.

"Nicho! By the abyss, am I glad to see you."

"Hello, Yaz." He wrapped an arm around her. It felt good to see one of his oldest friends again. She looked as sumptuous as always, and he quickly drew his eyes away from the plunging cleavage.

She laughed. "A bit more than Highborn Missy Shara has, right, Nic?"

"Sure is, but shouldn't you be covering up a bit with all these men around, Yaz?" How easy it was to fall back into the playful banter they used to share.

"No." She looked around. "They love it. And Colos makes sure they stay in line."

"Colos? The tall fellow?"

She smiled. There was a spark in her eyes as she found the proprietor in the crowd. "Yes, that's my Colos."

"You mean you're—"

"*Really* good friends." She slapped him on the shoulder. "Have I broken your heart, Nicho?"

"Absolutely!"

"What brings you back? Grotto not all it's made out to be?"

"No. The Grotto is amazing. It's not the reason I came back." He swallowed and looked away from her. How did you tell someone her brother was dead?

"No?" She dipped her head to the side. "And everything's fine with you and Miss Shara?"

"Well, it was fine. She didn't really understand why I left, though."

"That makes two of us then." Yasmin laughed. "Who would believe I'd agree with a Highborn?"

"I . . . I don't know how to say this." He grabbed her hand and squeezed it, and suddenly her expression turned serious.

"What? What is it Nicho? Not"—she put her hand to her mouth—"Pearce? With all that fighting he was doing, it sounds—"

"No, Pearce is fine," he interrupted. "But Derry . . ." The shock in her eyes lodged a lump in his throat that suddenly made it almost impossible to speak. "Derry died on the way to the Grotto, Yasmin."

Yasmin squeezed his hand so tightly that he almost winced with pain. She whispered, "No, Nicho. It can't be. You're just saying it to make the fool of me. It's not true. Tell me it's not."

"I wouldn't be that cruel, Yasmin. You know that. Derry is dead. I saw his grave."

"No, not Derry, too. No!" The last word was a long wail, causing those around them to look over. The next keening wail brought Colos rushing to the table.

"What is it, Yazzy?" He cast an accusing look at Nicho as he bent down to her. "What has upset you?"

"Her brother Derry is dead," Nicho said softly.

"My love, my love." Colos soothed her, stroking her hair.

After awhile, he rose and declared the Wool and Wench closed for the night, shooing his grumpy customers out the door and promising them a free beer the next day. Then he made a hot brew of origo and held a shaking Yasmin in his arms, feeding her sips of it the way one did with a young child. When Yasmin was completely drained of grief, he continued to hold her but turned his attention to Nicho, and asked how he had learned of Derry's death. Again Nicho repeated the story he had told Rosa and his mother.

When he reached the part where Pearce told him about Derry, Yasmin let out another shuddering sob. "Why didn't I feel it the moment he died? Shouldn't I have felt it, Colos?"

"I don't know, my love. I don't have a brother, never mind a twin."

Sometime later, Colos suggested he see Yasmin home, but she clung to him so much that he decided she should just stay there the night. "I think you'd best be going, Nicho." The proprietor gently unfurled himself from Yasmin's grip and rose to unlatch the door.

"There's something I want to ask her, Colos."

"Can't it wait?"

"I'm a wanted man in Gwyndorr. The sooner I get out of this town, the better. It's the only reason I came back."

"Not to tell her the news?"

Nicho shook his head. "We would have sent word, of course. But I wouldn't have come myself."

"Ask her, then," Colos said reluctantly.

Nicho slid back onto the bench where Yasmin huddled. "Yaz?" He touched her shoulder and she looked up slowly. He spoke softly so that only she could hear. "Yaz, I promised Derry I'd look after Hildah and Jed. Do you know where they are?"

"Hildah and Jed?" She closed her eyes and shook her head slightly, as if the question confused her, as if Derry's death had swallowed everything she had always known.

"Yes, Yaz, remember Derry's son, Jed? I want to find him and take him to where it's safe."

"Yes, that's good, Nicho." She nodded. "Take Jed somewhere safe."

"But you have to tell me where he is, Yasmin. What did Hildah do with him?"

"Hildah . . . Hildah is working somewhere. I can't remember the place's name."

"Are you talking about that thin girl that was here a few weeks ago, Yazzy?" Colos asked.

"Yes. Do you remember where she went?"

"One of them fancy brothels on the other side of the alley." Colos shrugged. "Not the kind of place a Parashi just marches into demanding to speak to a girl. In fact, they keep their girls under a strict watch."

"I have to find her, even if it means knocking on every one of their doors."

"You say you're a wanted man?" Colos laughed humorlessly. "Well, that's a sure way to draw the attention of the authorities."

"I don't have any choice. I have to find her son."

"Her son? Why didn't you just say so?" Colos said. "The girl is lost to us, but I know exactly where the boy is."

CHAPTER 22

Lohlyn pinned up the last strand of Nyla's hair and stood back to admire her handiwork. "Very regal," she said. "What do you think?"

Nyla turned her head to look into the polished glass mirror. "Nice. But what about you?"

"What about me?"

"Aren't you going to do something with *your* hair? There are some very eligible bachelors coming."

"Pfft, you can't get rid of me that easily."

"I'm serious, Lohlyn. Sovereign Day is the biggest festival in Lydora. I'm sure I can introduce you to some handsome landowner ripe for the plucking."

"What makes you think I want a husband?"

"Don't we all?" Nyla said wistfully.

"Not me. My duty lies with you, not with some sweaty landowner."

Nyla laughed as she flung her arms around her friend. "He's a land *owner*! He has people to do the sweaty labor. Which leaves him plenty of time to be a wonderfully thoughtful husband."

"Is there even such a thing? And what would you do without me?" Lohlyn asked. "Who would make your hair look that remarkable?"

"You're right." Nyla's playful expression was suddenly gone. "Of course I don't want to get rid of you." She tousled Lohlyn's loose locks and said, "Leave it just the way it is, so nobody notices you."

The day was a full one, starting with a procession through the streets of Lydora. Lohlyn didn't like being in one of the last carriages while Nyla rode upfront with King Alexor in an open carriage. At least Klyden was part of the Royal Guard running beside the carriage.

The procession was slow because, despite the guards pushing them back, the crowd pressed in to see their king and queen. Lohlyn couldn't help but notice that Nyla received most of their adoration. Men and women alike called out to her, and petals dropped on her from the bridges and buildings above the route. Children tried to run forward and press gifts into the carriage for her. She was gracious, and often told a guard to allow a child forward. She waved and called out to those she passed by. The king's expression, on the other hand, was rather surly.

It was midday before they drove back into the palace grounds. Lohlyn's carriage door swung open and a man reached out to support her as she alighted. For a moment she thought Nyla must have convinced a wealthy landowner to act as her companion, but then she saw who it was, and a chill ran through her body.

"What a delight to see you again, Lohlyn of Lorren." Lord Lucian's fingers were as icy as the last time he had reached out to kiss her hand. Again, Lohlyn had to fight her instinct to flee.

"Lord Lucian." She curtsied and tried to draw herself away from his grip.

"Allow me to accompany you to the Sovereign's dinner."

"Forgive me." Lohlyn turned her head to catch sight of Nyla. "I need to find the queen."

"There are plenty of guards around her. You need not worry about her safety." Something flashed in those strange eyes as he said that last word. Excitement? Triumph? A sense of trepidation crept through Lohlyn.

She had little choice but to let the lord lead her into the banquet hall. Lohlyn was surprised to find herself seated at the royal table.

She was glad to be so close to Nyla. Only Lord Lucian sat between them. Klyden stood just behind the king and queen, staring unwaveringly ahead.

The program was tedious. Noblemen paid tribute to their king and queen. Musicians played songs composed in their honor. Servants brought platters of food and mead flowed abundantly. Lohlyn didn't touch it, and she couldn't help notice that Lord Lucian did the same. Toward the end of the afternoon, the king rose to speak, but before he had even begun there was a commotion at the door.

"Let me through!" shouted a royal messenger as a guard blocked his way. "There is treason in the palace."

At these words, the murmur of voices amplified to a roar. The diners pushed aside benches and drew their swords, turning to their companions to ask what this could mean. Lohlyn edged her knife into her hand and rose to her feet, inching closer to Nyla.

Lord Lucian stood in her way. "Going somewhere, Lohlyn of Lorren?" he whispered. There was a feverish excitement in his eyes.

He knows what this is about, Lohlyn thought. For a brief instant she considered plunging the knife into his side so that she could reach Nyla, but as she glanced past the lord, she saw Klyden standing behind the queen. Nyla was still safe. Lohlyn didn't need to expose herself yet.

The messenger pushed across the hall, sinking to his knees before the king. "Your Majesty, I have a letter from the Raven."

King Alexor had also drawn his sword, and all the Royal Guards except Klyden now stood around him like a shield.

"Who?"

Lohlyn sensed the smallest of tremors in the king's voice.

"Raven, the great master-spy, my liege. He has uncovered a plot against your life."

The hall had grown quiet as the messenger and king spoke, but there was a collective gasp at these last words.

"I will read the letter in my chambers," the king said.

"Why not read it out now, Your Majesty?" Lord Lucian said. "That way, none of those involved in the plot will have time to escape. Guards, secure the doors!" He strode toward the messenger and held out his hand for the letter. "At such an emotional time, it might be difficult for you to read it yourself. Could I read it on your behalf?"

King Alexor nodded.

With Lord Lucian out of the way, Lohlyn edged closer to Nyla. She squeezed the queen's shoulder and Nyla, wide-eyed, turned and gave her a grateful smile. Lohlyn looked across at Klyden and for a brief second their eyes met. She saw her own resolve mirrored in his eyes.

Whatever it takes, we protect the queen.

The hall was so quiet that Lohlyn thought she could have heard a bird shed a feather. Lord Lucian cleared his voice and began to read.

To King Alexor, sovereign of Tirragyl,

It has come to my attention that there is an assassin in your midst. She goes by the name of Lohlyn of Lorren. She is of the Charab tribe, daughter of the Charabian who rebelled against King Tausorlin. With her close ties to Queen Nyla, it is possible that the two are plotting to kill and overthrow Your Majesty, King Alexor. This knowledge came to me from the current Charabian, who will verify this information. The woman known as Lohlyn is extremely dangerous and should be apprehended with great caution.

In the service of Tirragyl's rightful King Alexor,
The Raven

Some part of Lohlyn heard the words, even as another part assessed the situation. Years of training under her father had taught Lohlyn to stay calm in a crisis, and as Lord Lucian read the damning letter, everything slowed down around her. She sensed every eye in the room turn toward her, as well as guards tightening their sword grips. There were four exit points, and in a heartbeat she knew that the one behind her was the best option for escape, for one less guard was posted there, and the two who were there were young and inexperienced.

The Charab were more than just individually trained assassins.

They were also a highly effective army. Training together as children, they were taught to think and act as a single unit. With subtle shifts in their bodies, they could communicate with each other, and this is exactly what Lohlyn relied on in that moment.

Her left hand made the small sweeping motion for "cover me" as her head tilted toward the exit. Klyden's almost imperceptible nod showed that he understood. Lohlyn knew what she was asking of her brother. He was to hold back the entire Royal Guard as she escaped with Nyla. Even for a Charab, the odds were impossible. There was no time for grief, however. That would come later.

She grabbed Nyla by the arm and pulled her toward the door. Her reaction was so fast that the guards had barely responded by the time she reached the exit. Here she met the first opposition, but, as she had suspected, the guards were unproven, and she cut the first one down with a single plunge of her knife.

The next one was on her before she had pulled her blade free, but she kicked the sword from his hand and, as he bent down to pick it up, lifted her now-free knife for the deathblow.

"Lohlyn! Stop!" Nyla screamed, twisting herself from Lohlyn's grasp.

"Nyla, they'll kill us both. Come with me," Lohlyn said.

Nyla backed away from her toward the guards now rushing forward. As the queen passed Klyden, who stood between Lohlyn and the rest of the guards, Lohlyn knew that their one chance of escape was lost.

Klyden saw it, too, and made the only decision he could. He turned on his sister and, in a lightning-fast move, threw his knife, knocking her own from her hand. It was an old trick, one he had always been particularly good at.

"Put up your hands," he shouted. "Surrender now or forfeit your life."

Lohlyn slowly lifted her hands above her head. Klyden was the first to reach her, but three other guards were close behind him.

"Don't harm her," Klyden said urgently. "There are many questions she needs to answer."

Two swords stopped short at these words, their points hovering at her throat. As a guard wrenched her arms behind her back, Lohlyn felt something crack in her shoulder.

She swiveled her head around, looking for Nyla in the crowd, but she caught only a glimpse of her friend through the sea of guards surrounding her.

"Well, well. An impressive show, Lohlyn of Lorren. Your skills are fearsome indeed." Lord Lucian intercepted the guards as they pushed her from the hall. "But how the daughter of Charab has fallen."

Lohlyn didn't reply. In fact, she hardly registered his words. Her father's deep voice filled her mind now. *Control is within you, Shorlrihoan. They will try to take it from you with words and pain, but never surrender it. Go inward and take it with you to your grave. Then you will know you are a true Charab.*

Lohlyn did as her father had instructed. She went deep into the silence, where nobody could breach her control. The Charab taught every one of their children to discover this silent place—their "heart-haven"—within. Lohlyn's haven was a peaceful blue lake, beyond which dark mountains towered. Here nothing could hurt her, which was why she hardly noticed the guards' twisting her arms as they shoved her onto a cold floor in the dark, damp dungeon. She was not aware of the blood dripping from her cut hands, or the bruise swelling her eye closed after one of the guards punched her. Her brother's voice berating the soldiers for their harshness had a distant, unreal quality. Only one image still penetrated into her silent haven—the fearful eyes Nyla had turned on her after Lohlyn killed the guard. No matter what she did, Lohlyn could not erase that one wounded look from her mind.

CHAPTER 23

Nicho followed Colos through the narrow winding streets that lay beyond the Wool and Wench. For the first time he realized that, although the Parashi slum was dirty, there was at least some space to move and breath. This was a different kind of slum, where rickety buildings pressed inward and upward, clammy and crowded, stealing light and sky and one's very breath away.

Colos had refused to take him to Jed the night before. Instead, Nicho had slept on the floor of the Wool and Wench, listening to Yasmin's soft cries and Colos's soothing voice from the room above the tavern. Yasmin's grief for Derry had reignited his own, and Nicho spent the night remembering his boyhood friend, wondering what more he could have done to keep him alive.

Colos stopped abruptly. "This is it."

They stood outside a rotting timber building that had no windows, only a single door, the bottom of which was gnawed away by either insects or rodents.

"The boy is *here*?" He could hardly imagine lively Jed in such a dark and decaying place.

"Well, he was. But that was a few weeks ago already, so I can't say for sure."

"Let's find out." Nicho strode toward the door and knocked loudly.

"I told you to let me handle it, didn't I?" Colos pulled him away just as the door creaked open and a middle-aged woman with unkempt red hair stared out at them.

"By Taus, Colos," she rasped. "We weren't expecting you already." She pulled the door open and stared suspiciously at Nicho. "Who's he?"

"Hello, Froll. This is Nicho."

"Why's he here?" She drew nearer to Nicho and studied him with narrow eyes. He could smell the beer on her breath.

"Thought he could help me carry the supply. Is Hanzer here?"

"Good for nothing sod!" She spat on the ground. "Probably spent the night with a wench. Taus cursed me with a lazy, no-good husband, that's for sure."

"Well, maybe I'll come back when he's here." Colos smiled and started to back away.

"No!" Nicho said, and Froll glanced at him sharply. "No," he said again softly. "I think we should get what we came for."

"I told you to leave this to me, Nicho," Colos said through clenched lips.

Froll looked confused. "You need more beer? You must have had some heavy drinkers to get through the last supply so quickly."

"It's been busy."

"Fine." She beckoned them in. "There's a small barrel that's just about fermented in the workshop. Will keep you going till the next lot's ready."

She closed the door behind them, then led them through a small room lit by a single candle. The room smelled of sweat, cabbage, and beer, and from the pile of straw that appeared to be a bed, Nicho could hear the rustling of insects. Dirty plates and turned-over goblets littered the floor.

Nicho suppressed a shudder. In all his years in the slum, he had never seen anyone living in such filth. The Parashi were poor, but they had their pride, unlike these half-breeds or lowlanders or whatever they might be.

Froll pushed open another door and led them into a large courtyard filled with plants. They wound through the verdant growth toward a long building that must be the workshop.

There was almost no light in the workshop, other than a thin shaft that fell from a gap between the wall and roof. The room was hot and airless. He might not have noticed the two small figures sitting against the wall, if Froll hadn't addressed them.

"Fetch Hanzer's small barrel of beer, Klin, before I give you a clout."

A boy of about eight jumped to his feet and hurried to the back. It was then that Nicho saw another boy, smaller than the first. He was sitting where the other had been, hunched over, concentrating on something in front of him.

In the darkness, he couldn't tell what the boy did, or if it was even Jed, but as Nicho took a step toward him, Colos put a restraining hand on his shoulder. For some reason, Colos seemed reluctant to tell this woman, Froll, why they were here. Nicho took a deep breath and edged back toward his companion. He would have to trust Colos to take the lead for awhile.

"How's the new lad working out, then?" Colos said casually, as the boy named Klin struggled toward them under the weight of a small barrel. Nicho lifted it off his shoulder.

"Useless one, that. I don't know what Hanzer was thinking taking him in." Nicho heard Froll spit again. "Spent the first five days crying for his mama." She stepped toward the boy and, by the sound of the small whimper, Nicho thought she may have kicked him. "He has a new name now, don't you, Blubber-Baby?"

"Working a full day peeling bitter-berries must be a shock to him," Colos said.

"Huh! He has it easy. Sits on his backside all day. Not like me, doing all the hard work while that sod of a husband plays around." She turned to lead them out again. "Is that all then, Colos?"

"Well, Froll." Colos hesitated. "The truth is, I wanted to talk to Hanzer about something else. Maybe I'll come back . . ."

Just then the door flung open and a short, thickset man stood framed in the light from outside. "Colos, my friend!"

The moment the light flooded the room, Nicho spun around to look at the boy on the ground. At precisely the same time, the boy looked up. His hair was matted and long. His eyes framed by dark rings. The fingers that came up to wipe away a lone tear were raw and ulcerated. But it was Jed, and Nicho's heart jumped with joy inside him. Jed's attention was on the man who had just arrived, but as his gaze slipped to Nicho, a look of astonishment came to his face.

"Ko!" he said loudly and began to clamber to his feet. Nicho placed his finger on his lips, and the boy understood. He sank back to the ground, his eyes, now filled with hope, never leaving Nicho.

Fortunately, no one else had noticed the interaction between them, for Froll was at that moment attacking her husband.

"Well, well. Look who crawled out of the sewer." She struck him on the face with her hand as her voice rose to fever pitch. "Who was it this time? That pathetic widow Violi, or maybe Blubber's thin whore of a mother?"

"A good morning to you, too, Froll." Hanzer's smile was brittle. "Maybe we can talk about this once our guests have left?"

"Why? You don't want Colos to know that you're a whoring son of scum?"

"I don't think Colos has much interest in where I find my pleasure, Froll. And it probably doesn't come as much of a surprise to him, either, since he has met you."

Colos shifted nervously. "It was good to see you again, Hanzer. I think we'd best be going now, Nicho."

"But what of . . . ?" Nicho hissed, looking back at Jed, now wide-eyed with worry.

Froll eyed them suspiciously. "Didn't you say you had some other business with Hanzer?"

"Well, yes. Maybe if he sees us out?"

"We'll both see you out," Froll said, heading for the door.

Nicho lingered as the others left, changing the barrel to the other shoulder. *I'm coming back for you, Jed*, he wanted to say, but he wasn't sure he could trust the other boy not to tell Froll. He almost expected Jed to come running after him, but the boy didn't move or speak as Nicho reluctantly followed the others through the door. It swung closed behind him, shutting Jed into his dark prison. At that moment, Nicho considered throwing the barrel at Froll, grabbing Jed, and running until the breath left his body.

"What's this business, Colos?" Hanzer asked as they walked through the courtyard.

Colos took a deep breath and glanced at Froll. "Froll tells me the new lad isn't really working out so well."

"Jed?" Hanzer scowled at his wife. "The lad is trying his best. He's young for such tedious work. Even Klin struggles at times."

"You just have a soft spot for the lad because you are so *intimately* acquainted with his mother," Froll said. "The boy is useless."

"No, he just has to settle down, and all your ranting against him is—"

"Why don't I take him back?" Colos interrupted.

"Back?" Hanzer and his wife both looked up incredulously. "Why would you do that?"

"This man here"—Colos tapped Nicho's shoulder—"was a friend of Jed's father. He made him a promise to take care of the boy."

Froll looked at Nicho through narrowed eyes. "I knew you two were up to something. Run out of beer, my pickled rat! You came to steal the boy."

"Not steal him," Colos said. "Reunite him with someone who loves him."

"What are you saying? That we don't care for the lad?" Froll thrust a bent, stained finger at him. "We're the only ones that would have him. Isn't that true, Hanzer?"

Hanzer nodded, the first time Nicho had seen him agree with his wife.

"So you can just turn your scrawny backside around, Colos," Froll continued, "and get this filthy Parashi out of my house."

"Please, Hanzer." Colos looked pleadingly at the man. "Do what's best for the lad."

"What's best for the lad is to have a home. Not to be with a Parashi troublemaker." Froll was now so close to Nicho that he felt the spittle on his face as she spoke. "You will never, ever get that boy away from us."

CHAPTER 24

The Raven had not expected to stand on this bridge again. The fear was once again present as he took those first steps across. Yet this time, when he neared the other side and saw Elxa and his men materialize from the shadows, he felt a surge of gratitude. It was a homecoming of sorts, and Elxa's grin confirmed that the Raven was not the only one who thought it.

"Back so soon, my friend?" the young man asked, slapping him on the back.

"Glad to see I am still welcome."

"To a Charab, once a friend, always a friend." Elxa winked. "It's in our Code."

This time his bag was not searched and his knife not confiscated. They made their way back to the village, where once more the Raven was welcomed into the Charabian's second home by Gria and her children. The Charabian was expected back the next day, Elxa told him.

After dinner, the Raven broached the reason he had come. He and Elxa walked through the village, from Gria's house to that of Elxa's mother.

"I found your cousin, Elxa." His words were soft, and something twisted inside him as he heard Elxa's sharp intake of breath.

"How can you be sure?"

"I saw her. Dark hair. Hazel eyes. Skin the color of polished

Chay'ets." *Strikingly beautiful*, he thought, and a fresh wave of guilt clenched his stomach.

"There must be many with those features." Elxa's gaze bored into him.

He sensed the young man's anger. This was not the news he had expected a friend to bring.

"More than that," the Raven continued, "I saw her in action. I was there as she grabbed the queen and pulled her to the door, so fast that not a single guard reacted. I saw her plunge a knife into the heart of a Royal Guard before he even had time to draw his own. Does that sound like her?"

Elxa's silence was answer enough. He finally asked, "Why would you tell me this when you know what is required of me?"

"She calls herself Lohlyn," the Raven said, as if he had not even heard the question. "She has been at the royal court, the lady-in-waiting to the queen. And now she has been exposed as a Charab and is accused of trying to assassinate the king." The Raven did not tell of his own role in exposing her or how every night his remorse kept him from sleep.

"Yes, her name is Lohlyn." Elxa said slowly. "But she would never assassinate the king."

"But wasn't the old king responsible for her own father's death? Perhaps it is a vendetta against the royal family."

"A Charab could never harm one of Taus's line. Our duty—and curse—is to obey them."

"But you said women are not blood-bound to the kings."

"It's who we are," Elxa said, "all of us. Men and women alike."

"But Lohlyn and her father broke away from all of that, didn't they?"

Elxa shook his head. "You don't understand. They were both . . ." He searched around for a word. "*Above* death. Not that they couldn't still kill, but they wouldn't unless they really had to."

"I saw her kill that guard, Elxa."

"Tell me what happened, from the beginning."

The Raven spoke of that day—Sovereign Day—when he had

slipped into the Royal Courts. He told of the messenger and the letter, although he did not mention that, under Lord Lucian's instruction, his own hand had penned it. He recounted how Lohlyn had tried to capture the queen, but how the queen had escaped before the guards took Lohlyn down.

Elxa's brow was furrowed when the Raven finished speaking. "If Lohlyn had been there to kill the king, he would have been dead today," he said with unwavering certainty. "That's not why she was there. I think she was there to protect the queen."

"Protect the queen? But why did she grab her then?"

"To take her to safety. What happened to the queen after that?"

"By Taus!" Suddenly it was clear to the Raven. "The queen was accused, too. She stands trial in the next few days."

"Someone wants her dead. Court intrigue. It's the danger of wearing a crown." His voice softened. "What happened to Lohlyn?"

"I don't know. I left immediately to come here. But," the Raven swallowed, "if the past is anything to go by, they will make a spectacle of her death."

"What do you mean?"

"The old king used to sentence his enemies to slow, painful deaths that everyone could watch."

Elxa turned away and stood in silence for a long time. Finally he turned back and his gaze found the Raven. "Now I see why you came, Raven." His eyes filled with an ache as ancient as his people. "You want my hand to bring a swifter death than the king's cruel judgment."

The Raven gave a single nod. "So she will not suffer."

Elxa had known this day would come, and yet it still took him by surprise. When the Raven was here the last time, Elxa had been careful not to ask too many questions and the Raven had divulged little. Elxa had suspected, of course, that the master-spy knew something of the location of his cousin, but since none of it had reached his ears, he had not been compelled to act.

But now? Now he *knew*. Everything the Raven had told him confirmed it.

Yes, it was inevitable. Elxa had no choice but to obey the words of the old king's arrogant man. He remembered them as if they had been spoken yesterday. *She will be Elxa's assignment. What better way to prove his loyalty to King Tausorlin?* And his father's reply. *As the king commands, it will be done.*

It will be done.

Long after his family was asleep, Elxa opened the chest that contained his weapons. He carefully selected two knives before slipping outside to sharpen them under a blanket of stars. As the steel glided rhythmically along the whet stone, Elxa wondered from which of these blades he would wipe Lohlyn's blood.

Back inside, he sheathed the knives before returning to the chest and selecting a bow and a quiver of arrows. If the Raven was right and Lohlyn was to be executed publicly, he might have to revert to shooting her from a distance.

Elxa would leave at sunrise. He regretted that he could not speak to his father before he left. The Raven insisted on coming with him, although the Charab had tried to dissuade him. He knew he could move faster alone, yet the spy was adamant.

In the end, Elxa relented, agreeing to take him as far as the city gates, at which time they agreed to split up. He did not want his friend to witness the execution. He did not want anyone to see him at a moment of such shame.

Elxa packed a few more items into his bag before lowering himself onto his sleeping pallet. He turned his thoughts away from all that lay before him the next few days, and slowly drew into his heart-haven. Yet, strangely, dark clouds built over the meadow of flowers in which he lay, and the normally peaceful stream swelled to a roar.

CHAPTER 25

Nyla stared, unseeing, from the window in her bedchamber. Once again, she replayed the last moments of the banquet, marveling how it was possible for an entire life to change so quickly. One moment she was receiving tributes and honor, the next she was being detained in her own palace. One moment her lady-in-waiting was her best friend, the next she was a ruthless killer. It made no sense. Nothing made sense anymore to Nyla.

"Your Majesty?" A voice spoke from the doorway. "The council is ready for you."

Nyla did not turn around immediately. She took a deep breath, trying to still the sudden flutter she felt in her chest.

Six days had passed since Lord Lucian read the letter accusing Nyla of orchestrating a plot to kill her brother. In that time, Nyla had been locked in her bedchamber, guards at the door. Three council members had questioned her, as had Lord Lucian. To each of them she proclaimed the truth that she did not know Lohlyn was a Charab. She begged them to send Alexor so he could hear from her own lips how much she loved him, that she would never harm him. Yet her brother did not come.

She turned. The man at the door was Lord Briskyl. She drew strength from his brief smile. At least she had one friend on the council that would decide her fate.

Nyla lifted her chin as she made her way to the door. She had deliberately worn her purple gown embroidered with gold thread, to remind them that they stood in judgment of a queen. Even though she sensed her subjects' loss of respect since her arrest, the fact remained she was Queen Nyla of the House of Taus, their rightful monarch. She would not let them forget it.

Her eyes flicked briefly over the face of the guard who accompanied Lord Briskyl. He was a striking young man, with prominent cheekbones and solemn eyes. Yet what caused her to notice him was the slightest incline of his head as she drew alongside him. She valued the small gesture. Not everyone had forgotten she was a queen.

"Wait." She turned back to him. "Aren't you the one who seized my lady-in-waiting?"

"Yes, Your Majesty." He dropped his gaze.

"Thank you. That was courageous, given how dangerous she is."

They walked in silence to the council room. She had walked this way many times before, but never with such a sense of dread. Just before they reached the entrance, she grasped Lord Briskyl's hand.

"Any advice, Lord Briskyl?"

He shook his head somberly. "Let us hope truth and reason prevails."

The council members were already seated. Nyla strode into the vast room straight backed, head lifted. She did not even glance at the twelve men seated on their chairs. It was to Alexor, sitting opposite them on his throne, that she marched. Her own throne was empty next to his.

"Alexor." She tried to gauge his thoughts, but his expression, always so open to her in the past, was hard and closed. "I did not know she was an assassin."

Somebody on the council barked at the guards to detain her, and Nyla felt strong arms grab her own.

"Drop your hands! I am the queen," she snapped. It was the handsome guard again.

"Step back from the king," he said softly, "and I'll be able to let you go."

Nyla reluctantly obeyed, drawing back and coming to stand

directly between Alexor and the council members. Slowly, defiantly, she let her eyes rest on each of the men, and then noticed Lord Lucian, seated on a thirteenth chair. Lohlyn had told Nyla once that the lord made her uncomfortable, that there was something dangerous about him.

Lord Briskyl unfolded the damning letter and reread it. Nyla looked at Alexor but he did not return her gaze. Why couldn't he look at her and know the truth? They had always understood each other so well. How could he suspect her of this?

"We have discussed this at some length, Your Majesty," Lord Briskyl said as he folded up the letter. "You have told several of us that you are innocent of this charge. Would you like to address the rest of the council now?"

"Thank you." Nyla knew how important this moment was. "There are three things I would say in my defense. The first is that I would like to meet my accuser. Who is this Raven? Where is he? Who does he think he is that he can accuse a queen of treason? Bring him to me."

Duke Frankyl rose. "We have made attempts to reach the masterspy, but he is particularly elusive. However, there is no doubt that the letter is his. The seal is well-known—a bird's claw—and several people who have used his services verified it."

"It is irrelevant. Can the man be trusted? Who on earth would put his word over that of their queen?" Lord Briskyl nodded. She had made her point well.

"His words can be trusted. He said your lady-in-waiting was an assassin, and look at what she did. She killed a highly trained Royal Guard," said another council member.

"And then she tried to kidnap me. Why would she do that if we were working together?"

"Once she realized your plot had been exposed, she tried to fight her way to safety, taking you with her. The fact that she did that merely proves you were working together," the man answered.

"What is your second defense, Your Majesty?" Lord Briskyl asked.

"The letter states that it is *likely* we worked together, correct?" She looked at the council, several of whom nodded. "*Likely* doesn't sound very certain to me. This Raven, who we can't even find, thinks I *might* be working with my lady-in-waiting. There is no proof."

"Your motive is proof enough." Alexor finally looked up. "Just like Prince Juwer. He held the throne for two years. How long were you planning to hold the throne once you got rid of me?"

By Taus! He believed her capable of murder? A chill ran through Nyla at the thought. Even if the entire council believed her innocent, if her brother didn't, she was doomed.

"I'm already on the throne. I don't need to resort to treachery like Juwer did. You've known me all my life. How can you even think I could do something like that?"

"I don't know you at all anymore, Nyla."

The silent moments stretched on as Nyla and Alexor stared at each other. She could speak a thousand words for the next thousand days, and he would still think her guilty. It was clear to her suddenly. Alexor *wanted* to believe her guilty. So did Lord Lucian, Duke Frankyl, and most of the men on this council. They had never wanted a queen. She was an inconvenience.

What were the last words Lohlyn had said? *Nyla, they're going to kill us both. Come with me.* With the flash of insight about her brother, Nyla suddenly understood something about Lohlyn, too. Her lady-in-waiting had never meant to harm her, or even Alexor. Unlike Nyla, Lohlyn had not been blind to the queen's precarious position in the palace. Even Mada had tried to warn her. Why had she not seen it sooner?

Lohlyn had been trying to save her. The thought ricocheted through her until it settled heavily at her very core. Except, Nyla had stopped her. Nyla had condemned them both.

"By Taus, what have I done?" she whispered.

"Aha!" Duke Frankyl was on his feet. "She has confessed. She plotted to kill the king."

"That is not what she said," Lord Briskyl shouted, and the council broke into pandemonium.

Through it all, Nyla thought only of Lohlyn's eyes the last time she had looked into them—filled with sorrow and the kind of love Nyla had only ever seen in Mada's eyes. What had they done to Lohlyn? Would she be too late?

"My third defense is this," she shouted over their raised voices, which suddenly died down. "Bring Lohlyn of Lorren to this council now. Question her motives. Hear from her own lips that I did not know who she was. Ask her why she was here."

A voice echoed through Lohlyn's heart-haven. She resented the intrusion, and for a moment was surprised that mere words had breached her defenses, until she realized the voice was singing an old lullaby her father had always sung.

She took a deep breath and began to draw away from the peace of the lake and mountains to the place where she could once again feel her body. The first thing she noticed was the fire in her shoulder. She let out an involuntary groan.

"Easy, Loh," the voice whispered. "You have many injuries."

She tried to open her eyes, but even this was a struggle. Only a small slit of light was visible. She moved her head slightly until she could just make out a man with a torch kneeling over her.

Klyden.

"Lohlyn, listen to me carefully. There is a council meeting happening right now to decide the queen's fate. It was not going well when I left." He reached out and stroked her face. "She still needs you. I wouldn't have drawn you from your haven for any other reason."

"What can I do for her now? It's over." Her words cracked off dry lips. She should have felt sorrow, Lohlyn realized, but there was none. Didn't every Charab know that death was nearer than the next breath?

"Nyla asked the council to send for you. If you tell them that your mission was to protect her, maybe they won't believe this Raven's accusations. Maybe you will both be saved."

"I promised Mada I wouldn't speak of the mission."

"But that was when no one knew anything. It's all different now. Mada would want you to tell the truth to save Nyla's life."

It was true. The Charabian creed was a highly valued system of honor, but it was never placed above a mission. Mission over creed, her father always said. If breaking her word to Mada meant she could save Nyla, Lohlyn would do it.

"You're right. Let's go." She tried to raise herself off the cold, hard floor, but her body would not obey.

"Let me help you, Loh," her brother said, drawing her up.

"Why am I so weak? How long has it been?" In their heart-havens, Charabian prisoners merely weakened and slipped away over the course of several days.

"Six days, but the guards were brutal." As she moved she felt the pain in her side, legs and arms where they had kicked her. "I wasn't always here to protect you."

"Don't worry." She smiled at him. "I wasn't here either."

He helped her up the uneven steps.

"You are going to be taken, bound in chains. They fear you and only let me come in alone because they thought I would fail to wake you. Several have already tried, including Lord Lucian."

Klyden pounded on the dungeon gate. Two guards appeared and stared incredulously at the pair. "By Taus, Klyden! How did you do that?"

"Don't you know I have a way with the ladies?"

"She's not a lady. She's a Charab."

The burly man turned a key in the lock and the gate rattled open. The other guard inched closer nervously, and snapped manacles on Lohlyn's arms. He looped these through another chain which was attached to his waist. Her legs were also chained together in such a way that she could only shuffle her feet.

This was how they led Lohlyn to the council chamber, her captor leading the way, Klyden supporting her, and the other guard following with a sword held to her back. Several other guards joined the procession, too, just in case the dangerous Charab managed to kill the three Royal Guards assigned to her.

CHAPTER 26

Lord Briskyl offered Nyla a seat while they waited for Lohlyn to be brought. She refused it, choosing instead to stand in front of Alexor and all her accusers, staring them unblinkingly in the eye.

"It is unlikely the assassin will come," Lord Lucian said after a considerable length of time had passed. "I tried to speak to the girl myself, and she appears to be in a death-like stupor."

Nyla looked at him sharply. "She is injured?"

"No." He did not meet her gaze, directing his words to the other council members. "These Charab have a technique of withdrawing from everything around them. They hear no sounds and appear to feel no pain."

He seemed frustrated at the thought, but Nyla felt relief. If Lohlyn could feel no pain, she could also feel no fear at what was to become of her.

As if he sensed the comfort she drew from this, Lord Lucian said, "Of course, this means that we will never know just what passed between the two of you."

"Nothing passed between the two of us, Lord Lucian." Nyla tried to keep her voice steady. "Lohlyn brushed my hair and prepared my clothes."

"Let us wait to see if the girl awakes." Lord Briskyl waved a placatory hand in her direction. "Then the truth will be known."

They lapsed into another long silence. Eventually the door swung open. Nyla looked up. At first, she saw only a young, nervous looking guard, but as he entered the room, she noticed the chain around his waist. It drew taut, and Lohlyn, manacled to its ends, stumbled in behind him. Several other guards clustered around her, although only the guard who had bowed to Nyla earlier offered her an arm for support.

The last few days had taken a toll on Lohlyn. Dark bruises were visible on her now-hollowed cheeks, her eyes were swollen, and her normally beautiful hair was matted with dirt and blood.

A wave of pity drove Nyla toward her friend, but the supporting guard's almost imperceptible shake of the head stopped her in her tracks. No. It would not be wise for the council to see their closeness. It would add weight to the argument that Nyla and Lohlyn conspired together.

Lohlyn did not glance her way, but steadily followed the guard, coming to stand a few paces away from her. In her bearing was none of the cowering fear that Nyla had expected. Even though her body was battered, Lohlyn still stood with a dignity that imbued Nyla with a surprising sense of courage.

Lord Briskyl rose. "Lohlyn of Lorren, both you and the queen stand accused of a plot to assassinate the king. Your own punishment will soon be decided, but today the council meets to decide the fate of the queen. She has asked that you speak in her defense. Answer every question truthfully, knowing that you stand in the presence not only of the king but of Taus himself." He stared sternly at Lohlyn and then cleared his throat before continuing. "The king will be your first questioner."

Alexor did not even look up. Instead he studied his nails and asked, in a voice as cold as a northern wind, "When exactly did you and Nyla agree to kill me?"

"We did not, Your Majesty. The queen never—"

He looked up sharply. "Answer my question!"

"The queen knew nothing of who I was, and I was not here to kill you."

"You expect us to believe that?" Alexor snorted. "Isn't it true that you are the daughter of the Charabian who rebelled against my grandfather?"

"I am."

"So? Are we to believe a rebel's word?" The king addressed the council. "Ridiculous! Let us decide on the events we all witnessed and pay no more attention to this traitor's lies."

A murmur of agreement followed his words, but Lord Briskyl rose. "Your Majesty, may I please ask the witness one more question?"

"Witness?" The king laughed. "Don't you mean murderous rebel?" But he waved his hand dismissively. "If you insist, Lord Briskyl. But I think we have all heard and seen enough to make our judgment, have we not?" Most of the men nodded.

"Thank you, Your Majesty." Lord Briskyl turned to Lohlyn. "If not to assassinate the king, why were you here?"

"I was put in place when the queen was a child. To protect her."

"Protect her?" The king flung the words back at her. "From whom? By who?"

"By your grandmother, Your Majesty. She understood how vulnerable Nyla's position was." Lohlyn swept an arm over the assembled men. "Perhaps she sensed this day would come."

The king's face contorted with rage. He pounded his fist on the armrest of the throne before he rose to his feet. "I've had enough of these insults and lies! Take her away!"

Throughout the questioning, Nyla's eyes had never left Lohlyn's face. Now, just before the guards closed in on her again, Lohlyn turned to look at the queen and smiled. After seven years of friendship, a single smile could communicate a ream of words, Nyla thought, for she almost heard Lohlyn's voice saying, "I failed you, forgive me. Be brave now, Nyla."

"You didn't fail me, Lohlyn!" she screamed as her friend was dragged back toward the door. "You didn't fail me!"

"Wait," the king's voice thundered, and the guards froze. "Since I never want to lay eyes on this murdering Charab again, I will pronounce my judgment on her right now."

The room grew still.

"Death," the king continued. "A slow traitor's death on the fire pole."

"No, Alexor!" Nyla screamed. "She hasn't done anything wrong."

"Do it tomorrow," he continued as if he had not even heard Nyla's words.

"Please, Alexor, no!"

"And take Nyla back to her quarters, Lord Briskyl." He turned to the old man. "We do not want the council to be swayed off course by her presence as we deliberate."

"This is most unusual, Your Majesty," Lord Briskyl objected. "The Tirragylin way is for the accused to be present for the sentencing. To stare into the eyes of the one you sentence brings a measure of mercy to the judgment."

"We are no longer doing things the Tirragylin way," Alexor smiled. "From now on we are doing things *my* way."

In that moment and that one cruel smile, Nyla remembered what Mada had once whispered about her husband, King Tausorlin. *He wasn't bad. He was weak. And power has a way of rotting the weakest of men from the inside out.* A shudder passed through Nyla's body as she recalled what people whispered about that time, a time known simply as "the black reign."

And she knew then that Alexor was weak, too.

"Can I see the prisoner?" Klyden stood outside Lohlyn's dungeon.

"Why, Loverboy? Is she one of the ones taken in by those brooding good looks?" The two guards standing at the locked gate laughed.

Klyden shrugged, laughing with them. "We had some moments together. But I wanted to tell her the queen's sentence. She was with her a long time."

"*We had some moments together,*" one guard mimicked, puckering his lips into a kiss. "What would you give to be that attractive to the ladies, Husk?"

"My right eye. By Taus, perhaps even both eyes!"

"That wouldn't be all that attractive, Husk." Klyden slapped the big guard on the back. "So just a few moments, lads?"

"Fine," Husk said, unlocking the gate. "But don't expect any kisses. She's back in that dream world of hers. It's dark in there. Take one of our torches."

Klyden felt his way down the short flight of steps. In the shadowy light of the torch, he could see Lohlyn curled up in sleep where the floor and wall met.

Grief clutched at his throat, raw and rage-filled. Why? Why would she, the very best of them, die at a corrupt king's command? Klyden could still stop it, he thought. He could pick her up right now, kill Husk and Sirtle at the inner door and the three guards positioned at the outer door. He could try to make it to the stables before they sounded the alarm, and they could dash to the palace gates where—

"Klyden?" Lohlyn's voice startled him.

"Loh!" He dropped to his knees by her side and lifted her head, cradling it in his lap. "I thought you were in your haven."

"No." She pushed herself up with every drop of her remaining strength. "I was pretending. I've been thinking of a way to save Nyla."

"Save Nyla?" The queen's name made him think of the council's sentence. "The council pronounced its judgment. Nyla is to be . . ."

"Drowned?"

Klyden nodded, startled that his sister had foreseen their decision.

"Of course. That way her half-spirit will return to Alexor. It's their absurd belief system," she said. "When?"

"I don't know. Lord Briskyl came to tell Nyla, but he was so upset that he didn't tell her much more, and she didn't ask."

"How was she?"

"Braver than I expected."

"I knew Alexor was selfish, but to do this to your own sister . . . can you imagine, Klyden?"

"No, Lohlyn. I can't imagine." He reached out and pulled a

strand of matted hair away from her face. "I can take you out of here, Loh. Or at least die trying."

"Even if you could, I wouldn't let you. You are Nyla's only hope. Now here's what I think you should do."

After she had outlined her plan, Klyden held Lohlyn. Their tears mingled as they spoke of their father and of how proud he would have been of them now. Of how they had prepared their entire lives for this precise moment. Of how grateful they were that they faced death in order to bring life, whereas every Charab before them had faced death only to bring death.

They were hardly aware of the guards calling. Only when Husk lumbered down the steps did Klyden give Lohlyn one last kiss on the cheek. Then, rising to his feet, he fled the dungeon.

CHAPTER 27

Kella's gaze held the same intensity as her father's, and Shara, unable to bear it, quickly looked down at her hands.

"Shara! I didn't know you were coming to the Deep Caves today." Her smile was warm.

"I needed the sunlight." It felt good to tell the truth again, after all these weeks of deception-weaving. The walk to the Deep Caves had been lovely, settling a brief feeling of joy on Shara as she walked in the sun's warmth.

"It can take a few months to acclimatize to underground life."

Shara didn't know how she could survive another day, never mind a month, buried in the Grotto, but she smiled and nodded. Andreo clambered down the rope ladder leading from the Chay'ets tree. Above them, Mikel was descending rapidly.

Kella greeted Andreo warmly, studying the hloring bush cuttings that he had taken above. She seemed genuinely interested in the medicinal properties of the bush as she led the way to the larger chamber.

"Will you show me how to brew it into a paste for wounds?" she asked Andreo as they filed around the table, where Kella's warriors played their favorite game of Garrison and Gallows.

"Do you have a cauldron we can use?"

"Later, Andreo," Kella laughed. "My father and I have some

decisions to make. My warriors will take care of you until we're done. Gruna, can you bring our visitors some hot origo?"

Shara watched Kella greet her father at the far end of the chamber. They ducked down into a low passage with some of the other warriors. Shara had the urge to follow them. Perhaps Mikel was whispering to his daughter exactly where he had hidden the Dusk Dreamer.

"Origo?" A woman's voice broke through Shara's musings. She held out a steaming cup. Shara took it with little enthusiasm. How this had become the Parashi's favorite drink she would never know. Sweet, but yeasty. If it hadn't been the only thing available at times, Shara would flatly refuse to put it to her lips.

Yet she cupped it in her hands, drawing its warmth into her. How cold these caves were. Gruna looked at her and Shara took a small sip and smiled false approval. Andreo, taking long swallows of his own drink, nodded with genuine enjoyment. His Parashi mother must have fed it to him from an early age for him to like it that much.

Andreo was soon deep in conversation with the game players. He quickly grasped the complicated game and was discussing strategy with them. There was a time, Shara suspected, when she would have enjoyed the game as much as her old tutor. She remembered, with a sudden pang of longing, the conversations the two of them had at Randin's house about history and war strategies.

Nnow her thoughts flitted around, restless as a moth. The longer she was apart from the Dreamer, the edgier Shara felt in body and mind. She would do anything to take away that feeling.

That was the moment she sensed something—a soft hum vibrating through the air.

She looked around for its source, but couldn't see anything out of the ordinary. The others were still engrossed in their game. She turned her head to the left and then to the right to try to pinpoint its source. The sound grew slightly louder as she turned her head to the left and Shara walked over to study the solid wall. There was nothing there.

She shook her head and wriggled a finger into both her ears. Walking back to the table, she tapped Andreo on the shoulder.

"Can you hear anything, Andreo? Anything . . . strange?" she whispered.

Andreo dragged his attention away from the game and gave her a surprised look. "Voices. Laughter." He pointed to the lamp on the table. "The hiss of the burning oil. Is that it, Shara?"

"No, it's more like a hum. A vibration. Something you feel more than hear." By then the sound was gone.

His brow furrowed. "I was concentrating on the game."

Shara thought that even if she had been engrossed in the game, the sound would have caught her attention. Maybe it wasn't that Andreo and the others *didn't* hear the sound. Maybe they *couldn't.*

She stepped back to the wall where the humming had been the loudest and stood very still, waiting. It took awhile before she sensed it again. Lower, but somehow more urgent this time. She looked up at Andreo and the players, now hoping that they hadn't heard it. Perhaps the sound was intended only for her—a message of sorts.

She put her hand out and rested it on the cold wall of the cave. A small tingle crept through her fingers, then her hand and up into her arm. The hum vibrated right into her body. Her fingers no longer felt the cold stone. They grew warm. Warm, like when she held the Dusk Dreamer.

And Shara finally knew what Mikel had done with her power rock.

It lay alone, hidden in a dark cavern of the Deep Caves, somewhere beyond these walls. A feeling of vindication settled on her as she realized that the Dreamer was calling to her. Yes, to her—its owner.

It was only a matter of time until she reclaimed what was rightfully hers.

<h1 style="text-align:center">CHAPTER 28</h1>

On the day Froll slammed the door shut in Nicho's face, he had believed it to be a temporary setback. Of course, he had been disappointed walking back with Colos, knowing that Jed was back in the dark room, pressing berries under the stern eye of Froll. Yet, he consoled himself, he knew where Jed was, and it was only a matter of time before he would rescue the boy. *Just a little longer Jed*, he had whispered into the air that night, as if his words could take flight and strengthen the boy.

Now, a few days later, it was dawning on Nicho that rescuing Jed would be more difficult than he thought. To begin with, Colos refused to help him any further.

"His mama gave him to Hanzer and Froll. Simple as that. You have no rights to the boy," he said for the umpteenth time.

"But you saw him, Colos! He's in a dark room surrounded by dirt, with Froll's sharp tongue and fist for company. That's no life for the child."

"At least the boy has food in his stomach. Many would be grateful for that much."

"Take me back one last time, Colos, then I won't ask you again."

Nicho had returned to the oppressive slum that lay behind the Wool and Wench every day since he had seen Jed. The area was vast, and many of the timber houses were just as run down as Hanzer and Froll's had been. They all looked alike. Once or twice, he had stood in the shadows outside a house to see if the brewer and his wife emerged, but he had always been disappointed. He had even asked a few people where the brewer lived, but, if they didn't tell him to get his Parashi butt out of their streets, they just stared at him suspiciously and refused to speak.

"I told you already," Colos growled, "I'm not taking you back. We asked. They refused. Nothing more we can do." He wiped one of the tavern tables. His first clients should be here soon. "I've done too much already. It almost cost me my beer supply."

"Yes, how terrible it would be if you had to find another supplier." Nicho's sarcasm was lost on Colos, who nodded, a serious frown creasing his face. "I won't involve you at all," Nicho tried one more time. "Just point out the house."

Colos stopped wiping the table and looked up. Nicho sensed an anger brooding inside the usually docile man. "I won't. Now, it's time you left. Nothing here worth staying for, and you're starting to stretch my tolerance."

Nicho pushed his stool away and rose to his feet. He cast a long look at Yasmin, who, lost in her own grief, didn't seem to be paying them any attention. "I won't give up on the boy, Colos. I *will* find him, no matter how long it takes and no matter how many doors I have to knock on."

Colos shrugged. "Keep me out of it, that's all I'm saying."

A cold wind snuck through the alleys leading away from the Wool and Wench. Nicho turned in the direction that would lead him toward the taverns and hostelries frequented by the merchants, but at the junction, he stopped and looked back.

Jed was somewhere in that crumbling web of humanity. How could he walk away now? Knowing the boy was near these last few days had given him comfort. Leaving him tore at Nicho as much as leaving Shara had done. He couldn't go through that pain again.

If Colos wouldn't let him stay, he would find somewhere else, even if he had to sleep in an alley. And every day he would go looking, one street and one house at a time. No matter how long it took him, he would find Jed again.

Nicho turned back to the slum, pacing the road with new purpose. Dusk drew its curtain quickly in these alleys. He would have to find somewhere to shelter while there was some light. Figures shuffled around him. Men on their way to taverns. Women casting suggestive glances his way. Yet, in the distance, Nicho's eyes found the shape of a man and young boy, walking his way. Something leapt inside him. *Could it be?*

As they drew nearer, Nicho found his feet pushing into a run. The man cast a furtive glance behind him. Nicho had seen him before. It was Hanzer, and next to him, looking crumpled and afraid, was Jed.

A wave of love broke over Nicho. He dropped to his knees a few paces from Jed and opened his arms. Only then did Jed notice him. The smallest flicker of hope lit up the boy's eyes.

Hanzer let go the boy's hand. "Go, lad," he said gruffly, pushing Jed forward.

Jed hesitated and looked up at him, and the man smiled and nodded. Then the young boy broke into a run and threw himself into Nicho's arms. Nicho could feel Jed's ribs and the small, silent tremors in his body.

"I'm here now, Jed," he soothed. "I won't let anything hurt you."

"You must go," Hanzer hissed. "Froll will discover this soon enough."

Nicho stood up, keeping hold of Jed's small hand. "Thank you," he said.

Hanzer nodded. "It's the right thing for the lad, and it's what Hildah wants." The name sounded tender on his lips. Now Hanzer was the one to bend down to Jed. "Lad, your mama says she loves you." He cleared his throat. "She . . . she says to be strong like your papa."

He straightened up and frowned at Nicho. "Leave Gwyndorr soon. You've made a spectacle of yourself these last few days, and I fear the town guards will come looking for you, especially if Froll has anything to do with it."

Nicho nodded and turned, leading Jed toward the road. He did not know how they would slip out of Gwyndorr, but there had to be a way. He had escaped Gwyndorr's chains once before, and he would do it again.

CHAPTER 29

Death has many facets, Nyla learned. As her own approached, a strange stillness settled on her. At times it felt heavy and smothering. At others, she could almost pull it around her like a comforting blanket.

On the first day of her sentence, her thoughts had raced wildly. Memories, regrets, unspoken words, unfulfilled longings—they tumbled around, unruly and unfocused, until her temples ached. She had tried to record some of them on a scroll but gave up. One was not meant to die at eighteen. There was too much living still to be done, far too much for a single blank page.

After that insight, a burning rage lit inside her. It consumed the wild thoughts and dying dreams and scalded into a painful loathing against everyone and everything that had brought her to this place.

Her parents, who had only really wanted Alexor.

The council of men, who had resented bowing their heads to a woman.

Lord Lucian, who had turned Alexor against her.

And finally Alexor, her constant companion, even before birth, whose betrayal ripped like a knife through skin. She had loved him most of all and still did not know how to hate him, even though the rage enticed her to. *Alexor, her brother.*

Finally, her hatred found its true target—Taus. Years of reverence were undone as she fumed against Tirragyl's god. If this put her in danger of losing her soul, so be it. Hadn't she lost it already? Everyone said it rightly belonged to Alexor. He could have it back when he drowned her in the Adriel River. Taus had made a terrible mistake giving it to her.

So it was that a dark, frayed acceptance finally settled onto Nyla. Not a peace—it was more ragged than that and stained with sorrow—but it would have to see her through to the river, one step at a time. She would approach her death like the queen she was. Everyone would see her dignity and stand amazed. Alexor, too, for he would be in the river with her as the last air bubbled from her body. He would be there watching, waiting for the fragment of her soul to be released.

Tomorrow it would all be over.

"Your Majesty?" The soft voice startled her. Her chambers were dark. She was lying on her sleeping pallet, fighting the tiredness. With so little time to live, she resented sleep stealing these few precious hours. She wanted to breathe the air filtering in from her window, tinged with the sweet smell of the xora blossoms. She wanted to listen to the croaking of frogs and chirping of insects. She wanted to soak in life, this one last night.

"Your Majesty?" Slightly louder.

"Yes?" She detected a figure near the door, but had not sensed him slipping into her chamber.

He moved closer and for a moment she was frightened.

"Don't be afraid," he said. "I'm here to help you escape."

"Who are you?"

"Klyden. You've seen me before. I'm the one who captured Lohlyn."

"I remember." He was the one who had supported Lohlyn as she was brought to the council. "Why would you help me?"

"I am your protector," he said as if he was merely informing her that he had brought her a meal. "As Lohlyn was. Mada assigned us to you."

"Mada?" Nyla's thoughts reeled within her. "But then why did you capture Loh?"

"She couldn't escape," he said sorrowfully. "They would have killed her."

It was true. Nyla thought back to that moment and realized that, if Lohlyn had not been seized, the guards would have attacked her with their swords.

"Are you a Charab, too?"

"Yes." There was a long pause. "I am Lohlyn's brother."

"By Taus!" She had thought often of her lady-in-waiting these last few days. No news had come to her, but if Alexor's commands had been carried out, Lohlyn would have been tied to the fire pole for three days already. "What has—how is—?" She did not really want to hear the answer.

"There was some delay finding a pole." His voice was low. "They only tied her to it yesterday afternoon."

"She still lives?" Nyla let out a single warped cry. "Can't you do something?"

"We talked about it. If I save her, I can't save you."

"No!" For the second time, Nyla realized that Lohlyn's death would be on her head. The weight was too heavy to bear.

"It's what we do." He was astute at sensing her emotions. "We kill and we die. But the most honorable Charabian death is on behalf of another." He was silent for a long time. "Lohlyn will be at peace."

Peace? True peace in the face of death? The last days had shown her it was not possible.

"Is she in her—what do you call it?—sleep state?"

"She wasn't the last time I saw her. We discussed how we could save you and"—again Klyden's voice wavered—"I fear she might be waiting to hear news of your escape."

"How long does the fire pole take?"

"It depends how strong the person is, and Lohlyn has grown weak. Three days maybe." He let out a deep, shuddering breath. "Hopefully less."

"I'm sorry." Nyla's grief and rage broke through in a deluge of tears. Klyden stood by silently.

"Your Majesty, we need to plan your escape." His note of urgency drew Nyla back.

She wiped her eyes, ashamed of her weakness. "Do we go now?"

"No. There are too many guards around. Even slipping in here was difficult. I won't be able to get us out. Loh and I decided there's only one way, and it won't be easy." His voice grew solemn. "You are going to have to trust me completely."

"If you are Lohlyn's brother, I trust you."

Lucian turned his gaze from the girl on the fire pole. The day and a half had already taken a toll on her. The branch-pole was the home of a fire ant colony and, ripped from their usual food source, the insects quickly turned to the victim tied to the pole. This cruel form of execution was the creation of the old King Tausorlin, and Lucian thought it rather barbaric, even by Tirragylin standards.

Not that he minded seeing an enemy suffer, but watching the Charab girl filled him with some remorse. He had tried to speak to her while she was in the dungeon, and again as they brought her to the pole. He had whispered that he could save her, that he would become her guardian, if she let him. Lucian could not shake the image of her dark, glowing skin and mysterious eyes. Never before had he felt such strong attraction.

Yet, in the dungeon, he had been unable to wake her, and on the way to her execution, she had merely turned reproachful eyes on him, hissing, "I'd rather die than serve the man who desires to kill my queen."

She was lost to him now. He glanced around the almost empty square. A few revelers sang a rowdy song in one corner, but other than that, only the four guards remained at their posts around the execution pole. How different from the festive feel during the day, when the townspeople had milled around, staring at the assassin. They would be back the next day to watch her slow demise.

Lucian yawned and ambled in the direction of the palace. He would not see the Charab girl again, for the following day he would travel with the royal party to the river. The queen would be protected from the prying eyes of her subjects. Only members of the royal court would be present as she breathed her last.

The queen's death did not fill him with regret, only anticipation. Once the king was the sole ruler of Tirragyl, Lucian would finally have the influence he needed to attack the Guardian Grotto and unite the two guardian rocks. With such power in his hands, Lucian would be unstoppable.

CHAPTER 30

The Raven had not earned the title of Tirragyl's master-spy without reason. His skill at trailing people was legendary, so he had no trouble following Elxa through Lydora's dark and quiet streets. Not that he even needed to. He knew exactly where the young Charab was going.

They had travelled to Lydora faster than he had ever thought possible. He had been skeptical when Elxa informed him they were taking the treacherous mountain route, and he had argued to take the safer route through the Enderite Kingdom.

"You can go that way, Raven, but my path lies over the mountains," Elxa had said.

In the end, he had stuck with Elxa, and there were moments when he cursed Taus and wished he hadn't. Yet Elxa's prediction proved true. They had made it to Lydora's gates at the close of day, a mere three days from the time they had set off.

Every part of the Raven's body had ached and all he wanted to do was curl up on his sleeping pallet.

"You look like you need a good night's rest, Raven," Elxa had smiled as they slipped through the gates. Then he grew solemn as he placed a hand on the spy's shoulder. "We say farewell here, my friend."

"Thank you for coming, Elxa."

"You know I have no choice."

"Lohlyn would thank you, too."

Elxa had shrugged, as if he was not so sure. "I need to do this alone. You understand, don't you?"

The Raven had nodded.

Yet here he was, a few hours later, following his friend to Execution Square. Briefly, he wondered why he wanted to bear witness to this event. It was for Lohlyn, he realized. He had been the one to expose her and he would not shy away now from what he had brought about. He owed her at least that.

He knew where Elxa was going, for the Charab had already scouted out the square earlier, in daylight. An alley snaked toward the square, joining it about sixty paces from where the fire pole stood, and this is where Elxa took up his position. It would be a difficult shot for it lay slightly to the side and the pole obscured most of Lohlyn's body. Yet the Raven had no doubt Elxa could do it.

The Raven found another alley to shelter in. From here he could see both Lohlyn and the dark outline of Elxa, although if he had not known where the assassin stood, he would not have seen him in the early evening shadows. The Raven's heart pounded loudly in his chest. Now that he stood here, he wished he had listened to Elxa's request and stayed away.

That morning, Elxa had explained that his cousin had probably gone into her "safe haven" where she would feel no pain. Yet the Raven could see from the girl's expression that she was conscious. Four guards were posted around her, seemingly oblivious to her pain.

Do it now. He willed Elxa to take the shot that would end Lohlyn's pain.

But nothing happened. There were some loud men drinking in a corner. Perhaps Elxa was waiting for them to leave? The Raven's eye caught sight of a nobleman slipping away from the square. The moments stretched on, his body aching from standing so still. Watching. Waiting. His eyes sought out the shape of the assassin, but he could not see him anymore. Had Elxa become aware of his presence and aborted the mission? He looked one more time into the face of pure pain and prayed to Taus that, if he was still there, the Charab would take the shot.

• • •

Elxa melted into the shadows of the alley and waited. It took a long time before several men, singing a bawdy tavern song, stumbled out of the square. From the time they could walk, Charab children were taught about death. One of their first lessons was to respect it. In the presence of a dying person, be they friend or foe, one was silent and reverent. To watch such blatant disrespect in the face of his cousin's death filled Elxa with a quiet rage.

The other person in the square—a well-dressed nobleman—at least showed some remorse. Elxa had seen him in the square earlier that afternoon, watching Lohlyn with a burning intensity. The man made him uncomfortable, and he was glad to see him turn and leave.

Now only Lohlyn and the four guards remained. The time had come. Elxa had been running from this moment for nine years. It had stalked him through his days and haunted him in his nights. Would he be free after this, or would his cousin's blood cry even louder than the king's command?

His hand trembled as he drew out an arrow and meticulously notched it onto the string. He lifted the bow and judged the distance to the pole, drawing the string back to the precise point. He sensed a light breeze, and adjusted the bow slightly to the left. In his mind, he could see the trajectory of the arrow through the air, knowing exactly the place it would hit. Death would be instant and painless.

Elxa hesitated.

Ra'aph-aqeb. The word grated in his head, demanding obedience. He clenched the bow tighter, fighting the force as he had done years before, when he had looked up into the messenger's eyes. "*The arming word's force is stronger than your will, Elxa,*" his father had reprimanded him after that day. "*It is futile to fight it.*" What, then, of his uncle? He had fought it and won, hadn't he? There was something more powerful than Taus and his arming word—Lohlyn's father had proved it.

His arm shook now with his effort at rebellion. *Ra'aph-aqeb.* To Elxa it felt as if the word was no longer merely in his head. It was around him, shrieking through the square, ricocheting off the walls of the alley, pummeling him with its force. Still, he managed to lower the bow. If he took the shot now, he would miss. He would injure Lohlyn and cause her more pain.

He waited for the shaking to subside, taking deep breaths to steady himself, as his father had taught him. Finally, he lifted the bow back into position, drew the arrow back, and released it.

The Raven heard the soft swish of the arrow through the air before he saw it hit its target. For a moment, he was baffled. What was Elxa doing? Then the next arrow found its target with chilling accuracy. A startled shout rose from the square. A third arrow cut it short.

Three guards now lay unmoving on the ground. Only one guard still stood near the fire pole. The Raven watched the last man's expression of alarm, and his sudden jerk to the right, as he attempted to escape. Yet even though he was in motion, the fourth arrow culled him as easily as it had done the standing men.

A chill of fear ran down the Raven's spine and he recalled the Charab boys at their early morning training sessions. He had never seen such concentration and skill in children. Yet that was how they became, like Elxa, such fearsome killers.

He watched the Charab's dark figure slip from the alley and kneel briefly at each of the bodies, almost as if in prayer, before turning to Lohlyn. The Raven held his breath as he watched Elxa standing silently in front of his cousin. He didn't see the moment at which the Charab drew his knife. Only when the blade glinted in the torchlight did he understood the assassin's intentions.

The pole was not high off the ground, and Lohlyn was a mere head above him. Elxa looked up into her face. She was watching him.

Ra'aph-aqeb. The word taunted him. *You can't escape what you are. You are in bondage to me forever. You are mine.*

He grasped the knife a little tighter and moved toward his cousin.

Not once did she look away. Pride surged through him. No Tirragyl king faced their death with the courage of a Charab.

"Elxa, you found me." Her words, barely audible, cracked off dry lips.

"I didn't want to, Loh."

His knife-hand shook as it lifted up, almost of its own accord. Only now did Lohlyn close her eyes. He slashed down, through the ropes that tied her hands to the pole, and grabbed her as she toppled forward. She groaned as his hands touched the raw wounds inflicted by the fire ants. How beastly were these Tirragylins, prolonging death for their own pleasure!

As he held her, he leaned down to slash the ropes that bound her feet. He spread out his cloak and gently lowered her onto it, then lifted her head to trickle some water into her mouth from his water skin.

"Why aren't you in your safe haven?"

"Waiting for word—" She stopped. Shook her head. "I . . . I couldn't reach it."

"You are my assignment," he said solemnly. "The king . . ."

At mention of the king, the arming word surged through his body once more. He clenched his fists. He wouldn't be able to fight its force much longer.

"I'm glad you're here," she whispered. "The pain is great." She jerked her head in the direction of a guard. "But why them?"

"I wanted to say farewell. To tell you how much I always . . ." He stopped and swallowed. How did you tell the person you came to kill that you loved them? Still, Lohlyn understood, for he caught the faint trace of a smile on her lips.

"And I wanted to ask . . ."

Ra'aph-aqeb. Ra'aph-aqeb. Ra'aph-aqeb. It seemed the force was trying to prevent his next question, so great was the onslaught on his mind and body. He threw the knife to the side and curled his body up tightly. He forced the words out, slowly and deliberately, knowing it would be his last act of defiance, for he could no longer keep the command at bay.

"How? How did your father . . . break free . . . of the arming . . . word?" The word was screaming so loudly now that he feared he would miss her reply, but she reached for his hand and pulled him back to her with her urgent tone.

"Elxa! Seek the Gold Breast bird. Only its power is greater. There is no other way."

"Where is it?"

"Seek it with your whole heart, and it will find *you*." She closed her eyes. "I'm ready now, Elxa."

And Elxa finally gave in to the ancient curse that bound his people.

The Raven watched from a distance, grief clawing at his throat. What had he started by taking on Lord Lucian's assignment? What had he done to this fine young Charab man, now weeping over his cousin's lifeless body? And why, oh why, had he stayed to watch?

He dragged his gaze away from the sorrowful scene and slowly felt his way back down the dark alley. He felt a pressing urgency to get away from Lydora's darkness, but the gates were locked for the night. He would have to return to his quarters on the eastern side of the city, but in the morning, he would flee and never come back.

Perhaps he would return to the farmlands of his childhood, or perhaps he would seek out the Bent Bandit and become one of his men, drinking berry beer at night and singing outlaw songs around the fire. There was something naïve about the Bandit's men. Their misdeeds were childlike compared to the evil that stalked through Lydora's palace.

He heard the sound of marching boots moments before he caught sight of the four palace guards filing toward him. They must be on their way to Execution Square. *Elxa!* Would he be gone by the time they arrived?

The Raven darted into a side alley that connected with the alley where Elxa had stood, and ran toward the square. The guards were not far behind him. Elxa was wrapping Lohlyn's body in his robe and putting his arms under her to lift her up. The Charab was trying to take her body with him!

As the Raven burst into the square, Elxa reacted. He lowered Lohlyn's body and drew his long sword with his right hand, even as the left lifted a knife into a throwing position.

"It's me," the Raven hissed, coming to an abrupt halt and lifting his hands. "There are guards on their way. They are mere moments behind me."

Elxa cocked his head to the side, and turned to look down the alley where the Raven had stood earlier. "From there?"

"Yes."

Elxa gazed at the body of Lohlyn.

"You don't have time to take her," the Raven said. "Come. Quickly!"

One last time Elxa bent down, this time to place a curved ceremonial knife on Lohlyn's body. Then he turned and followed the Raven from the square.

"To arms! To arms!" the captain's voice rang out through the barracks in the middle of the night.

"What the—?" Husk clambered to his feet and cursed as his toe hit something hard.

Klyden lay still, breathing deeply. Unlike his companions, sleep had not yet come to him, although he knew he needed rest for what lay ahead the next day.

"What is it?" another groggy voice asked. Somebody lit a lamp, and all around him, men staggered to their feet.

Klyden rose cautiously, slipping his knife into his robe. Had his plans been discovered? Only the queen herself knew of them. Had she betrayed him in the hope of saving her own life? No. It made no sense. Her fate was sealed with his. If he failed, they died together.

"Assemble in the courtyard with your weapons," the captain bellowed.

The men dressed hastily. Klyden's initial fear subsided. Perhaps it was a mere drill. This captain enjoyed keeping his men in a constant state of uncertainty. If they had discovered his plot to free the queen, surely they would have come for him alone in the night? They wouldn't give him a chance to arm himself first.

The men silently fell into position in the courtyard. Klyden stared straight ahead, but sensed the captain's agitation as he paced before them.

"Guards," he shouted when they were all in formation. "We are under attack. This very night four of our own were cut down in cold blood on Execution Square. From this moment, consider that there is an enemy stalking toward the palace with the aim of killing the king and overthrowing the throne." The captain stopped his pacing and lifted his sword in the air. "From this moment on, consider that we are at war."

Four guards killed in Execution Square? Strange, but surely this didn't constitute an act of war.

"We are not sure who the enemy is," the captain continued, "only that they are ruthless killers, for their arrows took down our men with unerring accuracy. What's more, there are many, for our highly trained guards didn't stand a chance against them. So now"—he began to pace again—"we will have a full complement of guards at the gatehouse and another on the walls. We will double the guards that accompany the queen to her execution tomorrow, and only they are to return to the barracks for sleep now. Any questions, men?"

"Sir?" Klyden raised his hand. "What became of the prisoner the men guarded?"

"Strange you should ask." The captain's forehead furrowed with consternation. "She was found dead, too. Wrapped in a cloak, with a curved knife on her chest."

Even as the reality of his sister's death struck him, Klyden understood the truth. There hadn't been an enemy army in the square, only a single Charab. And it wasn't the king who was in danger, it was himself.

CHAPTER 31

Nicho was beginning to feel desperate. He had spent the last two days studying Gwyndorr's town gate from a distance, watching the flow of traffic in and out of the heavily guarded exit. Every cart was searched, every person questioned. The guards spent the most time on the Parashi travelers, and if they did not have a letter from a Highborn stating their legitimate business outside Gwyndorr, they were sent away, usually with a beating to remind them not to try it again. He'd even seen a few arrested, destined for a Rifter Gang.

He turned into the road leading to Rosa's house and looked around to make sure no one was on the street. The curfew hour was near. The street appeared empty. He knew he couldn't stay here much longer. Rosa was at risk for hiding a fugitive, and now that there was a younger boy in her house in addition to her son, her neighbors would soon suspect something was amiss.

Rosa had taken to Jed as naturally as if he were her own kin, and Jed was responding to her, too. Just this morning, Nicho had found the two of them huddled in the kitchen, Jed smiling shyly at something Rosa had just told him. Thinking of that rare smile pierced Nicho with a sorrowful love. The boy had nobody left. He could not let him down now. He had to find a way out.

He knocked at Rosa's door, but she did not come. The door handle pushed down without resistance, and a prickle of unease crept over Nicho. It was unlike Rosa to keep the door unlatched.

He opened it slowly and looked around the first room. A flickering oil lamp stood on the bench where Rosa normally sat, but there was no sign of her, Simhew, or Jed. Could they have gone out? No, she wouldn't risk it.

He closed the door quietly and crept to the door that led to Rosa and Simhew's sleeping quarters. Jed shared Simhew's bed now. Perhaps they had fallen asleep early?

"Rosa?" he whispered.

Then he heard the whimper. *Jed.* He flung the door open and his eyes found Jed, Simhew, and Rosa sitting on a single sleeping pallet. But they were not alone. Rising from the other pallet was a young town guard and behind them, sword drawn, stood the man Nicho had hoped never to see again.

Randin.

Confusion coursed through Nicho's mind, followed by a blow of despair so heavy that it might have pressed him to the ground if a heavy pair of arms hadn't grabbed him. The pain as this third guard twisted his arms upward could not compare to the anguish Nicho felt. He had done this. He had brought this upon these three people he cared for so much.

"Well, well," Randin smiled, trudging toward Nicho with his arms behind his back, savoring this moment of power. "News reached us of a Parashi loitering around, looking for a boy."

Nicho cast his eyes down to the ground, as he had always done when his master spoke to him.

"My runaway returns. Where exactly have you been, Nicho?" he asked mildly.

"I . . . I . . . just to Lydora and back, sir."

"You did not like it in my employ?"

"It . . . I did, sir."

"But the pastures were greener in Lydora? Or did your leaving have something to do with the fact that we discovered your forbidden activities?"

"No, sir. I was not—"

"Don't lie to me, Nicho." Randin's voice was soft, menacing. "Were you teaching the Parashi boys to read and write?"

Nicho met his eyes for just a moment. "It's true, sir." Perhaps they would just take him, and leave Simhew and Jed with Rosa. Perhaps she could raise Jed as her own son.

"And this woman has been hiding you these last few days?" Randin pointed to Rosa. "She let you teach in her house. Right, Nicho?"

"She did nothing wrong, sir." Nicho looked up pleadingly. "She was merely—"

"Nothing?" Randin's laugh was humorless. Cold. "I think the captain will disagree. But tell me. Who is the young boy?"

"He is the reason I came back, sir. My friend Derry died, and this is his son. He has nobody now. Only me."

"He won't have you for much longer, either, Nicho. I'm sure there's a Rifter Gang that needs a good rooter. He's the perfect size, wouldn't you say?"

"No, please, sir," Nicho's voice broke on the plea. "He's so young and has been through so much. Let him stay with Rosa. Take me. But please let him live, sir. He has lost everything already."

"Then nobody will miss him."

A guard stepped forward.

"Found this in the other room earlier." He thrust Nicho's knapsack into Randin's hand. "Think it belongs to the fugitive. Captain might want to see it."

"I doubt it." Randin tipped over the bag, spilling its contents at Nicho's feet. He kicked the threadbare blanket and several husks of dry bread. "Nothing of value here." He gave the bag one last shake, and it was then that a long narrow object wrapped in oilskin fell to the ground. "What's this?"

Nicho had forgotten about that reed pipe. What had Eliad said about it? Something about it being extraordinary. That you could play it and call . . .

A wave of cold prickled over his skin. The pipe called Tabeal. Tabeal, who had helped him and Shara avoid capture at the town gate and aided their escape from Lord Lucian's manor. If there was anybody who could have led him and Jed out of Gwyndorr, it was the Gold Breast. How could he have been so foolish as to forget this treasure tucked into the bottom of his bag?

"Just a reed pipe, sir," he said quickly. "My father carved it. Hardly even makes a sound. Can I show you?" Maybe it wasn't too late to call Tabeal. Even now he could blow it, and she would come.

"No." Randin cast the pipe aside. Nicho watched it rolling across the small room. "We're wasting time. Let's take these outlaws to the barracks. The captain can do with them what he wants."

As Nicho was jerked backward toward the door, he watched Randin grab Rosa's arms. She didn't even struggle, but tears brimmed in her eyes. Jed did not cry as the other guard gripped his shoulder with one hand, holding Simhew with the other. The numbness that Nicho and Rosa had worked so hard at breaking down was back on his face.

Nicho had failed him again.

CHAPTER 32

"You don't think we should postpone the . . . um . . . soul-transfer until these unknown enemies are found?" King Alexor asked as a servant lifted the heavy golden robe onto his shoulders. "They could be lying in wait along the road, or by the river."

"It's exactly what they want, Your Majesty," Lord Lucian said. "They want you to remain weak. Once you are whole and strong, they won't be able to touch you."

"Delaying it by a week won't make too much difference. It will just give us some time to root them out and be rid of them." Alexor impatiently shook off the servant's hand and fastened the robe himself.

"Much can happen in a week, Your Majesty. I think it's too great a risk to wait. And the guard troop accompanying us to the river has been doubled. Nobody will get near you."

"They don't need to get near. You heard how accurately they took down those guards in Execution Square."

"You won't be on horseback, sire, but rather in a secure litter, surrounded by your men."

Lucian quelled his annoyance. Of all the men who could have been king, Alexor surely had to be the weakest of all. Of course, he reminded himself, a stronger man might not have been as easy to influence.

"I think it will be good to get this behind you, my king," Lucian said soothingly. "It is the final unpleasantness needed to restore things to how they should always have been. You are the rightful heir to the throne, and you should not have been subjected to all the pain flowing from the unfortunate circumstances of your birth. Let us not allow anything to stand in the way of correcting the wrongs of the past."

"Yes." The king nodded. "It will be good to have this over with. To become the strong king I am meant to be."

Lucian glanced out the window. The guards and elders were already assembled. "It is time, King Alexor. Time to fulfill your great destiny."

Klyden watched Queen Nyla approach. Her face was pale as a sun-bleached sky and her body flimsy as a reed as she emerged from the palace. Lord Briskyl walked next to her and two palace guards trailed behind her. A hush fell over the group of noblemen and guards wait-ing to accompany her to the river. She paused and looked up at them, her chin rising defiantly and her eyes flashing with derision.

Good, Klyden thought. She was stronger than she looked. All that had gone before, and all that still lay ahead, would not crush her spirit.

"Your Majesty, a litter has been prepared for you," Lord Briskyl said softly, pointing toward the curtained box carried by four guards.

"I will walk."

"It is not possible. The events of last night show that there are crown-enemies in Lydora. It is not safe to go on foot."

"I am going to my death. I hardly fear a crown-enemy. In fact, I might consider them an ally."

"Please." The lord dropped his voice even lower. "Preserve your energy. It is a long way."

Briefly, Nyla's gaze met Klyden's. He was standing next to the litter and drew the curtain aside. The lord was right. She would need her strength.

"Fine." She stepped into the box, letting the curtain fall back to hide her from the staring eyes. After awhile, she pulled it open just a slit. "Why aren't we going?"

"We are waiting for the king," Klyden answered, glancing at the palace door.

She nodded, but continued to look at him. What was she doing? He had told her not to draw any attention to him. "Lord Briskyl told me what happened in Execution Square last night," she said softly.

"A tragedy," he said through clenched lips.

"Yes. Yet for Lohlyn, a welcome release."

He said nothing more and was grateful when the curtain closed again.

The king emerged at that moment, accompanied by Lord Lucian. He looked around furtively as he was escorted to his own litter.

The group set off. Winding their way to the river, slowed as they were by the weight of the litters, would take time. The procession moved in almost complete silence, as if the solemnity of what was about to occur had finally dawned on them. Their queen was about to die, and they would soon bear witness to it.

The Raven pushed through the crush of people waiting at the Friar's Gate, listening to their murmuring discontent. This was the fourth gate of Lydora that the Raven had scouted this morning. The Merchant and Water Gates were closed and heavily guarded. Steeps Gate, the smallest entrance to Lydora, was still open and allowing a small trickle of foot-travelers out onto its narrow, stepped trail. Royal Guards were present even there, searching and questioning each person who left the citadel's confines.

Crawling with guards, Friar's Gate was chaotic. Only well-known nobles and merchants were permitted passage. Most travelers were turned away after a thorough interrogation.

Elxa was definitely not leaving the city today, the Raven thought.

He turned and headed back to his dwelling in the wealthier part of Lydora. Elxa had been asleep this morning when the Raven slipped onto the city streets. Now a sense of urgency pushed the

Raven forward. What if Elxa had awakened and decided to leave? The city was in uproar. Guards were stationed everywhere. They even pounded on doors, demanding entry. Obviously the events of last night had shaken the palace to its core. Not for the first time, the Raven wished Elxa had only killed the girl and let the guards be.

He was relieved to find Elxa standing at the small window, shutter open, staring out onto the road below. The young man turned as the Raven entered. Normally his face showed little emotion, but this morning sorrow had stolen into his green eyes.

"Is Lydora always this frenzied?" he asked.

"No." The Raven slung his leather pouch over a chair and moved to the fire circle, where a few embers still glowed. "Only when four Royal Guards are shot in the middle of the night."

"They are looking for me."

"Word is they are looking for the horde of rebels who have come to murder the king."

"Horde?"

"A single man isn't meant to bring down four highly trained guards with such ease."

Elxa nodded. "Why would someone want the king dead?"

The Raven, on his knees blowing life back into the embers, straightened. "There is always discontent brewing in Lydora and beyond. Surely you know that?"

"The Charab don't pay too much attention to Tirragyl's politics."

"Well, you should. The Rif'twine is still steadily moving south, taking over large tracts of land, and even the Rifter Gangs can't push it back completely. Then there is the threat that the Enderites pose."

"Threat? Those short mountain goats?" Elxa laughed. "Cowards must reside behind those palace walls to consider *them* a danger."

"And the Parashi grow discontented," the Raven continued.

"Possibly," Elxa said solemnly, as if he could taste their dissatisfaction himself. "But they have no weapons or structure. The king could crush them like ants."

"Our timing wasn't too good, either. The palace is on edge already with the soul-transfer taking place today." He saw the question on

Elxa's face and continued. "You know the king and queen are twins? Well, the queen is to be drowned today, allowing her part of their joint soul to transfer back to her brother."

Elxa shook his head. "And they think *us* barbaric. Do you honestly believe that hogwash, Raven, or do you think the king might just want all the power for himself?"

The Raven looked uncomfortable. "I suppose it works to his advantage, but it is also part of what we Tirragylins believe."

"What's she like? The queen?"

The Raven conjured up a picture of the queen. "Serious. Clever, I think. And maybe"—the sudden insight surprised him—"stronger. Better than the king in many ways."

"Perhaps they should drown the king instead."

The idea was so ridiculous it caught the Raven off guard. Why did the thought of drowning the king appall him more than the thought of drowning the queen? Because she was a woman? Didn't her life have as much value as that of the king? The injustice of what was about to occur today struck him as never before.

"By Taus, Elxa. It *is* an outrage, isn't it?"

"Charab are taught that every hour of life is precious. A gift. To take it away from someone is a weighty matter." He looked up, staring deeply into the Raven's eyes. "We never do it lightly."

"Then why . . . ?" The Raven stopped. Last night was not something he wanted to think about, much less discuss.

Elxa understood, however. "Why did I kill the guards? I'll tell you why, Raven. We are bound to death. It whispers to us. Taunts us. Last night I fought it with all my might, and still I lost." He stood silently for a long time, before he spoke again. "Only one of us has ever managed to defeat death's cruel grip and break free of Taus's curse."

"Lohlyn's father."

"I had to speak to her and ask how he did it."

"Did she know?"

"She told me there is one more powerful than Taus and his curse."

"More powerful than Taus?" The thought was astonishing to the Raven, sacrilegious even.

"I'm going to find it." Elxa said, determination in his voice. "It's a bird. A Golden breasted bird."

CHAPTER 33

Sometime before dawn, Nicho fell into a restless sleep on the stone floor of the cell. There were voices in his dreams. Men pleading. Women screaming. But worst of all was the one silenced voice of a boy with vacant eyes. How Nicho wished that boy would speak or shout or cry, as he stood silently in the corner of Nicho's dreams.

I've let you down, Jed. Why don't you just scream it out for all of Gwyndorr to hear? Yet that boy's face, as unfathomable as an old man's, showed no anger, no pain.

A stone rattling against the bars startled Nicho awake. A voice bellowed, "On your feet!"

Around him men groaned, struggling to their feet. Nicho was too slow. A whip's tail caught him across the face. His cheek burned as if an open flame licked it. Almost as painful as the hot branding iron they had used on him last night to sear a number onto his lower arm. *12753.*

"Better get used to the whip, lad." The guard laughed. "It's one of the kinder things you'll encounter in the Rif'twine."

A withered hand lifted him to his feet and he looked up into the face of an old, wiry man with white hair. Guards shoved them from the cell. From farther down the darkened passage, he could hear women weeping.

The guards brought them to the barrack's quad. After the dark of the cells, the morning light pierced right into the back of Nicho's eyes. Yet he immediately spotted Jed and Simhew in the small group of children, huddled together under the watchful eye of a Town Guard. Nicho moved toward them, but an arm caught him from behind.

"It's useless," the old wiry prisoner said. "They'll just whip you again. Wait till we are on the road and you might get closer."

They set off as soon as the four female prisoners joined them. A wave of guilt assailed Nicho as he looked at Rosa. Her hair and clothes were in disarray. Both eyes were bruised. *What have they done to you, Rosa?*

Still, as she met his gaze, she smiled briefly—a quivering, courageous smile. How strong she was. Rosa, who had defied the Highborns and let him teach Simhew and the other boys letters in her house. Rosa, who had hidden him and Jed, and helped to draw the boy back from his silence. *You don't deserve this Rosa, I'm sorry.*

He hoped the old man was right, and he would have a chance to draw alongside Rosa, Simhew, and Jed. He wanted to say how sorry he was that he had brought this upon them. He wanted to say good-bye.

The sun burned down on them as the guards herded them out of Gwyndorr and along the road to the Rif'twine. Over the course of the long march, prisoners were pushed toward the large platforms that were the bases of the different Rifter Gangs. At one stage on the long trek, Nicho managed to slow down and fall back to where the women walked. He moved in next to Rosa.

"I'm sorry for bringing this on you, Rosa," he whispered.

"Don't be a fool." Her eyes filled with tears. "We defied the Highborns. We knew this day might come, didn't we?"

The remaining children marched behind the women. Nicho strained around, trying to see Jed, but he couldn't find him. Had Jed already been dropped off at a platform, and Nicho hadn't seen him go? Would he never see him again?

The group stopped. A guard pulled a woman forward and pushed her toward the platform.

"You!" The guard pointed at Nicho. "This is your final stop, Parashi. A room with a forest view. Who could ask for more?" Only a few guards guffawed at the joke. They must have heard it many times before.

Nicho followed the woman, aware of the point of a sword near his back. Perhaps he should run. Perhaps a quick plunge of the sword was better than the slow death that lay in the forest. He suddenly remembered his father—one of the few men to return from a Rifter Gang—and his dead eyes. What darkness lay in this forest that seeped the life out of your soul, even before it stole it from your body?

"Ko!" It was Jed's voice. The remaining prisoners parted and Jed came hurtling toward him. He was too fast for the guards as he threw himself into Nicho's arms.

"Jed." He held the boy's small, thin body against his own, so tightly he feared he might crush the very life out of him. "Jed." Sobs wracked through his body now. He should be strong. For the boy. But he could not hold back his grief. A guard reached for Jed, tugging at him, but still the two held on to each other.

A gruff voice said, "Have a heart. Give the man a moment with his lad."

"Ko," Jed whispered. "Remember the wooden horse Papa made me? Mama sold it."

"I remember."

"I didn't want you to be as sad as me, so I got this back for you. What your Papa made."

Jed reached into his shirt as a guard again began pulling him away. "Good-byes are over," the man said roughly.

Jed had something in his hand, and even as the guard wrenched him from Nicho's grip, he held it out toward Nicho.

It was the pipe. The one that called the Gold Breast.

The Hope-Caller.

Nicho grabbed it and lifted it to his mouth, even as the side of a sword hit him across the shoulders. He blew—one long, silent breath, brimming with every one of his failures and hopes. The guard's next strike was much harder, knocking the pipe from his hand and driving him to the ground.

Come, please come, Nicho whispered as everything went dark around him.

CHAPTER 34

The litter stopped. The curtain parted.

"We are here," Klyden said.

"Give me a moment." Nyla looked down at her shaking hands as the curtain fell back into place. She wondered why the air felt so very thin suddenly. No matter how hard she breathed, it did not seem to fill her, almost as if the very elements no longer wanted to nourish her.

Dignity. Show them you are a queen. You are not a coward. You are their queen.

She took one last, long breath before pulling the curtain apart. Lord Briskyl stood there now, his face grave. He dropped his gaze as he offered her his arm.

"I don't think I ever thanked you for supporting me, Lord Briskyl," she said. "It's meant a great deal to me."

"I'm sorry I couldn't"—he swallowed—"couldn't do more."

"The king's will always prevails." She sought out her brother in the group of noblemen, but caught only glimpses of his rich, golden robe as men crowded around him. He wore their Sovereign Day robe, she realized. Her matching one hung in her own wardrobe at the palace.

"We are to go this way." Lord Briskyl pointed to a small path. "There is a pool down there where . . ."

"Where I am to be drowned," Nyla finished flatly.

She held her head high and marched down the path, aware of the hush that had settled over the noblemen. They were watching her. Was Alexor watching, too? What was he thinking? She used to be so good at knowing his thoughts.

As the path wound steeply downward, she caught sight of the river. It appeared to flow lazily toward the waterfall that ended in the dark, deep pool where she was to die. Yet, as she grew closer, she could see the water ran faster than she had first thought. The dark pool fed into another waterfall, the final drop before the river coursed south toward the ocean. A shudder ran through her as she looked at that falling water and sensed the strength of the current.

Lord Briskyl must have felt her tremble because he squeezed her hand. "Soon this will be over. You and the king will be joined forever."

By Taus! Even her ally had come to accept her death. Well, if she was to die today, it wouldn't be as easy as they all expected. She would fight them until her very last breath.

They waited on the large, flat rocks next to the pool. Three guards stood around her. One of them was Klyden. Other than his clenched jaw, his expression gave nothing away. For a moment, she felt afraid. Had he changed his mind? Would he just stand by and watch her die so as not to endanger his own life?

No! He was Lohlyn's brother. Her protector. Hadn't he said that the Charab's most honorable death was in the protection of another? She had to believe he would help her today, even if they both died.

She turned to watch Alexor navigate his way down the steep path to the river. He looked regal in the golden robe, a crown resting on his thick mane of hair. She loved him still, she realized. Was it too late to throw herself at his feet and beg for mercy? Was every ember of his love for her dead? Couldn't they turn back, undo all these weeks, and walk arm-in-arm through the palace gardens again? How had they come to this place? By Taus, how had this happened?

As he reached the rocks, Alexor looked at her. For just an instant, she saw something in his eyes. Sorrow? Remorse? Yet almost instantly it was gone, replaced by the cold indifference that had crept over him since . . . she couldn't even pinpoint when. He turned to Lord Lucian and said something that caused the lord to smile. Then he undid the clasp at his neck and lay the golden robe in the lord's arms.

"Your Majesty, it is time."

Something quiet settled deep in Nyla at Lord Briskyl's words. The moment was here. She nodded. Her hands no longer shook as she undid her outer robe. She glanced back at the path, seeing the many bowmen positioned there and along the ridge, where the litters had stopped. She and Klyden were unlikely to survive, much less escape today. Yet, she would remind every one of them that she was a queen, born from a long line of warriors. Warriors who did not die easily.

The two guards who would accompany her into the water had been chosen for their strength. They moved to her side now, taking her in their vice-like grips.

"I can walk to the river myself," she said.

"We are under orders from the king," one said, not releasing her as they edged toward the water.

At the river, they stopped, taking turns to unbuckle their knife belts as the other held on to her. Nyla used the opportunity to look for Alexor. He stood with Lord Lucian and several of his attendants at the pool, a few paces away from her. A servant was undoing the clasp of his leather shoes. When his feet were bare, he took a few tentative steps forward onto the slippery rocks.

"Here, Your Majesty," one of his men pointed. "There is a submerged rock right here where you will be able to stand up to your chest in the water."

"Will that be deep enough for the transfer to occur?"

"You will just have to go under for a brief while as the soul is released. It will find you, its rightful owner," Lord Lucian said.

She watched him slide into the pool. Neither of them had learned to swim as children, and for a moment, he thrashed around in the water until his feet found the promised rock. He rose up a little then, and she heard his soft instruction. "I'm ready. Put her in."

The guards firmly guided her into the pool. The water was

shallower here than where Alexor stood. At first, the cold water only reached her knees, but within a few paces it was up to her waist, then her chest. The water was breath-stealing cold, but Nyla welcomed it.

Suddenly she could see all the surreal events of this day in stark and crisp reality. She was simultaneously aware of the beauty of this place, the blue sky, the quiet watchful eyes of the men on the bank, and Alexor waiting with trepidation, awe even, for their fragmented souls to be joined.

"Deep enough," one of the guards said. He looked at her with some discomfort before his large hand grabbed her behind the neck and he pushed her face down into the water.

It happened so quickly that she didn't have time to take the large gulp of breath Klyden had told her to. She struggled—a savage, primeval battle for breath and life. The guard's grip did not loosen. The pressure in her chest and her head grew. Still she wrestled, thrashing against the water, the guards, the injustice of it all.

Soon she felt the weakness stealing into her body, her movements slowing. Terror and darkness now lapped at the edges of her consciousness, like the murky waters of this pool. She wondered if Alexor was going under right now. If this was the moment when he would steal away her soul.

Klyden had not expected it to happen so soon. He had anticipated some formalities, words from the king or Lord Lucian, which would distract the crowd, giving him time to get into position. Yet there was none of that. One moment the guards led the queen into the pool, and the next, they held her thrashing body under the water.

How long did he have? A minute, at most. Less if the queen hadn't managed to take a large breath.

He moved toward the edge of the pool. No one noticed. Every eye was on the trio in the water. He eased the two circular throwing blades from his belt and hid them in the palm of his hands as he stepped into the water. Briefly, he skimmed his eyes across the noblemen and guards on the bank, but if they saw him in the pool, they thought nothing of it. He waded closer to the guards. About eight paces away, one of them sensed his approach and turned questioningly toward him.

"There is a fleeting moment," his father always said, *"that is the right time to act. The skill is in knowing when that is."*

Klyden had hoped to be closer to the men before he threw the blades. Not because he was afraid he'd miss, but rather because, in the time it would take him to reach Nyla from here, an arrow from a bowman could fell him.

But he could wait no longer. The ripples in the pool grew still. He was out of time. The moment had come.

He threw the circular blades within a second of each other, fast and with deadly accuracy. One guard jerked to the side, shock written on his face, before he splashed forward into the water. The other stood a moment longer. Klyden could not see his expression. Then he, too, sank into the water.

Klyden was now five paces from them. Because he expected a reaction from the shore at any moment, Klyden dived under and, with powerful strokes, closed the gap between him and the queen. He bumped into something and when he opened his eyes, saw it was the arm of one of the guards.

He spun in the water, trying to catch a glimpse of the queen through the green-brown murk. Something plunged through the water just to his right. An arrow. Another three followed in quick succession. The attack had started. Klyden dived deeper, even as his lungs burned and every instinct told him to surface for a breath.

Then he saw the queen. Her eyes were open, but glazed and lifeless, and a small trail of bubbles rose from her lips. Her hair and white robe billowed around her, wraith-like.

Klyden grabbed her around the chest. His feet nudged the ground and he pushed off as hard as he could away from the shore and bowmen. He couldn't risk surfacing here, even though he knew every second they stayed under reduced the queen's chances of survival.

When he sensed he was nearing the waterfall, Klyden knew he could not afford to wait any longer. He broke through the water.

There was a good distance between them and the shore, but he heard the shouts and, almost instantly, a bevy of arrows flew toward them. He dove under again.

The queen was limp in his arms. He swam a little farther before surfacing again and putting his lips onto hers, blowing air into her mouth. It was an ancient Charab trick that an elder had shown them once. He remembered debating with Elxa who they would like to practice the life kiss on. Klyden could never have known it would be a queen.

He heard the roiling waters and felt the current tug them toward the waterfall. He had almost no control over this part of the escape plan. *Success does not lie only with you. Some days, the Ancient One kisses you with his favor, and others He turns to hide his face.* The old Charab proverb rang in his ears as Klyden grabbed the queen and held her as tightly as he could.

Don't hide your face today. She doesn't deserve to die.

The water dragged them over the edge, and then they were tumbling down, with only the Ancient One's hand to break their fall.

CHAPTER 35

Afamiliar voice was calling him, urgent and high-pitched. "Ko! Ko! Ko!"

And another, more soothing voice. "I think he's coming around, Jed. Look."

Nicho opened his eyes to a circle of faces, but it was Jed's he looked at. The boy's mouth lifted into a tentative smile.

"Ko! You won't believe what happened!"

Nicho remembered. The guards marching them to their Rifter Gangs. Jed breaking through to say good-bye. Blowing the silent pipe. And then a blinding pain as something hit him on the back of his head.

Nicho's fingers found the swelling and he winced. He struggled to sit up, ignoring the warning pain that shot through his head.

"Did she come?" Now he focused on Rosa's face in the crowd. "Did she?"

She shook her head. "Who's *she*, Nicho?"

"Tabeal."

"Ko! You know what happened?" Jed's voice could barely contain his eagerness. "There was a flash in the sky. And then a horrible sound that hurt our ears. And the guards fell over and wriggled. I think they are dead."

"They're not dead," Rosa said. "Just asleep."

"Are they going to wake up?" Jed asked fearfully.

"If they do, it won't matter because Frintin tied them up. See?" She turned to point to the old wiry man. He was tying the unconscious guards together.

"She came!" Nicho tried to clamber to his feet, but the dizziness forced him back to the ground. "Where is she?"

"Sit awhile, lad. That was a hard blow to your head," one of the women said.

"No. The pipe called the Gold Breast bird. That's who knocked the guards over."

"A *bird* knocked them over?" Frintin had ambled over to look at Nicho.

"Not just any bird." Nicho was growing impatient. "A powerful bird of ancient lore. The pipe calls her."

"The pipe didn't make a sound, Nicho," Rosa said softly.

"The bird hears it, though." He looked around frantically. "Where is the pipe?"

"I got it for you." Jed held it out again proudly.

Would the bird come again if he blew it? Or did she only come in desperate situations, and they would think him a fool if he tried?

It mattered little if he looked foolish. Nicho wanted Jed, Simhew, and Rosa to see the Gold Breast. He could still remember the first time he had seen the bird, in the stable with Shara, and the joy he had felt.

Show yourself again. They need to know your hope for themselves. He blew it.

Almost immediately, something shimmered in the sky above them, drawing their gazes. The bird was even more majestic than Nicho remembered. He heard the gasps around him and saw Jed joyfully stretch out his hand to the bird. Yet there was something deeper, something just between him and Tabeal.

Why did you forget me? The soft question filled his heart and brought a fresh awareness of the sorrow he had inflicted on Rosa, Simhew, and Jed.

Forgive me. If I'd called you earlier, you could have saved us all this pain.

I can also restore and heal. In time.

He sensed the forgiveness. Joy flooded into him at the promise of healing. Jed's eyes would light up again with hope. Rosa's last night of shame and humiliation would wash away, replaced by days of dignity.

And his own pain? That, too, Tabeal would heal. His grief at losing Derry, his ache and longing for Shara, his anger toward Pearce. Nicho knew that he would be free of it all. One day.

Thank you.

Around him, faces were alight with joy, as if the golden light that shimmered from the bird's chest had found its way into their hearts.

Lead them to the Guardian Grotto, Nicho.

Will you come with us?

You should know by now that I'm closer than your very breath.

CHAPTER 36

Sky. Water. Sky. Sharp rocks lashed and cut. A force pulled them down. Deeper. Deeper.

As he tried to claw back to the surface under the waterfall, Klyden's first instinct was to let go of the queen. She was probably dead, and her weight was pulling him down to his own watery grave.

But he held her anyway until the dark water above him began to shimmer with muted light. The surface was near. It took every grain of willpower to keep kicking his leaden legs.

Finally he broke through, breathing loud, ragged breaths. Disoriented, it took him longer than it should have to assess the situation. The strong waterfall had pushed them under, but also closer to the far bank—something to their advantage. Already the king's bowmen would be on the move, probably trying to cut off their escape route downriver.

More pressing than the bowmen was the unconscious queen. He sliced through the strong current pulling them downriver. He had to reach the bank. Eventually he dragged the queen onto a rock along the waterside.

Klyden cast a quick look up to the pool, but saw no one. He bent over the queen, lifted her head back, and blew breath into her body, watching her chest rise as he did so. On the fifth breath, her arms twitched. Then she sputtered and retched.

Blessed Ancient One—she is alive!

He held her up until her fit subsided.

"What . . . where am I?"

"We made it down the waterfall."

"I feel so . . . so weak."

"You almost died."

"Oh." Her forehead creased at the memory. "I . . . I didn't take a breath like you told me to. It all happened too fast."

"You did well, Your Majesty." Klyden reached for her hand and squeezed it. Deathly cold, it reminded him of the need to get her to a safe place where he could warm her.

"I fought them, Klyden."

"You did." He glanced up to the far bank where a small flock of birds took flight. Could the king's guards be that close already? "We need to keep moving, my queen. They will be here soon."

"Which way do we go?" She peered anxiously at the wall of trees hemming in the river.

He shook his head. "Not through the trees. The river is the fastest way out of here."

"Back into the water?" Her voice trembled.

"Just for awhile until we're far enough away."

"I can't swim."

"I will help you."

Back in the water, they clung to a log and allowed the river to sweep them away from the execution pool and the king's guards. The cold, fatigue, and approaching darkness finally forced them out of the water.

Klyden carried the shivering queen from the riverbank into the forest. Her body felt icier than marble and her pale skin now had a bluish tinge to it. A fire might bring their pursuers to them, but if he did not warm her soon, he feared she would not make it through the night.

He found a small clearing, and used his hands to dig a burrow into the soft ground. He placed her in it, piling soil and leaves on top of her, before he went looking for dry kindling.

When Klyden returned, the queen's eyes were closed. He felt a momentary surge of fear. Her skin was as translucent as a snow-gem, and she lay so very, very still. He had spent his life in the presence of death, and for a brief instant, thought the queen had slipped into its grasp while he was gone.

But when he bent down and put his ear to her lips, he felt the small breaths. Klyden sat back on the ground and let out a long, jagged breath of his own, studying the woman in front of him. The queen's face, normally set in a worried or wary expression, was peaceful in slumber. There was something childlike in the way her wet hair stuck to her skin. He had the urge to reach out and release it. She stirred, and Klyden hastily rose to his feet. It wasn't right to be staring at a queen while she slept.

He turned his attention to making a fire, laying the kindling and wood out just as his elders had taught him, before setting to work on the flint stone. If there was one thing Klyden hated, it was making a fire. He had done if often enough, but it always took him longer than Lohlyn or Elxa.

"You're just not as fiery as the two of us," Lohlyn used to tease him.

Pain shot into his chest at the memory. If only Lohlyn were here now, protecting her queen and friend. If only he could have been the one to die on the fire pole. But such thoughts were a distraction and he buried them under layers of pain, as he had been taught to do.

What would happen one day if something cracked into the deep places of his hidden feelings and thoughts? Would they come rushing out, overwhelm him, slay him with their magnitude? Or would he become like his father's cousin Swen, who had lost himself in that dark world, crying, mumbling, and drooling, unwilling to live yet unable to die? That thought, too, Klyden pushed aside.

He focused again on the stones, willing them to produce sparks. Finally, a spark fell into the kindling and he carefully blew it into a flame. He fed small twigs and grass to the flames, then larger sticks and branches, watching the fire grow stronger until he felt the heat. Only then did he realize how cold he was. He stripped off most of his wet clothes, and rigged some branches together near the fire on which to dry their garments. Rather useless, for tomorrow they would probably take to the river again.

By the time the queen awoke, Klyden had boiled some river water in the small tin he always carried in his pack. He added some aromatic herbs to it and passed it to the queen.

"Here. This will warm you."

"What is it?"

"Yoran tea. An old remedy for anxiety."

"Ah, it's good to drink something warm." She cupped her hands around it as she drank. "Lohlyn knew all the strange herbs, too."

"Part of our training, my queen."

"I'm not a queen anymore, Klyden. Call me Nyla." The shifting shadows cast an angular hardness onto her face.

"You're still *my* queen." He hoped she could sense his respect. From what Lohlyn had told him, the queen had done everything in her power to make a difference. Perhaps the few short months of her reign had been more valuable than every year of every monarch before her.

She was silent for a long while before she said, "Thank you, Klyden. Now, as your queen, I order you to call me Nyla."

He smiled. "As you wish . . . Nyla."

Nyla came to sit by the fire with him, and they silently ate some dried meat and fruit. Klyden hadn't been able to bring much with him, so he would have to hunt or scavenge for berries and roots in the morning. He would have preferred to sleep in shifts that night, with one of them awake to guard against pursuers, but Nyla was in no state to stay awake, and he knew he needed rest. So, once Nyla climbed back into her burrow, he dug another one for himself and, just before he gave in to his exhaustion, entrusted them into the watchful care of the Ancient One.

CHAPTER 37

"Elxa. Wake up!"

Elxa's hand grasped the knife at his side as he sat up, but only the Raven stood over him.

The spy noticed his action. "By Taus! Remind me not to wake up a Charab too quickly."

"Sorry," Elxa mumbled. "We're a highly strung people."

"You need to be." The Raven, in cloak and boots, looked rather smug. "Listen, I checked on the gates this morning. There are only two guards at the Friar's Gate. It's the perfect time to slip out."

"Really?" Elxa pushed himself off the sleeping pallet. He couldn't leave this royal citadel soon enough. He hated the sounds and sights of the city. Hated the memories of Lohlyn that crept into every waking hour, and the sleeping ones, too. Perhaps he could shake off some of his guilt if he put distance between himself and the place of her execution.

"Indeed." The smugness was still on his friend's face. He obviously had more to tell. "And you will be happy to know that it seems the queen did not die yesterday."

"Did the king issue a last minute pardon?"

"No." The Raven walked over to the table. Cutting off a husk of bread with his knife, he threw it to Elxa. He took his time, relishing his role as news-bringer. "All went according to plan, it seems. The procession made it to the river. They say that the queen stepped from her litter with great dignity."

"She sounds like a woman of courage."

"The king climbed into the river. Some say he almost slipped and drowned himself doing so." The Raven let out a small chuckle. "Then a few strong guards took the queen into the river and held her under. That was when she started to fight for her life."

"She got away from them?"

"No. They were too strong. But then the strangest thing happened." He sliced a piece of cheese and held it up. "Cheese with that bread?"

"No, Raven." Elxa quenched his impatience. "What happened?"

"Well, there are differing accounts. Some say several guards—at least two on the shore—threw the knives that killed the men holding the queen, and then another one who waded into the water to rescue her."

"By the Abyss." Elxa felt a surge of energy prickle through his body. "The king's guards turned on him?"

"Not all of them, it seems. And they weren't trying to harm the king, only protect the queen." The Raven chewed thoughtfully. "The rescuer in the water dove down for the queen before swimming to the waterfall. Several witnesses saw them surface there just before they dropped over the waterfall."

"Festering figs! How high is it?"

"A good thirty feet, I think, but they must have survived, because there was no sign of them when the king's men arrived down there."

"Perhaps their bodies swept down river."

"Maybe," the Raven said. "My man in the palace says that the king went into a rage last night, the likes of which they have never seen. Screaming that everyone failed him and that they've always favored the queen. Ranting on about his stolen soul escaping. Sounded like a real madman, they say."

Elxa shook his head, trying to imagine the scene. "Did they capture the guards on the shore—the ones who threw the knives? The king will have their lives for that."

The Raven shook his head. "No one seems to know who they were. And my informer in the Royal Guard says they haven't begun to root out the traitors. They're too busy trying to find the queen." He flicked a piece of the hard crust across the room. "Some in the Royal Guard speculate that the rescuer was acting alone, for there is only one of their number missing. But for one man to take out two guards so quickly and still grab the queen . . ."

Easy, Elxa thought, remembering his training with circular blades. You could throw two or three of those together with ease. Some of the Charab were so good they could even throw four or five. Since the blade had multiple points, you didn't have to concentrate on ensuring the knife point hit the target, and so you could focus solely on your aim.

"The strangest story of all" the Raven continued, "comes from one of the lord's wives who accompanied her husband to the river." "She didn't want to see the drowning and had wandered over to the waterfall to look at the view. When she heard the shouting, she turned to see the commotion in the water. She was about to head back when suddenly she heard a splash and saw a man rising from the water, pulling the queen up with him."

"He must have come up for air before dropping over the waterfall."

"According to her, he was coming up for more than air." The Raven winked. "Apparently he and the queen were kissing."

Something droned in Elxa's ears. The Raven's mouth was still moving, forming a word that might have been "lover," but Elxa could only hear what sounded like a river coursing through his body. A river . . . and two young boys' voices.

"The only one's mouth I'd blow into is Triola."

"Not me. I think I'd rather practice on Chella."

Gradually, Elxa became aware of the Raven standing over him, his head furrowed in concern. The spy's voice broke through those of the past. "What's wrong, Elxa?"

"Did anyone see what those blades looked like?" Elxa asked.

"Blades?"

"That killed the men in the water."

"Oh yes." The Raven nodded. "My Royal Guard says he's never seen anything like it. Round—wheel shaped, with four or five points."

Elxa turned to the window, looking out over the city of his grief. As much as he wanted to, he could not escape it yet. Slaying one beloved cousin had been bad enough. Now he knew that another awaited him.

"It's an unusual blade, Raven. We call it a circular," he said softly. When it was obvious that his friend did not understand, he added, "It is a Charab blade."

Lucian rolled the round blade across the table with the edge of his dagger. He had seen the weapon before—many, many years before. The ancient Parashi had favored it and used it against the invaders four hundred years before. For awhile after the Great War, the invaders had tried their hand at throwing the blades and, never quite mastering the skill, returned to their familiar swords and daggers. The surviving Parashi had been relieved of all their weapons, including these round blades. The blade had become extinct, or so Lucian thought. Until today.

The Lord of Gwyndorr had a suspicion. At the time of the Great War, the Charab were just another family of particularly skilled Parashi fighters. The Charab were the only Parashi who had kept their weapons as assassins in service to the king. What if these weapons had included the round blades? Could it be that the blades, so deeply and accurately imbedded in the two dead guards, came from the hand of a Charab? Did the queen have more than one Charab protector?

The thought unsettled Lucian. Could the Charab, after four hundred years, finally have learned the secret to breaking the curse that bound them? Would they turn against the king? They were a formidable force and not to be taken lightly. If they led a Parashi rebellion and possibly trained the Lowborns to fight, the Highborn minority, no matter how well armed, would struggle to defeat them.

No, it must never come to that. Now that the queen was out of the picture, Lucian would direct the king to finding and destroying the Guardian Grotto. With both Guardian Rocks in his possession, Lucian would be invincible. And once Shara and Maldor were wed, he could set his sights even higher, far beyond the borders of Tirragyl.

He let the ancient blade fall to the table, watching it spin before it finally came to rest. In time, the Charab would have to be crushed. He would make sure of that.

But first he had to find the Grotto and the Guardian Rock. After all these long years of preparing and waiting, Lucian was close. So very close. He was just a single Dusk Dreamer away from his goal.

CHAPTER 38

From the time she sensed the Dusk Dreamer in the Deep Caves, Shara watched and waited for her chance to reclaim it. Today the moment had come.

Mikel had taken sick and, unable to make his usual visit to Kella, sent Andreo and several commanders in his place. Shara caught up with them as they made their way to the exit of the Grotto.

"Brother," she called. "I'm desperate for some sunshine today. May I come along?"

Andreo turned, hesitation on his face. No one was meant to leave the cave without Mikel's knowledge.

"I promise I won't lag behind. Nobody will even know I'm missing. The children have the rest of the day off. They're preparing for some festival."

"Tomorrow is the Parashi new year celebration," one of the warriors said with a smile. "There is always much excitement, especially for the children."

"Yes. They paid no heed to me whatsoever this morning."

"Come along, then, Shara," Andreo said. "We will return this evening. We have an urgent message for Commander Kella."

One or two men murmured at Andreo's decision, but Shara fell in behind them, walking so silently that they soon forgot she was there. How good she had become at deception, the insight flittered through her mind. She pushed the guilt away. Hadn't they all brought it on themselves when they turned against her? Mikel by confiscating the rock. Eliad and Andreo by supporting him. Even Kella, who knowingly or unknowingly guarded Shara's rock. If Shara had mastered the art of lying and deceiving, *they* had forced her to it.

Hope surged through her as they left the dark, dank cave behind. The anticipation of holding her beautiful rock again drew her forward. She would have twirled around joyfully under that blue sky, reminiscent of her blue stone, if it hadn't drawn attention to her. *I'm coming, my love. I'm coming.*

By the time they reached the Chay'ets Tree, she thought all of them would surely hear the loud pounding in her chest. She was so close to her beloved rock now. Lowering everyone down into the cave took some time. Shara waited her turn, making lighthearted conversation with Andreo while fighting her rising impatience.

"Your turn, Shara." Andreo finally took her hand and guided her to the ladder. His smile was warm as always. Andreo, who had risked his very life to rescue her from Lucian's mansion on her wedding day.

Again, an uncomfortable guilt sought to enfold her. No! He was Mikel's ally in keeping her from her rightful possession.

She descended into the root-clad cave, for once paying no attention to the dizzying height. Her arms and legs moved of their own accord, speeding her toward the Dusk Dreamer.

"By the sword," said one of Kella's warriors as Shara's feet touched the ground, "I don't think I've ever seen anyone take the ladder at such speed."

"Are the others in the common room?" Shara didn't have time for small talk.

"Yes."

Shara forced herself to walk slowly to the central cavern. She considered darting off right now to follow the voice of the Dreamer, for as her feet touched the base of the root cave, she had felt the small vibration and sensed the air humming around her. Yet the others would miss her if she didn't arrive in the common room.

Kella smiled in welcome as Shara reached the others. "Welcome,

Shara. It's been about a month since we saw you, I think. You don't visit enough."

That's because your father keeps me away, Shara thought as she returned the greeting.

When Andreo, Kella, and the other commanders were deep in discussion, Shara slipped away unseen, following the Dreamer's hum. Would she be able to find something Mikel had hidden in these vast caves?

As if in answer, the air hummed a little louder. *Come to me,* the Dreamer beckoned. *Follow my voice.* Shara wasted no time.

Mikel twisted restlessly on his pallet. He burned still and his lips felt parched, no matter how much water he drank. His body ached and every way he turned felt uncomfortable. His mind was just as restless and unsettled. By the abyss! He could not bear lying here another moment.

He sat up, fighting the wave of weakness that warned him not to rise, and reached for his sandals and robe.

"Sir, are you sure you should be up?" the Warrior at the door asked as Mikel shuffled from the chamber.

"Just going to the War Chamber for awhile." Mikel forced his voice to sound stronger than he felt. "Will you tell Pearce to meet me there?"

"Right away, sir."

Mikel watched the young Warrior stride down the passage and cursed his weakened body for not following at the same pace. By the time he finally reached the War Chamber, Pearce was already waiting there.

"Sir." He rose. "There is nothing urgent that requires your attention. Are you sure you shouldn't be resting?"

"Flaming arrows! Will you all stop reminding me how bad I look?"

"Sorry. It's just that—"

"I'm not getting better lying around like an ailing old woman."

"Of course not, sir. Andreo did say you should—"

"Andreo is good at herbal teas, but he doesn't know much about commanding a fighting troop, Pearce."

"No, sir. But all is well. The scouts have not sent any warnings. The Grey Unit returned last night. They didn't encounter any skirmishes so there were no casualties or injuries."

Mikel sat down before his second-in-command could see the tremble in his legs. Pearce and Andreo were right, of course. He should be in bed. Commanders should never be seen in their moments of weakness. It diminished them in the sight of those they commanded.

But Mikel could not shake off the sense of menace, warning him something was amiss. Perhaps it was just a symptom of his illness. Further proof that he should be doing as Andreo instructed.

"Did the party leave for the Deep Caves this morning?"

"Yes, sir. They plan to be back this evening."

"And are the preparations going well for the New Year celebration?"

"They are. Much excitement, as usual." Pearce smiled.

"So all is well, Pearce?"

"It couldn't be better, Commander."

Pearce's words should have instilled Mikel with confidence, but they didn't.

What was he missing? What in the abyss was he missing?

Finding the Cerulean Dusk Dreamer was easier than she expected. Its warm hum led her forward like a mother's voice calling through a maze.

Shara understood now why they called these the Deep Caves, for the twisting passages led her deeper and deeper into the earth. These were narrow, little-used passages. Unlike in the Grotto, feet and time had not yet smoothed them down. She paid little attention to the direction and turns. Only one thought consumed her—reaching her rock.

Finally, she reached a small cavern. The candle she had brought from a higher passage cast ominous shadows on the walls. The rock was here. She knew it now, as surely as she knew the sun would rise in the morning.

"Where are you?" she whispered, dropping to her knees to feel the space where the wall and floor met. When she could not find it there, she began to search higher on the wall, carefully feeling for a crack or a gap that would hide her rock.

The light of her candle glinted off something far above her head. It was the Dreamer, carefully tucked away into a hole in the wall.

Joy pulsed through Shara. Joy, and a deep longing. She cast aside the candle and clambered up the face of the cave, paying little heed to her bleeding hands and broken nails. The flame sputtered out but she hardly noticed, for the Dreamer cast a warm light to show itself, and nothing else mattered.

Her hand closed on it. Searing heat jolted through her hand. Painful. Exquisite. She cried out, shocked at the intensity, yet the thought of dropping the rock didn't cross her mind. She had the one and only thing she had been longing for throughout these months. She had her Dreamer.

She jumped down to the cave floor and sat, cradling the rock with her body. The heat and pain did not diminish. Perhaps the rock's power had accumulated over the last few months. Still she held it.

Time wavered and changed course, taking hold of her thoughts and weaving them into a dream. Initially she saw only red flames around her. They consumed her, burned her with their hot fury. Soon she would be nothing but ash. She allowed it, knowing she deserved this punishment, for she had failed the rock. As she relinquished herself to the flames, she was thankful that her death would come through the Dreamer. Only the Dusk Dreamer had ever wanted her this completely. She belonged to it now, and if the Dreamer would destroy her, so be it.

The Dreamer's fury abated slightly. A hot breeze blew away the flames. A desert wind now engulfed her in its shimmering haze of heat, pummeling her with sandpaper sharpness. She bowed before it, shielding her face but unable to protect her body. The wind cut into her over and over again, until she felt worn down and paper-thin. If her voice could have been heard over the wind's wailing, she would have begged for the flames to return and finish their work. But she was powerless. All she could do was surrender herself to the Dreamer's wrath.

Something shifted between her and the Dreamer. The wind dropped and then died completely. Shara sensed another presence. She should have been relieved, for whatever had joined her and the Dreamer may well have saved her from the Rock's chastisement. Yet she resented the intrusion.

A figure walked toward her through the shimmering heat. For a moment she thought Nicho had returned to her, but as he drew closer she saw through the illusion.

Lord Lucian.

In that blinding moment, she understood that it had always been him in her dreams. Only her longing for Nicho had obscured his true identity.

She should have been afraid standing before him, but the flames had burned away everything inside her, even longing and fear.

"My love, you have returned to me." His eyes filled with false tears.

"I know who you are, Lucian."

Momentarily, he seemed taken aback. Then he shrugged. "I see the Dreamer holds your heart now, no longer the groom."

"Why are you here?"

"For you, of course. You and the Parashi Warriors."

"Take me. Leave the Warriors."

He threw back his head and laughed. "Still a seed of valor. Very admirable, Shara. Your father would be proud."

"I don't have a father."

"Oh, but you do."

"Why do you want the Warriors?"

"They have been a thorn in my flesh for far too long."

"The Guardian Rock will protect them."

"Nothing can save them now. You and your Dreamer saw to that."

Fear fluttered inside her then. Perhaps the flames had not burned all of her away. She thought of Mikel and the love in his eyes as he looked at Kella. She thought of the children in her care, tugging at her dress for attention. She thought of Andreo's excitement as he brewed a new remedy.

"No. You won't find us." Shara knew what she had to do then. She had to let go of her Dreamer right now and never touch it again. Even though her heart would break to never again feel its embrace, it was the only way to keep those she cared for safe.

She willed her fingers to open slowly. Slowly.

Lucian laughed again. "Are you willing to give it up. All that power? All that comfort? Just so I won't find you?"

Shara gritted her teeth and straightened out her fingers. Any moment now the Dreamer would drop from her grasp and they would all be safe. Any moment now.

"Open your hands, Shara. Let it go." Lucian leaned forward, so close that she felt the heat of his breath.

As the rock tumbled from her hands, Lucian's last jeering words echoed through the strange spaces of her dreams.

"It's too late, Shara. I know where you are."

CHAPTER 39

Power pulsed through the Deep Caves as the stone flew from Shara's hand. Andreo felt it as a current, surging through the floor and up into his body. Kella felt it as a fearful tightening in her chest, making it difficult to gulp for breath. All around her, the warriors turned frightened eyes to her, their leader, as the vengeful force throbbed through the Deep Caves.

In the distant cavern where Mikel lay fighting the fever, fewer people felt it. But the High Commander was jolted awake from his shadowed half-sleep, knowing instantly what his earlier sickbed premonition had tried to warn him of. And he rose from his bed and fell to his knees, face to the ground, weeping for everything lost in that one moment of sleep.

Near midnight, Pearce appeared in the War Chamber where Mikel and Eliad had set up a watchful vigil.

"Sir, Commander Kella is here. And Andreo."

Pearce stepped aside as Kella entered the War Chamber, followed by Andreo and two men bearing a stretcher on which Shara lay still as a corpse.

Eliad ran over to the stretcher as the men lowered it to the ground.

"Shara!" He looked up and met Andreo's gaze. "Is she . . . ?"

"She lives, Eliad, but we could not rouse her."

"Tell me what happened," Mikel said, looking at his daughter.

"We were in the gathering cavern when we felt . . . something.

As if something dark had crept into the cave and grew bigger and bigger. So big that it sucked the very breath and warmth out of the air."

"Yes, I felt it, too," Mikel said. "A dark power was in the cave."

"Then it was gone," Kella continued. "We were all dazed, but I immediately ordered the warriors to take up arms, make sure everyone was fine, and do a thorough search of the cave. Only then did Andreo notice Shara was missing."

"You let Shara go to the Deep Caves with you?" Mikel's question held no blame, only sadness.

"I did, Mikel. I'm so sorry. I had no idea that the Cerulean Dusk Dreamer was there."

"It was my responsibility, Father," Kella said. "I knew and yet I thought the rock so well hidden that she would never find it."

Mikel nodded. "What did you do when you realized the girl was missing?"

"I suspected what had happened. Andreo and I went to the cave where you had hidden the rock. We found her there lying on the floor. I thought she was dead, for she was as cold as the stone floor on which she lay."

"But I detected a shallow breath and felt the flutter of a pulse," Andreo said. "We called her name but could not wake her."

"Even as we took her from the caves and across the highlands, she didn't move," Kella said, shaking her head sadly as she looked at Shara's unmoving figure. "Forgive me. I failed you, Father."

"No, my love." Mikel drew his daughter into an embrace. "The failing was mine, for I underestimated the rock's power and left it too close to her. I failed both our people and Shara."

A wave of weakness trembled through Mikel and he moved away from his daughter, back to his seat behind the high table. "What then, Kella? Did you pry the rock from her hands?"

"She had thrown it away, Father." Kella patted her robe. "I have it with me."

"She let go of the rock willingly?" Mikel asked. "Remarkable, considering the power it had over her."

"And maybe the only reason we're not burying her right now," Eliad said. "Is there something you can do for her, Andreo?"

Andreo let out a ragged breath. "I've never dealt with anything like this before."

"It is not an ailment herbs can cure," Eliad said softly. "But as long as she breathes, there is hope."

Kella fumbled in her robe and brought out a bundle of brown cloth. "The Dusk Dreamer." She stepped over to her father and held it out to him "I covered it."

He took it from her as if it was something too heavy for him to hold and placed it, unopened, on the table. Unwillingly, it drew all their eyes.

"The breach last night," Kella started hesitantly. "Was it worse than the last time, Father? Or did the Guardian Rock protect our location?"

"The last time, I sensed but a fleeting presence," Mikel said. "No one else even felt it. But this time, the enemy was fully here and over a longer period of time." He swallowed and his words dropped heavily between them. "I believe this man knows where we are."

And the ancient prophecy once again crept through Mikel's mind:

> *The Guardian, once strong, grows weak*
> *As evil pierces through the Dusk.*
> *Midnight darkness follows.*
> *And mountains shake at the wrath of the foe.*
> *Before Dawn releases her light.*

CHAPTER 40

Nyla and Klyden spent a few days following the course of the river. At times they clung to a log in the water, at others they picked their way over boulders or hiked through the thick vegetation bordering the river. Nyla noticed how alert Klyden was, and it added to her own uneasiness. But the more distance they put between themselves and the execution pool, Klyden's wariness eased.

After another long day, Nyla crouched near the flames, watching Klyden roast the rabbit he had caught. "Am I safe now, Klyden?" she asked.

"None of us is truly safe." He didn't say it, but she sensed the rest of his words. *Especially not those running from a powerful king.* "But the Ancient One has protected us this far. I don't think He will let us fall now."

Rage surged through her. The Ancient One? How she wished Klyden would stop talking of his god. Surely he knew that, from birth, her allegiance had been to Taus?

"Your Ancient One didn't do much to protect Lohlyn, did he?"

Klyden recoiled as if she had thrown stones instead of words.

She softened her tone. "It's not the Ancient One protecting me, Klyden. It's you."

"No. I am a mere man. An instrument in His hands."

"Maybe Taus is protecting me," she said belligerently.

Only the crackle of the fire and the sizzle of meat broke the long silence that followed.

"Do you know anything about my people? Of our history?" he finally said, his voice deepened by sadness. "Four hundred years ago, our country was invaded from the north. Before that time, the inhabitants of this region were landowners. Rugged, strong mountain people and skilled horsemen. We lived in close-knit communities that cared for one another. Our winters were harsh, but no one went hungry. We laughed and danced and were known for our wisdom with herbs and medicines. We were at peace, under the rule of a wise king whose territory stretched far beyond our own borders. Some called him *Ab'El*, others The Ancient One."

Nyla shifted uncomfortably. Her ancestors had invaded the country and established the throne. Guilt wanted to creep over her as Klyden spoke, but she reminded herself that this was only *his* version of the events.

"Then the invaders came. They were well-disciplined and trained in the use of weapons. We, on the other hand, had seldom needed weapons, and few had much skill with them. It seemed that the Parashi—the horse people—were doomed.

"The invaders were cruel. They pillaged and burned villages, often taking young women as unwilling brides. But there were two things to our advantage. First, we knew the mountains well. We could spirit ourselves away in the mist of its passes."

"What was the second thing?" Nyla couldn't help being swept up by his account, no matter how one-sided it was.

"Two Parashi brothers who had been in Ab'El's army and were renowned for their courage and skill. These two, Chaorlin and Rabnin, began to train the young men and formed a band of battle-warriors unlike any the invaders had ever encountered." He turned the meat over the flames. "From that time, the invaders struggled. Every foot of land they took cost them dearly in lives."

Nyla had never heard it told from this perspective. The history lessons she remembered spoke of the two rebel leaders, Chaorlin and Rabnin, as enemies of both the invaders and their own people. In delaying the inevitable victory of the invaders, their own people had paid the most dearly.

"Eventually the Parashi were outmatched by the sheer force of the invading army. In the last battle of the war, Taus captured Chaorlin and Rabnin at the Bloodbush grove."

Nyla recalled the name from her history lessons. The Bloodbush grove—where the uprising had finally been crushed and the leaders executed. "They were executed there?" she asked softly, suddenly ashamed at her predecessor's cruelty.

"Yes, slowly and painfully. But that was not the worst thing Taus did to them." Klyden swallowed. "Both leaders had sons and, even though they begged to die alongside their fathers, Taus saw something in them that he wanted. The boys, barely men, had their fathers' natural skill with bow and sword, so Taus decided to make good use of it."

"Chaorlin and Rabnin." Suddenly Nyla understood. "The Charab!"

"Yes. Taus used his powers to place the boys under his control. They were to become Taus's assassins, and their offspring would be the assassins of the kings to follow him. With just one word—the arming word—Taus could control them to do his bidding. He used them mainly against their own Parashi people, wiping out almost all the pockets of resistance that remained. The Parashi have hated us for it to this day."

"Surely they understood it was not your own will?"

"Perhaps. But, from that day, we were outcasts. Hated and feared by both sides. And completely under the control of the king."

A long silence stretched between them as Klyden took the meat off the flames and carved it into pieces. As he handed Nyla a piece, he spoke again.

"Do you understand now why I cannot believe Taus would do anything to help us escape?"

"What of this Ab'El, this Ancient One you speak of? Why didn't he save you from the invasion?"

"I don't know, Nyla." As he looked up at her, his eyes danced with firelight and hope. "But He is saving us now. Of that I have no doubt."

"What makes you think that?"

"He freed my father from Taus's curse. For the first time in four hundred years, a Charab disobeyed a command to kill. You know what else? I believe He has helped us escape. He has a plan for you."

"Aren't I one of the enemies?"

"No, you do not hate and destroy. You care for your subjects. The Ancient One knows that. Do you think it a coincidence that in all our days fleeing the king's men, not one of them has seen us?"

"There haven't been any soldiers, have there?"

He laughed. "I've heard them and seen evidence of their footprints. But our paths have not crossed. Only the Ancient One could bring that about, Nyla."

"Sheer luck."

He smiled. "It's easy to think that of the Ancient One's ways."

The meat tasted better than palace food. They ate in silence, Nyla thinking of all Klyden had said. *Hated and feared by both sides.* Those words churned in her mind as she thought about Lohlyn's love and friendship, and Klyden's devotion to her. She—Taus's descendant—didn't deserve it.

"Why did you and Lohlyn choose to come and protect me once you broke free of Taus's curse?" she asked at length.

"My father was on the run from his brother, the new Charab."

"Why?"

"Your grandfather issued an arming word decree to kill the three of us."

She let out a small hiss of disbelief as he continued.

"The only reason we weren't at the Charab village when the order came was because the queen, your grandmother, sent a messenger warning of the king's intentions."

"That sounds like Mada." Nyla smiled. Her father had always said his mother meddled where she wasn't wanted.

"She was a shrewd woman and had far more than our interests at heart. From the beginning, she planned to bring me and Lohlyn to the palace. My father saw the wisdom of it, for who would think of hiding right under the nose of the king trying to assassinate you?" He looked at Nyla for a long time. "Lohlyn and I made our oaths to your grandmother. She cared for you deeply."

"Yes." Nyla choked back a tear, remembering how her grandmother had tried to warn her of Alexor, but she hadn't believed it. She hadn't *wanted* to believe it could be true. "What happened to your father?" she asked, desperate to change the subject.

"He died a few years after Loh and I left for the palace."

"At your uncle's hand?"

"My uncle tracked him down to the island where he was hiding, but my father knew his brother was coming long before he set foot on the beach." Klyden looked deep into the flames for a moment. "Think about it. This was his younger brother, whom he loved dearly. My father knew that one of them would die and the other would live with the guilt of it forever. He wouldn't let that happen to his brother. So he took the only other course open to him."

A shudder ran through Nyla. "You mean he . . ."

"He took his own life."

"By Taus!"

The Tirragylins believed that a soul released by its own hand would never find peace. The northwestern Wailands, mountains now covered by the Rif'twine, echoed with the cries of these souls, forever alone, forever restless. Even reuniting her soul with Alexor's seemed like a better outcome to Nyla. But perhaps the Charab thought differently on these things. She was suddenly curious.

"What does your Ancient One say of such a death?"

"Our life is never ours to take," Klyden said softly, "but in this instance, I think Ab'El understood."

CHAPTER 41

After Tabeal appeared and told Nicho to lead them to the safety of the Grotto, he shared her instructions with the small group of Parashi prisoners.

They stared at him, wide-eyed and open-mouthed, still stunned by their recent sighting of the Gold Breast. Tabeal was gone now, but there was a glow on their faces, as if they had been standing by a hot fire for a long time.

Frintin was the first to respond. Nicho liked and trusted this tough old man, the one who had helped him to his feet in the cell and kept the guard at bay when Jed threw himself into Nicho's arms.

"I think we should take the Rifter Gang, too."

Nicho stared back at the platform that stood just outside the encroaching Rif'twine. A shudder of apprehension went through him. This was the place where he would have spent the rest of his life, if Tabeal had not come. There were others who, like him, had been brought here and were now deep at work in the forest. He knew Tabeal would have approved of Frintin's suggestion.

"Right. But how do we get to them? It's the middle of the day and they're all in the Rif'twine."

"We'll call them from the edge of the forest," Frintin answered.

Nicho fought a surge of fear, but agreed to go with Frintin.

Every step closer to the forest felt more difficult than the last. He could suddenly see the dark eyes of his father in his mind. Most of the time, those eyes had been dull and empty, as if there was nothing left in the world worth looking at, not even his young son.

But occasionally his father's eyes had been filled with terror, and it was those eyes that Nicho thought of as he neared the forest. What he dreaded more than all the vile things crawling through the Rif'twine, was seeing those horrors etched into the rifters' eyes.

He wanted to run back and tell Frintin to leave these long-gone people, that the forest had probably already killed the deepest part of them.

Yet Frintin's voice boomed toward the forest. It echoed back to them, warped and strange, as if voices in the Rif'twine mimicked and mocked them.

"Freedom! Freedom!" Frintin called. "You are free, rifters! Come out of the forest!"

They stood silently waiting for the rifters to come, and apprehension once again crept down Nicho's spine. Something was watching them. Something cold and dreadful.

Frintin took a few steps closer to the forest and repeated his shout of freedom and hope. Could the rifters still understand such concepts? Or did freedom seem like captivity, and hope like doom, to minds altered by the Rif'twine?

"Let's go," Nicho said, hiding his relief. "They are too deep in the forest to hear us."

"We'll just have to go in after them."

"But it's the Rif'twine."

"It's where you would have spent the rest of your life, boy. Me, too, if that bird hadn't saved us."

He didn't want to follow the old man, but his pride wouldn't let him turn back. So Nicho trailed after Frintin into the gloom.

"This is the Dimzone." Frintin's whisper pierced the eerie silence. "Farther in is the Darkzone. That's where the rooters work."

Nicho squinted into the forest. He thought he sensed movement but, in the gloom, he couldn't be sure. The forest was cold, the air grimy and heavy. No matter how much he gulped for breath, he couldn't fight the sense of panicked light-headedness. The smell was almost as bad as the lack of air. As a groom, Nicho had picked up his fair share of dead rats, and walking into this forest, Nicho was sure there must be a whole colony of the rodents rotting in the undergrowth.

Just when he couldn't stand it any longer, a shadow peeled off a tree.

Tall and thin, eyes filled with a quiet wariness, the man introduced himself as the Overseer.

"What is your name, lad?" Frintin asked.

Nicho assumed the man was at least double his age, but possibly the pain and fear, rather than the passing of time, had caused the deep ridges around his eyes and sunken cheeks.

"They call me Gruel." His voice was as gritty as the air.

"We have come to take you out of the Rif'twine, Gruel," Frintin said gently. "Can you call the others?"

"Have we done something to displease?" Terror flashed momentarily in Gruel's eyes.

"No. We are Parashi like you. We have come to take you to the Guardian Grotto."

"The Grotto?" Gruel's face creased with even more consternation. "We have tried our best, even though we are one rooter short. Many were lost when the western wind blew the delirea bloom's scent our way. Forgive me, I should have—"

"We are not here to punish you. We are here to set you free, Gruel," Frintin said, reaching for the man's hand. "Now call the others. We want to set off before nightfall."

"Set us free?"

"Yes. We have come to take you out of the forest." The words were soft and patient, as if spoken to a child, and Frintin's gentle tone finally broke through where the meaning of the words did not. Something replaced the terror in Gruel's eyes, and Nicho knew then that, indeed, rifters could still feel hope.

He and Frintin returned to the light and waited for Gruel to call the rest of the gang. One by one, they emerged from the Rif'twine. Nicho looked deeply into their eyes as they made their way past him.

News of their liberation brought no joy to those eyes, only quiet resignation or numbed despair. Just like his father's eyes, Nicho thought, and a sense of trepidation again crept over him. This was a mistake. These people were beyond saving.

Several days into their trip, Nicho became certain of it.

To begin with, the rifters were slowing them down. Many were sick, and only a few were likely to survive the long trip to the Grotto. At night, huddled in a copse of trees, their hacking coughs kept Nicho awake. Sometimes, when he had just fallen asleep, a terror-filled scream would pierce the night. The strain was visible on their whole party.

The real trouble with the rifters started with some edible roots. The rifters were good at scavenging for food, but instead of sharing what they found with the whole company, they only shared the food among themselves.

Jed saw one of the rooters—a boy of about nine called Liamo—eating and asked him for some.

"Find your own food, townboy," Liamo spat out. "We haven't all been living like kings, you know."

"What do you know?" Simhew came to Jed's defense. "You think you're the only one who knows tears? I can tell you this boy has had his share of them."

"Oh, if it isn't Mama's Boy," Liamo scowled. "Run back to her skirts. You know nothing about pain. Nothing." As if to highlight the point, Liamo kicked Simhew. The kick took the older boy by surprise and his yelp of pain drew the attention of the adults.

Rosa was already on her feet, but Nicho pulled her back.

"Let them sort it out, Rosa. He won't want you coming to his rescue." However, as Nicho watched Liamo's leg pull back for another kick—this one aimed at Jed—he let out a sharp cry. "Stop that right now!"

Liamo merely looked over, sneered, and kicked anyway.

In that moment, a red rage filled Nicho's mind. He leapt up and would have grabbed the rooter, if the Overseer Gruel hadn't stepped in his way. Gruel had turned out to be quite a different man than the one they had seen in the forest. Gone was the terrified, pleading man they had first encountered. Gruel was proving to be as tough and gritty as his voice.

"Leave him be," Gruel said.

"Did you see what he did? Did you?"

"Your boys provoked him."

"They did not! If anything provoked them, it was having to watch you all eat when we are on strict rations."

"I don't think you can begrudge us a little extra food. Food *we* found. We haven't exactly been feasting like all you outsiders."

"Feasting?" Nicho felt Rosa's restraining arm on his shoulder, but the rage simmered to a boiling point in his body. "We're Parashi, Gruel. Parashi don't feast. I think you've been gone a little too long to remember how things are."

"I remember. Freedom. Blue sky. Walking in air that doesn't stink of death. Waking up, unafraid that some one has died next to you in the night."

"I didn't put you there," Nicho said. "In fact, I got you out of it. Maybe a bit of gratitude for that?"

"*You* got us out?" Gruel smirked. "I don't think so. If it was up to you, we'd still be in the forest, isn't that true?"

Nicho recalled his reluctance to call the rifters and his urge to go back when nobody appeared.

"Just as I thought," Gruel said. "You're not quite the hero you make yourself out to be."

And as the group of rifters turned their backs on Nicho and the "outsiders," Nicho silently cursed Frintin for his kindness. It was going to be a very long journey to the Grotto.

CHAPTER 42

The Raven opened the door to his quarters as silently as always.

"Any news of the queen and her protector?"

The low voice startled him, even though he knew Elxa was home. He peered into the shadows where the young man sat with his usual attentive stillness. The Raven moved forward and threw the window drapes aside.

Wan light spilled onto Elxa's face, showing dark circles under his eyes and the pained pinch of his mouth. Guilt clenched at the Raven. If only he had let things be. With every passing day, the strain of what he had been forced to do took a greater toll on Elxa's body.

"Isn't it time you went home, Elxa?" It would be a relief to be rid of the lad, to no longer have to face the damage he had wrought with his meddling.

"My assignment is not complete."

"Lohlyn's brother, you mean?"

Elxa nodded curtly.

I thought only she was your assignment. Her father and brother, the Charabian's."

"It's not how it works. Lohlyn was given to me as a special assignment by the arming word-bearer. But her father and brother were given to us as a group. Any of the Charab can fulfill the obligation."

"Go home and tell your father what you know. Let him deal with it."

"I am to be the next Charabian. I can no longer hide behind my father's swords." He looked steadily into the Raven's eyes. "Is there news of them, Raven?"

As usual, the spy had been speaking to his network of informers at the palace. He had heard of the king's steadily worsening moods. The day before, the monarch had ordered his cupbearer whipped on the castle grounds for a simple act of negligence. Two days before that, a man was executed for bearing a stubbornly worded message from a lord.

Fear crept through the palace. The Raven saw it in the furtive glances and the hesitant voices. Guards who previously laughed and shared a story or two, now looked down and shook their heads emphatically as they passed him. It reminded him of another era, another tyrant.

"Nothing much to report. They have been scouting around the Adriel river for more than a week now, but the queen and your cousin have disappeared. One unit reported seeing some tracks in the area of Celtra, but no one gave it much weight. Unlikely they would head that way, after all."

"Do you have a map?"

The Raven rustled through a chest and pulled out an old chart. Elxa unrolled it, placed some heavy books on the corners, then began poring over it with deep concentration.

"Do you think they are still alive?" the Raven ventured.

Elxa looked up briefly, the corners of his mouth twitching. "He's a Charab. What do *you* think?"

"Then why no sign of them? There must be close to three hundred men looking for them."

The young man didn't respond. His attention was back on the map.

"Part of your training, right? To disappear like a ghost?"

Elxa peering closely at a point on the map. "Here?" He looked up at the Raven. "Is this where they saw tracks?"

The Raven bent over to look where the Charab was pointing. "Celtra. That's it. But it's in the middle of nowhere. Surely they would have headed to the border or a road that could take them away quickly?"

Elxa's finger trailed from the spot, travelling downward toward the Rhorhan Sea.

"Where would you have run to, Elxa?" the Raven asked with a sudden burst of inspiration. "Wouldn't you have headed for a border?"

"Too obvious," the young man said distractedly. "There are better hiding places, ones where King's Guards wouldn't think to look."

"But another Charab might?"

"Yes." Elxa rolled up the map, smiling wistfully. "It's part of our training."

"Have you had breakfast?" The Raven set plates on the table and tore two large chunks of bread from a loaf. The warm, yeasty smell reminded him of home. "Bread from the palace kitchen."

"The palace?" Elxa bit into the bread. "Isn't stealing from the king punishable by death nowadays?"

"Some of my friends still have a fragment of courage," the Raven mumbled, mouth full. "When will you set off to look for your cousin?"

"Only when the power of the arming word becomes too strong to fight." Elxa's mouth pinched as if in pain. "Soon, I think."

The Raven considered his friend with new interest. Not guilt alone caused the dark circles under his friend's eyes. It seemed Elxa struggled with the very forces that bound his people.

"I had hoped to discover more about this bird Lohlyn spoke of," Elxa continued. "If I could find it . . ."

"You would be free and you wouldn't have to hunt down your cousin?"

Elxa nodded.

"I have asked around," the Raven said. "No one has seen the bird Lohlyn described."

"Surely someone must know?"

"Yesterday I spoke to an old forest ranger. He patrolled the western forests for close to forty years. If there was anyone who would know the bird you seek, it is him."

"Perhaps it is not found in those parts."

"He knows all the forests. If it is to be found in Tirragyl, he would have been able to tell me."

"Maybe its territory is outside the borders. My uncle could have encountered it on one of his many trips."

"What exactly did Lohlyn say about it?"

Elxa closed his eyes. "That its power was greater than the arming word. She told me to seek it with my whole heart."

"So it has powers. It's no ordinary bird." The Raven furrowed his brow in concentration. "It can do magic? Perhaps the Brethren of Taus will know of it. Their order is the only one I know which uses magic. Other than the power rock bearers, that is."

Elxa considered this before shaking his head. "Taus set up the Brotherhood. They even bear his name. Why would a bird linked to them fight Taus's power? No. This bird was Taus's enemy, not his friend."

"So who was Taus's enemy? Other than your own people, that is?"

Elxa shook his head in defeat. "I don't know. It happened more than four hundred years ago."

"And surely you seek something with your eyes, not your heart. What does that even mean—seek the bird with your *heart*?"

"I don't know, Raven. I really don't."

Elxa was back in the mountains with a dome of blue sky stretched above him. Realizing he was close to the bridge, he began to run, overwhelmed by his longing for home. Yet when he stopped at the edge of the cliff, the bridge was gone. He looked down into the deep gorge and the unbreachable space stretching between him and his homeland.

Now he saw figures moving on the other side. One had the bearing of his father. The shorter two could have been his brothers. He felt sure that his mother was in the crowd, too. Their arms waved furiously in warning and their mouths moved in silent screams. All he heard, though, was the pounding of his heart, wild with longing.

The waving of his family seemed to grow more frantic and, with a sudden premonition, he turned to face the danger lurking behind him. Only the old king's messenger stood there, his face set in a sneer.

"You have no home now," the messenger whispered. "You belong to the king and will do his bidding."

"No!" The word tasted harsh as gravel in his mouth.

The man laughed wildly. Enraged, Elxa reached for his knife and threw it, determined to cut the laughter short. But the knife travelled right through the man and the laughter only grew louder.

"I will find a way to break your power."

The hysterical laughter echoed all around him now.

"I will find a way."

The laughter changed, took on a rhythm that filled him with dread. *Ra'aph-aqeb Ra'aph-aqeb Ra'aph-aqeb Ra'aph-aqeb*

Elxa fell to the ground, trying to cover his ears, but now the arming word exploded inside him, louder than he could bear.

"I . . . will find . . . a . . . way." His voice was a mere murmur now as the arming word pushed all the breath out of him. "I . . . will."

Another sound pierced the air, cutting through the guttural, angry arming word. Just one note, pure but powerful.

A bird's call.

The echoes of the arming word died away. The silence returned. Slowly, Elxa looked up. The Gold Breast must be here. He looked around but saw nothing.

"Where are you?" he shouted angrily. "Stop playing games! How can I find you if I don't know where to look?"

He gazed across the abyss. His family was gone.

Elxa awoke with a start. The sense of loss and loneliness lingered throughout the day.

CHAPTER 43

Nyla's knuckles were white as she clung to the sides of the boat. A wave crashed over the bow and she sucked in a sharp breath. Curses above, the sooner she was off this leaking bucket, the better it would be. She had already spent at least half the journey hanging over the edge, stomach heaving through every trough and wave.

"Enjoying the sail, Your Majesty?" Klyden's eyes sparkled with mischief. He had never looked better, Nyla thought, with his reddened cheeks and wind-tousled hair. He looked as if he belonged here, as if the steady southeastern wind had blown his every care away.

"I've been better."

"Sailing is really something they should teach royals. How are you meant to defend our waters if you can't even sit on a boat on a calm day like this?"

"This is calm?"

"I've seen worse."

Nyla looked away, finding the horizon. Focusing on something far away seemed to help. She thought back over the last few days.

They had left the Adriel River and steadily headed south to the sea. At first, walking seven or eight hours a day had exhausted her, but every day she grew stronger. Her legs were muscled now, her skin a warmer tone than ever before.

She had come to enjoy the long trek with Klyden by her side, waving occasionally to a peasant shepherd boy or a farmer plowing his land. This was her country. These were her subjects. It felt good to see it with new eyes, to be part of it, part of them.

When they had finally reached the Rhorhan Sea, its vastness took her breath away. They had sat side by side on a hill looking out over the churning waters, breathing in the fresh, salt-laced air, and pointing at seabirds circling far above them. Nyla could have sat there for a lifetime, soaking in the peace of the place, but as the sun sank lower, Klyden had insisted they move on.

It was dark by the time they reached the little cabin tucked away beyond the tide mark in a copse of trees. A weathered, bearded man had answered at their first knock. Catching sight of Klyden, he had uttered a single, sharp curse and thrown his arms around him.

"Klyden! By the abyss. I thought you were dead."

"Greetings, Nowl. Still very much alive, as you see."

"Festering fish! You're taller." Then he had turned thoughtful eyes on Nyla. "You must be the queen."

Klyden had merely smiled and shrugged as she looked at him. "Nowl's a sharp one. You can never hide anything from him. Believe me, Loh and I tried."

"Where is your sister?" Nowl had peered out into the darkness as if expecting her to appear. But when his gaze returned to Klyden's face, Nyla saw sorrow clouding his eyes. "Ah, my boy." He had pulled Klyden into another embrace as silent tears poured down his weathered face.

Inside his small cabin, Nowl had prepared fish over the coals, smiling when Nyla told him he made a feast fit for a queen. She had known then that she could grow to love this man, this father figure who did not seem at all overawed by who she was, and whose obvious devotion to Klyden shone in every word and glance.

She had fallen asleep on his pallet that night, listening to the two men's voices speaking about the years since they had seen each other and, for the second time that day, had wished time could stand still.

In the morning, Nowl had rigged up the boat for them and pushed them out onto the waves.

One of these crashed over the bow right now, soaking her already cold body and drawing her mind back to the present.

"It's not so much longer now, Nyla. Look." Klyden pointed at a spot on the horizon. "That's Lira, the first island in the group."

Nyla nodded numbly. After a few hours on the Rhorhan Sea, she could hardly remember what it felt like to stand on solid ground. "Does anyone live there?"

"One family used to, until the father drowned in a storm. His wife took her children back to the mainland then. It happened shortly after we arrived."

"Where does Nowl fit in?"

"He grew up fishing these waters. He spends a lot of his time on the islands. His sailing skills are legendary among the island folk. In fact, they call him Myshmar, the Keeper. He is always the first to respond to a distress signal, and he's brought a few half-drowned fishermen home to their families It's the kind of thing that endears him to the islanders."

Klyden smiled as he continued. "My father had a gift for finding trustworthy people. Long before we even left the Charab, he befriended Nowl. Maybe he was already thinking of an escape plan then. When we ran from our home, we knocked on Nowl's door."

"Did he know what you were?"

"Not then. That would come later. My father told him only that we were enemies of the king." A brief smile flitted across Klyden's face. "The islanders have never been very partial to the crown. Nowl took it upon himself to hide us on one of the remote islands and eradicate every trace that we were there."

"Only he knew?"

"Over the course of time, the other islanders became aware of our presence, but we were Myshmar's friends, so they accepted us and helped to protect us." Klyden changed course slightly as the wind shifted. "These are good people, Nyla. The very best."

The wind picked up then, making talk difficult. The dark smudge that Klyden had pointed out to her earlier grew in size and solidity. Nyla could even make out a tumble of buildings on slightly higher ground. She tried to imagine what it would be like to live here at the end of the world, waving good-bye to your husband every morning, scanning the skies and seas, hoping he would return.

She looked back at Klyden and a pang of sorrow lanced through her. Is that what her life would become, hiding on these islands? Watching. Waiting. Hoping. It was a bleak thought.

As they rounded the small island, the wind died down slightly. "We're in a channel here, protected from the wind by the largest island of the group, Zurai."

She looked over and saw the distant dark land rising from the sea. "This is where most of the islanders live."

Klyden picked up the story he had abandoned earlier. "So Nowl settled us on what the islanders call *Azab* Rock. The Forsaken Rock. Then he visited us every few weeks, initially bringing supplies. Often he would stay with us a day or two. He taught me about the sea and tides. How to tie knots and set a sail." Klyden laughed. "Lohlyn was like you. She didn't like the sea. But Nowl said I had salt in my heart, that I was an islander to the core."

"When did he find out you were Charab?"

"My father continued our training with great intensity. The plan to become your protectors was already in place, and we suspected we might not have so much time." He swallowed. "Nowl arrived one day when we were practicing our knife throws. As you know, Lohlyn was particularly accurate."

"She was a master," Nyla agreed, an image of the knife-imbedded wildwood pig surfacing in her mind. *Lohlyn*. How many times had her friend saved her?

"Nowl was impressed. He asked where she had learned such skills, and when she told him our father had taught us from an early age, Nowl laughed. I remember him turning to my father and saying, 'It is time to share your secrets, my friend.' Surprisingly, my father did. He told him everything."

Klyden pointed. "There is Azab Rock." His expression was suddenly darker, unreadable. Nyla followed his pointing finger to a small island that rose defiantly out of the sea.

"Have you been back since . . . since . . ."

"Since my father's death? No."

Nyla kept her eyes on the Forsaken Rock. The question that had haunted her seemed to grow ever larger, just like the island. Finally, she could contain it no longer.

"What will we do, Klyden, if they come for us here the way they did for your father?"

His green eyes found her own. "I will fight them. To the death, if I must."

CHAPTER 44

The girl was taking a long time to die. She'd already been sick when they rescued her from the Rif'twine, but for a few days she managed to keep up with the group, even though a constant cough racked her body. Then she began to lag behind. The rifters took turns supporting her, but she refused any help from Nicho or the "outsiders."

Finally, Nicho and Gruel worked together to make a rough stretcher, and the stronger men took turns carrying her. She no longer had the strength to argue about the identity of her stretcher-bearers.

Nicho was one of them now, carefully picking his way over a narrow path and wondering how they would carry the stretcher over some of the more difficult mountain terrain.

"Go."

Her voice startled him. He had assumed she was asleep. In the last hour, her eyes had been closed. He looked at her now, the girl called Hildor. She might have been Shara's age, although her face was thin and pale, her body sunken in, wisp-like.

"Wait, Frintin. The girl wants something." Nicho didn't try to disguise the irritation in his voice. They now covered only a third of the distance they should in a day.

The older man stopped and lowered the stretcher. There was concern in his eyes as he bent down over the girl. "Hildor, do you want water?"

She shook her head, her eyes still on Nicho. "You should . . ." A breathless coughing fit rattled her whole body for a few moments. Her struggle for breath made Nicho's own body yearn for air. "Should . . . leave me."

"No," Frintin said. "We're taking you to the Grotto. They have medicine there."

"He . . . knows it's hopeless." Those haunted eyes, so like his father's, were on him. They held an accusation.

"Nicho wants to take you there," Frintin said. "He has been to the Grotto himself. Right, Nicho?"

"Right." He looked away. The girl was dying. She would never reach the Grotto.

Hildor wasn't the only sick rifter. At least three others were coughing or breathless and lagging behind. At this rate, they would never reach the Grotto. He would never reach Shara. And every day they spent out here, the danger of discovery grew. They would have been at the Grotto by now if the rifters hadn't been with them.

Gruel and another of the rifters came over and offered to carry the stretcher. Nicho didn't argue. He didn't want to be near those accusing eyes that seemed to look into his very heart, seemed to know his dark, selfish thoughts.

When they stopped for the night, Nicho busied himself with starting a fire. Gruel sauntered over to watch.

"Hildor looks weak," Nicho said, arranging rocks into a circle.

"She's in the final stages. I've seen it many times."

Nicho looked up at him, surprised to see tears in Gruel's eyes. "Are you . . . close?"

"No, not like that. But we arrived in the Rif'twine bout the same time. She's a friend. A good one."

"I'm sorry." Nicho meant it. Until that moment, he had thought of Hildor as an inconvenience, but she was someone others cared about.

Gruel bent down and threw some kindling on the infant flames. "Where to tomorrow?"

Nicho turned and pointed to one of the higher mountains. "The trail leads around and over that. But I don't think we'll make it."

"With the stretcher, you mean?"

"We have no choice but to wait until . . ." His voice trailed off as he realized how callous the words sounded.

"Until Hildor dies?" The hard edge was back in Gruel's eyes.

"You said yourself she was in the final stages."

"You're quite something, you know that, Nicho?"

"What's that supposed to mean?"

"Maybe you would prefer to just leave her here. Hildor and everyone else slowing you down from reaching your precious Grotto." He kicked sand onto the kindling. "In fact, maybe just leave all the rifters behind like you would have preferred to do."

"By the abyss! I'm tired of your self-pity!" Nicho rose to his feet. "You keep yourselves separate but accuse us of not including you. You claim to be the only ones who have ever felt pain. You only think of yourself, Gruel. That forest stole your humanity!"

"And you've never had any to steal."

"What do you know about me? That forest stole my father, my childhood, my innocence. I found my father dead with poison berries in his hand. Did you know that?" Nicho shoved Gruel's shoulders. "What do *you* know?"

Gruel stumbled back, but recovered his balance and strode toward Nicho, face red and fists clenched. "Don't push me. You haven't lived in near darkness the last three years of your life. Don't you push me!"

And suddenly they were onto each other with a wild, animal-like ferocity. Punching. Clawing. Growling. Every fiber in Nicho's body wanted to hurt this man.

He was dimly aware of voices shouting, of arms grabbing his own. He fought them off, clawing forward toward his opponent. Nicho pulled Gruel down to the ground. They rolled a few times before he was on top of Gruel, punching him over and over, satisfaction surging through him at the sight of the blood pouring from the overseer's mouth.

Then he heard a small, frightened voice. "Ko! His blood is coming out."

Finally he looked up to see Jed, standing just inside the circle of onlookers, his eyes filled with terror.

"What have I done?" He found Rosa in the silent crowd, her eyes large with shock. Frintin stood next to her. Nicho looked back at Gruel. He wasn't moving. "Help him. Frintin. Help him!"

The old man knelt by his side, feeling for a pulse in Gruel's neck. He nodded briefly. "He lives still, Nicho. He lives."

Under Frintin's vigilant care, Gruel awoke the next day. Nicho sat by his side when he finally stirred.

"Wha . . . 'appened?" he mumbled, his lips thick and swollen.

"I . . . I hit you. I'm sorry, Gruel." Nicho couldn't meet the other man's gaze.

Gruel said nothing for a long time, then let out what sounded like a chuckle. "I 'member now. A townboy with a strong fist. Who could'a guessed?"

That night, just before the sky changed from deep blue to black, Nicho slipped away from the campfire into the dark hills. The day had been strained, although Gruel's recovery lifted the mood in the camp. The rifters huddled on one side around Gruel and the dying Hildor. The "outsiders" had mulled around aimlessly, voices lowered, eyes downcast. Everyone seemed to be avoiding him.

On a hill, Nicho found a ledge with a distant view of the camp. He pressed himself into the uncomfortable, shallow hollow in the rock wall.

What now? Should he run? Leave them to find their own way to the Grotto? Frintin and Gruel would manage, wouldn't they?

He thought of Jed's terror-filled eyes and a deep sob shuddered through his body. He failed the boy over and over again. What kind of man did something like that in front of a child? A child who had seen so much pain already?

"I can't do this. I just can't do this," he whispered into the star-filled sky.

Then Nicho wept. For Jed and Derry and Shara. For Hildor and

Gruel and the rifters in pain below him. For Rosa's night of shame. For himself. His father. His mother. For all the sorrows around him.

His throat and eyes ached and his face felt salty and tight when the tears finally dried up. Then he lay on the ledge and stared at the stars that seemed so close. Slowly the wonder of that night sky spilled its ancient light into his heart. It whispered that time and seasons and kings would pass, but those stars and their Ancient Creator would stay the same.

Finally, as the stars chartered their steady course above him, peace enveloped Nicho.

CHAPTER 45

Elxa had delayed long enough. He could delay no longer. As soon as he heard the Raven leave for his morning scouting, he rose. The ashen dawn light spilling through the window was not yet bright enough to pack by, so Elxa lit a lamp. He reached for the bag beside his pallet and meticulously packed his few belongings. He added the Raven's map. Maps were valuable and he felt a stab of guilt.

He slung his bow and quiver of arrows across one shoulder before throwing his thick cloak over it. Finally, he reached for the two knives hidden under his bed. Those first few days in Lydora, Elxa had compulsively polished the knife with the grunite handle until he could see his own reflection in it. Yet even as he picked it up now and slid it into his belt, the vivid memory of its blood-stained blade returned. In the long years of training, nobody had ever taught him how to forget the last look in someone's eyes. The blood. The guilt.

Elxa rummaged through the Raven's food supply, choosing some cheese and dried meat and adding this to his bag. He topped up his water bottle, doused the lamp, and slipped out into the cool morning air. Lydora's streets were quiet. Only the odd merchant pushing a cart of wares passed him by.

It felt good to leave this city of death and madness. He had hidden here too long, haunted by the past and taunted by the future. Today, he was just another traveler on the road. Today, death might not stalk him. He quickened his pace as the longing to leave overwhelmed him.

His only regret was leaving the Raven without a word of parting, yet he suspected his friend might be relieved to find him gone.

Elxa had expected some of the same resistance as before at the town gate. The Raven's stories of the king's paranoia were foremost in his mind as he approached the guard tower. The main gate was not yet open, but he spotted the small opening of the pedestrian gate. Two guards stood on either side of it.

Act as if you have every right to be there. His uncle's words rang through his mind. He strode purposefully forward.

"You're up early," one guard said.

"Long way to go."

"Where would that be exactly?" the other asked.

"Rhorhan Sea."

"Be off with you, then," the first one laughed. "'Tis a journey and a half!"

Elxa smiled and dipped his head, grateful that he didn't have to bloody his knife again. Not for awhile, at least.

"Good news, Your Majesty." Lord Lucian bowed as he entered the throne room.

Alexor sat on one of the double thrones, staring broodily at the candelabra hanging from the roof as his right hand picked at a scab on his face.

As usual, it took awhile for the king's mind to leave its muddled roamings. When it did, his eyes narrowed on Lucian with burning intensity.

Careful, Lucian reminded himself. Lately, the king was like an unpredictable grubear. Such volatility could be dangerous, as many had come to experience in the last few weeks.

"What did you say?" Alexor's voice seemed higher, more piercing, recently.

"Your Majesty." Lucian bowed low again. "I came to tell you that I have some good news."

"Good news?" The king's eyes burned with fevered excitement. "You have found my treacherous sister?"

"No, Your Majesty." Lucian lowered his voice to a soothing purr. "But it's just a matter of time. There is nowhere for her to run, and your men—"

"You have been saying that since she escaped!" Alexor kicked out at the other throne, as if his sister still sat there. "This was all *your* idea, wasn't it? The drowning that failed so miserably?"

"Your entire council felt it was for the best. It was, after all, the only way that your souls could be reunited."

"By rotting Taus!" The king was on his feet. "If you tell me one more time that I am a simpleton half-soul, I will have you slain right here before my throne!" He looked up at the guard standing by the door, as if contemplating giving the order right away.

"You are nothing of the sort, King Alexor." Lucian's smooth tone belied his pounding heart. "You are the rightful heir of Taus. A great warrior king that your people will remember through the generations."

Alexor slid back onto the throne, his gaze narrowed on Lucian.

"In fact, this is the good news I come to bring you, Mighty King. You are about to do what no king has managed to do before you. You are about to destroy the Guardian Grotto and all the filthy rebels scuttling in its depths."

Alexor's face puffed into a sulk. "How will that help me find Nyla?"

"Deep in the Guardian Grotto lies the Guardian Rock—the most powerful rock in this and any other kingdom."

"So what? I already have half of it and it hasn't helped me one bit."

"When the two halves are joined, you will become the most potent king of any age."

"Then will I be able to find Nyla?"

"Indeed, there will be nothing you cannot do, Your Majesty. But you will be so powerful, you will not even need Nyla." Lucian paused for effect. "I have come to tell you that we know enough to attack the Guardian Grotto. I recommend that we prepare the army and set off as soon as Your Majesty deems fit."

Alexor twirled his long golden hair around and around his index finger. He seemed to be looking right through Lucian.

As the long moments wore on, Lucian tried again. "You will forever be remembered as the king who overthrew the Parashi rebellion."

"Mm," Alexor's gaze was back on Lucian. "The Overthrower King. Yes, perhaps I will consider it. Once I find Nyla."

"All in your immense wisdom, Your Majesty." Lucian bowed, quenching his impatience. It was a positive beginning, he told himself as he left the throne room. Slowly, he would rein the king in to do his will. But he would have to be very, very careful indeed.

CHAPTER 46

Since the breach, the Grotto had become a frenzy of activity. Weapons were now made around the clock. Horses were shod. The weapons training of the older boys and girls had been intensified. Even the younger children were assigned tasks as messengers or couriers. One of these now shyly held out a note to Mikel. He took it from her with a smile and told her she could be off.

It was from Andreo, asking for Mikel to spread the word that he would be demonstrating the uses of some of his plants in wound and pain care. Already Andreo's classroom had been changed to a makeshift infirmary.

"Mikel?"

Eliad stood in the doorway. The old man looked more stooped over than the last time Mikel had seen him, weighed down by the grief of all that had happened with Shara.

"Eliad. Good to see you." He folded Andreo's note. "How is Shara?"

"She sleeps still," Eliad said, shambling forward.

"I am sorry."

"Andreo continues to care for her. She has regained some color in her cheeks." Eliad nodded, as if to encourage himself. "He remains hopeful that she will awaken. How are the preparations going?"

"There is much to do, but every day finds us stronger and better prepared."

"How I wish we had taken a different path from Gwyndorr. One that did not lead to the Grotto and all the trouble we brought to your people." The old man shook his head, confusion etched on his face. "Yet it was the way Tabeal led us."

"Do not allow these regrets to take hold, my friend. We do not always understand why things come to pass, but victory often lies at the end of the path of struggle and pain."

"Something the years have taught us, have they not?" Eliad smiled. "Still, I fear I let my own desire for rest overtake me, lulling me into a false sense of peace. I believed Shara would be safe here, that it could be a place of refuge and peace from those wishing to harm her. A place to recover and prepare for the long journey ahead. But instead, the Grotto has become a trap where the darkness of her enemies entwined her."

"Evil's reach is long indeed." Mikel nodded somberly. "No place is safe from it."

Eliad held out a roughly bound leather book. "I have completed the task you asked of me. The ink on the last word is barely dry."

"Shara's book? I am surprised you already finished the transcription." Mikel took it from the old man's hands and opened it, admiring the fine penmanship. "A wonderful addition to our collection. Although it is hard to think what might become of our ancient Parashi literature if Tirragyl's army penetrates the Grotto."

"It is more than just a book for your collection," Eliad said. "In its pages are hidden the secrets of the past and the hope for the future."

"So you have told me before." Mikel laughed. "Why, then, have you not already started reading it to us?"

Now it was Eliad's turn to laugh. "If all I did was read it to you, you would gain nothing." His fingers trailed reverently over the book. "The words need to open in your heart like the petals of a flower."

"And for that to happen?"

"We need Tabeal."

"Ah yes, the Gold Breast." Mikel sighed. "And where exactly is this elusive bird of yours?"

"Always close, Mikel. And always just on time."

. . .

The dream held Shara heavily in its arms. Initially, she had tried to fight it, but she knew now it was useless. She could not escape. It was best not to struggle. So she let herself be swept away into dark waters and even darker skies, falling and falling and falling with no place to land. She let the colors—purples and browns and greys—swirl and streak through her vision, even though she longed for the colors of a brilliant sunrise. She listened to the groanings and creakings and wailings, only sometimes wondering if it was more than just the wind, if it was actually the voices of others trapped in the endless darkness of the dream. If, in fact, it was not her own voice that made the plaintive, haunting sound.

At times she was vaguely aware of a world beyond the dream. A soothing word. A light touch on her hand or face. That was when she wrestled the most, trying desperately to find the portal of that world, sensing it held light and color and hope.

But even as she groped toward it, the mercury-thick darkness would wrap its arms around her, pulling her back with jealous intensity, stifling her with its cool kiss. And she would let it take her again, never wondering what right it had to do so. Not remembering what had brought her to this place. Knowing only that she was here now and there was no escaping its grasp.

But, suddenly—

A piercing sound.

A call, louder and purer than all the groaning voices.

Red. Gold. Rending through shades of black.

A shaking. A shouting. Then a shuddering of fear as she sensed the seeds of her own betrayal.

Leave me here. She may have spoken, or only thought the words. *Leave me here. It's what I deserve.*

A pulse of golden warmth enfolded her lightly. These were the arms to which she belonged. These, and no other.

And finally she yielded to their comforting embrace and they drew her back to the light.

The first thing she noticed were the voices. They no longer groaned or wailed, but were soft and soothing. One of them hummed a melody so beautiful it made her cry.

She opened her eyes and saw lamplight swimming through her tears. And then she noticed the walls, reminding her of her long, dark imprisonment. Terror lashed through her.

"No, no, help me. I don't want to . . ." Her voice was so weak.

"She's awake, Andreo." A silver-haired man bent over her, his eyes creased with joy. "Welcome back, dear Shara."

Shara? Had she heard that name before?

"Where . . . ?"

"You're at the Guardian Grotto. Look, here's Andreo, too."

Another smiling man now knelt by her side, holding a goblet in his hand. "Have a sip of this, Shara." His intelligent gaze was so familiar. She had a sudden memory of him teaching her history lessons.

She took a sip of the herb-infused drink. Its warmth soothed her throat. "Did I miss the lessons, Brother? I didn't mean to but—"

"We're not in Gwyndorr anymore. We're at the Guardian Grotto. We came here with Nicho, remember?"

Nicho. The name brought an ache to the center of her chest, the pain of longing and loss. "Where . . . where is he?" She tried to sit up, but her head spun. Why was she so weak?

"He went back to Gwyndorr to fetch Derry's son."

"He left?" Why couldn't she remember that? "What happened, Brother? Why is everything so . . . confusing?"

The two men shared a wary look, then the older one spoke. She'd seen him before, too, she realized, with a bird. An unusual bird.

"You have been in a death-like sleep for close to two weeks. It was brought on by a power rock. The Cerulean Dusk Dreamer. Do you remember that rock, Shara?"

"Dusk Dreamer," she repeated, but no image came to her mind.

"A particularly beautiful rock. Deep blue in color."

Blue. *The color of the night sky just before all the light has seeped away.* As the words filled her mind, so did an overwhelming and frightening desire. "The Dreamer," she whispered. "I remember it now. It tried to burn me. She looked down at her shaking hands, expecting to see scalded flesh. "It would have burned me to death, but then . . . then . . ." Something happened.

"Then what, my child?" Andreo coaxed.

She shook her head. "I think I dropped it."

"You did drop it, Shara," the silver-haired man said. "But before you dropped it, what happened?"

She closed her eyes, trying to remember. Someone had come. To save her from the fire? No. There had been menace in his approach.

"Someone came," she said. "At first I thought he was a friend. But he wasn't. And he said . . . he said my father would be proud. But I was trying to let go of the rock then. To cut the connection between him and . . ." She shook her head in frustration.

"What connection did you want to break, Shara?" Andreo asked. "Between him and you?"

No. It had been more than that. So much more. So much at stake.

"Between him and"—suddenly she knew—"and the Guardian Grotto."

Her eyes flew to Andreo's face. "Lord Lucian. He was laughing. Laughing, Andreo! I let him in, didn't I? Into the Grotto?"

"Yes, Shara." Andreo's eyes filled with unshed tears.

Guilt pulsed through her, so raw and deep that she wanted to bury her head in the pallet's straw and beg for the dark arms of her long dream to come back and claim her. She had no right to live in the light anymore—she, the one who had opened the door that would bring death to the Grotto.

But now her friends' arms held her and wouldn't let her go. The old man's voice again hummed the beautiful melody, drawing out all her cleansing tears. And when the melody finally stopped, his voice whispered, "We're going home, Shara."

CHAPTER 47

Nyla carved notches into the tall sapling behind the cottage. One for every day they had been on the island called Azab Rock, the Forsaken Island.

As she finished the twelfth notch, she looked up, taking in the sea beyond the high ground on which the cottage stood. Today it was white-capped, reminding her of the day they had arrived. Her eyes scanned the horizon where the sky and sea met, and she wondered again if Alexor would send a single ship or an entire fleet to find her. Would she see them coming, or would they storm onto the beach below without any warning?

Behind her was the small wooden cottage Klyden, Lohlyn, and their father had built in the first months of their own exile. Sturdy and well camouflaged in the trees, it was not a fortress to withstand the wrath of a king.

At times Nyla liked the seclusion of this island. Too long she had been surrounded by courtiers and advisors and lords. Always there were eyes trained on her, expectant and demanding. Here, she could breathe. She could sit an entire morning and look at the azure sea without someone criticizing. She could go for hours without hearing another voice, soothed by the waves and the calls of the island birds.

There were moments of loneliness, though, especially when Klyden left the island to go fishing or when he disappeared for long stretches into the coastal forest. He returned from the forest pensive and wrapped in sadness.

Similar, in fact, to how she was when she couldn't keep the past at bay. Alexor, raising himself up to his full fourteen-year-old height and telling his father that Nyla should come hunting, too. Alexor, laughing at an unspoken, shared joke or winking at her over the boring speech of an elder. That cold, unknowable Alexor who stared right through her on the day he sentenced her to death.

Lohlyn also pressed into her thoughts. Over and over Nyla returned to that moment when Lohlyn had tried to save her and Nyla had resisted. What if they had both escaped? Could her best friend still be alive?

"I'm going to the forest this morning, Nyla."

She spun around, cursing.

His lip curled into a rare grin. "Sorry. I should warn you before I creep up on you."

"At least crack a twig or something."

"Old habits die hard." His expression was serious again. "I'll be back before sundown."

"Klyden?" He turned back to her. "Can I come with you?"

She saw the struggle on his face. "I'm not sure. It's just . . ." His words trailed off.

"Fine. Go yourself, then." She turned away, angry at her own moment of weakness.

His touch on her shoulder was gentle and unexpected, his expression soft when she turned to look at him.

"I'm sorry." He hastily let go of her shoulder. "The last I heard, these islands were part of your realm. The forest is yours to walk through any time you want."

"Of course they are," she said haughtily. "But that's not what I asked. I asked if I could come with *you*."

He dropped his head in deference. "Yes, you can come with me."

She followed him down the coastal path with a hollow sense of victory. Yet the salty tang on the wind and the warm rays of sun soothed away her restlessness. Anticipation filled her as she finally stepped into the cool of the forest.

It was a beautiful place, verdant and lush. The sound of the sea was dulled here, replaced by the sounds of insect and birdcalls. It felt as if they had stepped into a new and mysterious world. As they walked deeper into the forest, Klyden occasionally broke the silence to point out a bird or small mammal. He often stooped to pick a few leaves or berries for a remedy.

Every now and then he stopped and ran his fingers over the bark of a tree. There was something tender and reverent in the action that caused Nyla to keep silent. As he started off again, she bent down to gaze closely at the trees and saw the small indents his fingers had sought out—arrow marks.

As they moved deeper into the forest, Klyden spoke less and seemed to forget her presence. Only when they reached the clearing did she understand.

In the middle of the clearing stood a large upright rock with a symbol carved into it. Around the rock lay an assortment of weapons —swords and knives, a bow and arrows. Rust coated the blades and arrow tips.

Klyden approached the rock slowly, then sank to his knees. She wasn't sure why, but Nyla, who had never lowered herself before another, had the urge to do the same. She stopped slightly behind Klyden and dropped to the ground, sitting cross-legged in silence.

"My father's tomb," Klyden said after a long silence. "I found it a few days after we got here."

She recalled Klyden's quietness on the day they'd arrived and entered the hut. He had looked around at the cottage, his brow furrowed, perhaps remembering. There had been no personal belongings in the hut. Yet, here, at the grave, lay the most prized belongings of the old Charabian – his weapons.

"Did Nowl bury him?"

"No." He took a deep breath. "My uncle."

"Why here?"

"It's the Charab way. Our home is in a forest. It provides

protection, nourishment. It shields us. My uncle would not have wanted his brother to lie for eternity on a cliff overlooking the sea, exposed to the elements." He paused, a long, sad moment. "My father would never go home again. This was his brother's way of putting that right."

"The brother who came to kill him?" The words slipped out unintentionally as she thought of her own brother.

Klyden looked at her for a long time. "The brother who loved him."

"What of the symbol?"

He rose to his feet and stepped toward the tombstone.

"This," his fingers traced the round symbol, "is a circular blade. The same type I used in the river. And this"— his fingers found the outline of the longer shape—"is our forefather's, Chaorlin's, sword. Its hilt was encrusted with snow gems, or so the legend goes."

"Snow gems!" She thought of her coronation crown. "One of the rarest gems of all."

"Only because the invaders made them so." He turned back to the symbol. "The blade and sword are the symbol of my people."

"It is a good resting place, Klyden."

"I wish I could have said good-bye." He swallowed painfully. "But at least I didn't have to bring him news of Lohlyn's death."

"I wish it had been different with Loh, Klyden." Suddenly she couldn't meet his eye. "If only I hadn't—"

"No." He closed the gap between them and drew her into his arms. "Neither of us could have changed what happened to her."

She rested her head on his chest and savored his comforting warmth, drawing strength from their shared sorrow. He pulled away from her after awhile.

"I'm sorry. This place—this forest—there are so many memories. I shouldn't have—"

"I'm glad you did."

Elxa spent a few days prowling around the small coastal village of Portas, an easy place in which to hide, for travelers came and went, mixing freely with the locals over goblets of mead and ale. Elxa struck up several conversations and gained some valuable insights.

There were, he learned, six inhabited islands within a day's sail of the mainland. There used to be seven, but one family had been forced to move when the husband died in the waves. A common enough occurrence on these rough waters, his local drinking companion had informed him morbidly.

The islanders sometimes came to the mainland to sell fish from the deeper waters. But on the whole, they were a taciturn lot who kept to themselves. No, the locals did not take boats of produce to the islands. The islanders grew their own produce and had fresh water, so there was no need.

A foreign sailor told him, in a broken tongue, that his ship, and all the others from distant waters, avoided the islands. "Bad water. Sharp. Break boat." He shook his head and Elxa saw the terror on his face. "Many boat and man die there."

From another drinking companion, he discovered that there was only one local man who visited the islands regularly—an old man, a very experienced sailor, who did not fear the treacherous rocks lurking beneath the waves. "Many islanders believe he is more than a man." Here, his companion leaned closer, dropping his voice. "Some think the wave spirits whisper to him as if he is one of their own. His name is Nowl, but they call him Myshmar."

Outside the tavern, a woman with rouged lips and hard eyes swayed over to him and pressed up against him. "You look like a sailor who's been on rough waters too long," she murmured huskily.

No, he informed her, he wasn't looking for a place to sleep. He was looking for the one called Nowl. She pointed, rather sulkily, to the western road and told him the old man lived some distance from the village.

Elxa slipped silently down the road and found the lone cottage, just under an hour's walk from the village. He slept that night in the forest, in a place that gave him a view of the man's door. Over the next two days he watched this Nowl, the one he sensed was the key to reaching his cousin.

Now, as the third day broke, Elxa tried to recall what his father had told him about his assignment to kill his brother. Very little, for even as time passed, Elxa had sensed the raw grief beneath his words. Elxa did not know how his father had reached the island or where the island was, only that he had found his uncle's body.

"How did my uncle know, old man? How did he know his assassin was coming?" Elxa said quietly under his breath, as he watched Nowl returning with a bucket of fresh water. The man led a life of routine. Every morning started the same way—catching fish, fetching water, and feeding his gulls, even before he ate his own meal to break the fast.

Elxa watched him push open the cage. The five—no, six—gulls flew to him and ate the fish from his hands. Elxa wondered where the other gull had come from. Yesterday there had been only five. He watched Nowl closely as he held a gull and drew it from the cage. Nowl attached something to its leg, then tossed it in the air.

It was a carrier bird. A messenger. *That* was how his uncle had known his brother was on the way—the old man, Nowl, had warned him.

With the insight came sudden clarity. There was only one way to get to the island, and this old Wave Whisperer was the key.

CHAPTER 48

The Wave Whisperer opened the door slowly. His gaze took in Elxa's face before dropping to his hands.

"Good day, sir," Elxa said quickly and as reassuringly as he could. "Are you the one called Nowl that Klyden told me about?"

The old man seemed unsettled at the mention of Klyden's name. "I am Nowl," he replied warily.

"I am glad to finally find you. The path has been a long and treacherous one. May I?" Elxa pointed to the interior of the cottage, and Nowl reluctantly opened the door wide enough to let him in.

The old man did not move from the door, as if he might bolt out of the cottage at any moment. "Who are you?" he asked.

"Elxa, Klyden's close friend from the palace." Too late, Elxa wondered if giving the old man his real name was a mistake. Had Lohlyn and Klyden spoken of him to Nowl? "We guarded the queen together."

Nowl's appraising eyes roamed over him. Elxa knew he was a convincing liar—all the Charab had to be—but would his story hold up under this sharp scrutiny?

"Why are you here?"

"To warn Klyden. The king is a mere day or two behind me." Elxa noticed the subtle widening of Nowl's pupils—a sign of fear—but Nowl's next words did not betray Klyden.

"I have not seen Klyden for many years. Not since he left for the palace."

"Strange. He told me he would bring the queen here to safety."

"He must have changed his plans."

"He said you might lie to protect him, Nowl," Elxa said gently. "He told me what a good friend you have been to him and Lohlyn." Sorrow crept over the old man's features at the name of Lohlyn, and Elxa suppressed his own last image of his cousin. *Every person has a weakness*, his uncle used to say. *You only need to find and exploit it.* He suspected that he had just found Nowl's, and he carefully felt his way through the man's defenses.

"Lohlyn loved you dearly, Nowl."

The old man nodded, cheeks puffed out as if to keep the pain and loss bottled inside.

"I went to see her before she died, and she spoke of you."

This was too much for the Wave Whisperer. He sank against the wooden door, dropped his head into his hands, and wept.

Elxa came alongside him. "I loved her, too," he said, finally speaking words that held no deceit.

He knew then that he was close to having the Wave Whisperer under his control, but the thought gave him no pleasure. *Ra'aph-aqeb*. The word mocked him, mocked the liar and killer it made of him.

When the man's sobs subsided, he shuffled back to his feet and offered Elxa the customary drink and seat at his table. They spoke no more words until their cups, containing potent mead, were drained. Elxa's head spun slightly and he cursed himself for drinking it so fast. He needed a sharp mind.

"You, too, are a Charab?" the old man asked eventually.

"No, sir."

"You have the look of one. And the manner."

"Perhaps from spending so much time with Klyden and Lohlyn. They taught me everything they knew."

The Wave Whisperer appeared unconvinced. "How did they

come to take you into their confidence? No one except the queen's grandmother knew they were there to protect Nyla."

"It was the grandmother who drew me in." Elxa was grateful for the old man's tongue-slip. "My father was her most trusted guard, and she had seen him train me from a young age. She trusted us." The lies slipped easily off Elxa's tongue—the trait of a true Charab.

"If both you and Klyden were there in the end, why couldn't one of you have saved Lohlyn while the other saved the queen? Klyden told me that Lohlyn made him choose Nyla over her."

So, the old man *had* spoken to Klyden since Lohlyn's death. Still, his question was a good one. The Charab never left one of their own behind. *The best lies are always closest to the truth*, his father used to say. Elxa knew what to say.

"I tried to save her." He saw himself running to the fire pole. "She was on the fire pole already. I shot the guards around her. I ran to her. Cut her down." He remembered how the arming word had taunted him. The look on Lohlyn's face as she saw it was him. "The ants had already eaten into her flesh. She was weak. As I tried to carry her out of the square, a new group of guards arrived. She told me to leave her behind. She knew I would never outrun them if I had to carry her."

The Wave Whisperer sat silently for a very long time after that, as if the questions—and answers—had worn him down. Elxa finally broke the silence.

"Nowl, every moment we spend here brings the king's forces closer. I need you to take me to Klyden and the queen. Together we can protect her."

Nowl glanced up. "How will two of you withstand the forces of Tirragyl any better than one? I will send word to him so that he will be prepared." The old man rose and started for the door. Elxa could not let him release a gull.

"Wait. Do not give him warning. I know him well enough. He would not want me to put myself in danger. But if I am there, on the island with them, I will be able to help him protect the queen.

I might even be able to protect him. Once I'm there, he won't send me back."

The Wave Whisperer considered these words before nodding curtly. "I will prepare the boat. The tide is favorable and we will leave in the hour."

CHAPTER 49

Lucian did not often enter the king's throne room. Few men did, for to do so might end in a tongue-lashing—or worse. Yet he knew what was at stake. Every day delayed meant the Parashi Warriors at the Grotto would be better prepared for an attack. And every day gave Shara more time to escape.

The time had come to act.

"Lord Lucian of Gwyndorr requests an audience, Your Majesty." The guard sounded wary. He, too, had borne the brunt of the king's anger these last few weeks.

"Lucian!" The king, pacing at the window, turned and his face lit up with a strange, bright smile. Lucian recalled that the last time he had an audience with the king, the sovereign had been morose and unresponsive. "My friend! You have been away too long." The words tumbled over each other, fast and high.

"Your Majesty." Lucian bowed low. "It is good to see you in high spirits."

"Of course. Of course. We must make our own futures bright, must we not?"

"Indeed, sire."

"The time has come to take action, Lucian." The king pranced to his side.

"I agree, Your Majesty." Lucian felt his heart pounding faster. The Grotto was in his grasp now. The king was coming around.

"We are to root out the traitors from our midst."

"Sire?"

The king dropped his voice to a conspiratorial whisper. "It's that Lord Briskyl. I hear he is talking. Planning. He always favored Nyla. I think he knows where she is."

"Lord Briskyl, sire? He is but a—"

"He is plotting against me." A fevered brightness lit the king's eyes. "He thinks I do not know. But I have ears. I have eyes that he does not see."

"Plotting, Your Majesty?"

"Indeed. He wants me dead." Alexor made a cutting motion across his throat. "Then he will bring Nyla back to rule. I think they plan to use poison, Lucian. I fear to eat now. Fear the taster, my own cousin, is one of them."

Lucian contemplated this new twist in Alexor's mind. Perhaps it could be of use.

"Sire, I fear you might be right."

The king's eyes widened with surprise. Had a part of him known it to be a lie? Lucian wondered. That it was the mere wild imaginings of a crazed king? That Lord Briskyl, gentle and loyal, was the last man who would ever turn on an heir of Taus?

"You have heard the whisperings, Lucian?"

"I have heard whisperings of the whisperings, sire."

"Yes. Yes." The king nodded emphatically. "That is their way. We need to take action."

"Yes, Your Majesty. I came to warn you of this. But the network of their deception is wide and deep, with many involved. Knowing who to trust will be difficult."

"My fears are right! There are many involved, you say, Lucian?"

"Yes, sire. But the army is still completely on your side. This has caused the traitors to stay their hand."

"We will bring them in. Torture them till they confess. Their fire-poled bodies will litter the square—"

"There are too many to take such drastic action, sire. If you turn on one or a few of them, the others will turn on you. What we need to do is strengthen your position. Turn them *toward* you, their mighty and powerful king. Then they will no longer want Nyla as their ruler."

"How do I do that?"

"To begin with, we take you out of the palace, with its whispering traitors. We put you under the protection of the army, where every man's loyalty is yours."

The king nodded, thoughtfully.

"Then we attack the Guardian Grotto. Once and for all you, Mighty King Alexor, will obliterate the Parashi Warriors, those thorns in the flesh of Tirragyl's royal house. You will come back victorious. The people will shout your praises. They will fall at your feet in the street. And the traitors will not dare touch you."

"Yes, yes." The king nodded wildly.

"Because the danger of treachery is so close at hand, we need to move fast, sire. Can you call your men to arms within the week?"

"A week?" Alexor seemed startled. "It is little time, Lucian."

"It is only your safety I am concerned with. The more time you spend in the palace, the greater the danger becomes."

"Yes, indeed. This is a dangerous place for me to be." And finally the king spoke the words Lucian longed to hear. "I will call my men to arms. We go to take the Guardian Grotto."

CHAPTER 50

The gull did not come from the mainland, as Klyden had expected. Instead the messenger-bird he found at the feeder that afternoon was one sent from the island called Trill Rock, one of the closest islands to the mainland. Klyden's stomach tightened as he saw the bird. He knew it was a warning even before he coaxed the tame bird into his hand and retrieved the small note tied to its leg.

The childlike scrawl was Cruwen's, one of the island's elders. He had meticulously copied the warning just as Nowl and the Old Charabian had taught him to. *Nowl comes under a brown sail.*

For just a moment, Klyden felt panic clenching his gut. The peace of these last few weeks on the island had soothed him, lulling him into a false sense of security. He should have known better. The most powerful man in Tirragyl wanted Nyla dead. Inevitably he would find her.

Klyden wondered again if bringing the queen here had been a mistake. A fresh wave of longing overwhelmed him. How he wished his father was here to counsel him in this hour of danger!

Yet, he reminded himself as he hurried back to the hut, brown sails meant only that Nowl had a stranger on board and had been unable to send a gull of his own. It was a bad sign that the person forcing Nowl to bring him to the island had not allowed him to send a bird. Still, a single scout from the king would be easy to dispose of.

"Nyla!" He burst through the door.

Nyla's hand, bearing a stylus, jerked. Ink splattered over the scroll she had so carefully been writing on these last few days.

"By Taus, Klyden! You startled me." Her glare was that of a wronged sovereign. It might have amused him on another day.

"We need to make haste. Nowl approaches. He will be here before sunset, if my calculations are correct."

"Nowl?" Her face lit up momentarily.

"He does not come alone." He explained about the colored sails and how the islanders sent warnings if they sighted Nowl's boat bearing any sail that was not white.

Nyla's face paled as he spoke. "Alexor!"

"I won't let him hurt you, Nyla." He reached her in three large strides and drew her small frame into his arms. Every fiber of his body wanted to keep her safe, no matter what the cost. "I promise."

She pulled away after a moment, and his gaze slid to the ground as he mumbled an apology. This was the third time he had let the depth of his emotions show. She was his liege, not a mere woman. His queen. His father would have berated him for his mistake. He could almost hear his voice. *You are there to protect, not befriend. Feelings only hinder us from our goal.*

"Where can we hide, Klyden?" It seemed she had hardly heard his reassurances, as she looked frantically around the hut.

"Listen, Nyla. There is only one man with Nowl. He is probably a scout for the king, and I can easily deal with him. There is no need to hide or to be afraid."

"But Alexor can't be far behind. And if the scout does not return, won't it prove that he came across us? They will be on us before we know it."

"I will capture this scout tonight and interrogate him. Then we will know what the king is planning. We will leave the island before his fleet arrives."

"Leave?" Fear and hope waged war on her face. "Where to?"

He had not thought far beyond the island, he realized. *Always know your next step,* his father's voice berated. He had failed the old

Charabian several times over today. "Let us talk to this man, and then we will decide."

The sun was nearing the horizon by the time Nowl broke the long silence.

"There it is—Forsaken Rock."

The island was much smaller than the others they had passed, yet it rose steeply, almost defiantly, from the sea. Elxa scanned it carefully as they approached the sheltered bay where Nowl would anchor.

He had few advantages. This was Klyden's island. He had spent several years here and would know it as intimately as every Charab learned to know their home terrain. Elxa hoped that their approach had not been seen, but even this was doubtful. In his role as the queen's protector, Klyden would constantly be scanning the horizon for danger. Nowl's boat posed no threat, however, so perhaps his guard would be down.

"Does Klyden's hut lie on the high ground?"

The old man's eyes narrowed somewhat suspiciously as he nodded.

"How long is the walk from there?"

"Half an hour. Slower going up, of course."

Enough time to lay the trap he intended. Elxa's eyes passed over the old man as he lowered the anchor. He felt a wave of regret. He did not want to harm the Wave Whisperer, but his only true advantage was that he held a hostage.

"You can get out here. It is only waist deep," Nowl said, as he began to pull down the flapping sail.

"You are coming?"

"After I secure these ropes."

"I'll wait for you." It was important to have Nowl close to him. He scanned the deep-shadowed forest surrounding the bay. If he hadn't stopped Nowl from sending out a gull, Klyden would be lying in wait for him there, an arrow trained at his heart.

A sense of impending danger prickled his skin. *Never disregard your Charab instinct. It is a gift as valuable as the circular blade,* his uncle's voice warned him.

Elxa's gaze left the forest, returning to the old man. Nowl was looping the sail's rope into circles as he peered expectantly into the forest. It was the only confirmation Elxa needed. He moved as fast as a gazelle to reach the old man, knowing that if *he* had been standing on the shore, *this* would be the moment he released the arrow.

Yet no arrow felled him as he grabbed Nowl around the waist, pinning his arms behind him and pulling him around—a shield between himself and the shore.

"How did you warn him?" he growled.

The Wave Whisperer smiled. "Brown sails."

Klyden lifted Nyla up onto the limb of a tree where she was shielded by thick, dark green foliage. The hiding place was uncomfortable, but effective. For once he had covered both their tracks at the base of the trunk, even he would struggle to locate her.

He passed her a belt containing two sharp knives. "Just as a last resort," he whispered.

Then he drew into the deep shade of the forest and watched the shape of Nowl's boat grow larger. In the last light of day, he could just make out the two figures on the boat. Nowl at the stern, tiller in hand, and another man in a dark robe, face hidden by the dusk shadows.

Klyden focused on this man as the boat neared the shore. Without taking his eyes off him, Klyden notched an arrow into place and slowly lifted the bow, steadying it against the tree trunk. The shot was far, especially as the arrow had to fly against the stiff sea breeze. If he took the shot now, there was a chance it would fall just short of the boat. Anyway, he wanted the king's spy alive to tell him of Alexor's plans.

Klyden watched Nowl drop the anchor. The soft splash could be heard over the flapping of the loose sails. The other man gazed out toward the shore as Nowl fastened the anchor rope and began pulling down the brown sail. As he wound the rope, Nowl's eyes, too, turned inland.

Klyden sensed the stranger's plan before it happened. That was the moment—before the man dashed toward Nowl—that Klyden should have released the arrow. Yet Klyden froze, for it was the same moment he understood that this was no scout. Only a Charab would have sensed him on the shore, and only a Charab could move with such agility and speed.

Klyden lowered the bow and arrow and watched as the man pushed Nowl over the boat's edge and pressed him forward through the water to the beach. He knew he would not get another chance for a kill shot, not with Nowl in the assassin's hands, and he cursed himself for missing the one chance he should have taken. *Don't let your first mistake cost you another.* He had to think fast. Nowl's and Nyla's lives depended on it.

"Klyden!"

A chill ran through him at the sound of the voice the wind carried toward him. It was the voice of his childhood, of hide and seek and wooden swords, laughter and fights and pranks.

Elxa. Cousin. Friend. Close as a brother.

How could *this* be the one he had to face? Suddenly he fully understood his father's last sacrificial act. But his father had not had a queen to protect.

Klyden slowly backed away from the tree, moving steadily deeper into the forest. Losing sight of Nowl pained him, but he knew Elxa would not harm him. Yet. Klyden's advantage was that Elxa did not know his exact position. His cousin would find his tracks soon enough, but at least he had a head start.

He briefly wondered if he should leave Nyla in her hiding place, but the protector's first rule was "stay close to the one you guard," so he felt his way back to the tree.

"Sss." His call was a mere rustle, but her pale face appeared between the hanging leaves. Finger to his lips, he beckoned her to slide down into his arms. The branch creaked as she moved. Klyden glanced back from where he had come. No movement yet. Elxa must still be on the beach.

"Klyden." Elxa's voice was soft, but still carried through the trees on the sea breeze. "I know you are here to protect the queen. By the oath, I will not harm her. But I make no such promise for the Wave Whisperer. Show yourself."

"Who is he?" Nyla whispered as she slid into his arms.

"My cousin, Elxa." He lowered her to the ground, grabbed her hand, and began to pull her deeper into the forest.

"Did Alexor send him?"

"No, he isn't here for you. He is here for me."

"Why?"

"On the orders of your grandfather. Under the curse of Taus."

They were moving fast and too noisily through the forest. Klyden could still hear Elxa's voice coming from the beach, although distance now muted the words.

After they covered more ground, Klyden stopped and looked around. This would have to do. Here the blood would spill today.

"He will follow our tracks to this point, Nyla," he whispered. "I will backtrack and lie in wait for him. When he is past me, I will cut him down from behind." Klyden could hear the assassin's coldness in his voice. He had a job to do. The past, with its laughter and pranks, no longer mattered. All that mattered now was that Nyla, Nowl, and he live to see another sunrise.

"What about me?" Nyla's voice was thin as a butterfly wing.

I know you are here to protect the queen. By the oath, I will not harm her. An oath promise was binding to a Charab. It gave him one more advantage over Elxa.

"You, Nyla, are going to stand with the courage of a queen, and help me save Nowl."

CHAPTER 51

Elxa had waited too long on the beach for Klyden to step out of the shadows. His mistake had given Klyden time to slip away, to think, to prepare. Frustrated, Elxa twisted the Wave Whisperer's arms a little tighter behind his back until Nowl groaned from pain.

"You're not much of a priority for him, are you, old man?"

"You can't beat him," Nowl hissed. "Why not just surrender?"

Elxa knew he would find Klyden in the forest, even in this low light. Nobody's tracking skills had ever come close to his own. But he also knew what he would find—a trap. Klyden would lure him somewhere and then attack him from behind or above. It's what he would do in that same position.

He considered his options. Ideally, he should draw Klyden out onto the beach. Threatening to harm the Wave Whisperer had had no effect. Actually harming him might. The thought sickened Elxa, however. There had been the occasional Charab boy who had enjoyed inflicting pain. Elxa and Klyden had not been one of them. Like most of the Charab, their nature was to seek as much peace as they could in their violence-infused world. No, Elxa did not want to hurt the old man merely to illicit a scream that would bring Klyden running. There had to be another way.

Leave this island and never return? Leave Klyden and the queen in the peace they deserved? Even as the thought pushed to reach the surface of his mind, the arming word pulled it down, drowning it in a wave of hostility.

The Wave Whisperer let out another moan of pain. Elxa had unconsciously tightened his grip.

"Sorry, old man," he muttered, loosening his grip somewhat. Nowl looked at him and for just a moment there was a softening in the old man's expression.

"You Charab are a strange people," he said with a shake of his head. "So what are you going to do with me now?"

"It's not your concern." He shoved him forward.

There were worse things than dying at Klyden's hand, Elxa thought. At least it would be clean and quick. Yes, there were far worse things—like living under the curse of Taus.

The thought came to him then that today he would be free. He would kill his remaining cousin and the curse of the arming word would lift—at least until his next assignment—or Klyden would kill him and the arming word would die in his grave. Elxa wasn't sure which outcome he preferred.

A surprising lightness settled on him at the thought of such freedom. Elxa suddenly knew what he would do—find and follow the tracks, as the curse urged him to, then let the Ancient One choose who died and who lived. He would not hurt the Wave Whisperer. The old man would only hinder him anyway.

He let go of Nowl.

"What? No hostage? No threats of torture and death?" Nowl peered at him suspiciously as he rubbed the blood back into his arms. "Wasn't I your best chance to get Klyden?"

"You were, but I'm leaving it in the Ancient One's hands now."

Nowl reached out and squeezed Elxa's shoulder. There was tenderness in the gesture. "You remind me of Klyden. May the Ancient One surprise you with his wisdom tonight." He turned away. "I will wait in the boat."

• • •

Klyden waited on the limb of a tree, peering out of the thick foliage. Nyla waited below him for his sign. As soon as Klyden sensed Elxa's approach, he would indicate for her to start moving, heading north toward the hut.

"Go slowly and as quietly as a wood-worm," he had told her.

"Then he won't hear me. Aren't I meant to lead him away from you?"

"He will hear."

"I'm scared, Klyden. What if it's so dark that he mistakes me for you?"

"He won't. And anyway, I'll deal with him long before he gets to you."

Again doubts assailed Klyden as he waited in the tree. What was happening to him? He used to be so sure, so confident in his ability to protect. Perhaps feelings *were* clouding his judgment. Was he a fool to use Nyla to lure Elxa past him? Could he honestly trust his cousin's word that he wouldn't harm her?

He sensed a darkening in the forest just to the south. Perhaps it was the shadow of a branch blowing in the wind, but Klyden knew that Elxa was particularly skilled at tracking. Klyden wouldn't hear him coming until he was almost right on top of them.

On instinct, he threw the small acorn toward Nyla—the signal for her to move—and watched as she began to slink away. His eyes roamed to the south, expecting Elxa to materialize on the narrow path their feet had made, but he saw nothing. Panic prickled through him.

After a long time, he again sensed a subtle shifting of the shadows. This time, he let his instincts guide his eyes at the almost unperceivable change. He found Elxa then—a mere shadow, slightly more solid than the mottled forest. His cousin was not on the path below him. Instead, Elxa was skirting to the east of their tracks, taking a course that meant Klyden would not be able to attack him from this position. The tactic was clever if one expected a trap, for it meant Klyden would have to leave his hiding place to follow him, losing his ambush advantage.

He watched Elxa slip toward the next tree. Briefly he considered using an arrow to fell his cousin, but the thick foliage made a clean shot almost impossible. He let his cousin put more distance between them before he silently slid down the tree trunk.

Elxa had heard Nyla moving northward, because he now cut toward her. Klyden couldn't waste any more time. He would not allow Elxa to reach Nyla. The queen had been through so much already. He would not allow her to come face-to-face with a Charab assassin. He pushed to close the distance, hoping that Nyla's louder movements would cover the soft rustle of his own.

Ahead of him, Elxa stopped. Had he heard him? Klyden pushed behind a large tree, raised his bow into place, and notched an arrow. He peered around the trunk toward the trees that hid Elxa from his sight. For a very long time neither of them moved. Klyden heard the crackle of Nyla's footfalls in the distance. The sound seemed to galvanize Elxa into action, for he suddenly materialized from behind the tree.

It was the perfect shot.

This time Klyden took it.

As he stepped from behind the trees, Elxa sensed his mistake. Yet even as he spun toward the direction of the danger, a branch crashed down from above, smashing him to the ground. As he fell, his eyes found the feathered arrow quivering in the trunk of the tree where he had stood a moment before. It would have been a kill shot.

Move, his mind told him, but even though he strained against the weight of the branch, he could not budge it. He tried twisting free, but the weight of the branch pinned him down, heavier than the strongest Charab he had ever wrestled against.

This was it, then. This was how it would end. He stopped fighting against the weight of the branch. The Ancient One had chosen Klyden over him. To Elxa, it seemed like the right choice as he waited for his cousin to come and fulfill the Wise One's wishes.

"Elxa!" Klyden knelt by his side, concern on his face. A rush of feelings enveloped Elxa as he looked into his cousin's familiar face.

"Klyden." He smiled. "It's good to see you again, cousin."

"I could have done without seeing *you* today." Klyden's grin was as wry as Elxa remembered it. "Are you hurt?"

"Not as hurt as I could have been." His gaze turned to the arrow in the tree. Klyden followed it.

"A kill shot," Klyden said simply, before turning his gaze back to Elxa. "Yet it appears the Ancient One had different plans for you today."

"What do you mean?"

"He wanted you to live."

"No!" Elxa felt the arming word clawing through his gut. "He gave me over into your hands. You have to end this today."

"If He wanted you dead, the arrow would have found its target."

"I can't live, Kly." The arming word filled his chest now, angrier than ever before. "You are my assignment. Only one of us can survive." Now it reached his throat, constricting him, throttling him in its rage. And into his mouth, salty with blood, it exploded outward, a torrent of fury and death. *"Ra'aph-aqeb. Ra'aph-aqeb. Ra'aph-aqeb."*

But even as it burst out of him, something light and beautiful filled the air—a note so pure that it drew all the vile darkness of that word into itself, yet stayed as beautiful as before. A light, gold and brilliant, swallowed the dark, tormenting presence as if it was nothing more than a passing shadow.

Elxa saw Klyden's joy-filled face turn upward, bathed in a golden light that came from everywhere, yet nowhere, filling all the distant spaces and years between them.

"What is that?" Elxa's voice was warm with wonder.

"The Gold Breast, Elxa." His cousin turned tender eyes to him. "Today you are free."

CHAPTER 52

Nicho and his party arrived at the Guardian Grotto just before sunset. Of the eleven rifters they had saved from the forest, only seven remained. The bodies of Hildor and three others now lay under the boulders of the ancient mountains that had proved too much of an obstacle in their weakened state.

As they stood before the waterfall that hid the entrance, a bone-heavy weariness settled on Nicho. He had expected to feel light and joyful to be this close to Shara again, but the long stretch of traveling and the pain witnessed had sapped him of all emotion.

"We made it," Rosa whispered beside him, the smallest of smiles playing on her lips.

"What now?" Gruel asked.

"The path over the rocks to the waterfall is rigged with traps. We will wait for them to fetch us."

"Do they even know we're here?"

"Undoubtedly."

They didn't have to wait long. Something clenched inside Nicho when Pearce emerged from the water. He had hoped Mikel would send somebody else.

Pearce jumped deftly over the rocks and landed on the shore. His gaze took in the motley group before settling on Nicho.

"Well, well. Look who has returned from his little rescue mission."

"Pearce."

"I thought you were fetching the boy and his mother. But you have acquired a few more stragglers I see."

"Yes, I went to fetch *your* nephew." Why did everything Pearce say prickle anger through his body? "Anyway, the last I heard this was a haven for all the Parashi."

"Indeed, it is." Pearce's smile was brittle. "They are most welcome, of course. It's just that the last visitor you brought may be the Grotto's death."

"Shara?"

"Indeed, your beloved Highborn has set us on quite a destructive path."

"What are you talking about?" Nicho reached out and grabbed Pearce's arm. He shook it off.

"It's a long story. All I know is that it would have been better for all of us if the two of you had never set foot here." Pearce turned his attention to the party then, calling out in a commanding voice for them to form a line and follow his every move over the water.

Nicho suppressed his agitation. There would be time enough to speak to Shara and find out what Pearce held against her now. First he had to get the party safely through the waterfall. He steered the group into a line, and took up his own position at the back. At the front he saw Pearce tousling Jed's hair before jumping deftly onto the first submerged rock. One by one, Nicho's party followed him to safety.

When he finally broke through the waterfall, joy surged through Nicho. He had made it back to the Grotto, with Jed and Rosa and Simhew! They were safe. All he wanted to do was run to Shara's quarters, throw his arms around her, and feel her warm softness against him. He wanted to hear her voice and laughter, kiss her mouth, and ask her if she would be his wife. He wanted to promise her that he would never, ever leave her again, that he would stay by her side for the rest of his life.

He pressed past his dripping party, all staring around them with wonder. "Pearce will take care of you from here. There's somebody

I need to see." He sidestepped Pearce, too. "You'll give them better quarters than you gave us last time, right, Pearce?"

Pearce's face broke into a sardonic smile. "Such a hurry, Nicho. Somebody you want to see?"

The Commander's echoing laugh should have been a warning.

"Gone?" Nicho stood in the War Chamber, staring blankly at Mikel. "What do you mean *gone*?"

"Eliad, Andreo, and Shara left a few days ago, Nicho."

"Only a few?" Hope surged through Nicho. Perhaps he could still catch them. "Which way did they head?"

The High Commander shrugged. "Eliad said little, only that they sought the path that would take them home."

"Home? Which *home*, High Commander?"

"Nicho." Mikel stepped to his side and took him by the shoulder, steering him to the corner of the War Chamber, away from Pearce and the other commanders. "You must be disappointed. It's been a long journey but you brought your party to safety. Thank you for that. It's a great achievement."

"But if you just tell me what direction—"

"You can't follow them," Mikel interrupted. "You need rest. You need to help the new group settle. Your strength is sapped and you are required here."

It was true. The thought of taking another step filled Nicho with quiet desperation. But how could he let Shara go now?

"I can't let her slip away again, sir." Tears broke through his voice.

"I know. I'm not asking you to give her up." Mikel pointed to an oil-skin wrapped object that lay on a small chest. He pulled the cover off gently, revealing a book with a symbol that looked strangely familiar on the cover. "This is a copy of Shara's book. Eliad made it while you were away."

"So?"

"Eliad told me that the book holds the key to finding the path they will take. He called it"—Mikel frowned—"the *Poison Tree Path*."

"The *Poison Tree Path*? Where does it lead?"

"The old man was cryptic." Mikel shook his head and smiled. "And in a great hurry to leave. He said only that it was a difficult path to follow, but the destination made it worthwhile."

Nicho reached out and turned the pages of the book, staring at the strange script under his fingers. "It's in the same script as the original book. He didn't translate it for you?" He looked up sharply at the High Commander. "Can you even read this, sir?"

"Well." The High Commander hesitated. "It's similar to Ancient Parashi, so I am sure I could make out some of the words."

"You can't read it"—from the other side of the room, Pearce looked up sharply—"yet you expect it to lead me to Shara?"

"This isn't just about you." Mikel carefully wrapped the book back into the skin. "Has Pearce told you what happened with Shara and the Dusk Dreamer?"

Nicho glanced up at Pearce. On the way to the War Chamber, Pearce had filled him in briefly—and scathingly—on Shara's crime against the Grotto. *She will be the death of us all,* he had said.

"He told me Shara had a power rock that gave away the location of the Grotto to our enemies."

"Yes. A Cerulean Dusk Dreamer. And I believe that Lord Lucian knows exactly where we are now. He might be readying an army as we speak."

"She couldn't have known. She would never put you all in danger like that."

"I know." Mikel's voice was gentle. "The rock is alluring and powerful. She was completely in its grasp and the enemy was able to exploit that. What I am saying, though, is that in all likelihood the Grotto will come under attack. Soon. And we need every blade-bearing hand we can find."

"I'm pretty lousy with a sword, sir."

"That's something we're going to have to change."

Mikel looked up and his eyes seemed to roam beyond the walls of the Grotto, beyond the fear-lashed, tear-stained history of his people. For a moment it seemed that those eyes caught glimpses of something different, something hopeful. Yet, when the High Commander's eyes turned back to Nicho, they brimmed with the same sorrow as his words.

"We'll need your sword, Nicho, because the battle for the Guardian Grotto is almost upon us."

FREE BOOK

LEGENDS OF THE LORETELLER

In Tirragyl history is kept alive through the tales of the loretellers. Hwynn, too old to travel the roads and spin his tales, tells them one last time to the scribe by his side.

A collection of short stories set in Tirragyl, Legends of the Loreteller delves into some of the history hinted at in The Poison Tree Path Chronicles and is an ideal companion book to the trilogy.

It is available as a download on Joan's website:
www.joancampbell.co.za